The Habit

This fast moving financial thriller based a
clubs, takes you on a hunt for a serial rap
Taxi.

About the author

Richard Armour was a Stockbroker for sixteen years in London where he saw some huge changes, from the Big Bang and Crash of 1987 through to the recent development of electronic trading.

He left the City in 1999 and relocated to Somerset. He is married and lives in Bristol with his wife Nicola who rides Dressage horses, representing Great Britain on several occasions. They are expecting their first child in the autumn. Richard is now Head of Sales for an Internet Hosting company, NTWebhost.co.uk

James Patterson is one of Richard's favourite authors and main catalyst behind "The Habit". Richard is already working on his second book and has a website where you can find out more. www.richardarmour.co.uk

This book is also available in e-book format, details of which are available at www.authorsonline.co.uk

An AuthorsOnLine Book

Published by Authors OnLine Ltd 2002

Copyright © Authors OnLine Ltd

Text Copyright © Richard Armour

The front cover design of this book is produced by
Keryn Roach © www.kmrmedia.com

The moral right of the author has been asserted

All rights reserved. No part of this publication may be reproduced, stored in a retrieval system, or transmitted in any form or by any means, electronic, mechanical, photocopy, recording or otherwise, without prior written permission of the copyright owner. Nor can it be circulated in any form of binding or cover other than that in which it is published and without similar condition including this condition being imposed on a subsequent purchaser.

ISBN 0 7552 0058 6

Authors OnLine Ltd
15-17 Maidenhead Street
Hertford SG14 1DW
England

Visit us online at www.authorsonline.co.uk

*For Nicky and Stephanie with all my love
in loving memory of
Susan Margaret Cooper
and
John Armour*

Author's Note

Ever since I was a small boy I have wanted to write. It has been a long, but enjoyable journey and I would like to thank some of the people who joined me along the way. Some are still part of my life, some are new to my life and others have left.

I would like to thank my mother, Jennie for buying me my first typewriter back in 1977 and being my early inspiration. Thanks Mum!

Thanks to Ursula Lodge for proofreading my manuscript.

Many thanks to Dione Coumbe, LL.B(Hons) for her great help in final editorial and her review of my book.

To Authors Online and the 2 Richard's for helping me through the scary process of publishing my 1st book.

To Keryn Roach from KMR Media Communications for her fantastic cover design.

Thanks for all the support from all my friends, there are too many of you to name here.

I so wish my Dad, John Armour could be here to share this success with me. He sadly passed away in January 2000 having suffered from Cancer. You are sadly missed and I can never thank you enough for your support and endless enthusiasm for my crazy schemes. This one happened Dad!

For my sister Jane, for putting up with not being allowed to read my manuscript! I'm sorry I made you wait. I hope it was worth it.

Huge thanks to Oliver Lodge who has helped this book become a reality. Without his support I would never have completed it or had it published!

And to my wife, Nicky for her undying love, support and belief in me.

The Habit

By

Richard Armour

ONE

Using his platinum Amex card, he mixed the Cocaine and cut four neat, white lines. He picked up the fifty-pound note, rolled it tightly and let it unravel slightly. Grinning with anticipation he began snorting the white lines. Trembling as the blood vessels in his nostrils absorbed the drug, he finished the fourth line and sniffed heavily two or three times. He licked his finger and wiped up the remaining coke from the table and rubbed it round his gums. His eyes widened as the coke raced around his body. He breathed in deeply and fell back into his armchair, letting the waves of heightened pleasure and awareness wash over him. He had so quickly grown to love this feeling.

He jumped up out of the armchair and pulled out a CD from his collection on the pine bookcase. Switching on the stereo he whacked the volume up, skipping forward to his favourite heavy metal track, he began singing along. His voice was deep and gruff and he thought that he sounded just like the lead singer. He loved this feeling of being a little crazy and out of control. He rushed over to the coffee table and picked up the two white pills and swallowed them with a swig of beer. His cigarette had burnt into a long stick of ash and as he played the drums on the table it disintegrated into the ashtray.

He loved Ecstasy, it was only a couple of months since he had been introduced to the drug and it was becoming a very enjoyable habit. He always felt so horny when he took Cocaine and Es together. It was a tantalising cocktail of desire, love, excitement and adrenaline pumping passion. They had become a dangerous combination, which should have bothered him. It didn't. What he needed was the same thing he always did when he felt this crazy.

He picked up his Timberland jacket and let himself out of his Chelsea flat. The stereo was still blasting out as he called the lift. He danced around the hallway and sang along to the music escaping through his door. The lift arrived and he got in, hitting the basement car park button on the panel. As the doors closed he glanced in the mirror. His blond hair was a mess and the two days of stubble made the beginnings of a pitiful beard. His eyes that were normally bright blue were dull, dilated and enclosed by wide, black rings. He felt great but looked terrible.

The car park was full of magnificent cars; he loved the 550 Maranello and the Bentley Azure. Everyday he passed these cars on the way to his sports car and each morning he asked himself why he had to get up so early to drive to work, when the owners of these dream machines were still sleeping in. He didn't mind really, his job was rewarding. After all, it did pay for his two parking spaces, each one a twenty thousand-pound extra and more importantly it paid for his new habit.

He passed his first car and stopped by the five year old Golf GTI, six bays along. He never took his normal car on these trips. At times like this he didn't want the unnecessary attention, besides, the Golf blended nicely into the background and served his purposes well. He unlocked the driver's door and climbed in. Reaching across he opened the glove box and pulled out a plastic bag. Smiling, he looked in and took out the cotton wool, the small bottle of ether and the latex gloves. It had been just over three weeks since the Golf's last outing and that had been a great success.

Old Faithful started first time and he reversed out and up onto the Kings Road. He shook his head in annoyance as he switched on the radio; the stereo in his other car came on automatically with the ignition. He headed down towards Worlds End and past the Esso petrol station on the New Kings Road and turned left into Waterford Road and then around the mini-roundabout into Pavilion Road. He stopped on the left in front of a row of garages and got out. It was a fairly quiet Saturday evening, helped by the fact Chelsea Football Club hadn't been playing at home. He got out a set of keys and unlocked the garage door. He nipped inside and disabled the alarm with another key. Inside was a black taxi. It was one of those new, bubble shaped cabs with grey/yellow trim, electric windows and a driver intercom system. He was very happy with his new toy and grinned as he drove it out of its shelter. He replaced it with his Golf, set the alarm and locked the garage door.

His first fare of the evening was an elderly couple that asked to be taken to the Savoy Theatre. He drove from the theatre back towards Trafalgar Square, keeping his eyes peeled. He ignored the City yuppie who confidently tried waving him down. The radio was on and he started singing along smirking at himself in the rear view mirror, realising the Es were starting to take effect.

'The eagle has landed!' he shouted out loud, noticing how big his pupils were.

The light on his cab was glowing yellow, advertising it's availability, but he was being very selective this calm, summer evening.

'TAXI!' yelled the pretty brunette.

He'd been looking the other way and had nearly missed her. She was tall, slim and very elegant. She wore a pretty navy blue jacket and a suitably short, camel coloured skirt. *Suspenders or tights?* He wondered. It didn't matter; she was a babe, which is what counted. He took a couple of deep breaths as she approached the taxi.

'South Kensington please. Cranleigh Gardens.'

He nodded and started the meter as she got in and slammed the door. He didn't chat unnecessarily to his fares, too risky. Instead he just glanced at her in his rear view mirror from time to time. *She is beautiful, what a result!* He thought as he guided his cab through the evening traffic. On the last occasion he had picked up three fares and ignored six or seven others before succeeding. He felt very good about this evening.

As they approached Knightsbridge the traffic began building up, stopping and starting every few yards. *Excellent! Just the excuse I need.* At Harvey Nichols he turned left into Sloane Street and on to Sloane Square.

'I'll drive down here love, to avoid that lot.' He told her in his best cockney accent.

She nodded and smiled at him in the mirror. She wasn't concerned, why should she be? *I'm just a harmless London cabby who's off his face and feeling bad!!* He drove around Sloane Square and turned left into Pavilion Road and then right into a little mews. He stopped opposite a car showroom and switched off the ignition.

'Hope you don't mind, I've just got to pop a letter in here.' He pointed to the showroom. 'Won't be a tick.'

Before she could complain, he was out of the cab and across the road. Once out of sight, he slowly began putting on the latex gloves. He waited in a doorway for a few seconds then sauntered casually back to the taxi. He smiled at his latest catch who, unaware of her impending fate, smiled back. He made for his door but instead, suddenly ripped open her's and dived into the back. In an instant he was upon her. He quickly pulled out the ether sodden cotton wool and slammed it into her attractive face and held his hand in place. She struggled, kicking at him and thrashing out with her arms, trying to twist her head away from the intoxicating rag that was firmly clamped around her mouth and nose.

Her mind and heart were racing; why was this monster doing this? Oh Fuck! He's going to kill me! Get off me! Oh Shit! Please stop. Please don't hurt me. Stop! Please stop. Oh no! She thought as she uncontrollably wet herself. I can't breathe. Please...... She lost consciousness. Her body slumped down in the seat and he kept his hand in place a moment longer. He released his grip and she slipped lower and onto the floor.

He stared down at her and lifted up her skirt. He noticed the fresh, dark stain spreading over the carpet where she lay. *Excellent, nice and wet for me, and suspenders too! Good girl! Well that was pretty easy!* He was very pleased with his work and began laughing hysterically.

TWO

It was still very early, in fact too early I thought as I got into my car and headed off towards the City. I went smoothly up through the gears of my BMW. I had bought it six months earlier and it still had that new, fresh out the showroom smell to it. The strong aroma of leather was as fresh and crisp as the day I'd bought it. It had seemed a long time coming. I had wanted the M3 for over a year and had decided to wait until I had the cash. It was a dream to drive and although I could use the tube to get to and from my office in Cannon Street, a car like mine had to be driven.

I had always wanted to wander into a dealership looking really scruffy with a pile of cash in a briefcase and buy my M3. I didn't do it, too dangerous carrying fifty grand in cash, but I did turn up for a test drive looking like a tramp. The sales guy at the first place explained that there were no cars available and asked me to leave. I laughed at him and explained I had the money but he got really impatient and stroppy and escorted me to the door! I couldn't believe it. I left him my business card and said I would be in touch. I rang him a week later and informed him and his sales manager that I had in fact bought my M3 from BMW in Knightsbridge. I don't think that they really believed me until I turned up at their showroom in my car. Still looking like a tramp, I had my smelly painting gear on with rips in the shirt and jeans, I marched up to the sales manager and pointed at my car and said, 'Big mistake! Big mistake!' and walked out. The look on his face was a picture. I felt like Julia Roberts in 'Pretty Woman'.

My two-bedroom flat disappeared into the distance behind me, and I noticed the sun was just coming up so I slid on my Oakley sunglasses. I raced to work, carving up most of the other traffic, especially the cabs. They all thought they owned the roads in London and I detested them. As far as I was concerned, a car was for getting from A to B as quickly as possible. The journey each morning was a Grand Prix and I was the Ayrton Senna of commuters. My record time from the flat to Cannon Street was eleven minutes, twelve seconds according to my car's on-board trip computer.

There was no way I was going to beat it today. I'd had a fantastic weekend and felt totally relaxed. I was in love; I had found the lady of my dreams. Emma had beautiful blue eyes and a body to die for which came hand in hand with being an aerobics instructor. I had met her in a nightclub a couple of weeks ago and on Saturday she had stayed over for the first time!

The lift doors opened on the twentieth floor of Four Cannon Street, where Kaplan Stewart International was based. I'd worked in the City for fifteen years, since leaving school, the last eight years for Kaplan Stewart. I was now the head of the Gilt desk; we dealt in UK Government debt, which was normally very lucrative. My three-year guaranteed deal was a comfort and an incentive to keep the desk producing. The last couple of years had been very good for my desk until the fifty percent commission cut last month, and now that Labour were paying off the PSBR, liquidity in Gilt's was drying up. Not good news for our figures and it was going to get worse as we approached the inevitable union with the rest of Europe.

The dealing floor spread right across the open plan office and there were two more, one upstairs and the other below. Three floors dedicated to broking any financial product in the world. As markets disappeared others popped up. Emerging markets were all the rage at the moment. A couple of my customers who were feeling the squeeze had said that they were considering job offers, trading the bond markets of Korea, China, Russia and even Turkey! Maybe I should learn a new language, I thought as I sat at my desk.

I ran a team of fourteen brokers and we had a customer base of just sixteen firms. We were basically middlemen, paid a small commission to match a buyer with a seller. We operated an anonymous screen based dealing system and had three competitors. We were the market leaders. The phone boards started ringing at about seven thirty and stopped at around five thirty. It was seven o'clock; I liked to get in ahead of my team. That way I was free to do my paperwork and read the FT in peace.

I was amazed at how everyone suddenly wanted a bit of my time now I was the boss. I was promoted three months ago after my predecessor, Gareth Miller, had keeled over from a heart attack and died. He was only forty-two at the time and had been cheering on his football team at Stamford Bridge. He had been a very heavy drinker and his marriage was 'a roller coaster ride from hell' he had confided in me. High blood pressure, too much booze, rich food and lots of late nights had all added up to an early grave. I was asked to take over the reins the very next day and was determined to be different. I tried to get to the gym at least three times a week and Emma said she would keep me on my toes at the weekend from now on!

The phone rang. Five past seven. A bit early I thought, as I promptly picked up the line.

'Roger, we need to talk. Expenses are way too high again. See you in five.'

Click! The line went dead. Michael Irwin was never too keen on politeness. He was the big boss and I remembered being warned before I met him he was arrogant and very aloof. Since then we'd had lots of meetings and he was a hard-nosed businessman. As long as your desk was making money you were safe. The moment you started losing money, that was it, no leeway, just a simple 'you are surplus to our requirements.' At least we all knew where we stood with Michael! I thought as I took the lift upstairs. I laughed as I straightened my tie in the mirror.

I got out of the meeting at seven twenty. The expenses weren't too high, they were justified by the amount of business we were doing, I had told Michael. I agreed that the figure was high but still within five percent of turnover as required. We had to entertain our customers, wine and dine them, take them to the theatre, the odd Grand Prix, the big one this year will be tickets for the World Cup in France. If the customer wants to do it, they do it and we pay! It's a sad reflection of the business, but as a broker, you are only as good as your last entertainment trip! If I wasn't taking my customers out, the oppo would be and they would be doing all the business. I knew for a fact not one of my brokers would chose their clients as mates. The only reason they suck up to them is for business. For example, my man at Morgan Stanley thinks I'm his best mate. I think he's arrogant and boring and wouldn't choose him as a friend, but because he pays my mortgage and more, he's my best friend too! That's one of the downsides to the job. You have to be very two-faced. We got to go to some of London's finest restaurants and the best sporting occasions, but believe me, an evening in a box at Wembley watching England with a leery, foul-mouthed lager lout from Essex was not my idea of fun!

Mondays were always our worst day and most of the guys didn't bother getting in too early. Today was no exception, I noted, as I retook my seat.

'Morning Rog.'

'Morning Eddie.' I replied. I liked Eddie, he was hard working, loyal and one of Kaplan Stewart's good brokers. He was great fun to go out with and we often had a quick beer after work. He was thirty-six years old but looked a lot older, mainly due to his rapidly greying hair.

I nodded morning to Jamie and got up the Gilt comment on Bloomberg. We didn't have to be too technical but I liked to have a handle on the market, it was a talking point. Jamie Berry was a waste of space and on my list of things to do. It was a never-ending list. Jamie was a good-looking twenty one year old with blue eyes and blond, permed hair. On anyone else it would have looked ridiculous, but the perm suited him. It gave him a pop star quality. He was one of those old Etonian Sloane rangers and a lot of us were convinced he spent most weekends raving with his mates on Charlie or Speed. He was always tired, never ate and couldn't concentrate for more than five minutes at a time. He was still scared to go on and talk to his man at FDS and whenever his customer did come on with a price or a swap, Jamie was like 'Bright Eyes' in Watership Down; a frightened rabbit frozen in the headlights of an oncoming car! My old boss was too worried about Peter Jarvis at FDS and what he would do if we sacked Jamie, but not me. I didn't have room for dead wood, especially dead wood that did drugs.

'Rog, Frank for you.' Eddie shouted over the desk.

I picked up the outside line. 'Hi Henson. You still on for tonight?'

'Of course mate. Whose turn is it?' He asked playfully. I always paid for dinner whenever the two of us got together. He was a detective in the rape division of the Met. Police. He was very good at his job, one of the very best, but he was also underpaid and overworked, as always seemed to be the case outside the boundaries of the City. I would never let him pay but at least he offered. He never took me for granted. Frank was working on various rape cases and I was hoping for my weekly update.

'Your turn, I think.' I joked.

'Right. I'll rob a bank on the way home! Usual place, eight o'clock and there've been some developments.' He sounded excited.

'Excellent! I'll see you at the bar.'

THREE

The bar was unusually packed for a Monday night, I noted as I entered the trendy Putney restaurant. So many of the capital's new restaurants had expensive bars added on as an extra feature. I enjoyed them. They were all full of good looking totty and I appreciated a bit of scenery! I looked around the bar and couldn't see Frank so I squeezed myself into a gap between two groups of suitably pretty girls and waited to be served. I listened to the different conversations going on around me. One on shopping at Joseph in South Ken and the other, far more interesting, about boyfriends and men trouble.

'Yes sport?' The Aussie barman smiled at me amongst the bevy of beauties.

'Gin and tonic and a vodka, lime and soda please.'

'No worries mate.' The barman replied as he filled two glasses with ice. If it weren't for Australians in London, we would never get a drink. All bar staff seemed to be Aussies now.

'...bloody bastard! I knew he'd been seeing her all along. I can't believe I was so naïve. Why did I let him get away with it?'

'Don't be so hard on yourself Susie. I can't blame you, he was divine and what's more, great in bed, wasn't he? I think I would have ignored the signals too!'

'Eight fifty please' requested the bar man, as he plonked the glasses on the bar.

My gin and tonic was an inviting aquamarine, shimmering under the glaze of the bar lights. I closed my eyes and took two big gulps. First drink of the evening was always the best, I thought as I put my drink down and took out a Silk Cut. I was a social smoker, I could never smoke in the office, I hated being away from the desk and also the smoking room was at the far end of the dealing floor. But I loved a cigarette with a drink. Frank smoked too, but unlike me he was a professional. He smoked for England! During the course of one of our normal nights out he would smoke thirty-five to my fifteen.

'Excuse me sir. You don't by any chance have a light, do you?' I turned to see Frank with an unlit cigarette hanging from his moustached mouth. We had been mates since school. I had left after my appalling 'O' level results and started in the City at the age of seventeen, working for a firm of stockbrokers. My boss was a friend of the family and had been happy to take me on. Frank meanwhile, had gone on to sit his 'A' levels and then studied Psychology at Nottingham University. He'd become a policeman and had worked his way up to detective sergeant. He had always felt a little hard done by with me earning my 'fortune' in the City whilst he struggled to earn a half-decent living working his butt off. It was a standing joke between the two of us.

'Hey Frankie! How's it hanging?' I greeted him with the flame from my lighter and a phoney New York accent.

'Still struggling. How are you, you rich bastard?' He asked, blowing out a plume of smoke.

'Yeah, good thanks. In fact, very good. I'm so rich I got the drinks in!' I answered sarcastically, handing Frank his Vodka.

'I like your chosen spot at the bar mate. I think I'm in heaven!' Frank commented, surveying the surrounding talent, 'She's got great tits.' He whispered, nodding towards the redhead to my right.

'Too right and look at her legs. They'd look good wrapped round your neck!' I laughed.

'Yes please. Do you know how long it's been Rog?'

'What happened to that solicitor you were knocking off?'

'Far too intelligent for me and besides, she used to question me like the accused in a courtroom if I wasn't where I said I was going to be, when I was supposed to be!' Henson sighed. 'So I finished it last week and it's just been one long barren patch since!'

'Oh there, there! You're breaking my fucking heart.' I mocked, playfully stroking my imaginary violin. 'A whole week without sex. I can't begin to think what that must be doing to you! But I presume you've got a couple of girls waiting in the wings?'

Frank kept himself very fit in the police gym and had a great body, the kind I'd like if I wasn't sat on my backside all day at work. He had scruffy, brown hair and jet black, piercing eyes most women died for. He had a bushy, brown moustache and normally a couple of day's stubble on the rest of his face, as he did tonight. Looking at him reminded me of Tom Sellick. He was wearing a pair of black jeans, a white T-shirt and a black leather jacket. He was envious of my money and I was envious of his good looks. I had already noticed the girls around us eyeing up Henson and raising their eyebrows at his hunky physique.

'No, not yet mate, maybe by the end of tonight. I didn't get out at all last week 'cause of these fucking rape cases I've been working on. They've really begun to get to me, I've got so much paperwork outstanding.'

'What a nightmare.' I truly sympathised with him. 'How are things progressing? You said there had been some developments.'

'Well, we're not absolutely sure but we think all the rapes are connected. All four have been committed in the same area, Fulham, Chelsea, West Kensington and Parsons Green. But the big break is this. I know I don't need to say this but, what I'm about to tell you is classified. I could…'

'Fuck off Henson!' I cut him short. He always swore me to secrecy before telling me anything confidential and I hated it. 'Just tell me.'

'Sorry Rog. It might just be a coincidence but all four victims had been travelling in a taxi just before the rapes. We think they were all raped by a London taxi driver!'

I barely caught the last sentence; Frank had whispered it so quietly. 'Bloody hell! A serial rapist.'

'Well, I think so, but not everyone agrees. We haven't got enough evidence. One of the girls doesn't remember anything about her ordeal, and the one raped in Chelsea can only remember being in a taxi on her way home and the next thing she remembers is waking up in a gutter. The other two girls were raped by their drivers. Our councillors are trying to gain as much info as possible, but you can imagine it's not easy going.'

'Shit, the fact that two of the victims say they were raped by taxi drivers would be enough of a coincidence for me.' I was trembling. This was so exciting, being on the inside of a police investigation. I had always wanted to be a private investigator, like Mel Gibson in Lethal Weapon. Riggs and Murtar were my two favourite detective characters. I envied them and Frank, tracking down and putting away the scum that crawled around the streets. 'So how are you going to trace this cabby or cabbies? There must be thousands of them.'

'Roughly eighteen thousand! We have a lot of people working on it. We were lucky enough to get a specimen of semen from two of the girls. Its not often we are able to get evidence like that. A rape victim's first instinct is to scrub herself clean. We're waiting for the DNA analysis to come back from the lab so hopefully they will match. The Chief wants me to appear on Crimewatch on Thursday. You know, the usual stuff, appeal for witnesses, give a photo-fit, reconstruct one of the rapes, that sort of thing.'

'Can you imagine, my mate Frank on TV! Can I have your autograph now before you're famous?' I jabbed him in the ribs.

'Bollocks! I'm more excited about meeting Sarah Swan.' Sarah Swan was the young lady who hosted the show and most guys I knew thought she was lovely. I couldn't believe Frank was getting to meet her.

'You lucky bastard! Well, I hope something comes up for you.' I said sincerely.

'Oh I don't think I need to worry. It will if you know what I mean!' He pumped his arm upwards and made a perverted grin. We both fell about laughing. 'Anyway, enough about work. Look at all these women waiting for me.' Frank said, eagerly rubbing his hands together. 'You get the drinks in again and we'll go have some fun!'

FOUR

He had made it back to the safety of his Chelsea hideaway but not without the odd moment. He always struggled to concentrate after the excitement of the drugs and the euphoria of being close to the edge. *The following through and doing what millions of men dream of doing everyday but don't because they haven't got the balls! All men would love to rape a pretty bitch! But they would never follow through like me!* He had panicked when he'd been exchanging the Golf and taxi, and accidentally set off the alarm in the garage. He had been feeling really paranoid as it was and the screaming siren made him drop his keys. He'd fumbled about for them and had finally managed to run in and turn off the alarm.

The Golf was now back in the basement and he allowed himself a smile as he got into the lift. As the lift doors opened on his floor, he was met by the music from his stereo, still blaring out. He grimaced as his head throbbed painfully in time with the beat. He had left the CD on repeat and the whole floor had been subjected to the entire Motorhead album over and over again. He checked his watch, eleven-twenty. He had been out for six hours. He laughed at the thought of the other residents pulling their hair out and the incessant complaints to the police. As he approached his flat he noticed an envelope sellotaped to the door. He unlocked the door and as he entered, ripped the envelope off and shut the door behind him.

The effects of the drugs were beginning to wear off and his headache was getting worse. He hated the fallout of coming down, it was the only side effect of his habit but he still felt the highs were worth it. Now, as he turned off the stereo and collapsed into his armchair, he wasn't so sure. He felt dreadful. His head really hurt and he was tired and pissed off. He hadn't eaten all day and his stomach was cramping, but he still wasn't hungry. His jaw was beginning to ache, he had been clenching it for the last five hours and even now he found he couldn't stop.

He recognised the handwriting on the envelope. It was from Mrs. Laidlaw, the interfering old battleaxe from across the hall. *What the fuck did she want?* She was a pain in the ass but seemed to like him for some unknown reason. As he didn't want anyone to be suspicious, he made an effort to be nice. It proved very hard at times because she was so nosey, but he tried. He opened the letter. It was to inform him she had come to his defence when the police had threatened to break his door down. Mrs. Laidlaw had told them a 'white lie' and said she had a spare set of keys and she would find them and turn the music off. The police had left satisfied and Mrs. Laidlaw had prayed for his quick return. He had a stale box of Quality Street somewhere, *the old bag won't notice the sell by date*, he chuckled. *She's probably in bed but what the fuck!*

He knocked on her door and waited with the chocolates hidden behind his back.

'Daniel, do you know what time it is?' She looked at her watch and tightened the cord of her dressing gown. 'What have you been up to? You look terrible. I should put you over my knee. Do you know I've had the police in here three times tonight?' His sweet little, grey-haired neighbour began raising her voice. 'Are you alright dear?'

'Yes, I'm fine. Just had too many late nights this week. I've brought you a little something to say thanks for coming to my rescue earlier.'

'How wonderful! Thank you very much.' Her eyes lit up at the sight of the chocolates. 'Would you like to come in for a cup of tea?'

'I'm so tired. I won't if you don't mind. I am so sorry about my music this evening. I was late for dinner and just rushed out without realising my stereo was still on.' He sounded very convincing.

'Never mind me dear, I don't mind. My hearing isn't what it was and I told the policeman what a nice young man you were and how quiet you are normally. So I don't think you have anything to worry about. Are you sure you won't come in? I've got some lovely Dundee cake.' She almost pleaded with him.

'No thank you Mrs. Laidlaw, I'm off to bed. Good night.'

'Good night Daniel.'

He wandered back into his flat and reached into his jacket pocket. He took out the roll of Fuji film, got himself a Bud Ice from the fridge and opened the door to his darkroom.

The darkroom and its annex were the favourite rooms in his flat. He spent most of his time in them, developing his latest shots, reliving many of his best memories and enlarging his best pictures. He walked through his photo lab and unlocked the door to his annex. He had the only key to the door. *You can never be too careful. Too many nosey neighbours.* He had turned the annex into a shrine of all his rape victims. On the long wall in front of him were photos of each of his seven victims. The photographs had all been taken in the back of his taxi. There were also close-ups of each of the girl's vaginas. The pictures would be very distressing to anyone else. The girls were all obviously unconscious, with no expressions showing on their faces. He loved sitting there looking at his collage, he especially liked the close-ups, remembering how they had been unable to stop him. Underneath the photos there were details of where, when and how he had raped them. There was a photo of his taxi at the scene of each rape. There were spaces ready and waiting for the next victims. He was going to fill the wall.

One day somebody would find the annex and all his secrets would be out. That day was a long way off yet. He would only let himself be caught when he was ready, when he had finished his work. He was preparing the room so the police wouldn't have to tie up any loose ends. He really wanted to be remembered. *I will be the most famous rapist of this millennium and the next.*

Not Dan Crosby. Fuck Dan Crosby! He would surpass Dan Crosby's re[cord] of sixteen victims. Until then, there was much work to be done.

FIVE

...ith one of those hangovers from hell. Frank had led me astray ...ldn't remember the whole evening; there were lots of little bits ...lled phoning Emma at one point and telling her how much I ...missed her. I think I then asked if I could go round and make love to her. I may well have dreamt that bit, no doubt I would find out later. Right now I needed to fix my hangover. Monday nights were not good nights for going out and getting pissed.

I slowly pulled the duvet back and swung my legs over the side of the bed. I sat there for a couple of minutes. My mouth was so dry and my tongue had that early morning, bottom of a birdcage feel to it. I could still taste the last cigarette I'd smoked. The taste triggered a coughing fit. Shit! My throat hurt. Why did I smoke so much last night? I had no fucking willpower. I stood up and wobbled. As I caught my reflection in the mirror, I suddenly became aware of the blood pumping inside my head, not good. I staggered into the bathroom and opened the cabinet. A box of plasters and my deodorant fell out and clattered into the washbasin below. I left them there and ferreted around for some Alka-Seltzers. I found a packet and zigzagged my way into the kitchen. I poured a cold can of Lucozade into a glass tumbler and dropped in two tablets. The best hangover cure perfected with practice over the years of drinking with Henson.

I sat at the breakfast bar in the kitchen and turned on the TV. It was just after six and the business news had just begun. Six am, oh God, far too early. I sat there trying to focus on the screen. It was too painful to concentrate. The business news finished and the sport came on. The World Cup commenced tomorrow. That stirred my mind into action. I hadn't had a bet yet, I thought as I sipped my hangover medicine. I would have to look at the spreads later on and decide what I was going to do.

During every World Cup we would all have bets ranging from winning team to the number of yellow and red cards. You name it, you could bet on it. I remembered from four years ago, that everyone was betting on the number of seconds that the Brazilian commentator could scream, 'G O A L' for! I had an account with a company called Sporting Spreads. They would quote a two-way price on yellow cards for example, of 310-320. You could sell at 310 or you could buy at 320. The minimum unit you could trade in was £2. So if you thought there would be more than 320 yellow cards in the tournament, you would buy £2 or more per yellow card. So for every yellow card over 320, you would make £2. If there were 350, you would make £60! The difference between 350 and 320 multiplied by your stake. It was very similar to dealing in stocks and shares, only far more volatile.

I fancied Brazil, Argentina, Holland and maybe the host nation, France. I didn't think England would score many goals. In a pre season friendly with

Saudi Arabia the score had been 0-0. An early indication of England's inability to score goals. I would sell England goals and buy some of the others if they were cheap enough. I liked the idea of selling yellow cards too, I'd read so many articles that all said the referees would be very strict and all tackles from behind would be penalised. I thought there had been a lot of overkill and therefore the price would be artificially high.

I struggled through my morning ablutions and arrived at my desk at ten past seven, feeling slightly better. I'd taken a taxi, with all the booze still in my system it was safer and I couldn't face the usual race in. I sat there sipping the latté I'd bought from one of those new, fashionable American coffee shops. They were springing up all over London and we had a very good one downstairs. It was great coffee but at the wrong price, one, seventy-five for a large cup. I didn't begrudge having to pay, it saved me having to make my own and besides I hated instant.

I logged onto Bloomberg and looked up the Sporting Spread pages. I found the code for the page I needed and keyed in the four letters. Immediately displayed on my screen were the prices of all the team goals. England were 7.0-7.3, a definite sell! Brazil were 10.5-10.8; Argentina were 9.0-9.3; Holland were 8.5-8.8 and France were 9.1-9.4. A shade high I thought, but the French were the host nation and I did think they would do well. I couldn't deal until nine-thirty when Sporting Spreads opened. So, as the rest of the desk arrived in dribs and drabs, I worked on my strategy.

At nine-forty I rang my bookmaker and gave them my account number and password. They quoted their live prices and I gave them my instructions. I went long of Dutch goals at 8.8; I bought France at 9.4 and Brazil at 10.8. I did nothing in Argentina and I sold England at 7.0. I dealt in £100 per goal. Every goal scored would make or lose me £100 depending on my position. I got a little bit of stick from the boys on the Forward Yen desk behind ours; they were staunch England supporters. I didn't mind. I wanted to see England do well too, but I really couldn't see them scoring a lot of goals. Anyway, I had an interest now and I was very content with my trades.

'All I need now is for Brazil to beat the Jocks 5-0 tomorrow!' I joked.

'More like Scotland 2, Brazil 0!' David retorted. He was born and bred in Edinburgh. His family had moved here when he was young but he still had a small trace of an accent, and he supported his homeland in everything that they did.

'Roger, one out.'

'Thanks.' I acknowledged. 'We'll have a side wager, Mactavish!' I shouted at David as I picked up the outside line. 'Hi Roge…'

'Shh! Shh! Don't shout you fucker!' Henson groaned. 'I feel like shit, I can barely open my eyes and my throat is killing me.'

'Oh and I suppose you want my sympathy? Well you can whistle! I'm really glad you feel crap too. You were the one that wanted to go on.'

I heard moaning down the handset. 'What time did we leave Putney Bridge?'

'I don't remember! But I do remember the blonde you were chatting up and her ugly mate I got stuck with. "Go on Rog, pretend you fancy her." You kept saying to me.'

'What did the blonde look like?' Frank almost sounded excited.

'No idea mate. I think we took them on with us. I looked in my wallet earlier and I found a credit card slip for seventy quid. Some place called New York, New York. A cheap night-club in Fulham I think.'

'So we had fun then? I'm not suffering for nothing?' Frank laughed hoarsely.

'We must have done. My hangover's one of the worst I've had in a while! But Frank, let's not do Mondays again.'

'Sorry mate. It was my only free night this week. What time is it?' He asked hurriedly. 'Shit! Fuck! I gotta go.'

The line went dead. Frank was late for work again. He was so often late after one of our sessions. I didn't fancy being in his shoes, having to work on those rape cases with his hangover. At least I could hide behind my screens and nurse mine. And that was exactly what I was planning to do for the rest of the day!

SIX

Louise Rutherford hadn't travelled on the tube for ages. Her grandfather had set up a trust fund for her and she was truly grateful. It meant that she could afford to take taxis everywhere. She detested the tube but her best friend, Amanda had insisted. She had called Louise that afternoon and asked her to come round that evening.

'Lou, whatever you do, please promise me you won't come by taxi. Please. Promise me now.' Amanda demanded.

'Why not? What's happened Manda? Are you all right? I always travel by cab, you know that.'

'It's just so awful! Oh God! Please don't ever travel by taxi again. It's so aw...' Amanda started crying hysterically.

'Sweetie, what's wrong? Please tell me.'

Amanda didn't answer, but continued sobbing.

'I'm coming over right now and I promise I'll take the tube.'

Louise told her boss she had a string of appointments and would be gone for the rest of the day. He didn't question it. She only had to go four stops, with a change at Earls Court. She hadn't travelled on the tube in months maybe even years. As she walked into the ticket hall, she was amazed at how modern it all looked. The ticket machine proved too complicated for her and she asked a member of staff for assistance. She made her way down the stairs and onto the platform. There was a digital display hanging from the roof that showed the destination of the next tube and time of arrival. The next one was due in one minute. As she waited she took in her surroundings. There were adverts all along the wall of the platform. The new Lethal Weapon movie was advertised on one, the opera on another and there was even one for a dating agency called 'Pulstar Dates.'

The tube arrived and Louise stood well back. She was amazed at how close to the edge some people stood. The single door whooshed slowly open and she got on. There weren't too many people in the carriage. She didn't bother sitting down, she only had one stop to go. She was slightly startled by the driver announcing their arrival at Earls Court. 'Change here for the Piccadilly line and the east bound District line. This is a one stop only train to High Street Kensington.' Louise smiled; the driver's accent was very Indian and very high pitched. A lot of the other commuters were wincing at the noise.

She finally arrived at her friend's flat in South Kensington at five-thirty. The tube had been an experience and actually not as bad as Louise had anticipated. Amanda lived around the corner from the station in Cranleigh Gardens. They had met a couple of years ago through work. Louise was an estate agent at Foxtons in Fulham and Amanda had started as a temp for the manager, Jeremy. Louise and Amanda used to spend their one-hour lunch breaks in the local Café Metro, smoking and gossiping. Amanda was twenty-three, a year older than her friend. They both had the hots for Jeremy. He was thirty and just married, but that didn't stop either of them from drooling over his Latin looks and tight bum! Amanda really enjoyed working there and when Jeremy had offered her a full time position she'd accepted without hesitation.

Louise pressed the buzzer marked Amanda Worthington.
'Who is it?' Asked a nervous voice.
'Hi Manda, it's me, Louise.'
Come on up. Make sure you close the door.'

The door clicked and Louise pushed it open and shut it firmly behind her. She made her way up to the second floor and was surprised not to see Amanda waiting for her as she usually did. She knocked on her door, which was rapidly opened. Amanda pulled her inside and slammed it.

'Oh Lou. I'm so pleased to see you.' Amanda said, with tears in her eyes. She grabbed her friend and hugged her. She began crying again.

'Manda, what on earth has come over you? Tell me what's happened. Why haven't you been at work? Everyone's been really worried.'

'I don't know if I can.' She said, drying her eyes with a tissue. 'I'm not sure I want to. I am still so ashamed.'

'Ashamed about what? Please tell me what's happened.' Louise was very concerned.

Amanda had stopped crying. 'I will try and tell you. I want to. That's why I wanted to see you. I'm all right, I promise. But first, let me get you a drink. Tea, coffee or a Bacardi and Coke? I'm going to have a Bacardi.'

'I think I'm going to need one too, yes please. Let me help.'
'Don't worry, it won't take two secs.'

Louise plonked herself down in one of the sumptuous, blue armchairs. It was a beautiful apartment. The living room was a vibrant yellow with blue and yellow curtains. It was very elegantly decorated. Amanda had paid a fortune for an interior designer to come in when she'd first bought the place. Like Louise, Amanda's trust fund had come in very handy from time to time! She was very worried about her friend. Amanda hadn't been at work since Friday. No phone calls, nothing. Louise had called five times and left messages and when Amanda had finally returned her calls, she had seemed very different, upset and troubled.

'Sorry I took so long. I couldn't get the ice out of the freezer.' Amanda said, handing Louise her drink. A large Bacardi and diet Coke; their usual tipple.

'Right, now please sit down and tell me what's troubling you.' Louise ordered.

'Oh God. It's so awful. Please help me, I don't know what to do.' She was fighting back the tears and trembling. 'I haven't spoken to anyone since

Saturday. I've been so scared. I feel so cheap and dirty.' She broke down again.

'Sweetie, I'm so sorry.' Louise leapt up and over to comfort her.

'Lou, I was rap... rap...,' she tried to speak between sobs. 'I was raped.' She wailed uncontrollably into Louise's shoulder. Louise hugged her hard, shocked at her Amanda's devastating news. She too burst into tears, imagining how her friend must be feeling. She was speechless.

Amanda spoke first. 'I'm okay Lou, honestly. I just feel so ashamed.'

'Fucking hell! Jesus Christ! Oh my God!' The expletives continued, as Louise let all her shock and anger out. She grasped at her Marlboro Lights, fumbling the packet open. She offered one to Amanda who took it and lit it quickly, forgetting to light Louise's. Louise lit hers with her own lighter and smiled at her friend.

'You have absolutely nothing to be ashamed about. Why didn't you call me?'

'I wanted to tell you. I just felt so dirty and confused. I didn't know what to do. It was so horrific. Horrific. Fucking horrific.' She closed her eyes as she relived the events of Friday night.

'Have you been to the police?'

'God no! I haven't spoken to anyone. Mummy's called twice and I haven't even spoken to her. I just can't face anybody. I definitely can't face the police.'

'You have to Manda. You can't just let the barbarian who did this get away with it. Who was it? Do you have any idea? Can you remember what he looked like? Where were you?' She had so many questions and they all came tumbling out at once.

'Lou, please calm down. I know you're angry. Believe me, I was at first too.' Amanda was very composed. She'd spent the last four days trying to come to terms with her ordeal. 'I got a taxi from Trafalgar Square. I'd been to see Daddy for afternoon tea. The traffic was really heavy and so the driver turned off Knightsbridge, down towards Sloane Square.' Amanda paused to take a sip from her glass and a gently knocked the ash from her cigarette into the ashtray. 'He said he needed to drop something off at some garage. Next thing I knew, he was in the back of the taxi with m... with m... me.' Amanda grimaced and closed her eyes. 'It was him. He raped me. It was the taxi driver.'

SEVEN

'Hi honey. It's me. I'll see you in the bar at six.'

'I can't wait. Where are we eating? Emma asked excitedly.

'You'll have to wait and see! I gotta run.' I quickly picked up Andrew from Morgan Stanley, who had been squawking.

'Roger, I'll sell sixes, buy babies, dropping twenty-four and a half. They pick up twenty-five on Walters. My terms should trade. I'll do up to a hundred.'

'Thanks mate. I'm on it.' I clicked out and repeated the terms to the room. We worked on an open outcry basis. Every order had to be shouted out by the brokers. A) To make sure the other brokers on the desk have heard the terms. B) The first to shout out the order trades, not the loudest. When the market was busy, it could be mayhem, with everyone shouting at the same time. But with good teamwork, it usually ran fairly smoothly.

'Rog, you're done! I'll do fifty babies.' Brian screamed across the desk. Brian Griffin had worked with me for about five years. He was my number two and in charge of the show when I wasn't around. He was a great broker, one of the best, certainly better than me. He was thirty-five years old with a full head of long, blond hair. I was three years younger and balding fast. Life just wasn't fair! Brian was very wealthy. He had been paid very well and had got some large bonuses over the past few years. He was single and lived in Chelsea and he also had a house in Hertfordshire. All the boys on the desk thought he was gay and I knew what they meant. Brian could be very strange at times and was very tactile but I didn't believe he was gay, just a bit strange. He was certainly good looking enough to be queer.

'Thanks Griff. I make that seventy-eight sixes of ninety-nine. Are levels of thirty-one plus and four and five-eighths okay?'

'I'll check. Do you go on?' Griffin asked.

I spoke to Andrew and he confirmed his balance. 'I've got another twenty-two sixes to go.'

It was great having customers like Andrew Duncan. He always gave me the lion's share of his business, and normally on very good terms. I picked up the outside line It was Frank.

'Rog, the DNA test results just came through. They were positive. Both samples match. I'm on Crimewatch tonight at ten thirty, don't miss it mate. I'll keep you posted.'

I sat there feeling a little disappointed. I had hoped the rapes weren't linked and just coincidences, but Frank's hunch had been right. We did have a serial rapist at large in London. Well I just hoped Frank's appeal on Crimewatch helped them catch the culprit. I wanted to record Frank's TV debut but I was meeting Emma straight from work.

We didn't manage to trade the balance of my swap but nonetheless we'd had a very good day. In fact, it was almost a record. £1.25 billion worth of bonds and at thirty-nine pounds per million that was £48,750 for a days work! Our best day was just over £95,000 and that was the day of the Election. I was really pleased and left the office, whistling.

I arrived at Holmes Place in the Barbican at ten minutes to six. I was early and sat at the bar and ordered a peach and strawberry smoothie. They made great fruit cocktails. I would have preferred a gin and tonic but the health club didn't serve alcohol. I sat slurping on my juice watching water-skiing on Eurosport.

'Hello handsome!' Emma greeted me with a big kiss on my left cheek. She looked awesome. Her cheeks were flushed from her recent bout of exercise and she smelled fantastic. 'Allure' by Chanel. 'Which smoothie have you got?'

'Peach and strawberry. Would you like one?'

'No, I'd like a drink, drink.'

'Brilliant!' I exclaimed. A girl after my own heart. 'Let's go. How was your day?' I asked her as I quickly polished off my drink.

'Great thanks. I had a wicked class at four. I really went for it and they all kept up. It was really good fun. I love it when I've got a class full of people who know what they're doing. How about you? Did you make a fortune?' She asked, draping herself over my shoulders and kissing me.

'One of our best days ever. I hope you're up for a late one?'

'For sure. Where are we off to?' Emma quizzed, hoping to catch me out.

'I haven't got a clue. TAXI!' I yelled and threw my hand up at the passing cab. I had booked a table at Gordon Ramsey's restaurant in Chelsea. It was the best restaurant in London and I knew Emma would love it. 'Hilton, Park Lane please.' I instructed the driver, making sure she couldn't hear.

'We're going on a magical mystery tour.' I joked, as I joined Emma in the back.

'I love you. What are we celebrating?'

'Your good day. My good day. We're celebrating our good days.' I leaned over and kissed her full on her fabulously, luscious lips. Her flame red hair shone in the sunlight that filtered through the rear window of the cab. As our lips parted company, she opened her eyes and I felt a sudden surge of passion as her stunning blue eyes were revealed. My heart skipped a beat. She was so beautiful. She had quite olive skin for a redhead and I loved all her little freckles.

'Roger, you're staring!' She laughed, going slightly red.

'Can you blame me? What does a looker like you see in a podgy bloke like me?'

'That's simple darling, money!'

We spent the rest of the journey talking and laughing. We arrived at the Hilton and I led Emma downstairs into Trader Vics. I loved cocktails and I was sure Emma would too.

'Oh no. Not a cocktail bar. I can't stand them. I'm sorry Roger, is there another bar we can go to?'

'Yeah, sure. We'll go upstairs.' I was disappointed.

'I'm sorry Rog. You don't mind do you?'

'No, not to worry. I'm the one paying, but we'll go where you want to go.' I said as I dropped my shoulders and slouched towards the lifts. She knew I was only kidding and kissed me as we got into the lift. We got out on the twenty-fourth floor and a waiter led us to a table by the window.

'The view is amazing!' Emma exclaimed, as we sat down. The waiter brought us our drinks and we sat and chatted. 'How's Frank? I can't believe those cases he's working on. It's so dreadful.'

'Shit! That reminds me. Frank's on Crimewatch tonight at ten thirty. I want to be back in time. He only rang to tell me this afternoon, so I haven't set the video.'

'That's okay with me.' Emma said, grinning. 'That gives us more time in the bedroom!'

We had a wonderful meal at Gordon Ramsey's award winning restaurant in Chelsea with some fabulous wine. Jean-Claude Bruton, the maitre d' was the perfect host, as usual. As I had guessed, Emma had loved it and we'd spent the evening getting to know each other's interests. It was our first big night out and I had wanted it to be a little bit special, but now, I felt very apprehensive. I had some strong feelings for Emma and I knew she had fallen in love with me, she had told me so many times already. It was all happening so fast, maybe too fast. We had only been seeing each other for three weeks. I did like her a lot. She had a body to die for but I wasn't sure if I was ready for anything this heavy. It was my fault, I thought I was ready. My last girlfriend had been seeing someone behind my back and when I found out, I'd been devastated. That was a year ago and since then I'd kept women at a safe distance. I would have to talk to Emma to try to explain my feelings, but not tonight. Not yet..Mum and dad were having a barbecue on Saturday and we were going. Maybe I could talk to her then.

EIGHT

He had been driving around Hammersmith with the roof down on his Ferrari 355 Spider. He wasn't trying to hide from anyone tonight. He didn't care that his yellow sports car turned heads. He didn't care about anything. It was hot. It was another one of those unbearable summer evenings when most people had trouble sleeping. Not him, he wouldn't be sleeping tonight. He was on a mission. Definitely not a mission from God, he thought then laughed out loud. He liked the Blues Brothers, it was a cool film. *'I've got a full tank of petrol, it's nine-thirty and I'm wearing sunglasses. Hit it!'* He roared up King Street and round the one-way system into Glenthorne Road. He cruised along the quiet road looking for the club. He had heard someone talking about it and thought he would check out the venue for himself. He knew it would be his kind of place. He grinned as he pulled up outside the table-dancing club.

'Can I leave it here?' He shouted to the doorman.

'Yeah, sure. We'll look after it for you sir. Nice plate!' The bouncer had noticed the number plate, "DAN 20".

He hauled himself out and slipped a twenty-pound note into the man's hand. He entered the club and paid the fifteen quid entrance fee. He was led into a low-lit room with a stage in the middle and tables and chairs around it. A DJ in the corner played all the latest chart toppers and there were naked women dancing everywhere and the smell of their perfumes hung in the air. There were two girls dancing on stage and they slowly began peeling their bikinis off in unison. There was a table free, next to the stage, where he sat down. He ordered a beer and watched the girl dancing for someone on the next table. She was beautiful, dyed blonde hair, fake tits and a fake smile. *What a great place,* he thought as he sat drinking his beer.

'Would you like a dance? My name's Wendy.' He looked up to see a very stunning girl leaning towards him. He couldn't divert his eyes from her huge cleavage. She was very fit and had lovely long legs.

'I've never been here before. What's the form?' He asked.

'I dance for three minutes and that costs ten pounds.'

'Do you dance naked?'

'Yes!' She exclaimed and giggled. 'Of course.'

'How much to fuck you?' He asked casually.

'I'm sorry. It's not that kind of place. We just dance.' She answered his questions as if she got asked it everyday.

'Is that all? What about a blow job then? If you get naked for a tenner, what does a blow job cost? Twenty-five? Fifty? I'll tell you what, come home with me and I'll pay you a grand for the night. How about it?'

The girl ran off in disgust. He laughed when he saw the two bouncers appear. They came over to his table with the girl hiding behind their huge frames.

'You been giving Wendy trouble?' The uglier one of the two giants asked, threateningly.

'No. I merely asked if I could fuck her. Is that a crime?' He stated.

'Don't get funny with me mate. The girls here just dance and that's all. When they leave here, they leave alone and they don't appreciate smart Alec punters.' He was trying to impress Wendy with his hard man act. *I'd like to get up and punch ten tons of shit out of this motherfucker. Bollocks, in fact, I'd like to stab him through the heart and shit on his head.* He laughed out loud at this thought.

'Right! That's it! OUT!' The two doormen grabbed him and hauled him out of his chair. As they whisked him through the club he winked at Wendy, 'If you change your mind, I'll be waiting for you outside.' He flicked his tongue round his lips and winked again. Wendy shuddered and turned away.

'Get out and don't come back, you sick bastard.' The bouncer threw him out, onto the pavement.

He beeped the alarm on his car and opened the door and climbed in. 'Thanks for looking after my car, spend the twenty quid on some plastic surgery for your ugly fucking face, you wanker!' He yelled at the doorman, as he sped away from the club. *I'll pay them another visit later.*

He headed for home and it was just gone ten-thirty when he unlocked his front door. He got himself a beer and plonked himself in front of the TV. He flicked through the channels on Satellite and then switched to TV; BBC 1, BBC2, *what the fuck!* He flicked back to BBC 1 and sat there wide-eyed and on the edge of his chair. It was Crimewatch and he was watching a reconstruction. It was of a black taxi parked in Waterford Road. He listened to the policeman talking about the rape! It was his rape! He couldn't believe it. He watched the reconstruction and laughed at how well they had done it. He'd liked Barbara; she had brown hair, and brown eyes, big nose and a big mouth like Kelly Lebrock. *Great for blow jobs. She had great big tits.* They finished the reconstruction off very nicely, he thought, with his taxi zooming away from the scene of the crime, leaving Barbara lying on the pavement.

Sarah Swan appeared with the copper who was a good-looking fucker. He thought they made quite a nice couple. The detective appealed for witnesses and described the rapist. He was five foot ten, in his late thirties to early forties, with grey hair. He was overweight and his voice was distinctive and deep. One of the victims commented the voice was exactly the same as the man who does all the Hollywood films voice-overs. A photo-fit appeared on the screen. He couldn't contain himself. He roared with laughter. The image looked nothing like him. It looked more like somebody's grandfather! The detective sergeant went over the finer points again. The police were looking for a taxi driver in his early forties who drove one of the newer style taxis. They believed the man was responsible for all four rapes. The police were very concerned that this man may have committed more rapes and appealed for any victims to come forward. All calls would be treated in the strictest confidence. The detective urged people not to challenge the man, as he was very violent and may be armed.

Four rapes! Nice to know that only four of the little bitches had gone running to the police. He wondered how long it would be before the other three went to the police. He lit a celebration cigarette and toasted himself with his beer. *Well done! Here's to many more. They haven't got a fucking clue. The taxi cover was working!*

He dabbed a wet finger into the white powder and then onto his tongue. He grimaced and shook his head. He hated the taste of Speed. He chased it down with a swig of beer and repeated the process. He had plans for later and he wanted to be awake and on his toes.

It was two-thirty when he drove the taxi away from his secret lock up. He was flying! He'd only had a couple of beers but he'd done a load of Speed and was very, very hyper. He shouldn't have been driving but he was a taxi driver and they never got stopped for spot checks. It was so easy playing hide and seek. Every time he took the taxi out he would change the number plate and his licence number. He drove down Glenthorne Road for the second time that evening and past the club, 'Paradise'. There were three black cabs outside on the taxi rank. He pulled into the next road, thirty yards further on and parked at the end. He had a perfect view of the entrance. Now he would sit and wait. It was two forty-five; he would only have to wait twenty minutes or so. He wasn't sure he could sit still for that long. He got out of the cab and lit a cigarette. He paced up and down by his cab not taking his eyes off the club, just in case she left early. *Come on Wendy! You little bitch! Come to Daddy!*

NINE

Frank was really pleased with last night's show. He had recorded it and watched it when he got home. His first thought was he and Sarah Swan looked good together. She was a honey. He had been introduced about two hours before the program and they had discussed how the rape slot would be recorded. She was very professional, but also very relaxed. She had a great sense of humour and Frank had done his best to turn on the charm. He was convinced by the end of the evening she had succumbed and had started to fancy him. He left her his number, purely for business reasons!

He arrived at the station at ten to ten and having got a coffee, sat at his desk and lit a cigarette. He wished the station were no smoking. There was no incentive to give up and he knew he should be trying. He smoked at least twenty during the course of a good day.

'Morning Guv. You were good last night. Did you get any decent leads?' One of the young constables asked.

'Thanks, Dave. A couple of bits of info seem quite promising. I think we got a few prank calls too. Quit the "Guv" bullshit, Dave. You know it winds me up! ' Frank insisted on his team calling him Frank and not Guv or any other condescending title. Those clichés were best left for the movies and TV series.

Frank went through the paper work from last night and tried to prioritise the leads. They had received over forty calls. He and his assistant had been in the studio until midnight taking phone calls and checking up on the info received. A lady from Essex called and she said she'd overheard a man bragging about the rapes in her local pub last weekend. His name was Barry Ramsey. He was a bricklayer and lived in Chelmsford. Frank had his address and phone numbers. This was a very promising lead. The rapes had been reported in the newspapers but nobody knew that there was a serial rapist, and yet here was a man claiming to have raped all the women. Barry Ramsey would be Frank's first port of call. The other lead concerned the photo fit. Three people had claimed the photo was of a Scotsman by the name of Archie Robertson. He lived in Edinburgh so Henson didn't hold out too much hope on that one. The chances of Mr. Robertson being the rapist were very slim. A sweet old lady had rung to say that she and her husband had taken one of those new shaped taxis to the Savoy Theatre last Saturday evening. Her husband had commented on how awful the interior of the taxi was. She also remembered that the driver had worn a hat and had grey hair. She was very apologetic about calling because she didn't know if the journey was relevant. Her husband had told her not to bother but she felt she had to call. Frank had thanked her but he didn't think the call was relevant. He had called the cab office and had discovered there were over a thousand of the new shaped cabs registered.

Henson kept all the details in folders. He had a folder for each of the rapes. There were details on everything; forensic evidence and results, text of each interview, copies of statements etc. He also had a main folder in which he kept all the key information such as his thoughts, profiles of each victim and similarities, all the photos his men had taken and he also kept the profile of the rapist in there. What the rapist looked like, his habits, time the rape was committed. Frank wrote down all his thoughts in this folder. He sat there, deep in thought with his cigarette in one hand and his coffee in the other. He put down the coffee and began scribbling on a piece of paper. He needed some notes for this morning's meeting with the Chief and he only had fifteen minutes.

The rapist was a taxi driver – grey hair- 35-45 years old – he only raped beautiful women – they had all been raped in a taxi – some in broad daylight – some at night – somebody must have seen something. Henson racked his brains for ideas and motives but his phone ringing interrupted him.

'Hey Frankie! How's it hanging? Did you score? Emma and I thought you and Sarah made a great couple!'

'Fuck you Hamilton! What did you think? Was it okay?'

'Yeah, we both thought you were excellent, very photogenic. Em thinks you should get yourself an agent and become an actor. How did it go? Did anything come up?'

'I think so. I've got to see the Chief now to discuss possible leads and our plan of attack. I'll give you a bell later.'

'Okay mate. I'm at lunch until three, so call me after that.'

'Easy life, you fuckers lead! Have a nice time. You driving home?'

'Yes, don't worry, I won't be drinking! Once a copper, always a copper!'

'Just thought I ought to check. If you do drink, leave the car and get the tube. I don't want you taking a taxi. Knowing your luck, you'll end up in the back of one with that rapist. I think he'd go for a pretty spam-head like you!'

'Very funny. Go on, piss off to your strategy meeting, you big stud!'

Frank laughed as he replaced the receiver. He enjoyed the repartee he had with Roger and he loved winding his mate up. He decided he would tell Roger that he was going for a drink with Sarah Swan next week. That would get him going! He tidied up his report and headed over to see the Chief.

Frank was with the Chief for less than ten minutes. His boss had complete faith in Henson's operation and had told Frank to follow up on all the leads. They both agreed there was little to go on. The Chief didn't think the cab driver lived in Edinburgh. The bricklayer in Essex needed to be spoken to and Frank said that was the first task on his list. The calls hadn't seemed too promising so far, but detective work was a funny old game. Just as you think you've turned into a dead end, something always happened to lead you down another route of enquiry. There had been four rapes they knew about but Frank knew that there would be more. They needed the rapist to make a mistake. They were desperate for some new evidence. He hated the early part of an investigation, it was like trying to piece together a new jigsaw but without knowing how many pieces were missing! There was never enough to go on, there was always a lot of guesswork. He felt so helpless. He shuddered at the thought of another beauty being raped and Frank and his team being powerless to prevent it. He wanted to catch the bastard. He may even have already struck again. A lot of rape victims didn't report their attacks. Frank sighed at his last thought; the cases were beginning to get to him. He lit another cigarette and went to the canteen to calm down.

Henson called Roger at three o'clock and was surprised to find him there. 'What happened? Not like you to be back this early.'

'Hi Frank. You know me; if I'm not drinking I see little point in supping mineral water all afternoon whilst listening to some big shot trader boring me stupid with his supreme trading skills! So, come on, tell me what's happening.'

'Well, not a lot really. Not as good as we'd have hoped. I followed up all the leads and nothing. We think he's aged between thirty-five and forty-five. One of the team rang the cab office and discovered there are over four thousand drivers in that age range. We need more info. Just two or three more clues and we could whittle the list down to ten or twenty. Someone called Barry Ramsey said he'd done the attacks and was the rapist. I spoke to Essex CID and it turns out that this muppet comes forward every time there's a rape, burglary or drug bust reported. Ramsey is their local nutcase. The detective I spoke to, said they've been trying to get him admitted for years, but the local loony bin is full and the social worker who sees him, says he's fine! So, apart from wasting bloody time, we haven't got that far, mate.'

'So, it's a bit like looking for a needle in a haystack at the moment?' Roger quipped.

'Exactly. We'll keep on sifting through the evidence. We may still get some leads from Crimewatch. A lot of people record it apparently, so some may not have watched it yet. How are you getting on with your World Cup bets? Making a fortune already, no doubt.'

'I wish! I'm not too sure yet Frankie, it's early days. Brazil scored two on Wednesday. I really needed them to score three or four. Tonight's game really matters. I need France to score bundles against South Africa.

'You should be all right. Have you done anything with Germany or Italy? They're my tips. They should meet each other in the semis so one of them will be there. The Germans should knock a load in against USA.'

'I had no interest in the Germans and I think the Itie's are shite! I watched last night's game and I thought that they were very lucky. The Americans are going to be tougher than most people think.'

'Maybe, I think that Italy are always a bit slow to get going but they'll be good. What did you think of the reffing? I thought he was very laid back last night.'

'That reminds me, I must go and sell some yellow cards. I'll speak to you later.'

Frank sat back in his chair looking at all the notes spread across his desk. What a mess! Sometimes he got very envious of Roger. He wished all he had to worry about were yellow cards and football. He wished that he could spend the afternoon dining in a fancy restaurant and have the company pick up the bill. He wished he drove a BMW like Roger instead of his clapped out Ford Sierra. Instead he was up to his armpits in a great big mess he saw no way of climbing out of.

The telephone ringing interrupted his feeling sorry for himself.

'Frank, there's been another rape!'

TEN

'Hi Mum. Emma and I are leaving now. We should be with you by eleven.'

'Okay Roger. Please drive carefully darling,' my mother fussed.

Emma was very nervous about meeting my family for the first time and she wanted to look her best. She'd been in the bathroom for fifteen minutes and I was beginning to lose patience.

'Come on Em. You look great, let's go.' I demanded, glancing round the bathroom door. She was dusting her eyelashes with a mascara brush.

'All right! Stop hassling me. I'm ready now.' She brushed past me without smiling.

I opened the passenger door of my blue BMW and Emma slinked into her seat. I closed her door and walked round to my side and got in. I turned the key in the ignition and hit the convertible button. The roof began peeling slowly up, down and away, revealing the car's inner cockpit. We were off to my parent's house for a family barbecue. My little sister, Penelope, three years my younger, was going to be there. I was really looking forward to seeing her. She'd been away travelling around the Far East and had returned two weeks ago. We spoke nearly every day but I hadn't seen her since my birthday in March. Mum had told me she was really looking forward to the extra company. My grandfather had been staying all week and by now my mother would be pulling her hair out! Dad had always got on well with mum's father but he and mum were too similar.

Emma didn't speak to me for the first ten minutes of the journey. It was an awkward silence. If she planned to make me feel guilty, it worked. I couldn't help the way I felt about women and how long they took to get ready. I could never understand what took them so long. I remember dad always complaining at how long mum took. It wasn't even as if Emma wore a lot of make-up. I put my hand on her leg and rubbed it gently along her silky, soft thigh. She was wearing a little white top with a short, summer dress over the top. She looked fantastic. The dress stopped about six inches below her pert bottom, revealing her long, tanned legs. She spent an hour every other day on a sunbed and her job had helped shape her legs to perfection.

'I only want to look my best for you in front of your family.' Emma stated, bluntly.

'I know. But you do anyway. I'm sorry; I just hate hanging around that's all. I'm sorry. You do look perfect and I'm so proud of you. I can't wait to show you off to my family.' I tried digging my way out of the hole I'd dug.

She leant over and kissed me. 'Thank you. I'm just really nervous. I know how famous your father is and I don't mean to sound funny, but I feel like I'm going to meet the Queen.'

'I understand. But my father is really relaxed and he's going to love you. You've got nothing to worry about.' I smiled, having dug my way out.

'I know I'm just being silly. I can't believe I'm going to meet him to be honest. My dad is going to be so jealous, he was a big fan. Why didn't you follow in his footsteps?'

'I wanted to, but I just didn't quite make the grade. I've raced Formula Ford and I had a crack at Formula three but I had quite a bad accident at Silverstone and lost my bottle. I thought I was going to die; I hit the tyre wall at over one hundred miles an hour. I broke my right leg and my collarbone and spent nearly two months in hospital. I never raced again. I just couldn't get back in the car.' For a split second I felt like a failure. I hated thinking about my motor racing career. I had become successful in the City thanks to my father putting me in touch with my first boss, who had been a friend of my father's for years. I had been determined to put my motor racing failure behind me and I was very proud when I had been promoted.

'I'm not surprised. I'm glad you didn't get back in the car, we would never have met! Tell me about your sister.' She squeezed my hand.

'I can't wait for Penny to meet you. She's got the same sense of humour as you. I've really missed her.'

'How long has she been travelling for?'

'About two months. She started in Malaysia and ended her trip on a beach in Thailand. She sent me loads of postcards and the one from Thailand was beautiful. She and her fellow travellers went round in a bus and stayed in some really cheap hotels and she even spent a few nights camping under the stars. She's going to be so brown, she only has to get a glimpse of sun and her skin darkens.'

'How wonderful! It sounds like a great trip. Did she go with some friends?'

'No, she went on her own. None of her friends could get the time off work. She'd just split up with her boyfriend of five years and she jacked in her marketing job. She had saved up quite a lot of money. She had been planning the trip for some time, she even offered to take me!'

'You and she are very close aren't you?' Emma asked.

'God, yeah! She's my little sister. She means everything to me. Mum and Dad's divorce brought us much closer. I used to lead her astray when she was a teenager. I started taking her to the pub when she was fifteen. I was responsible for her first hangover and she's never let me forget it!' I really loved Penny and I was so excited about seeing her. I loved the fact I was her big brother and she always rang me for advice and if she was in trouble, I was the first person she would turn to.

'She must love it. I've always wanted a big brother. I bet she really looks up to you.'

I couldn't believe Emma's statement. It was as if she were psychic! 'I don't know about looking up to me, but we do have a very special relationship. You'll love her and I know she will love you.'

The A3 wasn't too busy. We made good time and arrived in Windlesham just after eleven. My parents lived in a beautiful six-bedroom mansion with fifteen acres and a huge wrought iron gate at the beginning of their long drive. Dad had made his money in motor racing. He had been a Formula One driver, Mike Hamilton, and he had gone on to run the Brammer F1 Team. He was superb at marketing, no doubt where Penny got her talents, and he had done well keeping the second rate team afloat. He was a mildly successful team boss and was very proud to have taken Brammer to fifth in the World Championships of 1980. When his retirement came three years ago, he had a huge party held for him by all the other team bosses at the Grovesnor House Hotel in London. It was a very glitzy affair and made headline news and 'Hello' magazine. He was the talk of the town for about three months and he loved every minute of it.

He was a bit of a gigolo and it was the rumour of an affair with a tarty blonde that caused mum and dad's divorce. Dad had denied it vehemently but mum didn't believe him and immediately filed for a divorce. Penny and I were heart broken. We had to choose between mum and dad for who we wanted to live with. It was an awful time; some of the newspapers got hold of it and blew it out of proportion. Thankfully it happened in 1979 and the media circus of today wasn't yet established.

It was a very amicable divorce and Pen and I saw dad at least once a month. We had always gone to Monaco for the Grand Prix weekend and after the divorce dad still invited mum. Penny and I loved that weekend and looked forward to it every year. Although neither of us realised at the time, mum had begun to really miss dad and dad felt the same way. After three years apart, they got it together again and were remarried a year later. They have been happily married ever since.

As we approached the gates of 'Linden Lodge' I rang home on my mobile phone.

'Hello.' My father answered.

'Dad, it's me. Open up the fortress.' I joked.

'What's the password?'

'Lemon meringue!' I whispered. It was my favourite dessert.

'Come on down!' My father laughed.

The huge black iron gates swung slowly inwards. I waited until the gap was big enough and then headed along the tree lined gravel drive.

'Wow! This is gorgeous!' Emma stared, wide-eyed out of the window.

We followed the drive round to the right where it opened up into a big courtyard, revealing a beautiful white house. There were four white pillars holding up the roof of the grand entrance. There were trees everywhere and a tennis court just to the right of the courtyard. A stone statue of two swans entwined, spiralling upwards formed a delightful fountain in the centre of the courtyard. There was lush lawn around the fountain and an amazing array of flowers in the borders. Dad's Aston Martin Vantage was parked outside the house, with the number plate, MH 5, his best F1 finishing position in 1961. It was parked next to mum's Mercedes SLK that had been her latest birthday present. Penny's Golf was still looking quite good. She'd bought it six years ago and refused to part company with it. Dad had offered on various different occasions, to buy her a new car but Pen insisted that she loved her Golf and that she didn't want a new car.

'When can we move in?' Emma joked. 'I adore the house. But it looks like a car showroom out here!'

I laughed at Emma's comment. It had been a family joke for years. My mother had always complained about the number of cars that my father owned. 'You're going to get along just fine with my mum. She makes exactly the same observation every time she comes home.' I told Emma.

My parents had come out to greet us and I couldn't help noticing my father's reaction as he watched Emma get out of the car. Like father, like son, I thought!

'Mum, dad, meet Emma.'

'A pleasure to meet you Emma. I'm Mike and this is Janet.' Dad said, smoothly kissing Emma's offered hand.

'Nice to meet you both.'

'Come on in. I'm sure you would both like a drink.' My mother said, as she led us inside.

'Oh, and this is Jasper!' I laughed at our cheeky, black labrador licking Emma's legs.

'He's so cute!' Emma squealed, as Jasper rolled onto his back, waving his legs in the air. She knelt down beside him and rubbed his tummy.

'Just ignore him, Emma. He's such a big softy,' my mother commented.

'He's adorable, aren't you Jasper.'

I enjoyed watching Emma make a fuss of Jasper and smiled at Dad as he winked at me.

'Come on let's have a drink' my dad invited.

Dad served champagne on the terrace overlooking part of his huge estate. My sister was sat in one of the loungers, chatting with my grandfather. When she saw me, she leapt up, ran over and gave me a huge hug and a kiss.

'What a great welcome! Hi Pen. How are you? You look fantastic.' I stated, as I stepped back and looked at my sister.

'Hi Rog. I'm fine. I've really missed you. I've got some wonderful photos to show you.'

'Penny, this is Emma.'

'Hi, it's good to meet you, at last. Roger wrote to me in Thailand to tell me all about you. He didn't lie about your beauty. You're just as stunning as he told me.'

'Thanks Penny, that's really sweet of you to say.' Emma blushed. 'It's nice to meet you too. Roger doesn't stop talking about you, if you weren't brother and sister, I'd be worried!'

'Oh Rog. It's good to know that you care!' My sister playfully tweaked my cheek. 'How's that hunk, Frank?' She had fancied Frank since the day they met. Thankfully, Penny wasn't his type. I couldn't stand the thought of Henson with my little sister.

'He's feeling a bit sorry for himself at the moment. He's single again and because of all the cases he's working on, he has no time to go out pulling. I'm sure he'll survive though.' I pretended to feel sorry for him.

Penny got all excited at the news of Frank being single. 'What's his number?' She laughed and winked at Emma. 'I saw him on Crimewatch last week, he looked scrummy!' She was more interested in Frank than the rapes.

'Didn't he? Very good looking, I thought!' Emma agreed. I watched the girls laughing together and I couldn't believe how well my sister looked. She could pass for an Indian, she was so brown.

'Hey! Pen, don't lead Emma astray,' I said, trying to look as hurt as possible.

'Darling, relax. He's nowhere as good looking as you!' Emma screwed her face up and kissed me.

'Oh he is. Frank's much better looking!' Penny retorted and again the girls collapsed in stitches. It was going to be one of those days.

'Since when did you start fancying Henson?' I quizzed Emma.

'Since Thursday night!' She declared.

'That's my girl!' Penny and Emma clinked their champagne glasses.

ELEVEN

Frank held his head in his hands. It was not good news. He waved the young officer out of his office. He should be happy and excited; this was the break he and his team had been looking for. But with the break came the latest victim. Another pretty young woman violated by some arsehole for no reason apart from satisfying his own sick pleasure. Frank stood up and walked over to the window and stood staring into space.

A young woman had called to say her friend had been raped and she would be willing to give a statement. The victim's name was Amanda Worthington. She had been raped last weekend and her friend had seen Crimewatch and persuaded her to go to the police. They had arranged for Miss Worthington to visit the station at midday.

Frank arranged for a rape counsellor to be there and for a female detective to take her statement. These interviews were always very sensitive and he and his team had to play it very carefully. A woman who had been attacked in such a brutal fashion was very liable to change her mind and as a witness she could be vital to Frank's investigation.

Frank was informed Miss Worthington had arrived and that Susan Martin, the counsellor, had taken her into Interview Room 4. Frank took a deep breath and went to find DC Kelly Atkins.

Kelly knocked gently on the door and opened it. Frank followed her in and was introduced to Amanda Worthington by Mrs Martin. Her beauty stunned Frank. She had long brown hair and crisp, blue eyes. Her frame was very petite and her long legs were covered by her blue jeans. Frank could see the frightened look of pain in her eyes and he smiled to try to settle some of her fears.

Kelly took over and invited Miss Worthington to sit and she explained all about the process. One of the young female constables came in with a tray of tea and a coffee for Frank. He stirred the drink listening to Amanda Worthington begin her statement. Kelly was recording the interview with Miss Worthington's permission and she sat listening intently to the beautiful victim.

Amanda explained how she had been having lunch with her father and then caught a cab home from Trafalgar Square. The driver had taken a few turns to avoid the traffic then stopped to drop something off at the Volkswagen Audi garage just off Sloane Square. The next thing she knew he was getting into the back of the taxi with her and before she could do anything he slammed a rag in her face. She broke down in tears at this point and sat sobbing for a minute or two. Kelly asked her if she was okay to continue and Amanda said that she wanted to carry on.

The rag smelled of some kind of strong acrid chemical.

'Could it have been Ether?' Kelly asked.

'Maybe. I'm not sure.' Amanda said. That was all she remembered. She didn't mention she'd wet herself, she didn't feel that was important and anyway it was too embarrassing. She said as she came round she saw a flash of a camera going off and then the taxi drove off leaving her on the pavement.

When asked, she said she couldn't remember what he looked like, just that he had grey hair, but she thought he was quite young and he had a deep, husky voice. She also said her driving licence had been taken and her business cards, but no money.

Kelly and Frank left her with Mrs Martin for some counselling and Kelly took the tape away so she could quickly produce a typed statement for Amanda Worthington to sign.

TWELVE

The sun was up early and I had my Oakley sunglasses on. It had been a good weekend. Emma and Penny had got on famously and Emma really liked my family. My father had given her a signed photo of him in his racing car from 1961 for her father. She was thrilled with it and told my father her dad would love it. I knew that mum and dad approved - especially dad! My mother had pulled me to one side in the kitchen and told me so. Emma and I stayed over and dad and I had watched the Holland, Belgium game. Not a good result for me; a nil-nil draw. Holland would be easier this morning. At least I'd had a result on Friday night. France had beaten South Africa three, nil. Emma told me that I was pathetic gambling on football matches and I obviously had more money that sense. Women!

I'm not going to enjoy today, I thought as I sat at my desk. It was staff appraisal and bonus day. I always chose a Monday because we were never too busy. I had spent last night trawling through the figures. The bonuses were paid quarterly and this quarter had been a record. Michael Irwin had given me the total figure on Friday and the bonuses would be paid at the end of June. We had made over two million pounds and the desk got eight hundred and seventy five thousand to be distributed twelve ways.

I looked down at the list I had drawn up at home. I was to get three hundred grand, not bad for one quarter! Michael Irwin decided my bonus and I decided the rest of the desk. I had a list of every broker's turnover, their expenses and the turnover of each of the company's customers. I knew to the penny how much each broker was paid and how much he or she had made for the company. I was amazed, even Jamie had made money. It had nothing to do with his ability or his broking prowess; it was mainly due to the other brokers bringing in the business and Jamie feeding off it. I could have paid him twenty grand but I wasn't going to. I was giving fifteen of it to Michael Brooks who had worked really hard and done very well with his small client base. The lowest bonus would be five grand and the highest one hundred and twenty thousand, which I was giving to Eddie Pringle. He was the best producer by a long way. I was giving him twenty grand more than Brian Griffin, my number two. Brian wouldn't mind, he hadn't had a great quarter, but he was management and was also my friend.

Staff appraisals were considered very important at Kaplan. They were a very American idea. Most American firms lived and breathed appraisals and Dean Gilkey, the CEO, was no different. He felt appraisals were an invaluable opportunity for employee to meet employer on even ground and tell each other their thoughts. I didn't like them. I thought they were a potentially dangerous tool. I didn't like any of my guys coming into my office and trying to tell me how to do my job. Thankfully, most of my team didn't care about the politics of the firm, just as long as we were making money and they were paid fairly. A couple of the worst producers would always complain they weren't paid enough and spent the whole time slagging the rest of the desk off. I usually got very tense and would end up telling them what I really thought. The lowest paid broker was earning fifty thousand pounds per annum. I was always amazed at how they could complain. They sat in a very nice office and read newspapers most mornings. They had lunch provided for them everyday. They had an almost unlimited expense account and all received a car allowance and yet they were complaining about their salaries!

I logged onto my Bloomberg and accessed the Sporting Spread pages. I looked up the total goals for each country. As I had suspected Holland had been marked down, 5.75-6.0. I was already just over three hundred quid out of pocket. France were now 10.8-11.1 so I was up a hundred and forty quid there. I was okay on yellow cards, I had sold fifty pounds at 290 and the weekend games had been very tame. The price was now down to 275-285 so I could take a two hundred and fifty profit. Overall I was up small.

The morning's appraisals had gone much better than I had expected. We had a great little team and most of the guys had seemed pretty happy. Jamie Berry flew off the handle when I told him his bonus. 'Five grand? Do you think that's fair?' He had asked me. I told him that it was very fair and that he was lucky to get that. 'Well it's a fucking piss take! I've done loads of business and Pete's been giving us loads of swaps and stuff.' He informed me. I told Jamie Peter Jarvis had been mainly aggressive and Jamie had not been pulling his weight. He had been in late God knows how many times, had eight days sick and he just didn't concentrate enough. I accused him of being scared to pick up the phone and get business out of his people and if he didn't start trying harder he would be out. 'You are lucky to be getting anything at all.' I told him as he got up and stormed out of my office.

Brian had told me not to worry about it when I'd explained Jamie's reaction. 'You knew how he'd react Roger. Just bide your time and he'll end up making a big enough mistake that we can sack him. It's only gonna be a matter of time.'

I knew he was right but I didn't want to wait. 'Time isn't going to come into it Brian. I'll speak to Peter Jarvis when I can and explain we're going to have to let Jamie go.' I was still so angry.

'Roger, just leave it for now. Let's not do anything rash. As you said yourself, we do need Peter's business.'

I knew Brian was right but it didn't make me feel any better. As I sat at the dealing desk Mactavish came over to ask me how my bets were going.

'Not too bad actually.' I replied. 'No thanks to your second rate team!'

'They lost didn't they? What more do you want?'

'Brazil to have scored six or seven would have been nice.' I joked.

'Well you see, when they play a quality side like Scotland they have to adapt their game.'

'Do fuck off! Scotland, a quality side! That'll be the day!'

I picked up the outside line that had been ringing. 'Kaplan Stewart.'
'Roger, please.'
'Hi Henson it's me. What can I do for you mate? Are ringing to invite me out for drinks and dinner at some suitably expensive restaurant?' I joked.
'Rog. I wish. It's not good news. There's been another rape. Are you free this week?'

THIRTEEN

He left his work place at five thirty and headed for the newsagents for some cigarettes. His umbrella was at home and he smirked as he stepped outside and felt the rain on his face. He liked the rain. He looked up at the dramatically dark and sinister sky and thought; *this is going to be a majestic rainstorm.* He walked purposefully across the street, whistling loudly, oblivious to the glares from the passers-by. He didn't bother sidestepping any of the puddles; he just happily splashed through them in his Gucci shoes. He began to attract some strange looks but didn't care. He was soaked by the time he got back to his car and his feet were wet through. He slung his jacket onto the passenger seat and laughed as he put his foot on the clutch and felt his sock squelch! *I look like a fucking drowned rat!* He noticed in the rear view mirror. He slicked his long, blond hair back with the palm of his hand and wiped the wet hand on his now crumpled jacket next to him. *What a day! Time to go lap dancing again.*

He had sat in his taxi on Thursday night until about four am. Wanting to see how she got home he had watched the club from the side road waiting for Wendy to appear. The dancers had the choice of the sleazy mini cabs that hung around outside the club or the black taxis that waited on the rank. Wendy had taken a taxi with three other girls. *Good to see she was safety conscious!* He had followed the taxi to their destination. They had all got out together and gone into a nice looking semi-detached house in Clapham. It was good news Wendy had taken a taxi but he didn't like the other girls travelling with her. That was going to be a big problem. He decided he would stake out the club again later.

He squelched out of the lift and into his flat and threw his suit on the bedroom floor along with his shirt and socks. Half naked he walked into the kitchen and opened the fridge. He took out the bottle of Bollinger he'd put in the night before. *Tonight was going to be very cool!* He knew he would have something to celebrate later and couldn't wait. He opened the bottle carelessly; the cork flew out hitting the ceiling and a third of the contents spilt out onto the work surface. He didn't bother with a glass. He lifted the bottle to his mouth and took a big swig. *To dirty bitches everywhere,* he toasted out loud.

He opened his magic box and cut three thick lines on his coffee table. He snorted them in quick succession. He switched on his Bang and Olufsen music system and Black Sabbath's 'Paranoid' came thumping out the speakers at either end of the lounge. He sat down in an armchair and closed his eyes. He felt the stresses of the day begin to ease and ebb away and he imagined the events he had planned for later. A visit to 'Paradise', the lap-dancing venue in Hammersmith. He pictured Wendy in a small yellow bikini; her soft tanned skin and dyed blonde hair. Tonight would be her night. He felt a stirring in his crotch and took a sip of champagne. He sighed gently and grinned as he imagined her going down on him.

He jumped as the phone rang. '*Fucking Hell!*' He spluttered as he was brought crashing back to reality. The coke had heightened his senses and the shrill ringing had deafened him. The ansafone clicked in and took the call much to his relief. He couldn't face talking to his housekeeper. He knew it was her because she was the only person who had his number. He got up and turned the volume up so he could listen.

'…roof is leaking again. It's all this rain we've had up here, very unusual for June. We've had terrible thunder and lightening. I have put some pots and pans out to catch the big drips. Would you like me to call Arthur out? I assume you are still coming home on Friday. Please let me know what action you would like me to take.'

'*Fucking house!*' He swore. Olive had been in the family for years and was in her sixties now. His father had died when he was twelve and his mother had died in a fire in the house later the same year. He had inherited the house and a handsome sum of money. Olive had been out on the night of the fire and she had returned to find sirens wailing, blue and red lights cutting through the thick smoke and firemen rushing around the outside of the house. He had been found by one of the fireman hiding under a bush in the front garden. There was a picture on the front of the Daily Telegraph the next day of the fireman plucking the young boy to safety. They had saved the house and with the money he inherited, he'd had the whole place refurbished. Olive had stayed on to look after him. There had been a clause in his mother's will that paid Olive twelve thousand pounds to remain as his guardian. He was glad the ansafone had been on, it wasn't easy dealing with her when he was straight, never mind when he was high! She knew nothing of his habit; if she knew he did drugs she would have a heart attack. She was very straightlaced and had been very strict when he was younger but he was very glad to have her at the house now. He very rarely went there, but he would have to now. He would call her later.

He unlocked the door to the annex and sat at his desk. He looked up at the wall and remembered the photos next door. He jumped up and went into the darkroom, where there were eight or nine black and white photographs hanging on his drying line. He was a good photographer, he captured every moment, cleverly using the light available to give each photo real feeling. He had studied photography at College and would have chosen it as a career if the money had been better. He used a Nikon with a quick fire button, which enabled the camera to shoot a roll of film in eighteen seconds, two shots a second! He always used Fuji film and special Agfa developing paper. It was very hard to come by, but he had found a specialist shop in Hertfordshire he could order it from. He carefully unpegged the photographs and laid them face up. They were brutally graphic. They were of Amanda Worthington. *The posh little rich bitch!* He had gone through her handbag and taken her driving licence and looked through her purse. He found some business cards of hers. She worked for Foxtons, the estate agents. He was surprised to find over two hundred pounds in ten pound notes he left untouched. He was a rapist not a petty criminal! *I'll pay her a visit in a couple of week's time,* he thought as he noted the address on her business card down. *Always nice to see how my girls are getting on.* He spent the rest of the evening arranging Amanda's wall chart.

'Club Paradise. Good evening.'
'Can you tell me what time you close?'
'Last orders are two thirty, last dance at three.'
'Thanks.'

It was two o'clock when he pulled away in the taxi. *Time to pay Wendy a visit*

FOURTEEN

Wendy Winger hadn't always been a table dancer. She had started her career four years before as a glamour model. She had appeared in various top shelf publications. It didn't pay particularly well and most of the photographers she posed for were dirty old men. One bloke who worked for Penthouse seemed really nice at first. He had been good fun and very complimentary. These photographers saw so many naked women every day they rarely complimented their models. As she had taken her bra and knickers off he had sighed, 'Wendy, you have a great body.' He had sounded almost surprised.

'What did you expect? Some fat old bag?' she'd joked. His comment had made her feel good but by the end of the photo shoot he had changed completely. He had got his dick out and he had begun playing with himself.

'Wendy, how about it? You must feel horny after all that sexy posing? Come on baby.'

'Fuck off Dave! What do take me for? You're all the bloody same! You're all fucking perverts!' She'd exclaimed, quickly gathering her clothes and running out of the studio.

That was four months ago. She had been seeing a friend shortly afterwards who had just started table dancing. 'Wendy, come along one night and see what you think. The money's bloody good and there's no trouble. There are bouncers everywhere. It's a nice club and the other girls are really friendly.'

Wendy had started immediately and became an overnight success. On her first night, she had taken home eight hundred pounds. It was a Thursday night and the club had been packed. She made friends quickly and had moved into a house in Clapham with three other dancers. Trudy had bought the house a year ago and it was a refreshing change from all the hovels Wendy had rented in the past. It was a five bedroom terraced house near the common. Wendy's room had a double bed and a trendy Venetian blind. When she had seen the bed it reminded her how lonely she was. She knew she was good looking and had a great body but she hadn't had a boyfriend for over a year. She was sexually frustrated and ached for a passionate love making session. She told Trudy, who laughed and offered her services. 'I'll make love to you in a way no man could, honey!' Wendy knew that her friend had been joking but it had stayed in the back of her mind. She had never been with another woman but she did like the idea. A woman's body was so much more attractive and exciting than a man's was. She kept these thoughts to herself but they provided many fantasies over the past few months. Below the pine dado rail was dark blue wallpaper and above there were stripes of light blue and white. Wendy loved her room. She had a TV on top of her chest of drawers but she spent most of her afternoons downstairs with the other girls.

Wendy glanced at her Rolex, it was five thirty. Shit! She was late. She had been lying on her bed watching last night's episode of Coronation Street, which she'd recorded. She jumped off her bed and ran into Tina's room. Tina was twenty-two, a year younger than Wendy, but bigger up top. She was stood in the middle of her room drying her long, blonde hair with a towel. She was naked and had a perfect bikini mark, which she had spent many hours working on at Suntan City. The white was striking compared to her golden tan. Her body was great although Wendy thought her breasts were too big at 38C. A lot of the girls at Paradise had silicon implants because they thought the men that frequented the club liked them. Wendy would never get hers done. Hers were 34B and she loved them just as they were and she certainly wouldn't change them to please a load of drunken perverts.

'Tina, will you wait for me? I haven't even had a shower yet.'

'Sure. I don't care if we're a bit late. You know what Tuesday's are normally like, we'll be lucky if we cover our fee.'

The dancers started at seven pm and had to pay the club sixty pounds out of their takings. A dance lasted for one song and cost ten pounds. Last Tuesday Wendy had taken one hundred and thirty pounds for a profit of seventy pounds. That was a slow night and really hard work. She worked five nights a week and on average made about eighteen hundred pounds. That was nearly one hundred thousand pounds a year, for taking her clothes off. She didn't know anywhere else she could earn that kind of money. But there were certain drawbacks to the job, she was always being propositioned by the punters and sometimes there were some really pissed men from the City in the club who couldn't keep their hands to themselves. Most of the clientele were quite high calibre, either from the City or ad agencies. Occasionally Wendy would dance for a good looking guy which she really enjoyed but the odd one could be completely low life, like the guy who had asked her for sex last week. She'd told Tina he had offered her a thousand pounds.

'One thousand! Jesus, I would have jumped at the chance.'

'Not for him you wouldn't have. He made me feel really cheap, Tina. A real nasty piece of work.'

'How horrible. Was he one of those ugly, greasy pervey types?' Tina asked with her face screwed up.

'No, actually he was quite good looking, but he really scared me. He had a very deep, husky voice and his eyes, oh God his eyes! They looked straight through me and when the bouncers took him away, he didn't seem at all bothered and the way he winked at me, he was horrible. I asked him if he wanted a dance because he looked rich and smart. What a mistake. He was more like the kind of guy that wouldn't flinch whilst breaking your neck, you know?'

'Yeah, but a grand would have been worth the risk!' Tina joked.

'Yeah right! 'Here's a grand baby. Now kiss goodbye to the rest of your life, you little bitch!' Wendy mimicked the guy's deep voice.

Wendy was ready by six thirty and she and Tina made their way to Clapham Common tube station. Trudy and Debbie left at six and said they would see them there. The journey to Embankment took longer than normal. The girls loved living in Clapham but they hated their journey to work on the Northern line. It was the worst line on the London Underground system. The trains never ran on time and the carriages were always dirty, with litter and graffiti everywhere. At Embankment they changed onto the District line to Hammersmith. They always got the tube to work and because the tube stopped running at about one am took a taxi home when they finished at around three fifteen am.

They arrived at the club just after seven fifteen. They all shared a dressing room where each dancer had their own place in front of a long mirror. Debbie and Trudy were putting the final touches to their make-up when Wendy and Tina walked in. They sat chatting whilst they waited for their housemates to get ready. Once all four were ready, each in a different sexy outfit, they left the dressing room.

'Okay girls, let's work it. Let's go and frustrate the dirty bastards!' Wendy winked at her friends.

FIFTEEN

Frank had called me earlier that afternoon to arrange dinner. He had some news for me about the rapes and we planned to meet at TGI Fridays in Leicester Square. Lethal Weapon 4 had started last week and I was desperate to see it. I had the first three on video and I loved them. I had always wanted to be a plain-clothes cop who carried his Colt 45 tucked into his jeans, having high-speed car chases and catching villains.

I stepped out of the taxi and walked into TGI's. It was an American diner and had lots of old memorabilia covering the walls, number plates, traffic signs, American football gear, lots of different sports equipment going back to the fifties. There were screens everywhere beaming out MTV and sports channels. The greeter on the door was over the top as usual. 'Good evening Sir. Welcome to TGI's. Would you like me to reserve a table for you in our fabulous diner?' She smiled a really wide, sickly grin at me.

'No thanks. I'm meeting someone at the bar.'

'That's fine. Have a nice evening. If you would require...'

I ignored the rest of her company spiel and wandered up to the bar. The entire bar staff wore hats of all kinds and the chirpy barman that approached me was wearing an Aussie hat with loads of corks dangling from the brim. I ordered a bottle of Corona with a slice of lime in the top. I paid cash for a change instead of leaving my card behind the bar, as I knew we wouldn't be having our usual heavy session. There was nothing worse than sitting in the cinema desperate for a piss and then falling asleep half way through the movie.

I watched the American football on one of the TV screens above the bar and I didn't notice Henson sneak up behind me.

'TOUCHDOWN SAN FRANCISCO!' He screamed in my ear. I jumped a mile and dropped my beer. The bottle smashed, spilling it's frothy liquid over the floor and my shoes.

'You wanker!' I laughed. I turned to the barman and apologised.

'How are you Rog? You look well. You've got a really healthy, red glow about your cheeks!'

'Very amusing. Would Sir like a drink?'

'Do bears shit in the woods? Does Dolly Parton sleep on her back? Rolling Rock please mate.'

'A Rolling Rock and another Corona please.'

We sat on a couple of bar stools and looked around searching for any top totty that may have been lurking around. There wasn't a lot, much to Frank's annoyance.

'I'm not impressed with this Rog. Where's all the crumpet? How can a single guy like me survive?'

'Frank, never mind the girlies, we're not here for one of our big ones. We've got to leave in about fifteen minutes. Tell me the news. What's the latest?' I asked. I was desperate to know what Frank's update would contain.

'Well, there's been another rape. We got a call from a young lady. She's an estate agent in Fulham. She rang to say that a taxi driver had raped her friend but she had been too scared to come forward. The victim came in last Friday to give a statement, bit of a babe actually. Kelly and I interviewed her. It's such a shame. The poor girl was in fucking tears for most of the interview.'

'Oh no. You're kidding! How do you cope? How does a victim cope? It's all such bollocks! I sit in my comfy office thinking that I'm the best thing since the Internet, thinking what a difficult job I have to do, the pressure that us boys in the City are under. It's all a load of crap. You are the ones under pressure. Us City wankers haven't got a bloody clue about what goes on in the real world. There are all these psychopaths running about the place creating living hell for women. It just makes me so angry. I feel so fucking helpless!'

'Roger. Rog. Calm down.' Frank grabbed me. 'Calm down mate. How do you think I feel? I'm the one who's got to catch the bastard. It breaks my fucking heart too. When I see these women come in to give a statement, it's just fucking awful, you know. You realise they were just in the wrong place at the wrong time. It gets very depressing, knowing you haven't got enough evidence and you just have to wait for the next rape and hope some new clues come to light. Well this time he's gone too far. I'm going to catch this bastard.'

'And I'll be there beside you mate. You know that don't you. A real life Riggs and Murtar!' I slapped Frank on the back.

'Hi Roger.'

I spun round to find Brian Griffin's smiling face. His long blond hair was brushed back in a centre parting and his blue eyes twinkled in their usual confident way. He was another good-looking hunk. He looked good in a suit; his top button was undone and his tie had been loosened off which gave him a rough and ready, end of the day look. Great, I thought to myself, here I am stuck between two male models. I felt fat and ugly. 'Griffo, what the fuck are you doing here?'

'I'm meeting Bobby for a few drinks and then we're going to see Lethal Weapon 4.'

'No way? So are we. Frank meet Brian. Brian meet Frank. Brian works with me at Kaplan. He's one of my better brokers.'

'Hi Brian, nice to meet you.' I watched Griffo grimacing slightly as Frank shook his hand, squeezing the life out of it. Brian was fit but Frank was big and bulky!

'Call me Griffo, please. Any friend of Roger is a friend of mine,' he replied, gently massaging his right hand.

'Do you want a beer Griffo?' I asked him.

'Cheers Rog. A Bud Ice please.'

I caught a barman's attention. I was a bit pissed off Griffo had bumped into us. I wanted to know all about the latest rape but I knew Henson wouldn't feel comfortable discussing things in front of Brian. Hopefully Bob would turn up and we could leave the two of them to it. I gave Brian his beer and the three of us stood talking and eyeing up the odd girl that passed our way. By seven fifteen Griffo's customer had still not turned up.

'We'd better make a move Frank.' I said to my mate.

'Yeah. We don't want to miss the beginning,' he said excitedly. 'Nice to meet you Griffo. No doubt I'll see you again.'

'I might as well come with you guys. I don't think Bobby's going to show. He's always blowing me out. I'll try his mobile on the way. You don't mind do you Rog?'

'No not at all. Right you ready. We'll go on three!' I joked. Riggs was always saying that to Murtar when they were about to burst in on the baddies, with their guns blazing. We ran out of the bar and across into the cinema.

SIXTEEN

Louise Rutherford left her Fulham office and headed for Coniger Road. She had an appraisal at four thirty and a viewing at five. She got into her new VW Polo. It was a company car and Louise absolutely detested the colour, lime green! Her colleagues hadn't stopped winding her up about it. She and Amanda were having dinner later that evening and Louise just wanted the day to be over. Amanda had finally listened to her and gone to the police about her appalling rape. Louise was so proud of her friend and couldn't wait for their dinner date. Her mind had not been on the job lately and as she made her way along the New Kings Road she nearly missed the turning.

She pulled her little car up outside 14 Coniger Road and parked. The space was very tight and Louise wondered how some of the residents managed to park their BMWs and Mercedes. She began compiling her list of pros and cons as she walked to the front door. She rang the bell and as she waited her trained eye noted the flaking paintwork on the downstairs windows. An Indian lady opened the door.

'Good afternoon Mrs. Watkins. I'm Louise from Foxtons.'

'Hello Louise. Please do come in.'

Louise walked into a beautifully lavish living room that had obviously been recently redecorated. She hurried through each of the house's reception rooms and the five bedrooms and, having given Mrs. Watkins the good news her property was worth somewhere in the region of six hundred and fifty thousands pounds, she left.

Her next appointment was far easier. As she got into her little green bug her mobile rang. It was the office telling her the people had called to cancel the viewing. Louise was glad and she called Amanda to say she would be a bit earlier. Amanda was pleased, as she was very tired. She explained she hadn't been sleeping very well and she didn't want a late night. They agreed to meet at six thirty in the bar of the Bluebird Café and Amanda had insisted she was paying.

'We'll see about that. Take care darling and I'll see you there.' Louise spoke as if talking to a small child.

'Lou, don't be so protective. You make me feel about four years old. I'm fine now, honestly. I feel like a huge weight's been taken off my shoulders and I'm just getting on with things.' Amanda wasn't angry, she just wanted to make the point once and for all.

'Message received and understood. See you later.'

Louise rushed home as quickly as traffic would allow and ran a bath, pouring in far too much bubble bath. She liked a really foaming bath and wanted to lie and ponder. She felt really guilty for making Amanda feel like a kid. She knew she had a bad habit of being over-protective of her friends. As she lay in the bath she felt the stresses and strains of her day slowly ebb away.

She arrived at The Bluebird Café just after six-thirty and found Amanda waiting for her at the bar. She looked amazing, as she beamed Louise a huge, happy smile. Louise couldn't believe the change. Last time she had seen her, Amanda had looked depressed, very pale and about ten years older. This evening, Amanda looked like her old self again, and Louise told her so.

'Thanks Lou. I feel fantastic. I am so pleased I took your advice.' She replied, as they kissed each other on both cheeks.

They settled at a table in the corner and chatted non-stop. Amanda told Louise all about her trip to the station and went through the interview and how the police had recorded everything. 'They might need me to stand up in court if they ever catch the guy. I don't know what he looks like but the lady who interviewed me told me they had DNA samples from some of the other victims and…'

'What do you mean, other victims?' Louise interrupted.

'I was shocked as well. The police told me not to say anything to anyone. The taxi driver that raped me has raped four other women.'

'You're kidding! A serial rapist!'

'They don't have any real solid evidence yet but it can't be a coincidence when five women all get raped by taxi drivers.'

'I can't believe it. What did the police say to you? Were you able to help?'

Amanda was very calm. 'I'm so pleased I went, Lou, the lady that interviewed me was so nice and caring. I was in there for just over an hour. It was so harrowing at the beginning but she was ever so understanding.'

'God, I can imagine. You have been so strong through all of this.' Louise stopped herself from going too over the top. Amanda didn't need sympathy right now. 'Do you think you gave the police any clues?'

'You bet!' She sounded very excited. 'I told them he had a really deep voice and his hair was grey. The lady told me two of the other girls had said the same thing. One of the girls said she thought he was aged between forty and fifty. But you know, that's the really weird thing about him, I'm sure he was a lot younger. He was quite fit and muscular.' She shook her head in disgust. 'I don't want to talk about it anymore.'

The girls spent the rest of their evening catching up on everything else. Louise filled her in on all the latest gossip from the office and Amanda said she would be back at work next week. They both left the restaurant and drove home in their cars, having promised each other never to travel in a taxi again.

SEVENTEEN

I slipped my card into the service till and checked my balance. I took back my card and folded the mini-statement into my wallet. I whistled happily as I made my way back to the office. I was seeing Penny for supper tonight and had a little surprise in store for her. We were going to Sale Pepé in Knightsbridge. It was Penny's favourite Italian restaurant in London. The tables were just a bit too close together for my liking, but it was Penny's birthday and her choice. I took her out for her birthday every year and as my salary had increased so had my sister's choice of establishment.

I sat at my desk and Brian filled me in on what I'd missed. I thanked him and rang my customers just to touch base. I then rang the Volkswagen dealer in Battersea to put the final touches on my plan for Penny's birthday present. I had ordered her the new shaped Golf GTI in a beautiful royal blue. It had taken me ages to persuade the manager to agree to my demands. I got him down on price and for a bit extra the car was being delivered tonight on a transporter! The manager was having a pretty pink ribbon tied around the car and I couldn't wait to see Penny's face.

The table was booked for seven-thirty, which meant I had a bit of time to kill. Some of the boys were going for a drink downstairs and Brian asked me to join them. I asked him where they were going and he told me, Bar Excellence. I told him I would meet them there. I liked Bar Excellence; it was one of those new style bars as opposed to a pub. I didn't like pubs. I wasn't a great bitter or lager man unlike the average bloke. I much preferred bottled beer. And, even though I was a smoker myself, I always found pubs too smoky. The new bars in London had great ventilation. I tidied my desk and checked the profits for the day. I called Emma just to remind her I was having dinner with Penny and then headed for the bar.

The boys had a bottle of beer waiting for me when I arrived. They had found a nice little spot in the corner and looked as if they were going to be there some time. I congratulated them all on our day's work but then told them there wouldn't be many more decent days left. I was having a meeting with Michael Irwin next Friday and Dean Gilkey was coming over from the States to join us. Dean Gilkey was God; he was the Chief Executive Officer of Kaplan Stewart International. I didn't know what the meeting was about, but had heard from a good source the company was bringing in electronic trading. I had a hunch we would be the guinea pigs for the new system. I liked Dean Gilkey but he was a very hard man to argue with. I wasn't sure I was going to like what he had to say.

'I wouldn't worry about Gilkey too much Rog.' Brian gave me a reassuring squeeze on the shoulder. 'We're making money, he's not going to rock the boat too much.'

'I'm not so sure Griff. The liquidity in the market is drying up more and more everyday. You've seen the figures. It's only 'cause of our friends we're still doing some decent clips. I've just got a funny feeling about this one. I don't think we will still be a desk of fourteen by the end of the World Cup.'

'I don't like it when you get one of your feelings. Anyway, what will be, will be. How's Frank? Isn't he working on these rape cases I read about in the newspaper today?'

'Yeah.' I smirked, as I pictured Henson's pretty face in the paper. 'Did you see the picture of him in the Times today? He's turning into a real celebrity!'

'I thought he looked quite good. It was great to see him the other night. When are you seeing him next? I'd love to pop along for a quick beer.'

'Should be sometime next week, I'll let you know.' I replied, finishing my beer. 'Right I'm off. You lot look settled for the evening. Have a good one.'

'See you in the morning Rog. I hope your sister likes her surprise.' Griff shouted after me.

I jumped in a taxi and found myself wondering if the driver was the rapist. I had looked at his face very closely as he wound down his window. He was in his late fifties, far too old. The taxi made its way across London and I sat staring into space, thinking about Frank and the difficult job he had ahead. The hailstones that began beating down on the roof of the cab broke my thoughts. London was really miserable in the rain, dull and grey. I watched the tourists battling with their umbrellas as they walked along the Mall, towards Buckingham Palace. Even the Palace looked drab and dreary. I snapped out of my gloomy mood and started to look forward to my evening with Pen.

The taxi pulled up outside Sale Pepé. I paid the fare and ran into the restaurant. The bar was already busy and the umbrella stand was full of multi coloured brollys. The lady took my damp overcoat and checked my reservation. As she was putting my coat on a hanger, Alfredo, the manager, came bustling over. 'Ciao, Professorie! Comme sti?'

'Ciao Alfredo. Benne grazie mille.' I replied in a very poor Italian accent.

'How nice to see you. I 'ave a very special table for you by-a da window. I 'ave the champagne ready on the table.' He said, rolling his R's in the way that only the Italians could.

'Thank you. Is my sister here yet?'

'No Senhore, you are da first to arrive.'

I ordered a gin and tonic at the bar and waited for Pen. It was a very busy Italian restaurant, popular with Americans and the financial world. It was like all the successful places in London, you had to book at least three weeks in advance. There was supposedly a mini-recession going on in England but you would never guess it from the restaurants. I had a perfect view of the door and stood sipping my drink watching the other patrons rush in from the wet. By the time Penny came running down the street, the restaurant had begun to fill up. She had a Cartier Umbrella and shook it vigorously outside before entering. She wore a striking red suit with a skirt that I thought was a bit too short under a blue cashmere overcoat. Her blonde hair was in a very smart bob and her huge blue eyes were stunning against her newly acquired suntan. She noticed me at the bar and beamed a grin at me as the maitre d' courteously took her coat and umbrella.

'Happy birthday Pen.' I said as we kissed and I handed her a present. I had bought a watch from TAG Heuer which I wanted her to think was her only present. The transporter was due at eight o'clock, in fifteen minutes, I noted as I looked at the white face of my gold Rolex.

'Let's go straight to the table, I've ordered some drinks, they should be waiting at the table.' I said innocently. I wanted Penny to be sat down and relaxed by the time the car arrived. I also wanted her to know she was driving home! I didn't want her having too much to drink. Alfredo had sorted out a bottle of Krug, which sat in a bucket of ice.

Penny's face lit up when she saw the champagne and turned to give me another kiss. 'Roger, how wonderful.'

Alfredo opened the bottle and I toasted Penny's birthday. She sipped the champagne and then opened her present. She had a Swatch watch on and very quickly ripped it off and replaced it with her Tag. 'Wow! I just love it. Thank you so much. That is so naughty of you.'

'It's my pleasure. I knew you needed a decent watch and I told mum and dad that I was buying you one just in case they did. It looks really good against that bloody tan.'

'This?' She asked, rubbing her forearm. 'You saw me on Saturday and it's faded so much since then and I've started peeling on my back. Mummy and Daddy bought me a year's membership to The Sanctuary in Covent Garden. I am so excited.'

'Wow, that's wonderful. You'll be able to top your tan up on the sunbed then. How's the new job going?'

'It's fantastic. I really didn't think I would settle here again. I loved sleeping on the beach in Thailand and not having to get up at a set time every bloody day. But the people I work with are great and I've been given some good clients already. One of the girls has a flat in Fulham and I'm moving in next week. I think Mummy and Daddy will be pleased and I'm sick of the commuting already! I'm off to the Polo at Smiths Lawn, Windsor Great Park for the Cartier Championships in a couple of weeks. One of my accounts is Veuve Clicquot and they are sponsors, I am so excited. Oh! If you guys are free on Saturday, one of my new accounts is launching their new outdoor go-kart circuit. Would you like to come?'

'That sounds great. I don't think we've got any plans. I'll check with Em. Is it a nice flat?'

'Yes, it's really sweet and my bedroom's lovely and big. Lucy is so nice too. You'll love the launch party. I've got some pit passes for you and you can both race. We're running a four-hour endurance race. There are going to be lots of celebrities. I'm just finalising numbers at the moment.'

'Who's going?' I asked.

'David Coulthard, Johnny Herbert, Damon Hill, Vic and Bob, Denise van Outen, Ian Pattison, Dani Behr and Shane Richie, possibly the Spice Girls, and Robbie Williams. But the really big one is Tom Cruise!!!'

My sister was so excited and her eyes and mouth jammed wide open at the mention of Tom Cruise. I have to admit I was very impressed. 'What a guest list! And Tom Cruise? How did you pull that off?'

'He's been to the indoor track quite a lot and he and the MD of Daytona have become friends. So it wasn't really my doing but it really impressed my boss. Daddy helped with the F1 drivers, he even tried to get Schumacher along but he was busy.'

I was really proud of her and I told her so. It was great having a father like ours. We got invited to so many parties and mixed with lots of famous people from the world of Motorsport. I knew Johnny Herbert and Damon Hill quite well, I wouldn't go so far as to say we were friends but I'd had many a drink with them in the past.

'Have you been to any World Cup games yet?' she asked me.

'No but I've had loads of bets.'

'Why do you always gamble? Why can't you just put your money in a Building Society like normal people?'

'Normal people don't make the kind of money I do. It's good fun and exciting. Just having it sat in a building society knowing the exact rate of return doesn't do it for me.'

I looked out the window and saw the transporter pull up outside. There was a tarpaulin over the car as arranged. Penny had noticed too but thought nothing of it. Alfredo came running over and told Penny there was a phone call at reception for her. When she'd left the table, I got up and followed her and sneaked outside. I helped the lorry driver remove the tarpaulin. The Golf looked fantastic, it had a huge pink ribbon wrapped around it and there were balloons tied all over it. There was a huge sign that said 'HAPPY BIRTHDAY PENNY! LOTS OF LOVE ROGER xxx' I ran back inside and sneaked past reception. I had arranged for Mum to call Penny and keep her talking. I got back to the table and looked out the window. It looked brilliant. I was very pleased with the result and couldn't wait for Penny to get off the phone.

I rose out of my seat as Penny sat back down at the table. She told me it was mum and dad on the phone to wish her a happy birthday. She hadn't noticed the car outside. She took a sip of champagne and I told her that she had better not drink too much.

'Why on earth not? It's my birthday and I'll drink if I want to.' she sang to me.

'Well if you drink too much, you won't be able to drive that home.' I gestured out the window and watched my sister's face. She sat there staring, with her mouth open and eyes wide. She shook her head and tried to speak but nothing came out. It was delightful and I felt really great. Penny was overjoyed and having hugged me for five minutes went running out to see the car. I paid Alfredo for the meal we didn't have and went joy riding with Penny.

EIGHTEEN

He got there at two fifteen and parked his taxi on the cab rank behind two others. He was far too early and realised the girls wouldn't start leaving until after three. The first taxi left with a couple of men in suits. When the taxi in front was taken by the next fare it was two thirty five. As three men stumbled out of the club, he drove his taxi away, to leave them for the one behind. He would have to be very lucky to pick up Wendy tonight. *This is a fucking nightmare. How the fucking hell am I going to catch this bitch?* He drove round the block a couple of times with his yellow light off. There were no taxis on the rank now, just a whole load of mini-cab drivers in Sierras and Vauxhalls.

At five past three he stopped again on the cab rank. His was now the only taxi there. He bent down to his left and opened his 'magic' box. He picked out some of the powder and snorted it quickly. He was feeling very good and wanted a little extra buzz. He checked his pockets. He had the wadding and the gloves, now he just needed Wendy. The first of the dancers began emerging. There was a car park at the back where a lot of the girls parked their cars. He knew that Wendy would take a taxi but he didn't want her housemates to join her. He watched the doors of the club like a hawk, not wanting to miss his prey. The girls all looked really plain and drab now they were in their casual clothes and you would never guess what they did for a living. Most of the girls wore baggy tracksuits with training shoes. He was feeling really horny watching the girls and he decided if just one girl got into his cab, she would be the next.

Two girls approached the taxi and he glanced in his rear view mirror. His was still the only cab on the rank; he couldn't turn them away. They stopped right by his cab and the girls kissed each other goodbye. The shorter of the two with frizzy blonde hair, a perfect complexion and big platform sneakers walked briskly off towards a mini-cab. The other girl was stunning. Even though it wasn't Wendy, he couldn't believe his luck. *Yes! Come on in Darling, the water's lovely!* She had long, shiny brown hair and blue eyes. She too had great skin, sun-tanned like most of the dancers. Her nose was too big for her face but her teeth were the whitest, straightest teeth he'd ever seen. And when she smiled it took his breath away.

'Can you take me to Clapham please? Sullivan Road.' Her voice was so disappointing. She looked like she would be really classy, but her cheap, Essex accent didn't fit her face.

She jumped in and sat on the back seat. He glanced at her in his mirror and couldn't contain his excitement. He slapped the steering wheel and began sniggering. *I am the luckiest fucker in the world! What a fucking doll!* He looked back at her again and was overjoyed at the size of her tits. They were spectacular! *They couldn't be all hers; not even God was that clever.* He had to control himself when the smell of her perfume came wafting through the partition window. *She looks good, she smells good and I bet she tastes good!* He had a semi-hard on already and began thinking of where they were going to fuck. He had a spot in mind.

He heard her mobile phone ring and listened to the conversation. It was obviously one of her roommates calling, who had been locked out of the house. His passenger sounded concerned and promised she wouldn't be very long. She said she was heading south over Putney Bridge towards Wandsworth. She finished the call and then spoke to him, 'S'cuse me mate, put yer foot down, can ya? My friends locked out the 'ouse.'

He simply nodded and accelerated slightly. *It would be difficult to stop the cab now without her getting frustrated. Why were women so fucking stupid?* As he crossed the bridge he turned right and took the very next left and stopped outside an office block.

'My mate works nights here and he's a locksmith. Be back in a tick.' He rushed out the cab before she had a chance to stop him. He quickly put the latex gloves on as he walked away from the taxi and into the reception of the building. He asked the frail, old security guard for directions and then abruptly slammed the wet wadding into his face. He didn't want any witnesses and was very pissed off he'd had to alter his normal pattern. *At least this would give the police something to think about.* He left the old man slumped in his chair and headed back to the taxi. The girl was now stood outside the cab and looked really impatient.

'I don't need a bloody locksmith. I live there too. I've got a set of keys. Just take me home, please.' She instructed him, dangling her keys at him.

'Sorry love, I was only trying to help. He's not in tonight anyway,' He said, trying to keep the adrenaline rush under control. She obviously hadn't seen the incident with the security guard, *thank fuck!* 'Hop in love and we'll get going.'

He watched her climb into the back of the cab and he dived in after her. His heart was pounding and he couldn't breathe. He was upon her in an instant and in no time had the "sleeping juice" smothered into her face. She thrashed and kicked like they all did, but he was more than prepared for it. Her dainty little arms were no match for his muscular physique and he kept a careful eye on her long legs just in case. It didn't take long and once he was completely sure she was out cold, he got out and casually got back into the driver's seat. He didn't like being south of the river and had already got a love nest planned. He couldn't have gone straight to it because he hadn't wanted to alert her.

He steered the taxi towards its final destination, back over the bridge and right into the New Kings Road. He turned right again into Hurlingham road and turned into the small side road. It was a dead end and led into an industrial unit where he sometimes went to have his car cleaned. There were also various car workshops and MOT places based there. At this time of night the road was very quiet.

He switched the engine off and got out. He opened the rear door and climbed in. She was lying in a crumpled heap and he lifted her sweatshirt up. She had a Wonderbra on and he squeezed her breasts. *Fake. I knew they would be. Nice and firm though. You don't mind if I play with them do you darling?* Her friend could wait. In fact he might pop along to find her later!

NINETEEN

Jamie Berry didn't want to go out later. He was having dinner with Peter Jarvis, his man from FDS. Jamie had been out on too many benders recently and he just wanted a quiet night at home. Eddie was going with them and Jamie didn't like Eddie, mainly because he was Roger Hamilton's supergrass, which meant Jamie wouldn't be able to get too drunk. Eddie would always tell Roger if any of the guys came back late from lunch or if they'd fucked up during a trade. He was always grassing Jamie to Roger and Jamie knew that Roger had it in for him. Eddie didn't do drugs; his vice was women. Jamie didn't ever pay for sex, he didn't have to, but he did do drugs. He knew he was good looking and had never had a problem with women. The girl he'd taken home last night had been a right little raver. She lived in Chelsea, about two minutes from Jamie's flat in South Kensington. They had spent most of the night 'shagging' as Jamie called it. He was knackered now and regretted last night. She had called him twice already; both times he had pretended to be busy. I should never have given her my number, he thought.

'Right then, where are we meeting the boys?' Eddie came bouncing over.

'I don't know yet. Gotta speak to Pete. I thought we'd go up to the West End. Table's booked for eight at Mezzo.' Jamie replied, in his posh Sloane ranger accent.

'Great, let me know.'

Jamie and Eddie left the office at bang on five and jumped in the taxi that one of the secretaries had booked for them. They were meeting Peter and the rest of his team in the Pitcher and Piano in Wardour Street. Jamie was very worried about Roger's meeting with Dean Gilkey. He asked Eddie if he knew what it was about.

'I don't think it's going to be good news. I can't really say anything you know that. Just keep your head down over the next week or so and keep your nose clean.' Eddie had a very good idea what the meeting was about, but he didn't want Jamie to know. There were going to be redundancies and Jamie's name was at the top of the list.

They got there before their clients and stood at the bar smoking and drinking. Jamie found conversation difficult. He had little in common with Eddie, who was fifteen years older. Jamie loved going out clubbing and raving and he couldn't imagine when the last time Eddie had been in a night-club unless it was for sex. Jamie was bored and needed a little pick-me-up so he told Eddie he was going to the toilet.

Jamie walked into the gents and into one of the cubicles where he pulled out a small packet. He opened it and licked his finger and dipped it into the Speed. He finished half the contents and folded the packet back up. He unlocked the door and went over to the basin and washed his hands. He had a couple of pills he might pop later and he also had the Cocaine Peter had asked him to bring along. Even if Eddie was there Jamie knew it would be a good evening. He smiled at himself in the mirror as he straightened his tie. It was a beautiful Hermes he had been bought last week from the shop in Royal Exchange. He tucked it inside his blue, single-breasted jacket and strutted back into the bar.

Peter and the two guys that worked for him arrived fashionably late. It was always the same with all traders. They treated brokers like shit and as nothing but a meal ticket. They always went for a drink on their own first and would turn up at least half an hour late. Peter Jarvis was no different. They were nearly an hour late and Jamie had begun to think they weren't coming. He had tried calling Peter on his mobile but kept getting his ansafone message.

'I tried your mobile a couple of times.' Jamie said as he passed Peter his beer.

Peter looked uncomfortable for a split second and replied, 'Sorry mate, it was turned off. Cheers.' He raised his bottle. The other two guys from FDS smirked and clinked bottles with Jamie and Eddie. They stood at the bar talking about their days and the markets. Eddie was fairly good on market technicals and was very happy to stand chatting about yield curves and basis prices. Jamie on the other hand, just stood there listening and trying to look interested. He tried catching Peter's eye and finally managed it on the third attempt. Jamie winked and tossed his head towards the toilets and patted his jacket pocket. Peter knew what he meant and winked back.

Peter Jarvis was twenty-nine years old and had found success at a very early age. He had graduated from Exeter University with a first in Economics and Business Management. He applied to all the main banks in the City and was accepted by Barclays where he had two years learning how to trade bonds. He picked things up very quickly and had what it took. It helped that at Barclays, the size of positions the traders could take were almost limitless. Taking on a big position and running it and having complete faith in it, even when it went against you, took balls and Peter Jarvis had balls. In his second year he had been let loose on his own and had made the company just over two million pounds. The bosses at Barclays couldn't believe it. 'What's this guy's secret? Is he just lucky?' the Chief Executive had asked the head of bond trading. He was told the profit was exceptional. The market had been very volatile and a lot of firms had lost a huge amount of money. Peter Jarvis had been the only profitable trader at Barclays that year. That was five years ago and since then Peter had been headhunted twice, each time with a large Golden Handshake and massive salary. He had moved to FDS last year and had been made head of trading six months ago. He liked Jamie. He knew he wasn't the best broker in the world but he was very devoted, kind of like a dog, stupid but very faithful! He loved Jamie's sense of humour and the main thing they had in common was drugs. They'd had many a good night out on Cocaine and tonight would probably be another, Peter thought.

'I'm just going get some more fags, mate.' Jamie said to Peter and wandered off. Peter went to the toilet and met Jamie by the vending machine outside.

'There you go mate. Enjoy. It's fucking brilliant stuff. I've taken some Speed and I've got some tabs for later. Top fucking tastic!!' Jamie grinned and smacked his client on the back.

'Thanks Jamie. How much do I owe you?'

'Don't worry about it mate. I'll just whack it through on my expenses!' Jamie laughed and sauntered back to the others.

They got to the restaurant fifteen minutes late by which time the place was packed. The bar was crammed full of beautiful young ladies, some of which were hookers. It was a well-known fact that high-class hookers hung around the bar waiting to take advantage of the well-heeled customers. Terence Conran owned Mezzo and it was one of his more successful establishments. The reception area was vast with a cloakroom on the right with a suitably exquisite young lady taking coats. The bar swept round to the left and was overflowing with people. Most of the diners were young and trendy, from the world of media and advertising. There was café style dining upstairs and an a la carte restaurant downstairs. The boys went downstairs to their table, led by another attractive member of staff. The restaurant was very art deco but stylishly designed and the food was amazing. There was a live jazz band playing in the corner near the bar downstairs. The atmosphere was great and Jamie and the boys settled at their table, looking forward to the meal. Eddie nudged Peter and nodded towards the girl's legs as she passed out the menus. Jamie shook his head in disgust at the lecherous, grey haired, old fart. Eddie was married to a solicitor who was a very wealthy woman in her own right. Between the two of them, they were very comfortable. Eddie didn't have a mortgage and didn't really need to work anymore. But he loved the industry, he loved the social side and he loved sex. He would often tell his wife he was out with clients, when in fact he was in some brothel or sex club.

As they sat smoking cigars and drinking stickies at the end of their meal they discussed where they were going next.

'How about lap dancing?' Eddie suggested excitedly. 'There's a great club in Hammersmith. The girls are meant to be really rude.'

'How about going to a casino?' Jamie suggested. He was buzzing and didn't like the idea of sitting around in some dark club. He wanted to do something he could get a buzz from. He couldn't afford to lose but thought it would be a laugh.

'Bollocks to a casino, Jamie. We want some dirty birds.' Eddie told him.

'Yeah, let's go lap dancing, what d'ya reckon Pete?' One of the others said.

'Well, I'm not sure…..' Peter began, but was interrupted by Eddie.

'Paradiso! Or something. I think that's what it's called. It's in Hammersmith, fifteen minutes by cab. Come on Peter, you know it makes sense.'

'No!' Peter almost shouted. 'Not there.' He realised the rest of the party were looking at him as if he were mad. 'Um. It's uh. It's just that I've heard that it's shit in there.' He stuttered and fumbled over his words.

'Pete, you all right mate? You've gone very pale.' Jamie asked.

Peter undid his top button and loosened his tie. 'Yeah, I'm fine, just a bit hot. Look, I don't mind going lap dancing but I just don't want to go to Club Paradise.'

'Club Paradise! That's it. Well done Pete. I'd never have remembered that.'

'I just said no!' Peter glared at Eddie, who dropped his head and played with his brandy glass.

'Fuck me Eddie, you're going really grey!' Jamie burst out laughing, pointing at his colleague's head. Peter smiled and began laughing. Eddie joined in, glad that the awkward moment had passed. He wondered what Peter's hang up with Club Paradise was.

'Thanks mate. You'll be grey one day too you know?' Eddie playfully flicked his V's at Jamie.

'Oi Pete,' Jamie nudged Peter. 'How about the Windmill? That's only round the corner, and then we could go gambling after.'

'Done. Come on let's go and see some dirty little bitches and then make some more money!' Peter replied and aggressively downed the rest of his Kummel. 'Monte Carlo or bust!'

They all staggered out of Mezzo laughing loudly.

TWENTY

Wendy woke with a start. She sat bolt upright in bed. She was sure she had heard someone shouting or screaming. She listened and heard nothing. She got out of bed and slowly peeked between the curtains. The street was very quiet and empty. She thought that she must have been dreaming and climbed back into bed. Then she heard someone screaming downstairs. It was coming from inside the house. Her pulse quickened and she jumped out of bed and quickly put on her dressing gown. She slowly opened her bedroom door, scared of what she might discover downstairs. She heard someone crying and she peeked over the top of the stairs and saw Debbie lying in a heap on the floor, her shoulders jerking in time with her sobs.

Wendy rushed down to find out what had happened to her housemate. By now Tina had come out to see what the commotion was and also sped downstairs. They helped Debbie to her feet and slowly led her into the lounge. Debbie was too hysterical to speak so Wendy ran to the kitchen and poured a large glass of Rum from a bottle she used for cooking. She gave it to Debbie who sipped from the glass. She grimaced as the harsh spirit hit her throat. Colour returned almost instantaneously to her cheeks and she wiped the tears from her face.

'What happened Debbie?' Wendy asked in a soft whisper.

'I don't wanna talk about it.' She murmured into her hands that were hiding her face.

Wendy forced her friend to drink some more rum and handed her another tissue from the box of Kleenex. Debbie blew her nose and looked up at her housemates. 'I've been raped.' She stated matter of factly. 'I've just been raped by that taxi driver.' She started crying again and then, before Tina or Wendy could stop her, jumped up and rushed out of the lounge and upstairs to her room. By the time Wendy got there the bedroom door was locked.

'She's locked the bloody door. Debbie, are you all right. Do want to talk love?'

'Go away. Leave me alone.'

'Come on Tina. Let's leave her, she's safe for now. Do you wanna coffee?'

'I may as well, I'm not going to get to sleep now.' Tina followed Wendy down to the kitchen.

'Should we call the police do you think?' Wendy asked.

'I don't know. Would Debbie want us to call them? If we call the police, we'll have to explain what happened and Debbie may not want to go through all the pain of giving statements and maybe even having to go to court. I think we should wait and try to talk to Debbie when she's calmed down. I just feel so awful, slagging her off for leaving me stuck on the bloody doorstep. If you hadn't come home when you did, I'd still be out there! And the whole time she was being attacked. God how terrible.'

Wendy handed Tina a mug of piping hot coffee and sat down at the breakfast table. 'I know, it's best not to think about it. Do you think when she referred to *that* taxi driver, she meant the guy they are looking for on Crimewatch?'

'Maybe. Or maybe she just meant the driver that brought her home. How does she normally get home? In one of the club's cars or cab?'

'Normally black cab. She doesn't like the mini-cab drivers very much. Oh Shit! How ironic. I think we should call the police. What if it was the same guy? I read about him in The Mail last week. He's raped four or five women so far. We've got to call them. Debbie might be able to tell them something that will help.' Wendy was really concerned. She sipped her coffee and waited for Tina to reply.

'I still think we should talk to Debbie first. I know what you're saying but let's see if Debbie tells us anything and if she does, we can always call them but not give her name.'

The two girls sat staring into space with their mugs of coffee going through the events of the early morning. Neither of them wanted to sleep. Wendy was so upset for Debbie. She couldn't imagine how her friend felt. To be raped, the worst violation any girl could suffer. They talked about how awful it would be to be sexually assaulted and what kind of animal could commit such an act.

'There's no way I'm ever going to travel by cab again.' Tina stated.

'What and get in one of those bloody mini-cabs instead? No way! I'd rather risk taking a taxi than going in one of those smelly cars. There's that white Ford that always waits outside, you know, John I think his name is.'

'I know.' Tina interrupted. 'He smokes and his breath always stinks of drink. He's always hanging out with the doormen. He's such a slime ball. I couldn't travel with him, but some of the others are okay.'

'No way, I'll still travel by taxi. What are the chances of me jumping into the cab that the rapist's driving?'

'Maybe you're right. I'll see how I feel about it next time I'm outside the club. I'm gonna pop up and see if Debbie's okay.'

'Good idea.' Wendy got up and followed Tina upstairs.

Wendy knocked on the door to Debbie's bedroom. The two girls waited, looking at each other, concerned about their friend. The lock clicked but the door remained closed. Wendy tried the door. It opened and she slowly walked in with Tina following closely. Debbie was sat on her bed. The lamp on her bedside table was on and the TV was on too, but the volume was turned down. She was sat hugging her knees into her chest and rocking very slightly backwards and forwards.

Wendy sat down on the side of the bed and gently touched her friend's arm. 'Debbie are you alright?'

'No I'm not all right. Why the fuck would you think I'd be all right. I've just been fucking raped!' Debbie screamed.

'I'm so sorry Debbie. We're just both really concerned. Will you tell us what happened?' Wendy treaded very carefully not wanting to upset Debbie any further.

'Please talk to us. We want to help you.' Tina supported Wendy.

Debbie brushed her hair away from her face and wiped her eyes with the back of her hand. She sat upright and unfolded her long legs. Her neatly painted toenails were a sharp contrast to her face, which now had mascara smudged around her eyes and any traces of lipstick were long gone. She looked at her two housemates and tried to force a smile. 'Go to bed. It's gone five thirty.' She said looking at her watch on the bedside table.

'We are concerned about you Debbie. Is there anything we can do? Do you wanna talk about it?' Wendy asked.

'Maybe in the morning. I just want to be alone now. I'm okay. I need to get some sleep.' Debbie said crawling under her duvet.

The girls left the bedroom and made their way back down to their mugs of coffee. They had no choice but to leave Debbie until the morning. Wendy said she was off to bed too. She would persuade Debbie to go to the police. She didn't like the thought of some rapist being at large in London and shuddered as she closed her bedroom door.

TWENTY ONE

It had been a pretty shitty week and Emma and I had celebrated the end of it last night with a bottle of Chablis, a pizza and a video. I'd had my meeting with Michael and Dean yesterday afternoon and my fears had been justified. The company had been using an electronic trading system in the States for about six months. It was an overnight success and now they wanted it implemented on Gilts. It was a great system that enabled the Traders to input their own prices and trade themselves. The Stock Exchange had introduced a similar system into the Equity market a year ago called SETS. It had wiped the inter-dealer broking firms out of business within six months. The SETS system was free to use compared to the broking systems that cost fifty pounds per one hundred thousand traded. There had been talk of a free trading system on Gilts for some time now and many broking firms had decided to pre-empt it with their own cheap electronic dealing systems.

Dean had run me through the figures and how quickly the clients could have it on site. He expected it to be implemented by the Fourth of July, American Independence Day. How apt I had thought. He then broke the bad news I had been expecting. Our profits would be reduced by more than forty percent and therefore I would have to reduce the number of staff on my desk. He wanted the costs down by fifty-five grand a month. I had sat in my office working out staff costs and it looked like I would have to let two or three brokers go. If I knew Dean Gilkey, it wouldn't stop there.

I was up early and was preparing breakfast when Emma sidled up next to me. She reached inside my dressing gown and gently tickled my balls. 'Morning sexy! I see you haven't got your racing pants on yet.'

I laughed and kissed her. I gently undid her dressing gown and peeked inside. 'You're a fine one to talk. Racing in our birthday suit are we?'

Penny had invited Emma and me to a go-kart circuit in Milton Keynes owned by Daytona International. Daytona had just signed up Penny's company to look after their marketing and their new outdoor circuit was being launched in front of a star studded guest list. Penny had mentioned it over dinner. She was an account executive for Marble Mayhew, one of London's top PR companies and Daytona International was one of her new accounts. I was a bit pissed off as it meant I would miss the game this afternoon between South Korea and Holland. I had been to Daytona's indoor track in West London a couple of times and I had enjoyed it, but I wanted to watch the match.

Emma and I had breakfast in the kitchen watching TV. Emma was really looking forward to the day and had started winding me up.

'So come on then, why won't you have a bet with me? It's because you know I'll beat you isn't it?' She giggled.

'I'm sorry Em. I just can't seem to get that excited. You know I'd rather be watching the football.'

'Only because you've had a lot of big bets. Look, you might as well accept the fact we're going. You've got to go and you ought to start looking forward to it. You'll love it once you're there. Plus, you can't let your sister down, can you?' She reasoned with me.

'I know, but I'll be frustrated all afternoon, wanting to know the score.' I said, stirring my cereal with my spoon.

'They've got a big TV screen there you told me. You can watch it on that. So come on, five pounds says I beat you.' She held out her hand, waiting for my handshake. I playfully slapped it out the way. There was no way she would beat me, I had always loved karting but the novelty had worn off since I changed careers and more importantly I wanted to watch the World Cup.

'Okay, okay. Five pounds says *I* beat *you*.' I held out my hand and she shook it firmly, smiling coyly.

'We'd better make a move.' I said, looking at my watch. 'I'll start running you a bath and I'll jump in after.'

'Never mind 'after', you can jump in with me!' She jumped up of her stool and tried pulling my dressing gown off me as she ran out the room.

It was a beautiful day and I had the roof down as we made our way out of London, towards the M1. Milton Keynes was only 40 miles north of London but the trip would still take nearly an hour and a half. The slow bit was actually getting out of London and onto the motorway. I hated the north circular but it was more direct than going all the way round the M25. Emma selected the Simply Red CD from the stack system in the boot and began singing along. She looked great with her Gucci sunglasses on and the wind in her hair. As I looked at her sitting there I felt a sudden surge of panic. I had been thinking about the rapist and how I would feel if Emma were one of his victims. It had given me a horrible kind of stomach churning feeling. I knew I would find the perpetrator and kill him. I hadn't noticed my speed increase or my grip on the steering wheel tighten.

'Roger, are you okay?' Emma sounded concerned. 'You're doing over a hundred.'

'Sorry honey, I hadn't noticed. Just thinking about work, sorry.'

'Roger please try not to worry about it. Let's just enjoy our weekend together.'

I didn't want Emma to know what I had been thinking, I felt guilty. I was glad that Emma wasn't one of the victims; I was glad she wasn't one of the ones suffering. It must be so awful. I put the thoughts out of my mind and leant over to kiss her.

'Thank you! What was that for?' She grinned.

'Nothing. Just a kiss for my lovely lady. I am looking forward to today and I can't wait to meet Dani Behr!'

'In your dreams. You wait 'til Tom sees me. He'll be gagging for it!' We both burst out laughing.

We arrived at Milton Keynes at nine fifteen and the car park of Daytona was already really busy. I parked and we walked towards the entrance. It was all very impressive. There was a huge red awning over the entrance and a red carpet. There were two control towers at either end of the building. The one nearest the car park looked like it was race control. Inside, there was a bar and one of those huge Sony TV's and a big reception desk. A pretty young lady asked us for our invites and she checked us off on her list. She told us which team we would be racing in and then asked us to sign in. We were given a nice clean Sparco race suit each and shown to our respective changing rooms. As I opened the door of the men's, Les Ferdinand came sauntering out in a bright yellow race suit. 'Awight.' He said in a broad London accent, as he passed me. I smiled and made my way into the changing room.

My suit was a bit baggy but comfortable. I felt like a racing driver again and went up to the bar to get a drink. Emma looked great in hers. It was a perfect fit and her legs looked long and slim compared to the girl she was stood next to. 'What would you like to drink?' I asked her.

'Diet Coke, please. Guess what? I just got changed with Denise van Outen!' She exclaimed.

'I know, isn't it great? I bumped into Les Ferdinand coming out of the men's. Have you seen Dani Behr yet?' I asked, trying to wind Emma up.

'No, but I've just snogged Tom Cruise!'

'Was I good? I don't recall.'

Emma whirled round to find Tom Cruise stood directly behind her. She was so embarrassed. 'I am so sorry. I was just jok...'

'Don't apologise, please. Don't worry about it.' Tom Cruise grinned and walked off with his drink.

'Oh my God. How embarrassing! I can't believe that just happened. Oh my God! Did you see the way he grinned at me? He is divine.' Emma went from being mortified to excited in a split second. I couldn't stop laughing.

'Morning guys!' My sister ran over to us. 'How are you? I hope the directions were okay?'

'Hi Penny. You won't believe what just happened to me.' Emma gave her a kiss and began telling her. As Emma relayed her story I kissed my sister and threw my eyes up at the ceiling. Penny and Emma agreed on how divine Mr. Cruise was and laughed at me when I protested. Penny told Emma all about her new car and she thanked me again, for about the tenth time! I was pleased she loved it. Penny ran us through the day's activities and then explained she had loads of people to look after and left.

There was a race briefing at ten o'clock to be followed by practice, qualifying then a four-hour endurance race. We would then have a girl's race and a boy's race where it was every person for themselves. Everyone would be in teams of eight, which meant we would all get half an hour in the kart.

We each had a team number and were told by the race director to meet the rest of our team-mates by the kart with the team number on it. Emma and I were in team nine and as we headed outside we were handed a pair of gloves and told to select a helmet from the rack. Now I was getting excited. 'Well let's hope we're not in Tom's team.' I said jabbing Em in the ribs.

'Very funny! There's our kart.' She pointed.

It was tiny and didn't look capable of doing seventy-five miles an hour. It had two engines, one on each side and black side pods with a red chassis. They had Daytona stickers everywhere and looked like little formula one cars without the spoilers. There was one bloke stood behind the kart who introduced himself. We waited for the other five members to arrive. I couldn't believe it when Damon Hill, Eric Clapton and Dani Behr all pitched up and introduced themselves. Damon and I knew each other, I introduced him to Emma and we stood chatting, he asked after my father and I told him he was well. Damon joked my father should have been here today and I told him that he hated being in the limelight nowadays. Damon said he knew the feeling but he was really happy to help out Penny. The other two members were the owner, Jim Graham and Penny. I stood there in disbelief. I couldn't believe I was racing in such company. Emma had to whisper in my ear twice to tell me to stop staring. I think I was more excited about racing with Dani Behr than Damon Hill. She was better looking in the flesh than I'd imagined and I couldn't wait to tell the boys on Monday. Frank would never believe me but I made sure Emma took loads of photos.

We had a brilliant day and Penny was really pleased with the proceedings. Her boss was very impressed and he had spent the whole day chatting up Denise van Outen and Samantha Janus. The owners of Daytona were very happy with the publicity. Penny had arranged for Damon Hill and David Coulthard to drive some handicapped children round the circuit in a two seater go-kart between races and the day had raised over three hundred thousand pounds for Cancer Research UK and MenCap. There had been press photographers around all day and I had had my picture taken talking to Dani Behr. I just hoped it was going to be in Hello Magazine or somewhere similar. I wanted to get my own back on Frank after his wind up about Sarah Swan fancying him.

Our team had done remarkably well; we'd come fourth overall in the team race thanks mainly to Damon. I wished him luck in the British Grand Prix next month. He was racing for Arrows and he was quite open about his feelings and how unhappy he was with the car's performance. I asked him if he was looking for another drive for next year and he confided in me he had been having talks with Eddie Jordan, saying that he was always open to offers.

We had a drink in the hospitality tower after the race with the Daytona bosses and were reintroduced to Tom Cruise. He had told Jim Graham about Emma's slip and they had a good laugh at her expense. Emma didn't mind, she spent the evening drooling over him! I was very impressed with the circuit and told Jim. He seemed pleased and when he found out I worked in the City he took my business card and said he would get one of his sales team to call me on Monday.

Emma and I drove home and arrived at about ten o'clock. Emma didn't stay, she had to collect a change of clothes from her place. She said she'd be back in time for breakfast in the morning. I walked her to her car and we kissed goodbye. I waved her away and watched her disappear into the night. She lived above a night club and I couldn't stand the noise of the bass beating up through her ceiling, the one and only time I'd stayed there.

I made myself a pot of coffee and rushed into my lounge to get the football results. Holland had been playing South Korea and I needed Holland to have scored a plethora of goals. Fat chance after their performance against Belgium, I thought as I called up Teletext. I couldn't believe my eyes. Holland 5 South Korea 0! Excellent, it was exactly what I needed. I had a look at my positions in my diary. I was long of Holland goals at 8.8 so that result would definitely help. My France position was looking brilliant; they had beaten the Saudi's 4 – 0 on Thursday. Brazil had scored five so far but I still had a bit of a way to go to get up to eleven goals. I didn't care about my England position and Yellow cards were still coming my way.

I switched off the TV and regretted being on my own. I missed Emma and really wanted to be with her tonight. I dialled her number and got her ansafone. I left her a message, pleading with her to come back over tonight. I then tried her mobile but that was switched off. I sat there sipping my freshly ground coffee and thought about my feelings for Emma. I had never plucked up the courage to sit down with her and discuss how I felt after our night at Aubergine. I had slept on those feelings and over the last couple of weeks my feelings had changed. I had fallen in love. I now couldn't imagine life without her. I loved her boundless energy and her sense of humour. We were soul mates and as I sat there thinking this, I felt complete. I didn't panic about how I was losing control. It was right and it felt great. I was successful and it was good to have someone to share the success with. As the saying goes; 'behind every great man there is a great woman.'

My phone began ringing. I picked it up and knew it was Emma replying to my message.

'Open the door Rog.' She laughed into the mouthpiece.

I jumped up and rushed to the door. I unlocked the dead bolt and as I opened the door Emma bounded in, dropped her bag, shut the door and led me into the bedroom.

TWENTY TWO

He hadn't slept well at all. He had spent all night developing and arranging his collage for victim number eight. Her name was Deborah Williams and she had been the best so far. He had enjoyed himself and had become a fan of silicon implants. He held up the picture of Deborah's tits and sat staring at it. *They really were amazing; they sat up, begging like a couple of puppy dogs.* He applied the Pritt stick to the back of the photo and placed it on the wall below a photo of Deborah's beautiful face. He finished off her position on the wall and stood back to admire his handy work. He laughed as he took in her photos. At the top was one of her face, below one of her tits, then a close up of her belly button, which had been pierced and had a ruby sat in it and finally a picture of her pussy. He glanced at his watch. It was nine thirty and time he was on his way. He had told Olive he would be home by ten thirty.

He arrived at the house at ten forty and Olive was on the doorstep to welcome him home. He parked the Ferrari and walked into the house brushing her off with a curt 'Good morning.'

'So nice to see you. How have you been? Arthur's repaired the leaking roof and said he would come over to see you this morning. Would you like a cup of tea? The kettle's just boiled.' Olive fussed round him.

He ignored her and took his bag to his bedroom and sat on his bed. It was the same bed he'd slept in as a teenager. He unlocked a trunk in the corner of the room, raised the lid and removed a pile of old newspapers. The paper on top had a headline that read; 'FIRE DEVESTATES HOUSE KILLING MOTHER.' There was a picture underneath of the burnt remains. He sat on his bed and looked through the article, dated 1979. There was a photo of him and his mother, Mrs Denise Freeman, which had been taken when they had been on holiday in St. Tropez. The article mentioned him and that he was found by one of the firemen, hiding in a bush in the front garden. The fireman was acclaimed for his rescue and had been interviewed by the press and been treated like a celebrity for weeks.

He had been twelve at the time of the fire and now, as he flicked through the newspapers all the old feelings of hatred came flooding back. *The bitch deserved it. When had she ever been there for me? She was too fucking busy going out every night with a different man. All the guys she fucked around with thought she was beautiful. What the fuck did they know? Nothing, fucking nothing. She was nothing but a slut, a cheap little whore who never loved daddy or me. No sooner had daddy died, the whore was out fucking every man she could.* He chucked the papers back in their trunk, slammed the lid down and sat there looking out the bedroom window. His room was at the back of the house and overlooked the huge garden. He remembered picking apples from the orchard as a young boy at the side of the garden and that calmed him down. He had enjoyed most of his childhood. He had been a normal child until his father's death. He was his dad's little action man and they had been inseparable. His dad had been a Tottenham Hotspur fan and had taken him to his first match. He sat there reminiscing, looking at the orchard and the overgrown garden. The match had been the London Derby, Arsenal v Spurs and Spurs had won 2-0. His father was overjoyed and from that moment he was hooked. He looked up and smiled, seeing the Arsenal team poster was still stuck to the wall. He had a fixture list from 1979 and a huge poster of Alan Sunderland celebrating his goal in the F.A. Cup final. An Arsenal scarf was draped above, pinned in position by a couple of drawing pins. His dad had laughed at him supporting Arsenal, but deep down had enjoyed the rivalry.

'Daniel, Arthur's here to see you.' Olive shouted up the stairs.

He locked the trunk up. Arthur was waiting in the study. He was in his late sixties and had a thick white beard and a full head of hair to match. He wore little round spectacles and looked just like Father Christmas. He was short, about five foot and very plump. He was a very sweet old man and though he was retired did odd jobs for people in the village. His appearance fooled a lot of people. He was in fact very fit and agile for his age and had made light work of the leaking roof.

'Morning Sir. The roof will leak no more. I have replaced the missing tiles and I popped up to the loft and repaired the hole and insulated it with waterproof sealant.' Arthur stood proudly looking at his temporary employer.

'Great. Thanks Arthur. How much do I owe you?'

'I think eighty pounds will cover it. It didn't take me very long.'

He got a wad of notes out of his pocket and gave Arthur two hundred pounds. 'Have a drink or two on me Arthur.'

'That's far too much! I can't possibly accept this,' Arthur said, trying to give some back.

'Arthur, just take it please. Thanks again.' He left Arthur shaking his head.

He headed out the house and got into his car and drove to the village of Harpenden and parked outside the parish church. He walked across to a little shop called 'Barry's Camera Shop', opened the door and a bell signalled his presence. There were shelves of cameras on two sides. Most were second-hand but there were some new models. He picked up a Nikon and was looking it over when the shopkeeper appeared through a door at the back of the shop.

'Morning, can I help you?'

'Yes. I ordered some Agfa Colour Signum II paper through your web site last Thursday. I arranged to pick it up today.'

'Ah yes. I had to order it specially. Not one we normally keep in stock. What did you think of our web site? It's quite new and we're still finding our feet.' The shopkeeper asked keenly.

'It's quite good. Did you design it yourself?' He asked.

'No. A Company called Motley.co.uk that does Web design approached me. A very nice guy called Jamie Forster runs the company. It cost me two thousand pounds but I've already made a thousand pounds from it. We've only had it running for three weeks.'

'Great. Can I have the paper I ordered, I'm in a bit of a hurry.'

'Sorry, I'm still so excited at the thought of selling things through my web site. I'll pop out the back and get it for you.'

He reappeared with a heavy looking box that he placed on the counter. 'There are two boxes of one hundred. That will be one hundred and fifty pounds please. It's terribly expensive paper, are you a professional photographer?'

'No just a very fussy amateur!' he replied, handing the shopkeeper one hundred and fifty pounds in fifty pound notes.

He drove back to the house and spent the rest of the day going through his post and sorting out his admin. Olive cooked him a roast lunch of beef with all the trimmings. He drove home in the early evening and went straight to his dark room.

TWENTY THREE

It was eight o'clock on Sunday morning and Frank was at his desk. He had been there since five o'clock. Last night he had gone out with some old mates from University who had been in town. He had hit the sack at two and hadn't been able to sleep. The rapes had been whizzing through his mind and in the end he had got up and driven into the station. He probably shouldn't have, being over the limit but it was too late by the time he'd thought of it. He was on his fifth cup of coffee and as he sat slurping the hot drink he realised he was probably addicted to caffeine. He drank over ten cups a day and couldn't function clearly in the morning until he'd had at least one cup. The coffee out of the machine in the station wasn't too bad. Frank had got used to it. He smiled as he thought about his mate and how Roger hated machine coffee and instant coffee. Frank hadn't spoken to his friend for a while and made a mental note to call him later.

He leafed through the notes spread over his desk. He held his head in his hands and read through his doodles and messy writing. He had written the names of the five victims; Fiona Stevens, Barbara Simpson, Samantha Keats, Kim Dodds and the latest, Amanda Worthington. Did they have anything in common? They were all beautiful and in their twenties. Were they all just simply in the wrong place at the wrong time or were they connected in some other way? Frank had gone through all these points and more with his team of detectives. He found no matter how many times you went over things, you could still miss a vital clue that had been staring you in the face the whole time. He lit a cigarette and sat back in his chair. There had to be something that would give him the needed break. Why didn't he use protection? Forensics had tested two semen samples and they had matched. Why wasn't he concerned about being caught? It almost seemed as if he wanted to be caught. Why were all the rapes in the Fulham and Chelsea area? The rapist must know the area. This had to be the key.

Frank made a note to start door to door enquiries. Someone must have seen something. The calls from Crimewatch had come to nothing. It had been a real let down. The new rape had shed a bit more light on things. Amanda Worthington had told them she remembered a flash going off as she came round. She thought someone had been taking her picture. Frank had asked the other victims if they remembered any flashlights. One girl, Fiona Stevens did. So was the rapist taking photos of his victims and if so why?

All the girls had been drugged before the rape. It seemed he used ether to knock them out. The girls didn't remember anything about the actual assault apart from the beginning and the coming round lying in a heap on a pavement. It was all very weird. Two of the girls had woken during the end of the rape and that was when they recalled the flashing white light. If he was taking photos of his victims where did he get the pictures developed? The photos must have aroused somebody's curiosity. He felt like he was going round in circles.

Frank threw the polystyrene cup in the bin and stubbed out the cigarette. He picked up the phone and dialled my number.

'Hello.' I answered still half asleep.

'Shit sorry mate. Are you still in bed?' Frank had forgotten it was Sunday. All his days just seemed like one. He hadn't taken a day off in seven months and he needed a holiday.

'Yes I am. It's Sunday. I don't do Sundays.'

'Sorry Rog. I'm at the station. I've been here since about five. I couldn't sleep. I just keep going through these bloody cases. What a nightmare. I'm sorry, I didn't mean to wake you. Is Emma with you?'

'Yeah. Sleeping like a baby.'

'What? Is she wearing a nappy?'

'Very funny! Go home. Go and get some sleep. You must be shattered. Did you call for a particular reason?

'Yeah I did actually. I wanted to tell you about my date with Sarah Swan. I'm going out with her next Thursday and wondered if you wanted to join us?' Frank was trying not to laugh.

'You're going on a date with Sarah Swan? No way! I don't believe you. When was this arranged? Bollocks mate! There is no way you could have kept this news to yourself until this morning. I'll bet…' I was fully awake now.

Frank interrupted. 'I've been so busy at work I haven't had the time. I finally had some free time yesterday and I tried you at home and there was no reply. I tried you on your mobile and that was switched off. Roger, you have to face up to it. You are a very important young man who is very difficult to get hold of!' He added plenty of sarcasm.

'Fuck off Frank! I forgot to leave the ansafone on at home yesterday and I had my mobile switched off. Emma and I were at that go-kart day in Milton Keynes. I did tell you we were going. The launch party Penny organised, remember.'

'Yeah, I do. How was it?'

'We had the best time. But I'm knackered. We were all racing in teams and Emma and I raced with Damon Hill, Eric Clapton, David Coulthard and Dani Behr! She is so fucking sexy mate!'

'Did you give her my phone number?' Frank asked eagerly.

'No way! She's not your type. Tom Cruise was there. Emma and Penny spent all day drooling over him! So sad.' Frank heard a murmur in the background. It was Emma stirring. She asked me whom I was talking to. 'It's Henson, honey. I'll make you a coffee in a minute.'

'You know something Rog? You are one lucky guy. I would give anything to change places with you. Lying in your huge king-size bed with a babe and not a care in the world. I'm sat here with notes and evidence scattered across my desk and I'm no closer to the truth than when I got in here.'

'Hey come on Bud. At least you've got your date with Sarah to look forward to.' I was convinced Frank was winding me up.

'Yeah that's true. We're going out on Thursday. You coming?'

'Call me at the office tomorrow and I'll look in my diary. Frank, do me a favour, go home and get some rest. All work and no play makes Frank a dull boy!'

'Ok mate. I'll give you a call in the morning. Have a nice day now.'

Frank put the phone down and lit yet another cigarette. He knew his friend had taken the bait. He looked back at his latest scribbling and tapped his pen on the desk. The rapist voice was deep and very gruff. All the victims had said the same thing. Was it his real voice or was he putting it on? Did he really have grey hair or could he have worn a wig? He had so many questions and no way of answering them yet. He needed to start answering them and fast before another young woman was raped. Someone, somewhere knew the answers and Frank was determined to find him or her. He tidied up his desk and made his way downstairs and into his car.

TWENTY FOUR

I got in at seven as usual and logged onto my Bloomberg terminal. The thought of the day came up; 'Time waits for no man, don't put off until tomorrow what you can do today.' Bloody right, I thought as I looked up my World Cup bets. My positions were looking very good now. Holland had beaten South Korea 5-0!!! Last Thursday France had beaten the Saudi's 4-0. Things were looking very good indeed. All I needed now was for England to be beaten by the Romanians in tonight's game and I would be happy. The boys were going down to watch the game in the pub with some customers. I had ducked it, as the game didn't kick off until eight. I planned to have a quiet night in front of the box with Emma. She had promised to come over and cook me a meal and I was really looking forward to it. I wanted a few quiet nights as I was meeting Frank on Thursday with Sarah Swan. I still couldn't believe it. He was such a smooth bastard. I didn't know of many women who could resist his charms. I hadn't told Emma because I still wasn't one hundred percent convinced myself. Plus I knew Emma fancied Frank and the truth was, I was jealous! She would be really impressed and I didn't want her to know. It sounds crazy, I know. He was my best friend but I really hated the way that Penny drooled over him and was always asking how he was. Now even Emma seemed more interested in Frank than me. I couldn't believe that I was getting wound up about my mate going out with Sarah Swan. I just hoped it was a wind up.

As I unfolded my newspaper I noticed the memo on my desk. It was from Lydia, Michael Irwin' personal assistant. There was going to be a modelling shoot for Vogue magazine in the dealing room later on this morning and all the desk heads were asked to keep their brokers under control. They were employed to make money and Michael Irwin asked for everyone to stay focused on their jobs and not the models. Yeah right, I thought. A load of Vogue models and the boys would be gagging for it! I smirked as I imagined the scene with the whole dealing room wolf whistling at the girls as they came strutting into the room. It would be carnage!

As the desks began to fill up and the word went around, the talk for the rest of the morning was the modelling shoot. There were a lot of young, good-looking guys that fancied their chances. It was a typical Monday morning, very quiet and slow to get going. Most of the morning was spent with the guys talking about their weekends. Michael had the desk in hysterics with his Viagra story. He had taken two of the impotency cure pills with his wife on Saturday night and it had been a nightmare. He didn't have a problem with his manhood but thought it might be fun to experiment. He and his wife had taken the pills at dinner and by the main course Michael's dick was rock hard and it had remained that way for the whole night. He and his wife had shagged the night away and he told us that it was fucking brilliant but bloody frustrating.

'I came and instead of just rolling over and going to kip, I wanted more and within two minutes it was up and raring to go again!! My balls are fucking aching this morning!' He grabbed his crotch and grimaced.

'How was it for yer missus?' Jamie asked.

'She loved every minute of it. She was wetter than I've ever known. It was like Niagra Falls in the monsoon season!! I kept calling her Viagra Niagra!!!!!!' The whole desk burst into hysterics. 'Tell you what though, I woke up this morning and my heart was beating at nineteen to the dozen. No wonder the doctors say that old people should be careful.'

'Where did you get the pills from?' Brian asked.

'A mate of mine who works upstairs on Forward Yen. He went to his doctor pretending to have a bit of a problem. He was prescribed Viagra and given six pills. If he needed any more the doctor told him to ring and he would be sent a new prescription. He didn't have to pay so he only charged me a fiver each for them.'

'Can you get me some for tonight?' Jamie enquired eagerly. 'I might need them for shagging the models after I've pulled them!'

'In your dreams mate!'

We were having quite a good morning for a Monday until the models arrived at eleven o'clock. The word slowly went round the room that they had arrived downstairs. You could feel the excitement in the air. Nobody was concentrating, myself included. I had just done a fifty million swap with Griffo and had sent one of the ticket boys downstairs to get me a coffee. It was good fun being in a dealing room environment at the best of times but when something like a modelling shoot was about to take place there was that certain anticipation. There were so many wind-up merchants on the various desks that you were never too sure what might happen. We often had TV cameras in filming during the budget and whenever there had been a major financial event or disaster. They always wanted to portray the City as a very serious place, which of course it isn't. I believed if anyone came into the office they would see it as it really is. A load of arrogant brokers and traders sitting around thinking they are special when all they really do all day is play games on their screens, read newspapers and do crosswords. I would love to pretend I deserve the huge amount of money that I'm paid but I'd be lying. Out of our eleven-hour day we're probably only busy for an hour. The rest of the time is spent staving off the boredom. As a broker I don't make any decisions myself. My clients instruct me what they want to do and I merely carry out the instructions. Sure, you could be quite pro-active and suggest trades but a monkey could do my job. It is without doubt the most mind-numbingly boring job. You get treated as the lowest form of life by a predominant amount of the traders. Job satisfaction is zero. I ask myself what I achieve on a daily basis and by and large it is Jack Shit! I bring in a shed load of money for the company each month, but there was no real sense of achievement. Now electronic trading was taking over we would have even less to do. The customers can now input their own orders. Great! I try to keep my mind on the job, I always watch my Bloomberg where I watch the Long Gilt Future and I don't like to be seen playing games on my screen. I don't mind the guys playing games because if I weren't the boss I would do the same! As long as we made money I didn't have a problem with any of it. Every single broker on my desk and each of the other desks would admit they hated their jobs but would tell you they were only there for the money. It is just one big bubble and maybe, just maybe the electronic system would be the pin that finally burst it.

I picked up the outside line. 'Kaplan Stewart.'

'Hamilton my old mate. I'm sorry I woke you yesterday. How are you?'

'Yeah good thanks. Just a typically dull Monday morning here. Mind you, *"we've got real excitement coming up!"* There are a load of cat walk models coming in here for a photo shoot later on this morning.' I used my best Murray Walker commentating voice.

'No way! Give them my number, give 'em my number mate, please?' Frank pleaded with me. 'You guys lead such a rich life. What a fucking giggle. I can imagine those animals you work with going mad when the girls walk in.'

'Yeah, so can I. I got a memo from my boss today about keeping the boys focused on the job in hand.'

'Job in hand, nudge, nudge, wink, wink!!! Can you make it on Thursday night?'

'Yes I can. Emma's busy, out with some of her friends. But if you don't mind me playing gooseberry I'll be there?' I still wasn't sure if he was winding me up about Sarah Swan.

'Great. I've told her about you and she says she's looking forward to meeting you.' Frank sounded very sincere.

'I can understand that. You're so dull you had to talk about me to make yourself sound interesting!!' I joked.

'That hurt. I'm meeting her at The Pitcher and Piano in Fulham at seven thirty. I'll see you there.' Henson was trying to sound upset.

'Yeah, great. I've got to go Frank, the models have arrived.'

'Roger, don't forget..' I cut him off.

There was a huge cheer and lots of wolf whistles. The models were both stunning. The two most beautiful creatures I had ever seen. Where did girls like that hang out at night? They were better than I told Frank. He had sounded gutted and rightly so, I thought as I watched the two babes. He would love this. Graham from our PR department led the team into the room. There were the two girls, a photographer and two assistants. The photographer had long, grey hair and was about forty-five or so. He looked a lot younger because he was very fit. He wore a white t-shirt and a pair of Levi jeans with cowboy boots. He was very cool and both the girls seemed to really warm to him. They based themselves in one of the corner offices and put up a black curtain for their privacy. This was met by boos from the brokers. The models came out dressed in pinstripe suits with short skirts and the photographer directed the shoot. He had them posing with telephones on the Repo desk pretending to be brokers. I doubt whether they got one serious photo. The whole time the girls were there, men were leering at them and brokers were pulling stupid faces and shouting out inane comments.

    The girls seemed very relieved when the photographer was finally done. They changed back into their own clothes and strutted toward the exit. I cringed when a guy from the Repo desk walked up to the brunette and thrust his business card into her hand. 'Hey baby! Maybe we can do lunch. Call me. I will make it worth your while.' Amazingly, she took the card and put it in her tiny handbag before disappearing into a lift. As the broker headed back to his seat, the boys from his desk pounced on him, grabbed him and threw him head first into one of the huge black bins that were dotted around the floor. The bin was full of half-drunk coffee cups, breakfasts and newspapers. The entire room cheered as he scrambled back out, covered in the morning's rubbish. Just a typical day at the office!

TWENTY FIVE

The collection was coming on beautifully. He had his back to the door and sat staring at his work, beer in hand and cigarette in the other. As he looked from girl to girl he noticed blotches had appeared on Deborah's photos. He had developed them on Saturday night and put them up on Sunday morning. They had been fine then so it wasn't the camera. He had checked the negatives and they were fine. *It was either the fucking fluid or the fucking paper.* He had experimented all evening and still didn't know what was wrong. It had to be the new paper he used for Deborah's photos. He had no other paper so couldn't check. The photos had a horrible grainy affect to them that made them look old and really dulled the colours. *Fucking paper! It had ruined them.* He had really enjoyed fucking her. *Why pay ten pounds to see her naked, when you could fuck her for nothing?* He ripped the wasted photos off the wall and threw them in the big bin he kept in his darkroom. He walked into his lounge and picked up the telephone. He began dialling and then swiftly slammed the handset back down. *You fucking idiot.* He never made calls on his home phone. He wanted to be caught in his own time and leaving clues on his phone bill wouldn't help. He picked up his mobile and began dialling.

'Thank you for calling Barry's Camera Shop. We are closed now but will re-open at nine o'clock tomorrow morning. Please leave a message and I will call you back as soon as I can. Thank you.' The ansafone bleeped and he left an angry message about the expensive Agfa paper being crap and could he call his mobile tomorrow. He threw his mobile phone onto the sofa and put his cigarette out in the ashtray on his coffee table. He turned on the TV and began flicking through the channels. The news had started on ITV and he sat listening to Trevor McDonald. There had been a siege in a school in Kansas and some lunatic with a gun was holding ten children hostage. *There are some freaks out there!* He laughed at himself but became serious as the next item was reported. 'The South west London Serial Rapist has struck again.' The black newsreader began. *Which little bitch had gone running to the police this time?* He wondered as the report started. It was Amanda Worthington. He knew as soon as he saw the location in South Kensington. That had been three weeks ago. *So they now knew that there had been five rapes and maybe more*! He couldn't believe how slow the girls had been to go to the police. There were still three girls that were obviously too scared. *They will never solve this!*

He went into his bedroom, stripped off and put on his work out kit. He wore Ralph Lauren pants, a white t-shirt, blue Russell Athletic shorts and Nike socks and trainers. He donned his knackered, old Timberland baseball cap and went into the kitchen. He filled his sports bottle with a light mixture of orange squash and took a little swig to check the consistency. Satisfied, he headed for his spare bedroom he had converted into a gym. There was a treadmill, a bike, a rowing machine and a stair machine on one side of the room and the weight machines were opposite. There was a mirror all the way along one wall and a couple of mats for stretching and in the corner he had a punch bag hanging from his reinforced ceiling. He wrapped bandages around each hand and put on his gloves. He did his stretches and began dancing around the punch bag. He took out his anger about the photographic paper, aggressively jabbing at the bag and nimbly dodging as it swung back towards him. He quickly worked up a sweat but continued punching at the swinging target. He stopped after fifteen minutes and caught the bag on the back swing and stood hugging it, trying to catch his breath. He felt better already and jumped on the rowing machine. He was out of condition and regretted not using the room more often. He had been preoccupied recently and didn't want to get out of shape. He pounded out two and a half thousand metres on the rower and then did some weights. An hour after starting he was stood in his shower washing off the sweat from his workout. It was an invigorating power shower with three jets powering water at him, one from above and two out of the walls.

He opened the fridge and took out a bottle of Evian and drank from it until he had to stop to catch his breath. He felt so much better after his hard work out and sat down at his desk in the lounge. He switched on his computer and waited for it to start up. He was still pissed off about the paper. It now meant he would have to make another trip to Hertfordshire. He logged onto the Internet and got into the camera shop's website. He sent Barry a message asking him to order some more of the paper and he made it perfectly clear he would not be paying for it! He left the computer on and picked up his car keys. *Time to check up on some of my old flames!*

He went down to the car park and drove the Ferrari out. He made his way towards Wandsworth and on into Clapham. He saw the house in the distance and stopped by the house next door and switched the ignition off. He turned the key back so that the air conditioning stayed on. It was really hot and sticky and even with the air con it was still stifling. He sat listening to Iron Maiden playing on his stereo waiting to see if any of the girls turned up from work. It was midnight and he was probably a bit early but he figured as it was Tuesday the club might be a bit quiet and the girls might get home early. He knew there were four living there. He had followed them from Club Paradise just over a week ago. He had hacked into the council's web page and found a list of all the registered council taxpayers. He had searched through the list and finally found the address. There were four females registered. Miss T. Lloyd, Miss T. Griffiths, Miss W. Winger and Miss D. Williams. *Four little vixens living together, only three to go!!* He laughed and pulled out his little box of 'snuff' and quickly snorted a finger full.

There were no lights on inside the house and he sat there wishing he were a burglar. *If I knew how to pick locks I could go up there and do Wendy right now. That would surprise her, she wouldn't be expecting a visit at home.*

Wake up you little bitch, it's time to party! He could imagine her face as she woke up to find him stood in his glory over her bed. He grinned in the rear view mirror at himself and brushed his hand through his blond locks. He couldn't do anything tonight and besides he wasn't in the mood. He wasn't in the taxi and he didn't want to break cover yet. He was still a long way from Dan Crosby's record of sixteen rapes in 1979. He was caught and convicted in 1980 and admitted to all twelve rapes and he informed the police of the other four rapes. They didn't know, as the victims hadn't gone to the police. The victims confirmed it but all four still refused to go to court to give evidence. Crosby went down for twenty years and no parole. He was due out sometime next year, *by which time I'll be way over his record and then I will be the most famous serial rapist of all time!*

It was one o'clock when a taxi stopped outside the house. He had been taking a leak in a bush opposite his car and had to hide as the headlights swept past him. He smiled and quickly zipped up his flies and watched from his hiding place. Three girls got out, one red head and two blondes. One of them was Wendy. His breathing increased with the excitement as he stood watching the girls. *Welcome home ladies. Aren't you all just the prettiest little things? Hey girls! Can I come in and play?* He whispered to himself. He noticed Deborah wasn't with them. *Poor little Deborah. I bet she's tucked up in bed fast asleep with her nightmares!* The girls closed their front door and he came out from hiding. He was going to get back into his car and head home but he was still buzzing from the Cocaine so changed his mind. *Time to come out of hiding!*

He walked casually up to the front door and rang the doorbell. He ran his hand through his hair a couple of times and brushed a leaf from the lapel of his sports jacket. The door opened and the red head asked 'Can I help you?'

She was more beautiful up close than he had imagined. Bright green, kind eyes and a few freckles sprinkled delicately over her cheeks. She looked very relaxed considering it was one o'clock in the morning. She should have been afraid, very afraid. He was upset that Wendy hadn't come to the door, he had wanted to see her reaction as she slowly recognised him.

'I'm really sorry to disturb you. My car has run out of petrol and I was hoping I could trouble you to call the AA breakdown service for me? I know it's late. I'm so sorry.' He smiled at Trudy stood on her doorstep.

Trudy couldn't help feeling attracted to the man standing in front of her. He was very good looking and very fit, a clean living sort of guy. He was wearing grey flannel trousers, a blue shirt and a yellow sports jacket. He had long blond hair swept back in a centre parting and deep blue eyes. His voice was very deep and gravely but somehow soft and gentle. 'Is that your Ferrari?'

'Yeah, great car shame about the idiot driver! I can't believe I let it run out of petrol.'

'I love the colour! Come on in. The phone's just behind me in the hallway.' She laughed.

He stepped across the threshold and smiled as the door closed behind him.

TWENTY SIX

It was still raining and had been since I'd woken up. It was so depressing listening to the sound of the windscreen wipers in the middle of summer. Sunday had been the longest day of the year and now it seemed as if autumn had already arrived. I put my Dance Anthems CD on and tried cheering myself up. I was seeing Frank later and looking forward to it, and I was actually excited at the prospect of meeting Sarah Swan. I had finally told Emma and she hadn't reacted as I thought she would. She wasn't surprised, as he was so charming but she told me that she thought he tried too hard. She didn't think it would work; Sarah Swan was very successful and in the public eye and Frank was a Detective with no money. I sort of agreed with her but I did hope that things might develop. I liked the idea of my mate going out with a celebrity! This morning I'm not going to get wound up by the traffic, I thought as I tapped the steering wheel in time with the "I like to Move It, Move It" song by Reel to Reel.

I got in at ten past seven, slightly later than usual due to the wet roads. My World Cup bets were making me a small fortune and I was contemplating closing off some of the positions. France had scored nine goals, Brazil had scored six, England had only scored three and the Dutch had scored five but were playing Mexico this afternoon at three o'clock. I would watch it on my small TV. The referees had been easy going on the whole and yellow cards had tumbled. In total I was up over a thousand pounds and the first round matches hadn't even finished yet! The second round of the tournament got under way on Saturday and France and Brazil had already made it through. Holland hadn't scored that many and seemed to struggle at times but I felt good about them. England on the other hand looked crap! They had lost to Romania on Monday night and the price in England goals was 4.5- 4.9 and I bought my position back at 4.9. I had sold a hundred pounds at 7.0 so I had just made two hundred and ten pounds. That would pay for a few beers tonight, I sniggered. It also meant that now I could support England in their match against Columbia on Friday night.

I went through my email and read an update on the electronic trading system. All systems were go for a launch across European Government bonds on Monday 6th July. All the traders had the system now and were in the process of learning how to use it. I had spoken to Andrew about it and he was very impressed with its capability. He would still talk to me with swaps and basis trades but he said that he would be quite happy to input his own prices. He promised to fill our screen with prices on Monday morning. The commission structure would change as all the brokers had anticipated. For normal trades on the telephone we would still charge forty pounds but for trades the clients input themselves we would only charge twenty pounds.

Frank called in the middle of the afternoon and confirmed we were meeting at the Pitcher and Piano on the Fulham Road at about eight o'clock. We were going to have a few drinks there and then he and Sarah were going off for a romantic twosome somewhere. Frank refused to tell me the location until this evening in case I tried to cancel the booking or something.

'What do you take me for Henson? I'm your mate, mates don't do that sort of thing. I was just interested to know where she was taking you.'

'She's not taking me anywhere, I am taking her to dinner.' Frank informed me.

'Excuse me! I hope the venue is suitable? I don't want you being out of your depth. MacDonalds or Burger King?' I asked, tongue in cheek.

'Fuck you Hamilton! I've been saving for this date all month. Give me a little credit. It is suitably trendy and expensive. It just means that I will have to stay in for the next few months, that's all!' he joked.

'Good for you buddy. I'll see you in the bar at eight o'clock.' I was about to put the phone down.

'No. Not in the bar. The manager has cordoned off a table at the back of the place for us. I told him that Sarah didn't want to be disturbed and that we just wanted a discreet drink. He was really pleased that we had chosen his bar and has promised to look after us!! I could get used to this treatment.' He laughed into the handset.

'That sounds great. I'm over the moon for you mate. Just don't let it take your eye off the ball. You still got that motherfucking rapist to catch, remember?' I pretended to sound serious.

'Get off my back Roger. I can't stop thinking about the fucking cases. I live, breathe and sleep those fucking cases. And you think I might forget that the bastard is still loose, free to rape again.' He had lost it.

'Frank, Frank, stop! I was playing with you mate.' I couldn't help laughing at him.

He saw the funny side and began laughing too. 'You wanker Rog. You got me! I'm going. I'll see you tonight.'

I leant back in my chair and smiled. We just seemed to spend the whole time winding each other up. I was always one step ahead of him. I think that comes with the territory. Everyone in the City winds his or her friends up, I don't know why. It was simply one of the character building traits of working in this environment. I hated it sometimes but it was also good fun. It was a boring afternoon made worse by the Holland result. They had played Mexico and as the market was quiet I let the guys watch it on TV. We had four TV's, one on each side of the desk. It had been a really scrappy game that Mexico could have won. The final score was 2 – 2! Not the result I wanted. Two Dutch goals helped but against the Mexicans I had hoped that they would have scored four or five. They now had a total of seven goals and I was long at 8.8. At least they had qualified and I could keep my fingers crossed for the second round.

I left the office at six o'clock having spoken to Emma and explained I was having a quick drink with Henson. I was really looking forward to meeting Sarah Swan I thought as I headed home. I got home at six forty five. The traffic had been very heavy mainly due to the road works on the Embankment. Emma had bought me a new pair of Nike running shoes. They were state of the art and I had promised to use them. I changed into my running gear, T-shirt, shorts and socks and put on the Nikes. They felt really comfortable as I did my stretching exercises. I lived in Cadogan Gardens, just round the corner from the main strip of South Kensington and I had planned a two-mile route around the tube station. I became out of breath much faster than I thought I would. I was nowhere near as fit as I had been a few years ago. It was depressing but I resolved to change that. I struggled through the effort of making it home. It had taken me just over twenty minutes and I was fucked. I got into my flat and collapsed onto the carpet, trying to catch my breath. I lay there for a couple of minutes and then staggered into the bathroom. My face was bright red and I was sweating profusely! I jumped into the shower and slowly brought myself back to life! I was fully refreshed and changed by half seven. I had a Ralph Lauren polo shirt on with a pair of chinos and felt like a million dollars as I jumped in the taxi I'd ordered. I was really pleased I had followed through and gone running. I felt invigorated now and sat watching the world go by with a slight smirk on my face.

I got to the bar a little bit before eight and went in to see if Henson was there yet. There was no sign of him, so instead of having a drink, I went outside and hid around the corner. I wanted to see if Henson turned up with his hot date and how close that they were. I didn't have to wait long. I spotted Frank walking along the Fulham Road and I ducked back into the doorway. He was on his own and I immediately knew it had been a wind up. I hid there for about thirty seconds, with a hundred ideas rushing through my mind. I knew she wasn't going to show and Henson would have an excuse already worked out. I would pre-empt him by playing a game with him. I slowly poked my head round the corner just in time to catch Frank walking into the bar. I came out of hiding and followed him into the busy bar. He was already stood waiting to be served as I approached him.

'She looks really good mate. I have to say I'm really impressed, I honestly didn't think that she was going to show.' I sounded really genuine.

'What are you talking about?' Frank seemed a bit confused. 'Oh I see! You mean Sarah Swan? I told her we'd meet here and she's probably just a bit behind schedule, that's all.'

'Not that behind schedule mate. I've just seen her parking outside Pizza Express. I expect she'll be here any second!' I tried not to smile as I watched my mate's face change. He didn't know whether to believe me or not. I had called his bluff and I knew from his expression that Sarah Swan was never coming.

'Great. I'll get her usual drink in. Gin and tonic mate?' He asked, having regained his composure.

'G & T would be great mate, but let me put my card behind the bar.' I handed my card across the bar to the guy serving us before Frank could argue. 'She's not coming is she mate? She never was, was she? You made it all up, you bastard!'

'Yeah that's right, I made it all up.' Henson said, looking over my shoulder towards the entrance. 'Hi Sarah. Meet my friend Roger Hamilton.'

I swung round as quickly as I could. There was no Sarah Swan. I heard Frank laughing uncontrollably. 'You're such a wanker.' I was gutted. I knew that she wasn't going to turn up and yet he had still got me.

'I'm sorry. But the look on your face Rog.' Frank was still laughing. 'I couldn't resist it. You had me sussed, but I still got you! You sucker!' He was leaning on the bar with both arms crossed on the bar with his head buried in them.

'A large gin and tonic please and whatever this wanker wants please.'

'I'll have a large vodka, lime and soda please.' Frank asked, between spasms.

'I knew she wasn't going to turn up. You fucking tosser Frank. I can't believe that I actually thought you were going out with Sarah Swan. Never mind, just one of our normal nights out then?'

'Yeah, let's get pissed. I'm sorry Roger, I wish I *was* going out with Sarah Swan. She was so lovely that night we filmed Crimewatch. She's got such a great sense of humour. Anyway, back to reality. What have we got over there then?' He flicked his head towards the huddle of pretty girls on my right.

'There will be plenty more like that in here tonight mate. Cheers. Here's to your wind up!' We clinked tumblers and swigged our drinks.

TWENTY SEVEN

He called the AA and waited for an answer, tapping his membership card on the work surface. Trudy was stood in the hallway watching him and smiling as he looked at her. He gave his details over the phone and read his membership number. Trudy was still smiling at him as he said 'An hour?' into the handset. He looked at her, shaking his head in disbelief.

'Would you like a cup of tea or coffee while you're waiting? You may as well wait here. My name's Trudy.' She extended her delicate hand.

'That's very kind, Trudy. Nice to meet you. Daniel.' He shook her hand and felt his dick flicker slightly. 'I could murder a cup of coffee, milk, no sugar, and thank you. I can't think that they can be that busy. An hour!' He shook his head again. 'Are you sure you don't mind me waiting here? I don't mind sitting in my car.'

'It's no trouble and I wouldn't want to sit in a nice car like that waiting for some thug to come along and pinch the car. I'm making myself one anyway.' She led him into the kitchen.

He couldn't believe he was in their house. It was such a buzz; he needed some more whizz and asked her where the toilet was. He shut the door and quickly undid a wrap of Speed he'd had in his pocket. He smudged it onto his tongue and screwed his face up at the taste. *Fucking awful stuff! It will do the trick though. I can't believe I'm here. This is fucking superb!* The walls of the toilet were bright red with black and white photos hung on them. Photos of young people enjoying themselves and a couple of black-tie parties. The naked light bulb was very bright and made the walls shine red, like a cheap brothel. It was an intense experience with all the drugs rushing through his system. He flushed the toilet and went back into the kitchen where Trudy was stirring his coffee. She was incredibly sexy and she kept playing with her hair, which he knew was a sure sign that she fancied him. He knew he was good looking. *They were all lucky that I had chosen them for my collection.* He knew that he could pull any woman he wanted. He was flattered that Trudy fancied him but he really wasn't interested. It was Wendy that he wanted.

'Thanks. Coffee, one of the great discoveries of this century. I live off the stuff.' He told her, as he took the piping hot mug and sipped from it.

Trudy smiled and reached for a packet of cigarettes that were sat on the worktop. 'Do you smoke?' She asked, offering him one.

'Yeah, but I prefer my own brand.' He pulled out his Dunhill and took one. He offered Trudy the flame from his Cartier lighter and then lit his. She put an ashtray between them and asked him what he did for a living.

'A bit of this and that. I run a couple of small businesses that keep me busy most of the time. How about you? What do you do?'

'I'm a dancer. Well, not one of those art type dancers, more like an erotic dancer. My official job title is table dancer,' she said very matter of factly.

'Cool! That explains your great body.'

She went bright red at his compliment and thanked him, looking away as another girl walked into the kitchen. His heart burst into his mouth! It was Wendy! The Speed was taking affect and his breathing had increased. He was struggling to keep calm, his jaw clenching tightly in spasms and took a drag on his cigarette.

'Hi Wendy. This is Daniel. His Ferrari has run out of petrol and he's waiting for the AA. Daniel, this is Wendy, one of my housemates. She also works with me.' Trudy did the introductions and he watched Wendy's face. She didn't recognise him at first but as she came closer and shook his hand her expression changed. *She was as stunning as I remembered. Her long blonde hair was perfect.* She looked like she had just stepped out of a Salon Selective advert. Her eyes were beautiful with a large black outline around each iris that helped the blue really stand out from the white of her eyeballs. She had a petite nose and yet another set of perfect teeth. *That mouth would look great sucking on my cock!* He had to fight back a smile. He saw the first hint of recognition on her face and then it dawned on her. She backed away slightly and turned to Trudy.

'What's he doing in here?' She sounded very agitated.

'Do you know each other or something Wendy? What's the matter?'

'What do you mean, 'What's the matter?' This is the animal that got thrown out of Paradise!' She raised her voice and glared at him.

Before Trudy could reply he stepped in to defend himself. 'Wendy, it's good to see you again. I had no idea that you lived here, what a pleasant surprise. I really wanted to apologise to you for the way that I behaved that night and never thought I'd get a chance. I had been on an all day drinking binge. I've been back twice and tried to get in but each time I was told to F off by the doormen.' Wendy's face had softened slightly but he knew she wasn't convinced. 'I had had some bad news about one of my businesses and I just got hammered. It's no excuse for my behaviour, I know, but please accept my apologies. I really didn't mean to offend you. I woke up the next morning feeling like shit and then kinda remembered my awful remarks. I am truly sorry.' He was really surprised at how well he had come across considering that he was flying. *The Speed always makes me talk for England. I had said far more than I meant to but I couldn't help it. I felt like Spud in 'Trainspotting' when he went for his interview!* He laughed to himself as he looked at the two girls. *I am the rapist and they have no fucking clue!*

'Is this the guy you told Tina about? The one that offered you a thousand pounds?' Trudy looked amazed.

'Yes, this is the pig!'

'I offered you a thousand pounds? What for?' He asked innocently, feigning embarrassment.

'What d'ya think for? To sleep with me!' Wendy told him, backing away slightly as she listened to his horrible voice.

'Oh God! I am so sorry. Look I really ought to go. This is really embarrassing for me. I really didn't mean any offence.' He got up and made for the door.

'Wait! Daniel, don't go. You don't have to go.' Trudy turned to Wendy. ' Come on Wendy, he apologised for what he said. He obviously didn't mean any harm. Why not let it go?'

Wendy was slowly coming round to Trudy's way of thinking, but not without a small protest. 'I don't know Trudy. No offence,' she said to Daniel. 'But I don't trust him.'

'Come on Wendy. Daniel was pissed and asked to have sex with you. It's not as if he raped you! It's not as if it's the first time that it's happened in the club. And it will probably happen again. I'm sorry Daniel. I don't think you look like an animal.'

'Thank you, Trudy. I'm not now and never have been an animal.' He looked at Wendy. 'I've said I'm sorry, what more can I say? You are a beautiful woman and I asked you for sex. Surely you can't blame me? I am only human. I couldn't find you one bloke who wouldn't want to sleep with you. You are stunning and I am sorry.' He got down onto his knees and tried looking as sorry as he could. *Women were so fucking gullible! Oh, Wendy, I am soooo sorry, that I haven't had the pleasure of sliding into your love tube!* He laughed inside.

Wendy began laughing and told him to get up. 'It's amazing how wrong you can be about someone.'

The doorbell rang and Daniel said it was probably his AA man. Trudy and Wendy led him to the front door and sure enough, when Trudy opened the door they found an AA patrolman waving his torch at them. The two girls said goodbye and he once again said he was sorry and turned to Trudy. 'Maybe I could take you out for a drink one evening?'

Trudy beamed a great big smile his way and said that she would enjoy that. She rushed over to the phone and quickly scribbled her number down and then handed it to Daniel. 'Call me.'

They closed the door and he wandered over to the Ferrari with the patrolman. 'Look I'm really sorry. I've wasted your time a bit.' He pulled out a fifty-pound note and put it in the hand of the AA man. 'I used you as a lame excuse so I could chat up one of those girls. Sorry! My car's actually fine.'

The AA man wasn't bothered. He looked down at the fifty quid and just grinned. 'Fanks mate. Any time you get another problem with yer motor, let me know.' He laughed as he walked back to his yellow van, putting the note into his pocket.

TWENTY EIGHT

Frank had a hangover. It had been one of their usual heavy sessions and once again Frank was regretting it. Perhaps I'm an alcoholic, he thought as he picked up the keys to his Sierra and left his flat. For the second time in a fortnight he was driving whilst under the influence. As he made his way to the station he wondered how many other drivers drove the morning after a night on the booze. Too many, that was for sure and he did it just as often as most. It had been a great night and he had got home at about three o'clock. Roger had taken him lap dancing, to some club in Hammersmith. The birds had been out of this world. It wasn't the sort of place Frank enjoyed. He found it far too frustrating, sitting in a bar watching a pretty girl taking her clothes off and dancing. He would rather be either just drinking or fucking or both! But drinking and watching did nothing for him. He had tried to drag Roger away a couple of times to no avail. Roger had been in his element! He had just sat there drinking gin and tonics all night, staring at all the naked women around him. Frank wished he'd had a camera, he could still picture Roger sat there.

He got to the station at nine o'clock and made his way up to his office. This morning saw the beginning of Operation Catwalk and he knew he should have had an early night. He didn't fancy traipsing round South Kensington making door to door enquiries. The plan was to start at the apartment block where Amanda Worthington lived. He had a team of four other officers to assist him and they planned to contact as many people as they could. He held a meeting at ten o'clock to brief the officers on the line of questioning and that he expected complete confidence and politeness whilst dealing with the public. Before they left in two unmarked cars he called Roger to see how he was feeling.

'Kaplan Stewart.' An abrupt broker picked up Frank's call.

'Roger please.' He heard the broker scream out Roger's name.

I tore a strip of the broker for shouting so loud. The room was fairly quiet for a Friday morning and his screaming didn't help my headache. 'Hello?' I croaked. My throat was sore from the mixture of gin and cigarette abuse.

'You sound like I feel. Why do we do it mate?'

I was glad that Frank had been suffering as well. 'Fuck knows! At least I can relax today; you've got your door to door day today haven't you? I bet you need that like you need a blow job from Freddie Mercury!'

'Too right. I feel like shit. I've had five coffees and three fags to try and kick start the system. No luck so far. Fag number four is in progress but I'm not too hopeful.' Frank tried a small laugh.

'At least we chose a Thursday this time. Far more sensible than bloody Mondays! Good luck with the hunt today and let me know if you have any joy. I hope you do mate. By the way it was great to meet Sarah last night, she was lovely!' I tried to laugh but the spasms in my stomach hurt too much.

What a couple of lightweights we were, I thought. But we had drunk from eight o'clock until about three or four. I didn't remember getting home.

'Had you going for a while though, didn't I? You were a pain in the arse last night do you know that?' Frank sounded half-serious.

'Why mate? What did I do? What time did we get home?' I had no idea what he meant.

'You. Last night in the lap dancing place. What a fucking nightmare! I tried to get you to leave about three times and you refused. You were just sat in your chair staring at every naked bird that came your way. At one point you got a fucking great wad of vouchers, which you put on that bloody platinum Amex of yours. You must have spent a fucking fortune mate. But I'll say one thing for you; you do know how to enjoy yourself. That little black bird I danced with was a dirty little cow. Her fingers were everywhere. Thanks for paying!'

'Oh shit. I haven't looked in my wallet yet.' I knew I had gone over the top last night. I had woken up on my sofa with my boxer shorts around my ankles and the telly buzzing at me. I checked the video and sure enough it was a porno film! I looked at the receipts in my wallet and winced when I found the bill from Hammersmith Club Ltd. What a fucking idiot! 'Frank, I've just found it. Three hundred and eighty pounds! What a fucking waste. Did I enjoy myself?'

Frank was now laughing at me. 'I guess so mate. From the smile on your face I presume you did. I really wished that I'd had a camera because you looked like you were in heaven! And anyway, it's not as if you are gonna struggle is it? You've made a killing on the World Cup and last night's game must have helped?'

'No not really. The three yellow cards made no difference and I could have done with the Dutch scoring a couple more and I could have done with spending a whole lot less! Never mind, I can't take it with me can I?'

'No but you could leave a lot of it to me in your will. Listen, I gotta go and make a start on the operation. I'll give you a call this evening and let you know how it went. Fag four is now complete and I still feel like shit. Have a nice day now.' Frank said, dropping his cigarette into his half-empty coffee cup.

'Hey Frank, you still okay for that blind date dinner party tonight? Emma has promised me that the girl's a babe. She said she wouldn't try to set you up with a complete moose!'

'Yeah that will be great, just so long as I get some sleep this afternoon, fat chance!! What time?'

'About eight at my place, and get rid of your six o'clock shadow mate! If you get as far as snogging, you don't want to sandpaper her face now, do you? If it's any consolation, I'll be knackered too. At least we can watch the England game!' I could hear his stubble scraping against the mouthpiece of his phone.

'Great! See you tonight then, Rog. Thank Emma for the invite, tell her I'm very grateful.'

'Will do. You have a nice day now! Good luck with the door to door stuff mate.'

'Thanks.' Frank replaced the handset and went down to join the rest of his team.

TWENTY NINE

I got home at about six o'clock after a very long cab journey home. Once again I had wondered whether the taxi driver was the rapist. It seemed that every time I jumped into the back of a taxi I wondered the same thing. The one this evening had been far too chatty, and he was in his early thirties, a bit too young and very skinny. I had just wanted to sit back and relax but the driver had insisted on talking to me the entire journey. As I paid the driver and walked away, he was still prattling on about how great the England side was! I laughed and thought, 'Now I know why I drive in everyday.' It was a luxury I appreciated and it meant I didn't have to travel on the tube either. I hadn't driven in because of my stinking hangover and I had given Frank a huge bollocking when he'd told me that he had driven to the station.

Emma was due round at seven thirty so I had time for a run followed by a long soak in my sumptuous bathroom. It was my favourite room in my flat. It had very thick blue carpet, not shag-pile. I couldn't stand shag-pile! It had his and her's sinks with a mirror above going along the whole wall. There was a Jacuzzi bath in the corner, which was big enough for about five people, and next to it there was a shower unit. The shower unit was one of my best investments. On those mornings I struggled out of bed still drunk from the night before, unable to open my eyes, I would feel my way into the shower and boom! I was hit from all sides with incredibly powerful jets of water. It was fantastic and a must have for anyone who rose at an unearthly hour.

My bedroom was next to the bathroom and I had an ensuite dressing room for my clothes and shoes. My bedroom was very simple, a king-size bed, two bedside tables with lamps and a chest of drawers. The door to my dressing room was mirrored, as was the whole of that wall. When it was closed you would never know there was even a door there. Emma and I had had some great nights of passion and I found the mirrors really kinky. She joked I should have the ceiling mirrored too but I had seen a movie where a couple had been lovemaking passionately, the bed head had been banging against the wall and the mirrored ceiling had come down on top of them nearly slicing the guy in half. Not my idea of a good time in the bedroom! I didn't feel like going running, but I knew I had to keep up my new routine.

I was as shattered when I got home from my run, as I had been last time. I did my stretches whilst the bath was running and I managed forty sit-ups. I climbed into the bath and slid down into the foam. The water was a little too hot but it felt good against my aching limbs. I lay there with my eyes closed, just relaxing. I was looking forward to the dinner party later. It had been Emma's idea and she said she would cook. She had a friend who worked as a beautician at Holmes Place who had been single for a couple of months. Emma had mentioned Frank to her and Isabelle had been quite interested. I couldn't wait to watch Henson as he went to work on his blind date. I hoped she knew what she was letting herself in for. I could just imagine the awkwardness of the first few minutes and I laughed as I thought of Frank having to make polite conversation!

I felt something moving about in the water and then, suddenly it was biting my balls. I sat bolt upright to find Emma with her arm immersed in my bath water. I had fallen asleep!

'Hi Darling! Sorry, did I wake you? It's nearly seven o'clock.' Emma smiled at me.

'Hi Em. I can't believe you. A gentle kiss on the forehead would have been a little nicer.' I smiled back, and reached up to kiss her mouth. She tasted sweet and clean and she smelt of Allure.

'I came round early to prepare the starter. I must get on.'

'What are we having?' I called after her, as she walked out.

'Wait and see, sweetheart.'

I got out the bath and shook my head in disbelief as I looked at myself in the mirror. I had been in the bath so long that my skin had wrinkled very badly. I looked like an old man! I towelled myself dry and got dressed. It was really warm outside still so I put on a blue silk shirt I had bought in Singapore and a pair of Dockers. I wore a pair of loafers with no socks and headed for the kitchen to get a glass of wine. Emma had beaten me to it, she was sipping a glass of Chardonnay as I walked in and asked me if I would like a glass.

'I feel like your wife, cooking for you, pouring you a glass of wine. It feels really good.' She raised her glass, took a sip and then kissed me passionately.

'I hope you're not expecting me to propose tonight?' I asked her, tongue in cheek. I was glad she felt so relaxed in my company but a little worried that she felt like my wife already.

'Oh relax! I was just trying to say that I love being with you. I'd say 'No' if you asked me anyway!' She poked her tongue out at me. 'Now go away and leave me to it please Roger.'

I sat in front of the telly and flicked through the cable channels. The England game kicked off at eight so I hoped Frank would be here by then. Emma had agreed we could watch the first half and I would record the second. I watched the match preamble and the pundits were saying good things about England. I was convinced England would lose and I was engrossed when the doorbell rang. I told Emma I would get it and as I opened the door had to quickly stop my mouth from dropping open. Frank's blind date was very pretty.

'Hi, you must be Roger? I'm Isabelle.' She extended her hand and I noticed the perfectly manicured nails as I squeezed it.

'Nice to meet you. Come on in.' I ushered her into the flat. 'Honey, Isabelle's here. What would you like to drink?' I asked the supermodel!

'A glass of wine would be lovely, please.'

I led her into the kitchen and Emma gave her a kiss and took the bottle of champagne Isabelle had brought. 'Will Chardonnay be okay?' I asked Isabelle.

'Yeah, great thanks.' She flashed a set of perfect white teeth at me as she smiled and took the glass from me. 'I love your flat Roger.'

'Thanks. Well, cheers. Here's to a good evening. Frank should be here soon. I presume Emma has told you all about him?'

'Yes and I can't wait to meet him! He sounds absolutely ideal. It is so difficult to meet the nice guys these days. We get so many posers at the club trying to chat us up don't we Emma?'

'I hope you don't!' I appealed, trying to sound jealous.

'Of course we do, darling! Wouldn't you be disappointed if we didn't? You shouldn't be concerned though Roger, they are all mostly, completely obnoxious. Just because they do a little bit a gym work they think they're all hunks! As for Frank, now there is a hunk!' She winked at Isabelle and then ran over to kiss me. 'Only joking Rog.'

I was about to remonstrate when the doorbell rang. 'Speak of the Devil!' I said as I made for the door. Frank had a bottle of wine in one hand and in the other a bouquet of flowers. I looked at the flowers in amazement and Frank just laughed. 'If she's the babe that you and Emma say she is, I thought I'd better start on the right footing!'

'And a bottle of wine too. Thanks mate, very generous. Not quite as generous as your blind date though. She brought champagne! Come on in.'

We joined the girls in the kitchen and Emma did the introducing. I stood back to watch Frank on his best behaviour. I could tell they liked each other from their body language. I had read a book by a guy called Anthony Robbins called 'Personal Power'. Anthony Robbins calls himself a personal success coach and the book was all about improving your life and helping you to take action instead of procrastinating. There is a chapter on body language and how if you mirror the body posture of someone you immediately create rapport with that person. Well, from what little I had learnt, Frank and Isabelle were definitely creating rapport! I poured Frank some wine and I ushered them into the lounge where I left them to get to know each other.

Emma and I watched through the doorway of the kitchen and Emma said, 'They really seem to like each other. I hope this works, Isabelle has been really unlucky in her relationships and it's about time she found Mr. Right.'

'And you think that's Henson? You've got to be kidding! He is just a dirty old man who's addicted to the opposite sex. I will be very surprised if this lasts more than a couple of months.'

'Well prepare to be surprised then, honey. I think Frank is ready to settle down. That awful job he does, he needs someone to share his problems with and he can't just keep having one-night stands forever. As you keep telling me: "Behind every great man there is a great woman' and I really think Isabelle could be that woman.'

'I think we're getting a little ahead of things. They've just met, let's wait and see what happens tonight shall we? Now can I help you with anything?' Deep down I hoped that Frank and Isabelle got it together too.

'Yes please. Can you drain the spaghetti and take the salad into the dining room. Oh, and have you got a bottle of red we can have?'

'Already opened and on the table. Barolo, Frank's favourite.' I winked at Em.

'And mine!' Emma blew me a kiss across the work surface.

I wandered into the dining room with the salad and then joined Frank and Isabelle to top up their glasses. Frank was telling her all about his job and the latest on the rapist. Isabelle sat next to him on the sofa, hanging on his every word. Her hazel eyes were concentrating on Henson and her pupils were huge with interest and excitement. She was wearing a short green skirt, very revealing I noticed, her legs were slim and I could see halfway up her thighs and there was no trace of cellulite, that would please Henson. Her breasts were trying to burst through the buttons on her yellow Lacoste blouse and I saw Frank glance down at them from time to time. It was great fun watching my mate in action, he was in his element, working his prey and slowly reeling her in. Isabelle told him she had seen him on Crimewatch and she had been impressed with him. She said she was surprised no decent leads had come from the show.

She asked him if he was any nearer to catching the rapist and Frank shook his head disappointedly. 'We have been going round knocking on doors near to where each victim was raped, to see if anyone can remember anything. We have a sample of the rapist's DNA, which is great news, but until we catch someone and get a match we are a bit stuck. What surprised me was there was no match on our files. We have DNA profiles of every criminal on record, that's over three million and not one match.'

'It must be so frustrating sometimes.' Isabelle was trying to say the right thing.

'Sometimes? You mean all of the time! It also gets really depressing, but hey, you don't want to hear about that. Maybe I should come into the club and have a massage! That would help me wind down.' Frank was desperate to change the subject.

'Dinner is served.' Emma shouted from the kitchen. 'Roger, can you help me please?'

I carried two plates into the dining room, each nearly over flowing with spaghetti Bolognese. There was garlic bread steaming on the table and Emma had tossed the salad with a French dressing. 'Help yourselves to Parmesan cheese guys.' I said, as I gave Isabelle her plate.

'Emma this looks fantastic, and it smells scrummy.' Isabelle told her friend.

'Just a little number I prepared earlier. Cheers.' Emma toasted with her glass of Barolo.

'To the wonderful cook, thanks for having us. Cheers.' Replied Frank, as we all touched glasses. 'To this evening being the start of something good.' He smiled at Isabelle, who blushed.

'You are too smooth for your own good Henson!' I punched him on the arm and laughed. 'Be careful Isabelle, don't fall for his cheap chat up lines.'

'Roger, please don't worry. I can look after myself and besides, I like his cheap chat up lines.' She smiled at Frank, who was now poking his tongue at me and flicking his fingers up.

By the time we had finished dinner the first half was over and England had a one, nil lead over the Columbians.

'I can't seem to do anything wrong at the moment. I made just over two hundred quid on England goals. I closed my position yesterday, so I'd like to see them win tonight. At this rate they could make the bloody play-offs.' I told Frank.

'You deserve to lose money, not make it. How could you not back your own country?' Henson was trying to wind me up.

'Don't you start. You're my mate. I can just imagine the stick that I would have got from the boys this weekend.'

'What's happening this weekend?' Henson asked.

'He's leaving me all alone in this big city Frank. Can you believe it?' Emma jumped in front of the TV. 'He's off on a golfing weekend with some clients. I begged him to take me but he said it was strictly business. They're staying in Cliveden!! I am so jealous!'

'Hey don't you worry Emma, I'll look after you.' Frank stood up and put his big arms around her. 'Only poofs go to a place like that.'

'Yeah, like I really want to go? I'd rather be with my honey in London than with a load of clients that think they deserve this kind of entertainment.' They had both succeeded in winding me up. 'I can just imagine them swanning around as if they own the place.'

'Darling, we're only having a laugh with you.' Emma realised they'd hit a nerve.

'I know. I'm sorry, it's just that I hate having to give up my weekends to go away with bloody clients.'

'Hey Hamilton, it could be worse. At least you'll have the winnings from your England bet to spend!' Frank was laughing.

I smiled and kicked out at him. 'Fuck you, Frank. Let's get pissed, I don't want to watch the second half, do you?'

'No, I don't care, beside I've got a date that needs converting!' he whispered and winked at me.

THIRTY

The curtains were still shut but Penny knew the thunderstorm that had woken her at two o'clock had passed, along with the rain, she hoped. She was entertaining Veuve Clicquot who were sponsoring the Polo at Smiths Lawn in Windsor and she had been praying for good weather. She got up and pulled back the curtains and was relieved to see the cloud dispersing and the sun trying to burst through. It was six o'clock, much earlier than she was used to, but she had to be in Windsor by eight and her train went from Paddington at seven, thirty-eight. She knocked gently on Lucy's door and asked her if she would like a cup of tea. Lucy was already awake and said she would love a cuppa. 'Shall I use the bathroom first?' Penny asked.

'No, I'll jump in now whilst you're making the tea. I'll only be ten minutes.'

Penny knew that was true. She didn't know how Lucy managed to be in and out in just ten minutes. It took Penny nearly ten minutes just to shave her legs and armpits! It didn't really surprise her though, Lucy was not the tidiest person and her clothes were always strewn over her bedroom floor and never ironed. Penny popped the kettle on and stood looking out the window, thinking how lucky she was. She had only been back in the country two months and she had landed herself the best job in the world. She had two really big accounts, one of which was Veuve Clicquot and she had five smaller accounts she didn't have to dedicate as much time to. Her job was to identify new sponsorship opportunities and forge relationships with all of her accounts, organise innovative events and create star-studded guest lists. Penny loved the people she spoke to, she was helping their businesses and they all spoke to her like she was their best friend. When her company came up with the idea for the launch party of Daytona and she organised the guest list they were very, very impressed. Penny's boss had received a letter from the Chairman saying how pleased he was with the day and that he hoped they could continue the good work. He mentioned Penny and said that she was the hardest working and most professional PR person he had ever worked with. David Walton, Penny's boss, had shown Penny the letter and he had given her a two and a half thousand pound pay rise. Penny was definitely a people person and she felt like sponsorship days were just one big party.

Today would be no different. Again she had had to organise the day and make sure that suitable guests had been invited and were in fact coming. Sarah Ferguson was the special guest of Veuve Clicquot and the company had given Penny a guest list to work from. She had managed to invite Tom Cruise and Nicole Kidman and the main man from Veuve Clicquot was over the moon. He was a big Tom Cruise fan and had loved 'Jerry Maguire'. Penny grimaced as she imagined him going up to Tom Cruise and shouting, 'Show me the Money!' and giving him a high five! She took Lucy her tea and dived into the bathroom.

Their taxi arrived at seven and the girls were at Paddington station at seven twenty. The train stopped at Slough where they had to change and get another train to Windsor. A forty minute journey if the trains were running on time. They travelled first class and had a light breakfast in the buffet carriage. They chatted about life in general and Penny talked about Roger and his job and his friend Frank, the detective. Lucy was especially interested in Frank, she thought he sounded divine. She asked Penny if he was single and Penny told her he was, but that he had gone to Roger's last night on a blind date, so maybe not for long. Penny told her flat mate about the rapes and Lucy asked if there was any inside gossip.

'No, not really. Roger and Frank are very close and Frank tells him everything but I don't think the police have much to go on. They have the DNA sample they need but until they catch the man, it's useless. The thought of some maniac going round London in a taxi raping women leaves me cold.' Penny shuddered.

'I know isn't it awful. I was talking to some friends and we just couldn't bear to think about it. My father says if it happened to anyone he knew he would have no choice but to take the law into his own hands and kill the man! My mother told him not to be so ridiculous but he said if this rapist is caught, he will probably only get sentenced to ten years and will get out after five or six for good behaviour! I do know where my father's coming from.' Lucy explained, taking a sip of orange juice.

'He's right I think. The law is an ass, as the saying goes. Now about today, I have the list of guests and the umbrellas should already be there. I confirmed most of the guests yesterday, there were a couple I couldn't get hold of, Tania Bryer, Tim Jefferies, Sting and Phil Collins but everyone else should be there.'

'So are Tom and Nicole definitely coming?' Lucy asked, excitedly.

'Yes! I'm really pleased. It's all mainly thanks to Jim at Daytona, I rang and invited him and his girlfriend and asked him if he thought that the Polo was something that Tom would be into. Jim said that he would get back to me and called me last week to confirm that the four of them would be attending. I couldn't believe it!' Penny was proud of herself and happy to share the fact with one of her colleagues.

'I bet David's pleased isn't he?'

'I think so but more importantly, the main man, Sir Christopher from Veuve Clicquot is, he's a very big Tom Cruise fan! I just hope he doesn't follow Tom around all day.'

'Like a pet dog, you mean? Can you imagine.' They both laughed loudly, much to the disgust of some of the other passengers.

The train arrived on time at Windsor and the two girls jumped into a minicab outside the station.

'We'll ask him for a number and I'll arrange for us to be picked up later.' Penny suggested to Lucy.

'I'm actually not going back to London tonight. Alex lives in Reading and he said that he would pick me up from the Polo at about six. I told him that it should be all over by then. I'm sure he wouldn't mind giving you a lift to the station.' Lucy told Penny.

'No, don't worry. It should be finished by six but just in case it's not, I'll catch a mini-cab back. Honestly, I don't want to hold you and Alex up unnecessarily.'

'Do you think I should call Alex and tell him to pick me up later? I don't want to leave early and get in trouble.' Lucy was concerned that she should be around until the end.

'No. The match finishes at four and I can't imagine too many people staying that late. Go at six, it will be fine.' Penny said. She felt important, giving her work mate permission to leave early. Lucy had been with Marble Mayhew and Co for five years and was highly thought of by the management. She also had her own accounts that she looked after but the Veuve Clicquot account was one of the company's biggest and she and Penny worked it together.

The huge gates at the beginning of the drive were open and the mini-cab slowly drove through. The tarmac was a light red colour and looked very regal against the green trees that lined the entrance of Windsor Great Park. Smiths Lawn was within the grounds of the park and that entrance was even more impressive. The gates were painted gold and the lawns were immaculately cut with sweeping shades of green stripes going vertically from the entrance to the huge marquee that had been erected next to the Polo field. David's Jaguar was already parked next to the marquee Penny noticed as they got out of the car.

'This is so impressive! It's beautiful.' Penny was really pleased that the Veuve Clicquot banners had been put up. They were everywhere. All the Cartier signs had disappeared into the background with the stylish orange banners blowing in the light breeze that remained from the storm. 'I don't think Cartier will be happy when they see the photos in Hello magazine and Tatler next week!' Penny joked.

'It looks amazing!' Lucy agreed. 'Come on, let's go inside, I can't wait to see the table settings.'

They walked into the huge tent and were greeted by David and some of their other colleagues. 'Penny, Lucy, you have done me proud. This is all very impressive. I think this is going to be a great day and to cap it all, I'm going to meet Mr. Tom Cruise!' David was stood between the two girls with his arms around them.

'Oh, don't you start! You sound like Sir Christopher, He's a big fan of Tom Cruise.' Penny threw her hands in the air, 'Show me the money!'

David laughed and pretended to strangle Penny. 'Help yourselves to coffee; everything seems to be under control. Well-done girls.'

There were five hundred people coming as guests of Veuve Clicquot and they would be having a Champagne reception followed by a demonstration on Polo, then lunch at twelve followed by the Polo match. The match was between Ascot Polo Club and a club from Argentina that was reputedly one of the best teams in the world. Penny knew nothing about Polo and was glad that Veuve Clicquot had requested a demo first.

The day was a huge success. Ascot had beaten the Argentineans by two goals and the crowd had gone wild. Sarah Ferguson, Prince Andrew's ex-wife had presented the boys with their trophy and Sir Christopher Lloyd-Palmer, the Chairman of Veuve Clicquot, had given a short speech. Penny was relieved that her hard work had paid off. She was sat at the back of the marquee drinking coffee with Lucy and a good-looking man from Veuve Clicquot. It was nearly six o'clock and the guests had gone and all the staff were now rushing around like ants, clearing up all the mess.

'Is that Alex, Lucy?' Penny asked, pointing over to the entrance. A scruffy looking chap had walked in and was peering around looking very lost.

'Yes, it is. Alex! Over here.' Lucy waved at him from our table. He came bumbling over, and he was obviously, a little embarrassed.

'Hi, hope I'm not late? I had a bit of trouble getting in without a pass. Was I meant to have one?' He asked Lucy, awkwardly playing with his black hair.

'No. I'm ready now. Penny are you sure you don't need me?' Lucy stood up and frowned at Alex as he went to sit down. Alex tried to cover up his mistake by reaching down to scratch his left leg. Penny winked at Lucy and smiled.

'Off you go. Have a good evening and thank you so much for all your help. We were a big hit.'

Penny watched them walked away and laughed as she watched Lucy telling him off. Poor Alex, she thought. 'Right, well I'd better get going myself.'

The young man from Veuve Clicquot stood and thanked Penny again for all her help and he explained Sir Christopher was so happy to have met Tom Cruise. Penny was just pleased that the film 'Jerry Maguire' hadn't been mentioned.

'Here's my business card, I'd love to see you again, maybe dinner?'

Penny took the card and noted his details. 'James Forster, Marketing Director. You *are* quite good at marketing aren't you?' Penny smiled at him. 'I may call you next week.'

James grinned. 'I know one shouldn't mix business with pleasure but it's not everyday one has the pleasure in business to spend time with someone so beautiful.' He ran his hand through his brown hair confidently.

'Don't overdo it now, James!' Penny blushed.

The headwaiter came over to inform Penny her car was here.

Penny tapped the business card and said, 'I'll keep this somewhere safe! Nice to have met you.'

She got into the mini-cab and went off to catch her train. She sat looking out of the window, content with herself. She was really pleased with the way the day had gone and she felt very flattered by the approach from James, but not sure she was going to follow it up. She caught the six thirty-five from Windsor and sat back thinking how lucky she was.

THIRTY ONE

He sat in his Ferrari with the engine running whilst he unwrapped a little parcel of Cocaine. He used a door key to spoon up some of the powder, he snorted one key's worth up each nostril and then popped an Ecstasy pill and he washed the concoction down with a swig of Evian water. He pulled out of the Chelsea car park and headed for the M1. The traffic wasn't too bad for a Saturday afternoon; he was on his way back to Hertfordshire to collect the photographic paper. He had received an email from Barry at the camera shop explaining that the paper was ready and that if he brought back the bad batch, Barry wouldn't charge him for the new batch. *Very generous.*

He zoomed up Park Lane and the Edgware Road and was on the M1 twenty-five minutes later. He unleashed the yellow beast and was soon doing over one hundred miles an hour. He felt good from the drugs and also because of his plans for the day. He was going to strike again tonight. It was very appropriate he thought what with it being a Saturday night, Lottery night. *I wonder which lucky, little bitch has tonight's winning ticket, a session in the back of my taxi with me! It could be you!* He thought as he pointed to a pretty girl driving a blue Audi, as he overtook her car. Motorhead was blaring out of the stereo and he was tapping along on the steering wheel.

It was four o'clock when he pulled up outside the parish church. He walked across the busy high street and into the camera shop. The annoying bell rang as the door opened and he waited for Barry to appear. 'Good afternoon, Mr Griffin, how nice to see you again. I am so sorry about the Agfa paper.' Barry fussed, rubbing his hands together nervously. 'I took the liberty of sending an email to Agfa and asking them if they knew of any problem. They explained the Signum II is one of their best quality papers and there should be no discolouring at all with it. They have asked me to send back the paper and if you could provide a couple of the photographs you developed.'

'That's very kind of you, but I just want my new batch of paper. I don't have any of the photos I developed, they were so bad I just chucked them away.'

'Never mind sir. I will email the company and explain if you like? Were the pictures grainy at all?' Barry asked.

'Look, I don't care about the old paper!' He shouted. 'I just want the new batch so I can get on with my day. Now surely that isn't too much to ask. And if I have a problem with Agfa, I will contact them myself!'

The shopkeeper was trembling. He had never met anyone so rude and over-powering in his life. He rushed into the back of the shop, stooped down to pick up the box of paper and staggered back into the front with it.

'You said no charge, right?'

'Um, oh ye… yes. Yes, that's right. No charge. Thank you Sir.' Barry stammered, nervously, trying to avoid eye contact.

He picked up the box and walked out of the shop, kicking the door shut behind him. He bleeped the alarm on his car and put the box on the passenger seat and drove off, as Barry watched through the door of his shop. Why did some people have to be so rude and abrasive? He thought. When he saw the man's Ferrari he wasn't surprised. It was always the rich people who were the rudest. Probably how they become rich in the first place, he thought, by pushing everyone else around and manipulating them for their own gain. Well Mr. Ferrari man won't be coming into my shop anymore, he thought.

He drove to his house to check everything was okay and then headed back to London.

He arrived in Pavilion Road in Fulham at six-thirty and swapped his Ferrari for the taxi.

As he drove off in the taxi he did some more Cocaine and then panicked slightly. *Why the fuck did I just do that? I'm losing it. I must be more careful.* He should have gone home first to get the Golf. He didn't want the Ferrari to be seen around the lock-up. He shook his head and laughed. He couldn't be pissed off for too long. *Tonight was going to be a good night! Who was going to be the lucky winner? Roll up, roll up, all the fun of the fair!* He shouted, as he headed along the Kings Road and past his flat. He had a new plan for tonight's adventure. He was going to try something different. He had decided to sit on a taxi rank outside one of the Capital's train stations. He was now driving through Hyde Park, which was London's biggest park with the Serpentine River cutting it in half. It was a stark contrast to the drab, grey buildings and roads that surrounded it. He had plumped for Paddington, as he knew it would be busy and it wasn't too far from the park.

He arrived at seven-fifteen and joined the back of the queue. There were seven cabs in front of his and there were only five or six people waiting. *Fuck! Not one babe. Not such a great fucking idea.* As he thought this, a beautiful young lady arrived at the cab rank. She was wearing a smart, Yves Saint-Laurent style suit, white with a blue border running round the edges. Her skirt stopped just above the knee, showing off enough of her long, slinky legs. Her blonde hair was slightly ruffled which gave her that just out of bed look. *Oh Fuck yes! Please let her be mine. Come on Darling, you pay your money, you take your chance. It could be you!*

He wound the window down as his passenger approached. 'Munster Road in Fulham please.'

There is a God! Thank you! This is my lucky night. Penny climbed into the back of the taxi and pulled out The Daily Mail and began reading. She was glad to be nearly home. It had been a long, tiring day and she couldn't wait to get in and relax in a hot, Badedas bath. *This girl is so fucking stylish and very up-market.* He couldn't believe his luck. *A little, rich bitch waiting to be taught a lesson.*

He guided the taxi back through Hyde Park and into South Kensington. As he got nearer to her destination, his pulse quickened. He couldn't stop jiggling in his seat and he felt the blood surging to his groin. He glanced at her in the rear view mirror and had a near perfect view up her skirt. He could hardly contain himself. He had a little location in mind. He would have to be careful as it was still quite early but he liked the excitement of doing her in broad daylight. He headed along the Kings Road and halfway down, he pulled back the window dividing him and his passenger, 'I've just got to pop in here love, I'll be two secs.' He turned the cab into the entrance of Marks and Spencers and parked, making sure the cab was hidden from the road. He jumped out and walked off towards the entrance. Once out of sight he put his gloves on and then walked casually back to the taxi. Penny was still happily reading her newspaper. *Honey, I'm home!* He laughed to himself and quickly ripped her door opened and jumped in. He slammed the ether rag into her face just as she screamed out in shock. She didn't fight as much as he had anticipated and soon she was limp and all his. He was going to drive to a safer spot but couldn't wait. *I hope you don't mind if I take your clothes off now, you sexy little bitch. You are about to be had by the most famous rapist of all. You're about to win the fucking Lottery, baby!*

THIRTY TWO

We had been busy and were having one of our best mornings in a while. Our bond market was rampant on the back of an Alan Greenspan interview on CNN. I was always so impressed how one person like Greenspan, he was the main man at the Federal Reserve Bank in New York, could have such a huge affect on the worlds financial markets. The Long Gilt contract opened up three-quarters of a point and continued rising during the first half an hour. It was our busiest start to a Monday for a long time and I could have done without it to be honest.

I had spent the weekend playing golf in Berkshire with the guys from Morgan Stanley and had drunk far too much and was feeling a little tender. Our great plans for golf had been a washout. It had rained from the moment we'd checked into our five star hotel and so we'd spent most of Saturday and Sunday in a state of semi-consciousness. We hadn't got to bed before 1am on either night. Not a great way to begin a hectic week, and it was about to get much worse.

I was in the middle of a fifty million swap with my best customer, Andrew from Stanley's when my mother called.

'Rog, one out.' David yelled across the desk.

'Hello!' I shouted abruptly down my handset.

'Roger darling, where have you been?'

'Mum, I'm really busy. I'll call you…'

She interrupted me. 'Roger please listen to me. It's Penelope!' My mother's distraught voice quivered down the line.

' Mum stay there!' I put her on hold and told Danny to speak to Andrew. 'What's wrong mum? What's happened?'

'It's Penelope. She's been …' My mother broke down in tears, sobbing uncontrollably into the phone. 'Roger please come home tonight, it's awful. We've been trying to get hold of you. Penelope's been raped!' Mum started crying again.

Raped. I couldn't believe it. 'Mum what did you just …'

I was interrupted by my father's voice. 'Roger, your mother's very upset, well we all are but please don't worry. Considering the circumstances, Penelope is going to be fine but she's been heavily sedated.'

'Dad, what happened?' I asked slowly, as the shock of my mother's news began to sink in.

'I've spoken to the policeman who found her. Penelope had been in a taxi on her way back from Paddington and that is all she can recall. She had been at the Polo in Windsor. The police found her wandering around the Kings Road at ten o'clock on Saturday night. The officer told me that she seemed very confused and in a state of shock. They took her to the local police station then to the Chelsea and Westminster Hospital for a check up. They called your mother and me late on Saturday night. I did try and call you but your ansafone was on and I couldn't get through to you on your mobile. I didn't want to leave you a message, I wanted to talk to you in person.'

'I'm sorry Dad. I was away with bloody clients all weekend and there was no reception on my phone.' I was so angry at the network I subscribed to.

'Anyway,' my father continued, 'they still need to ask Penelope some questions, but they have been very understanding. The doctor said she should sleep right through until tomorrow and I know how busy you are. Please don't rush down because you feel you have to.'

'Dad I'm leaving now. I want to see Pen. The guys here can cope without me for a couple of days. I'll see you soon.' I clicked the phone off and sat staring into space, my mind working overtime. Pen. raped! Why her? By whom? Why my beautiful little sister? This kind of thing didn't happen to people I knew. I'd read about plenty of rapes in the papers in the past. I knew all about the taxi rapist and Frank was trying to catch the bastard. But not my Pen. I never dreamt he would, could rape my little sister. I am going to kill him!! The man that did this was going to pay. When Frank and I find him I'll cut his fucking balls off!

'Roger, the fifty million sevens oh two, sevens oh one is done. You go on buying twos, selling ones, dropping twelve and a half.' Danny brought me back to reality.

'Danny you handle it and keep Goldman in touch.' I told him curtly.

'Griff.' I got up and tapped my right hand man on his shoulder and motioned for him to follow me. He closed the door of my office behind him.

'What's up Rog?'

'I've had some bad family news. I'm going home for a couple of days. Keep an eye on Morgan Stanley and Goldman and make sure Jamie's timekeeping doesn't slip. If Michael needs me just tell him I'll be back on Wednesday or Thursday.'

'Is there anything that I can do for you? Do you want to talk about it?' He seemed very concerned.

'That fucking cab driver has raped my sister. I can't believe it. I'm going to get that cunt if it's the last thing I do.' I slammed my fist down on my desk and one of my screens fell crashing to the floor. I noticed some of the boys on the dealing floor spin round to look. 'I'm sorry Griff. I'll call you tonight if I get a chance. Any probs call me on my mobile.'

There was nothing he could say or do to make me feel any better and as he walked out, I noticed the picture on my desk. It was of Pen and me playing with Jasper, our labrador, in mum and dad's garden. I had to fight back the tears. God, I loved her and I really felt for her. I had always been there for Pen. I remembered her first love, Chris Nettles and how I had been there to pick up the pieces when he dumped her. I had called him 'Stinging Nettles' and she had laughed. Her first hangover had been my fault and I had spent the whole night trying to sober her up with black coffee before I could take her home. Mum would have killed me. I was always there for her and I should have been there to protect her this weekend. Instead I was away, getting pissed with a load of clients. I felt so guilty. I had always hated rapists and I couldn't believe that one had come between my sister and me. Well, I wasn't just going to sit back and wait for Frank to catch him; I was going to get this fucking bastard of a taxi driver myself.

THIRTY THREE

He sat at his desk and watched Roger scurry out of the dealing room. He had gone too far now and he knew it. *How the fuck was I to know I was raping the boss's little sister? Fuck! This was getting way too complicated. Fuck I need a hit right now.* He reached into his jacket pocket, pulled out a small packet and went into the toilets. He looked at himself in the big mirrors as he passed. *God I look like shit!* His face was a white as a sheet and his blue eyes very, very blood-shot. He went into an empty cubicle and locked the door. He pulled his trousers and pants down and sat on the toilet so if anyone did look, they would think he was taking a crap. He started unravelling the packet but his hands were shaking too much. *Come on Daniel, get a fucking grip of yourself! Daniel Freeman or Brian Griffin? I don't even know who the fuck I am anymore.*

He finally managed to get the packet open and quickly pinched a big lump of the powder and snorted it quietly up his left nostril. He winced as the sharp crystals cut into the already tender membrane of his nostril and were immediately absorbed by the capillaries in his nose. He repeated the process, this time using his right nostril and sat back as the drug rushed to his head. *That's better. I need to relax and get through the rest of this motherfucking day and then I can think.*

He wiped his nose with toilet paper, checked his nostrils in the mirror for any traces of powder then walked back onto the dealing floor. The drug intensified the din of the brokers screaming at each other and he allowed himself a small grin as he sat back at the desk.

'Brian, are you okay mate? You look like shit.' Danny called over the desk.

'Yeah, I'm fine.' He replied, thinking to himself; *No, I'm pretty fucking far from okay!* 'Umm. Roger's had some bad news and will be away for a couple of days. As soon as I know more I will let you all know.' He felt a complete fraud. He was the cause of the bad news and he could imagine how the wankers he worked with would react when they finally found out he was the rapist.

'What d'you mean 'bad news'?' David asked, his broad Edinburgh accent cutting through the noise.

'I can't say at the moment. Roger didn't want me to until he calls me. Let's just get on with the job in hand.' He tried to sound assertive, but didn't feel it.

He was relieved the day had ended and as he got into his Ferrari, he allowed himself a smile. *Roger's kid sister! Fucking Hell! She had been the best by a long way. She should be one of those fucking lap dancers. She had a fantastic body and the cutest little cunt. Not like a lot of those pretty bitches with hairy bushes. Hers had been neatly trimmed into a very small triangle.* He sat in the car park below the office, recalling his evening with Penny

Hamilton. He had gone through her handbag and found her driving license but the name hadn't meant anything to him at the time. Now it seemed so obvious. He should have recognised her from all the photos in the press and 'Hello' magazine, but the drugs had obviously got him too excited to notice. *Shame, 'cause it would have been more fun if I'd known! At least she would be one victim easy to keep in touch with!* He laughed as he accelerated out of the car park and into the busy traffic.

He got home and went straight to the dark room where the photos of Penny were hanging on the drying line. He was pleased with the quality of the new paper and began carefully unpegging the photos. He laid them all out and stood back to enjoy them and then took them next door into the annex. He unlocked the door and went over to the place he had reserved for his latest victim, never imagining that it would be Roger Hamilton's sister. *Just a few to go and I will have broken Crosby's record of sixteen!* He spent the early part of his evening sticking Penny's pictures onto the wall and then he went into his gym to work out a plan of action. After two hours of hard exercise he showered and then slumped into his armchair at ten o'clock with a bottle of Bud Ice.

He had done a lot of thinking and hadn't got very far. He wasn't looking forward to Roger returning at the end of the week. He knew that Roger didn't suspect him and therefore it shouldn't be too big a problem. He just regretted that Roger was involved; he liked him. He had contemplated getting rid of the taxi and lying low for a while but he thought that might be a bit too obvious. The police weren't stupid and might wonder why the rapist had stopped after Penny's rape. So he decided nothing would change for now. He needed to keep in touch with the police investigations and he could do that through Frank Henson. He knew Roger and Frank would be talking and going out together and he needed to be there. He would try to get invited along for a few drinks next time. He was convinced he would be able to keep at least one step ahead of the police. He had had a sudden flash of inspiration; he would change his plan of attack for the next victim. *I need to put the fucking police off the scent a bit and this will throw a spanner in their investigation!* He laughed as he swigged the last of his Bud.

He would give Trudy a call and arrange to take her out. She had given him her number last week, and he jumped up to find his wallet. He pulled out the piece of paper she'd jotted it on, and smiled. *I'll spike her drink with Rohypnol and then have some fun with the slut.* He had obtained the sleeping drug from his doctor when he had gone to Hong Kong on business last year. It was great for taking on a long-haul flight; it would knock you out for about ten hours solid, but when mixed with alcohol it became a lethal, mind-altering drug.

About three months ago, he had experimented with the dosages of Rohypnol. He had poured himself a gin and tonic into which, he'd slowly added the drug. He knew he had to be very careful when adding the drug. He had been given the drug in capsule form and he had slowly opened the plastic, outer casing and poured the powder in. He had waited and timed how long it took for the chemical to alter the colour of the drink. The Drug Company that manufactured Rohypnol had only added the colour changing effect as a safety measure recently. The drink began turning blue after twenty-two minutes, *enough time for Trudy to have finished the drink and be like putty in my hands!* He had done this on five consecutive evenings in March, each time increasing the dosage until on day five he reached the right quantity. He had set up his camcorder on a tripod in his gymnasium to record his movements and each night he had the gin and tonic followed by a work out session in his gym.

On the fourth day he had blacked out just a couple of times and finally on the fifth day he couldn't remember anything he had done. He knew he had been moving around and had been conscious but he couldn't remember any precise details. When he had sat down to watch the video, he had been amazed. The video showed him looking and acting completely normally, firstly on the treadmill for twenty minutes followed by twenty minutes on the bike. He had finished off his drug-hazed work out with a series of stretches and about one hundred sit-ups. He had watched himself on the video finish off the stomach exercises and then just seem to lie back and fall asleep. He had woken up on his exercise mat at ten o'clock the next morning and felt like a bag of crap. He had a terrible chemical taste in his mouth, which he had finally got rid of with a serious session of brushing his teeth. Over the next two or three days he'd had various flashbacks and remembered bits of the evening workout. By the time he had remembered most of his movements three days had passed.

He was very excited at the thought of raping someone who seemed normal when in fact they were completely unaware of the whole thing. *And that someone would be Trudy!* He would have to be careful; he didn't want to get caught. He knew she would eventually remember everything, but he figured she wouldn't do anything about it. And if he was very clever, he would be able to ensure that she and the police were as confused as each other. *Time to ring the pretty little vixen and arrange that drink!* He laughed and picked up the telephone.

'Hi is Trudy there please?'
'Yeah sure. Who's calling?' A sexy female voice asked.
'It's Daniel.'
He waited whilst the sexy voice shouted, 'Trudy phone call for you.'
'Hello.' Trudy sounded out of breath.
'Hi, it's Daniel, I hope I didn't disturb you?'
'No, I was in my room watching telly. I ran down the stairs that's all. How are you?' Trudy sounded pleased to hear from him.
'I am feeling great. I was hoping we could go out for that drink we discussed, next week maybe?'

'That would be lovely. Wednesday would be good for me, I can't do Thursday, it's our busiest night at the club.'

'Wednesday it is then. Shall I pick you up at around eight, eight-thirty?'

'That would be great! I'll see you here. Thanks for calling Daniel. Good night.'

'Good night, Trudy.' *Sweet dreams you fucking slut.* He thought as he replaced the handset.

THIRTY FOUR

I had done nothing but think about my poor little sister, the whole of my journey down. I still couldn't really believe that some bastard had raped my Penny. Rape is something that you hear about everyday but you never think it's going to happen to anyone that you know. I just hoped and prayed that she would be able to cope and eventually get on with her life. I hadn't called Frank yet. I had decided that I would call him after I had seen Penny and anyway, I could talk to her and get as many of the details from her as possible. She wouldn't be ready to talk to the police yet, even if it was Frank. I'm sure he would find out soon enough from the officers who interviewed Penny on Saturday and Sunday.

I stopped by the fountain and rushed into the house where my mother and father were stood waiting.

'Roger, so good of you to come down so quickly.' My dad shook my hand and I kissed mum. 'Did you get any trouble from those bloody reporters?'

'No. If I had, I would have just run them over. How's Penny?'

'She's all right. She hasn't really talked about it. She's sitting up in bed and I took her a light breakfast earlier. She asked if you were coming home.'

'Can I pop up to see her?' I asked my mother.

'Of course you can darling. Just try to be strong for her, I don't want her being upset. I think it's best if you don't ask her too many questions yet.' My mother fussed.

I rushed up the huge staircase and up onto the landing. Penny's bedroom was on the left-hand side and the door was slightly ajar. I called through to ask her if it was okay to come in.

'Hi Roger. Come in.' Her voice was flat and carried no emotion.

I walked in and she was sat up, reading a book. She looked completely different, like the life had been sucked out of her. Her hair was a mess and her face was drawn and wrinkled. But she looked in control; she didn't seem near tears, she didn't look upset. She just seemed completely void of all feelings and emotion. 'Penny, how are you feeling? Are you okay?' I couldn't help the panic in my voice.

'Roger, I'm fine. I'm a little bit groggy from the sedatives but I'm okay. How are you?'

I was surprised by her reaction. I had expected her to break down in tears, not to be sat there looking fairly calm, and asking me if I was okay. I know people handle shock in different ways but I expected Pen to be really upset. I was upset and finding it really difficult not to show it. 'I'm okay thanks, Pen. Can I get you anything? Do you want to talk about it?'

'No, thanks Roger. I'm just fine thanks. I wondered whether you would come home, shouldn't you be working?'

'I had to come and see you. I don't care about work, I care about you!' I was beginning to get pissed off with Penny. 'Mum and Dad called to explain what happened and I came straight down to see if you were okay. You're my sister and I love you.'

'Roger, I don't want to do this right now. Please leave me be. I'm not ready for this yet.' She pointed to the door. 'Please go, Roger.' She was looking down at her book as she asked me to leave.

'I'll be downstairs if you want to talk about it Penny.' I told her as I walked out. I made my way down to the kitchen where my parents were sat drinking coffee.

'Would you like a coffee, Roger?' My mother asked. 'It's filter.'

'That would be great, thanks.' I kissed my mother on the cheek, as she rose to make me my drink.

'How was she?'

'She was acting really strangely. She didn't want to talk about anything, it was like she had switched off, you know? She asked me to leave! I just want to help.'

My mother could see the concern on my face. 'Roger, please try not to be too upset. Penny has been through an awful lot over the last few days and she is trying to forget the whole episode. Your father spoke to the specialist at the hospital and she said that the human mind is very complex. Penny has chosen to shut out the memory of Saturday night and to pretend it never happened, and I don't blame her.'

'I know Mum, it's just so difficult to imagine what it must have been like.' I still felt so angry and upset. My parents had had two days to get over it, I had only been told this morning. 'I am going to speak to Frank later and we are going to get the bastard who did this, if it's the last thing we do.'

'Roger, calm down. I don't want Penny being more upset than she should be. And I certainly don't want to see my son's picture in every goddamn tabloid newspaper as some heroic private eye.' I knew my father was right. If I was going to help Frank, it would have to be done subtly.

'I'm not going to do anything stupid Dad, I promise. But I will call Frank this afternoon. I don't want him hearing about this from anyone else.' I said, slurping the hot, milky coffee. 'Great coffee Mum. I always missed that about living at home; your milky coffees and your fantastic lemon meringue pie!'

'As you are going to be staying for a few days, I will try to find the time to make you one darling.' My mother winked at me. 'Now let's change the subject. How is work? Are you busy?'

'Yeah, too busy at the moment, but it won't last. The bloody Government's paying off debt like it's going out of fashion and the market is becoming less and less liquid. Plus, Kaplan is about to introduce this fantastic trading system that the customers can use themselves. That should make half the dealers redundant within three years. The City isn't the place it used to be. I enjoyed it when it was more 'old school-tie' and less Essex boys. It used to feel like belonging to a private members club, now it only seems to be loud-mouthed youths with huge egos that get the jobs.'

'It can't be that bad darling. You are just feeling sorry for yourself.' My mother tried to pacify me. She had always put me on a pedestal, telling all our friends that her little boy was "something in the City"!

'Mum, I promise you, it's not the great job you think it is. Yeah, sure I get paid well, but if you saw what I did on a daily basis you would be amazed. I spent most of Friday afternoon going through all my World Cup bets and adding up my positions and then I spoke to Emma for about an hour. Can you imagine what goes on when there are a load of guys sat around a desk! It just a big playground. When the big boss, Michael comes down onto the floor, everybody pretends to look really busy.'

'Roger, I think you are getting a little carried away.' My father interjected. 'Are you trying to tell me you command this huge salary and yet do no business to warrant it?'

'Toast darling?' My mother was poised over the toaster with two thick slices of white bread.

'Yes please Mum.' I turned back to my father. 'Of course we make money Dad; we make an awful lot of money for the company. But what I'm saying is it's like falling off a log. I don't have to go out of my way to extract that business. I just sit at my desk and wait for the phone to ring. It really is that simple. I can't imagine what it must be like to work as a salesperson earning twelve grand a year with a chance of earning twenty-five grand if I reach the ridiculously high targets the company set. Having to go and see MD's of companies and try to convince them my publication is the one that they should be advertising in. It must be bloody hard work and really soul destroying most of the time and all for a reward of twelve grand basic plus. My guys sit there doing crosswords, playing games on their PC's, they get lunch provided and a huge expense account and they have to do very little actual broking or hard work and the lowest paid broker earns fifty grand basic! It's bollocks.' I loved trying to convince my father I really didn't do an awful lot at work. I smiled as I watched him thinking about my comments. We'd had this conversation many times over the years and I had never quite managed to convince either of them.

'I do know what you are saying, but you are a special breed Roger. Not everyone could do your job. The pressure is intense and having to scream and shout all day long, I know I couldn't do it.'

'Dad, will you please come up and see the dealing floor one day and I'll show you what I mean?' I knew he still didn't get it. I think that most people outside of the City either knew we did bugger all for our money or they thought we were all some elite specialists that deserved our salaries. My father was definitely the latter!

'Sure Roger, I would love to. How long are you staying for?'

'Two or three days I thought. The guys have got it covered and I want to ask Penny about her ordeal. I think it's important she talks about it.' So I could find out what she knew. I wanted to get the man who had violated her.

THIRTY FIVE

I had been up to take Penny her lunch and she seemed fine. She still hadn't said much but appeared to be in better spirits. We both laughed when Jasper had rushed into the bedroom, his tail wagging and jumped up onto the bed and began trying to lick us both to death.

At two-thirty I left a message at the station for Frank. I was told he was out and would be back about four, so I gave the officer my parent's number and asked if he could get Frank to call me. I spent the afternoon trying to take my mind off things, swimming in the indoor pool and tried to beat dad at tennis, but he had been playing regularly since his retirement. I was thrashed! 6-1, 6-1, 6-3. The only reason that I had managed to nick three games off him in the last set was down to my age advantage! Mum had been in the garden watching and she had laughed all the way through the match. As we finished and came off the court, mum was waiting with a huge jug of lemon barley we polished off in no time. I sat with mum and dad in the garden just enjoying the peace of it all and talking about life in general. We led such a great life, no money worries, more material items than most people could wish for and dad was famous, which sometimes meant we got to go places we wouldn't otherwise. All in all, I enjoyed being me and yet even with all that, someone was able to enter our lives and completely fuck it up for us. We were still very upset about Penny, but I was determined to catch the perpetrator and kill him. I had no faith in the criminal justice system of this country and I'd had many debates with Henson on the subject. How I thought that we should bring back capital punishment and give longer jail terms and not let criminals have such a cushy life when in prison. Frank disagreed with a lot of my opinions but I think he agreed the deterrent needed to be more severe in most cases.

My parents' housekeeper, Susan, came out to inform me I had a phone call. 'I don't believe it! He's only been here for five minutes and he's already getting calls!' My father joked with my mother. I thanked Susan and went in to take the call.

'Hello.'

'Roger, it's Frank. What the fuck are you doing skiving off on a Monday? Long weekend mate?' Frank sounded his usual jolly self, and that made what I was about to tell him all the more harder.

'Frank, I need to come and see you. I'm surprised you haven't already heard the news. Penny was raped on Saturday night.' I felt the atmosphere change, and I waited for Frank to reply.

'Oh my God! I am so sorry Roger. I don't believe it! No way! Not Penny?' Frank stuttered.

'I know mate. I didn't find out until this morning. I was away all weekend with clients and had no reception on the mobile so dad couldn't get hold of me.'

'How is she? Is she okay? She wasn't beaten up was she? Where did it happen?' Frank was in detective mode.

'She was travelling back from Windsor on the train and she caught a taxi from Paddington. It was the fucking taxi driver that did it. It was him! It was that fucking rapist!' I was fighting back my anger.

'Roger, I can't believe it. Look, try not to worry, we will catch this guy, I promise you. Come in and see me. You said you were surprised I hadn't heard the news, why would I have?'

'The police found Pen in Chelsea, on the Kings Road looking very dazed and confused. They took her in and then into the Chelsea and Westminster hospital. Dad said a policeman had tried to ask her a few questions but she hadn't been very co-operative. The doctor told the police Penny needed rest and so they had to leave. I think they were from your station.'

'I wasn't working this weekend as you know and I'm doing lates today. I've got a pile of crap in my in-tray but I would normally have either a big note on my desk or a message on my phone. Very strange.' Frank said. I could hear the paperwork rustling as he searched. 'Got it! It was hidden under a folder. Miss Penelope Hamilton aged 25. Found on the Kings Road at twelve minute past ten on Saturday night. Yep. I've got it here. It's just a quick report from one of my constables. I'll go and see him now. Roger, come over whenever you want, I'll be here until two tomorrow.'

'I'll be there at about seven ish. See you soon mate.'

'Send Penny my love and tell her that I'm thinking of her.' Frank sounded quite emotional.

'Will do.' I put the phone down and went back into the garden. I told mum and dad I was going up to London and I would return later that evening.

'Drive safely, son and take care.' My father shouted after me.

Considering it was rush-hour, the traffic going into London wasn't too congested and I was in Chelsea by ten to seven. I pulled into the station car park and stopped at the barrier. An attendant came out of his booth to see what I wanted. 'I'm here to see detective sergeant Henson.' I told him. He asked who I was and noted down my number plate on his clipboard, before lifting the barrier. I parked my car in one of the visitor bays and went into the front desk. A cheerful constable whose bright red nose shone like a Belisha beacon greeted me. I told him detective sergeant Henson was expecting me, whilst trying very hard not to stare at his proboscis.

'Hi Roger. How are you mate?' Frank was very sullen, not his usual jovial self. He led me down a maze of corridors and suddenly stopped by the vending machine. 'Coffee? It is the best in the station and the nearest we can get to filter coffee mate,' he asked me, genuinely.

'Yeah great. Whatever. The way I'm feeling I don't care if it's instant.'

Frank handed me the polystyrene cup of piping hot coffee, got one for himself and led me into his office. The room stank of stale cigarettes and the white walls had faded to a yellowy-grey from all the smoke. The ashtray on

Frank's desk was full of cigarette butts and there were four empty polystyrene cups in amongst all his paperwork. There were folders piled high and pieces of paper everywhere. Screwed up balls of paper that had missed their target surrounded the bin in the corner.

'Sorry about the mess, mate. I don't know where all paperwork comes from. I have an in-tray and an out-tray but most of it seems to remain on my desk. Have a seat and let's talk.' He gestured to the chair opposite him.

'Frank, just do me a favour and run me through what you already know about this piece of shit. What he looks like, age, height ecetera.'

'Roger, it's all classified. I'm not allowed to discuss any of...'

I stopped him mid sentence. 'Look Frank, let's get one thing straight. I am now officially working with you on this whether you like it or not. I want to catch the bastard that violated Penny and I will, even if it's the last thing I do. I don't give a damn about all the red tape that goes on in here. Frank, you are my best mate and you must work with me on this, please.'

Frank sat there looking at me. 'Roger, you are too closely involved, your emotions will just get in the way. Please leave it to my team and me and I promise you we'll catch him. I don't mind briefing you from time to time but you have to just let it go.'

I wasn't taking no for an answer. 'Frank, just humour me. I want to help you catch this fucker and I am going to begin by asking Penny some questions. She told me she won't talk to the police, but I am sure she'll talk to me. Let me see what I can find out from her and I will give you a full run down as soon as I can. This could be fun mate; you and I working together. I can help you catch this guy, I know it.' I was now pleading with my friend.

'Okay, okay. Talk to Penny then come back and we'll go through everything. But I'm telling you now, if you get too emotional on me, you're out. Agreed?'

'Deal, partner. I won't let you down.'

THIRTY SIX

Frank Henson got out of his beaten up Sierra and made his way into the station. He was actually pleased Roger wanted to work with him. He felt honoured his high-flying mate from the City wanted to be an undercover 'agent'. Frank knew that he was breaking every rule in the book but he needed someone to work with who understood him. Frank was the Governor and the rest of the team never let him forget it. They didn't really confide in him and he certainly couldn't share all his thoughts with them. Dobson was good, but he was still young and lacked experience. He knew he could trust Hamilton and was looking forward to sharing his ideas with his friend.

He went through his usual routine when starting work, a stop at the coffee machine before settling into his office for the first cigarette of the working day. His desk was a mess and he made a mental promise to tidy it by the end of the week. He enjoyed the cigarette and sat, sipping on hot coffee hoping Penny would hold the clues he so desperately needed. He opened one of the many folders and pulled out a piece of paper with the list of all the girls that had been raped and added Penny Hamilton's name at the bottom. He felt real anger and took a deep draw on his cigarette and put the list back in the folder.

He picked up the report from the door-to-door inquiries they had carried out last week. The people they had spoken to had all been very helpful but no one had seen anything nor had they remembered a taxi being parked anywhere suspicious. Yet another brick wall, Frank thought. His next step was to interview every taxi driver that owned one of the new style cabs and who fell into the thirty to forty age group. There were four hundred and twelve and Frank had the list of names and addresses in front of him. The taxi drivers had all been sent a letter from Frank's department requesting an interview at their earliest convenience. Henson and his team would be spending the next week or so interviewing the taxi drivers and eliminating them from their list. Proof of alibi on any of the dates the rapes took place was all they needed. Frank was very hopeful the interviews would whittle the list right down. David, one of the constables had pissed Frank off with his comment, 'You know the rapist might not be a cab driver, don't you? He might just 'ave bought one and be pretending like, might he?'

Frank didn't even want to consider that yet. But he did make a note to contact London Taxis International in Kent. They were the sole suppliers of the new style taxi.

His telephone rang and he quickly stubbed out his cigarette before answering. 'Henson.'

'Hi Frank, it's Isabelle.' Her deep, sexy voice made the hairs on the back of Frank's neck stand on end.

'Hi Isabelle, how are you?'

'I'm feeling great thanks. I just wanted to call you quickly; I've got a client coming in any minute now. Are we still going out for dinner this evening?' She asked.

Frank had completely forgotten about the dinner date they had arranged, the shock of Penny's rape. He was so immersed in his fucking job he was beginning to let his social life slip. 'Yeah, of course we are. I've been really looking forward to it. Where shall we go?' Frank hoped his hesitation hadn't been too obvious.

'Well, I'm finishing at six o'clock so I can be over in Chelsea by seven, if you want to go somewhere near you?' She rebounded the question.

Frank had a dilemma on his hands. If he took her somewhere too expensive, she would expect to go to nice restaurants all the time. On the other hand if he took her somewhere too cheap, she would think he was a skinflint. It was a lose, lose situation and one Frank didn't like being in. He was also very overdrawn at the bank and couldn't afford to spend a lot. Honesty is the best policy, he thought and took in a deep breath before speaking. 'I would love to take you out for a really expensive meal, but to be truthful, I can't afford to right now. So would you mind if we went somewhere cheap and cheerful?'

'Frank I don't care where we go. I didn't expect you to pay for me anyway. I was going to suggest that we go Dutch.' She laughed.

'Great. Do you like Indian?' Frank loved curries.

'Yes, I do actually. That would be lovely. Tell me where and when and I will be there.'

Result! Frank thought, a girl that likes curries. 'It's in South Kensington, called 'Namaste'. Shall I meet you outside the tube station at seven o'clock?'

'I'll see you then. Have a nice day, Frank.'

'You too. See you later.' Frank put the phone down and sat back, smiling and feeling a lot better about life. He finished his coffee and went out into the corridor to get himself another.

Later that afternoon Frank's phone rang again. He picked it up and was pleased to hear his mate on the other end. 'Roger, how are you?'

'I'm okay, Henson. I have just spent an hour with Penny and she agreed to tell me everything she could remember. It was really difficult for her and I hated every minute of it.' I was feeling really jaded.

'Roger, can you tell me anything new?' Frank sounded really excited.

'Yes, lots. I really hope this helps you catch the bastard, Frank. I want him found so fucking badly! Penny was very aware that when the attack began, that he may be the serial rapist, so she took note of as much as she could. He clamped a rag over her mouth and she is sure it was ether. He was very strong and she thought he was very muscular. He was wearing an Arsenal baseball cap which Penny vaguely remembers knocking off his head. He had grey hair but Penny is convinced it was a wig; she said it just didn't look right. When she came round she was lying on the pavement but she has a hazy memory of being photographed. Thankfully, she doesn't remember any of the ordeal, which is a real relief. She also said he looked really fat, when he jumped into the back of the cab with her, but his face looked chiselled, as Penny put it.' I tried to relay the details as slowly as I could, so that Frank could make notes.

'That is fucking brilliant work, Rog. Send my love to Penny and thank her.'

I cut in. 'He must wear padding of some sort to appear fatter than he is. And he's obviously not as old as he's trying to make out. Oh, and Frank, Penny said he was wearing aftershave. It smelt expensive she said, quite musky. Not one that she knew, but she said she would definitely remember it if she smelled it again! I'll come in to see you and then we can go through everything.'

'Definitely. Let me know when and I'll make sure I'm free. I have to go and interview a couple of taxi drivers. Speak to you later mate. Hey Rog. I want you to know, I want this cunt as badly as you do. Together we *will* catch him, I promise.'

In all the excitement, he had forgotten to tell Roger about his date with Isabelle. It could wait, he thought as he replaced the handset.

THIRTY SEVEN

Frank was feeling good about the progress he had made that afternoon. Roger's phone call had been just the boost he'd needed. He made a list of clues and his ideas he wanted to go through with Roger. He was now really looking forward to his dinner with Isabelle. He closed and locked the door to his office at five to seven and skipped down the stairs that led to the entrance of the police station.

He reached South Kensington tube station at a little after seven and checked both exits. Isabelle was late but Frank didn't mind. He stood waiting by one of the Evening Standard newspaper vendors.

'Hi Frank. Sorry I'm a bit late. My last appointment was late turning up. Have you been waiting long?' Isabelle looked amazing. She radiated health and happiness and was a breath of fresh air for Henson. She wore a tight pair of Levi jeans that hugged her hips perfectly and a tight white T-shirt that had POP IDOL printed across her breasts. She wore the faintest trace of make-up and her long, brown hair was styled in a ponytail. As she kissed him on the cheek, he caught a subtle whiff of perfume.

'Only about ten minutes. Are you hungry?' He asked, dropping the newspaper back down.

'Famished. I skipped lunch on purpose, knowing I wouldn't be able to resist the naan bread and popadoms and everything!'

'Good. It's just around the corner. How was your day? Busy, I take it?' Frank asked, as he escorted her across the busy road.

'I'm always busy but it's nowhere near as exciting as your job. How was your day?'

'Good, but let's not talk shop tonight. I want to get to know you, deal?'

Isabelle laughed at him and shook his hand. 'Deal!'

The manager of the Indian restaurant greeted Frank like a long, lost friend and kissed Isabelle's hand. He sat them at the best table in the house, as he called it. Frank threw his eyes up at the ceiling and whispered an apology to Isabelle for the manger being so over the top. He came back with two menus and a wine list. 'Now what can I be getting you and the lovely lady to drink Mr. Frank?' The manager asked, with a thick Indian accent.

'What are you gonna have Isabelle? Do you want wine?' Frank asked.

'With Indian? No thank you.' Isabelle screwed her face up at Frank and turned to the manager. 'I would like a pint of lager please.'

Frank laughed. 'Same for me please and can we have four popadoms as well?'

'I am bringing it for you right away.' He scuttled off to get their drinks.

'Pints of lager hey? I love it. The only way to eat curry is with pints of lager. I'm impressed.'

'You're the first bloke I've known that's been impressed by it. Most men find it very unattractive. I'm glad you approve. I know we said we aren't going to talk about work but I'm curious to know what made you chose the police force as a career?'

'I studied psychology at Nottingham and when I left decided to use my degree for the good of mankind. There weren't that many interesting things I could do with a degree in psychology. Rape has always been one of my big pet hates and paedophilia. I knew the law was an ass but I thought if I went into the police force I would be able to make a difference. It was good fun at first, going through all the training at Hendon in north London with all the new recruits. It was hard work but we were all in the same boat. I've made some really good friends through it.' The popadoms arrived and he crunched his hand down on them, gently breaking them up.

'How did you meet Roger? Was it at university?'

Frank smiled and shook his head. 'My thick mate Hamilton wasn't bright enough to go to university so he went straight into the city. Clever bugger! Roger and I were at school together. We've been friends since we were little boys! He chose the rich trappings of a job in the city whilst I followed my nose into the police force and eventually I landed a poorly paid role as detective sergeant!'

'Money isn't everything Frank. I'm pleased you're not one of those wankers that work in the city. I wouldn't be sat here having dinner if you were. I want you for your mind!' She joked and quickly added, 'I don't mean that Roger is a wanker.'

'Oh, don't worry. He is most of the time!' Frank retorted, with a mouthful of popadom and chutney. 'I presume you know about Penny?'

Isabelle suddenly looked concerned. 'No. What's happened to her?'

Frank told Isabelle everything he knew and he was surprised Emma hadn't told her. Isabelle was shocked by the news and suggested that maybe Emma didn't know.

'I know she has been trying to get hold of Roger but she never indicated anything this bad was wrong.' Isabelle sat shaking her head.

'Maybe he hasn't told her yet.' Frank reached across the table to caress her hand.

'He can't have done. I can't believe it. Poor Penny, I haven't met her but I can imagine what she must be going through. How is she? Have you seen her at all?'

'No. Not so far. She told Roger she didn't want to see the police. She knows we know about it and now we have recorded it at the station. We need to ask her some questions, but Roger has talked to her and she did tell him a little of what she could remember. I think she will let me see her eventually. Normally we would be pushing to interview the victim but as I know her, I'm giving her all the time she needs.'

'Shit, it must be hard for all of you. How's Roger coping with it all?'

'He seems okay. Surprisingly, he's being really strong. I know he's fuming and desperate to catch the guy that did it. We all are. I'm pulling my hair out at the moment though. We've got a bunch of taxi drivers coming in to be interviewed over the next couple of weeks, so we are whittling the list of suspects down slowly, but this rapist seems to be the most prolific we've ever come across.' Frank shook his head. 'Anyway, let's talk about you. How did you get into the beauty business?'

THIRTY EIGHT

He got home at six o'clock and went straight into the darkroom to get his camera and make sure there was film loaded in it. *Tonight is going to be fucking special. I must call the hotel and check my reservation.* He picked up his mobile phone and called the Conrad Hotel in Chelsea Harbour. He spoke to one of the receptionists and she confirmed his reservation. 'Thank you for choosing the Conrad, Mr Lucky. Your room is ready and waiting for you sir.' He thanked her and waited ten minutes. He hit redial on the mobile and when the phone was answered he booked another room. 'Thank you for choosing the Conrad, Mr Freeman.' He turned off his mobile and went into his supply cupboard and got out a couple of Rohypnol and put them with his camera. He went into his gym for a quick workout and a shower to freshen up. He packed a small overnight bag and opened a cupboard next to his wardrobe and pulled out a grey wig and some foam padding, a crappy suit and shirt three sizes too big for him and a wallet.

He got out of the lift feeling refreshed from the exercise and walked into the underground car park. He pulled off the dust cover that protected his Ferrari and threw it into the tiny boot. He placed the camera and the drugs on the passenger seat and checked the glove box for his little box of tricks. He got out the latex gloves and the ether and put them in the inside pocket of his Timberland jacket. He started the car and let the engine idle for a couple of minutes whilst he snorted some Cocaine and popped an E. He drove to the hotel, which was only ten minutes away and pulled up outside the front doors. A concierge quickly approached and told him he would park the car for him. He gave the concierge a twenty-pound note and went inside to check into the room. The pretty girl behind the desk was very helpful and smiled sweetly when he winked at her. *If you're a good girl, I may come back for you one day. She would look great sat on my face!* He laughed as he pictured the pretty receptionist squirming on his face.

'You're in Room 312 Mr Freeman, on the third floor.'

He said he would find it himself and got into the lift with an elderly couple and a mother with her two children. The doors closed and they all stood in silence. He looked at each person in turn, holding his stare until the other person glanced away in embarrassment. He was really buzzing now and excited about later. He always found it amusing how people in lifts found it awkward to talk or show any signs of life. He purposely broke wind loudly, as he left the lift and laughed.

He walked along the corridor of the third floor and followed the signs to his room. He let himself in and checked out the interior of the room. It was beautifully decorated, as you would expect of a five star hotel, a huge double bed sat proudly in the middle of the room with a bedside table on either side. There was the usual TV with all the cable channels, desk, chair and mini-bar.

A door led into the marble bathroom, which was bright and very clean. He pulled aside the heavy curtains and looked out of the window. The view was of the harbour below and the surrounding residential apartment blocks. The harbour was full of boats of all shapes and sizes. There were a couple of big Sunseekers and he smiled as he watched a good-looking young guy, tying one of them up to the dock. He wanted to buy a big Sunseeker yacht one day but knew he would be spending the next fifteen to twenty years in prison. *Who needs toys like that when I can have all the pretty pussy I want? I will be so famous when I get out, I can sell my story to the News of the World newspaper for a fortune and then I can buy a big, fuck off Sunseeker!* He let the curtain fall back and looked around the room. He opened the small holdall he'd brought with him and took out the wig, padding, suit and shirt and quickly changed. He neatly folded his clothes and jacket in the holdall. It took a couple of minutes to stick the wig on effectively and he had to wrestle the foam padding into place. He checked his reflection in the bathroom and grinned, *You fat fuck. Go and check into your room!*

He picked up the holdall and put his room card in his wallet and left. He waddled into the lift and travelled down to the first floor. The bar led conveniently out onto a balcony over looking the harbour. He casually walked through the door and down the balcony steps to the harbour. He followed the path along and round to Belevedere Tower, where Michael Caine had an apartment. He walked as quickly as he could onto the road and waited for a cab. *All this fucking effort just to keep the fucking police off my back.* A cab came round the corner and stopped for him. 'Can you take me to the Conrad Hotel please.'

'The Conrad Hotel mate? You having a laugh? It's only just round the corner.' The taxi driver was about to pull away.

'I'm sorry. I am recovering from a heart attack and I'm having trouble breathing. I'm staying there and I've just had a little walk around the harbour and I'm struggling. I know it's not far but I'll make it worth your while. Will twenty pounds cover it my friend.' He had put on an Italian accent.

'I'm sorry Guv. Of course! Jump in and I'll take you.'

He waddled into the Hotel and checked in with a different receptionist. 'You are in Room 343 on the third floor Mr Lucky. Can I take a credit card impression please?'

'I don't use credit cards, I only pay cash. I will pay you for the room now and settle the sundries in the morning.'

'That's fine Sir. One hundred and seventy five pounds please.'

He found Room 343 and with great relief, threw off his disguise. Once again he changed and packed the disguise into his holdall. He took out the gloves and hid them under the bed. He left the camera and ether in the wardrobe. He quickly made his way along the corridor to Room 312 and let himself in. He put the holdall in the wardrobe ready for the morning and checked his watch; it was time to leave. He took a beer from the mini-bar and quickly licked some Speed from a sachet. He grimaced at both the Speed and the cheap beer he washed it down with. He would catch a cab downstairs and be at Trudy's by eight fifteen.

He jumped out of the taxi and bent down to check his face in the wing mirror, his pupils were huge and he noticed his hair was looking really cool. *Somebody stop me! I'm smoking!* He smiled at the taxi driver as he strutted up to the door of the girls' house and rang the doorbell. It didn't take long for the door to be opened and Trudy to appear. 'Hi Daniel, you look great!' she exclaimed.

'You don't look so bad yourself,' he retorted, with a smile. 'Shall we go? Are you ready? I thought we'd go to a bar round here. There's a cab waiting.'

'Oh, okay. See you later!' She shouted back into the house, just before she closed the door. 'There's a great bar on the Northcote Road, Bar Excellence.'

They got into the cab, which took them to the nearby bar. There were no obvious places to park in the busy street and he was glad that he'd left the car at the hotel. Parking in London was always totally impossible. It pissed him off there were so many parking restrictions everywhere. There were plenty of streets and roads with just two or three parking meter spaces and then just yellow lines, forbidding parking at certain times. He never understood why there weren't more spaces for parking, it made no sense on a wide road to limit the number of spaces. *No fucking wonder NCP car parks make so much fucking money!* he thought as he paid the cab driver. 'You're not that rapist are you?' he asked, with a straight face.

'Daniel! Don't be so rude.' Trudy smiled at the taxi driver, apologetically.

'Why not? He might be. Well, are you? Should I be calling the police right now?' He started to raise his voice.

'Yeah, I am. I'll be whatever you want me to be, mate. Here's your change, now sling your hook!' The taxi driver slapped the change into his hand and began pulling away.

'Daniel, what's wrong with you? Do you do that to every cab driver?' Trudy looked upset.

He smiled at her and put his arm around her. 'I'm sorry Trudy. I think it's just awful what that rapist is doing. I can't believe what it must be like for those poor girls. I think I'm just too sensitive sometimes.' He looked very affected and sad.

'I know, believe me. I know.' Trudy took his hand and led him into the bar.

He wondered whether she was about to tell him about Debbie and her rape. She was definitely thinking about something and he was sure it concerned her housemate. 'If I tell you something, do you promise that you won't tell a soul?'

'The one thing you will learn about me is that you can trust me. Go ahead, I'm listening.' *You can trust me and then I'll get you naked and have some fun with you, you bitch!*

'One of the girls I work with rents a room in the house. She came home alone last week and was raped by the taxi driver. She was left, lying on the pavement outside the house. I'm really scared this freak knows where we live. Her name is Debbie and she hasn't left the house since. Wendy wanted to tell the police, but Tina and I said we couldn't without consulting Debbie first.' Trudy shook her head. 'I know how I would feel, having to go to court and be asked questions by some old male chauvinistic judge. I don't think I could do it and we didn't feel it was fair to put Debbie in that situation, without her consent.'

'Bloody hell! Every time I travel by taxi I wonder whether it's the rapist driving, but I never thought I'd actually meet anyone involved, or who had been or knew someone raped by this bloke.' He exclaimed. 'Let me get you a drink and we can talk more. What would you like?' A barman waited for their order.

'I'll have a Jack Daniels and Coke please.' Trudy smiled, but she still looked uneasy.

'And I'll have a Bud Ice please.'

They got their drinks and found a table near the back of the bar. As he sat, he put his hand into his jacket pocket, just to make sure the Rohypnol was there, ready and waiting. He took a long swig from the bottle of cold beer and asked Trudy if she was all right.

'Yeah, I'm okay. I just can't stop thinking about poor Debbie.'

Poor Debbie deserved it. She was a beautiful little bitch who was gagging for it. She only got what she deserved. I wanna know how she is. Is she coping? 'You said she hasn't been out the house since?' He prompted her.

'That's right. She seems fine. She's up before the rest of us. Most mornings when I get up to make myself a coffee; she's in the lounge watching TV. But she won't talk about it, even when I've sat with her and tried to ask her questions. She just looks at me as if I'm mad and she doesn't know what I'm talking about. It's like she doesn't want to admit it happened. I think I'm more fucked up about it than she is!' Trudy was ripping a beer mat up into tiny pieces.

'Come off it! There is no way that you are more fucked up than she is. It's just her way of coping with her ordeal. It's a shame you can't get her to talk, I bet she could help the police with their investigation.' He reached across to stroke her hand.

'Anyway, let's change the subject. You told me that you ran a couple of small businesses. What kind of businesses?'

'One is an Internet company that hosts web sites for companies and the other is an investment company. I mainly concentrate on the investment side myself; I'm not one of these techno geeks. I have some very talented ones working for me though and they never cease to amaze me with their skills. I still don't fully understand the Internet but I do know all companies should be embracing it. Every company will benefit from having a web site. There are over ten million people hooked up in this country alone and that figure is growing every month.' Trudy looked fascinated. *I fucking amaze myself at times! I'm so full of shit, I'm surprised she hasn't smelt it yet!* He couldn't stop the giggle that popped out.

'What's so funny?' Trudy asked.

'Sorry, I can't help laughing when I think how much money I'm going to make from it all. It sounds very arrogant but it just feels so good. You make me feel very relaxed too.'

Trudy smiled. 'Your life sounds really great. I bet you get to go on some really exotic holidays?'

'No not usually. I'm always too busy to organise a holiday. Last one I took was to the South of France for a week, not very exotic. Plus, I haven't had anyone to take for the last couple of years.' He was getting bored now. *Hurry up and go to the toilet for fuck sake! Come on!* 'Would you like another drink?'

'I'll get this round.' Trudy tried to insist.

'No way. I know you are a successful lap-dancer but I can't let a lady buy me a drink. Same again?'

'Yes please. Thanks Daniel.'

It was half an hour before Trudy got up and went to the toilet. *Half an hour of talking crap and trying to seem interested. It will be worth it when I get her back to the hotel! Oh boy, oh boy!* He pulled out the drug, which he had measured to perfection and quickly slipped it into her drink. The dark colour of the Coke eliminated any chance of detection and he swilled the drink around a couple of times to make sure it had mixed in properly. He then sat back and waited for Trudy to return. He was jigging his legs up and down under the table and tapping the table with his hands. The drugs together with his sudden spurt of adrenaline were almost too much for him to control! *Let the fun begin!* He said as he watched Trudy heading back to the table.

THIRTY NINE

The door opened slowly and a lady's hand fell out and onto the carpet. The maid ran, screaming into the hallway. 'HELP, somebody help me! She's dead! HELP!'

A couple of the doors opened and heads poked out to see what all the commotion was about. A fat man in his late forties, with grey hair came rushing up the hall and the maid crashed into him. 'Oh mister, please help. It's so awful. Oh God, it's so awful. Please help me!' He asked her to calm down and to tell him what she was screaming about.

'It's the lady in room 343. She's dead!'

The man looked up the hallway and began walking quickly towards the room, closely followed by the maid. He walked in to find the lady the maid referred to. She was hanging out of the wardrobe with the top half of her body lying on the carpet. He bent down and placed his fingers on her neck. He felt her pulse beating strongly against his finger and looked up at the maid. 'You are right. She's dead. I'll call the police.' The maid burst into tears. He picked up the phone in the room and dialled reception. 'Hi can you call the police. There's a dead women in room 343.'

He told the maid to lock the door and to let nobody in until the police got there and then began walking away.

'Mister, who are you? What is your name?' The maid asked, between sobs.

'It's okay. I'm a doctor. Let no-one in.' He turned and walked down the hall way and into the lift that had just arrived. He turned to face the maid, smiled and waved as the doors closed. He looked at himself in the mirror and laughed. At the ground floor he walked out into the foyer and up to the concierge desk. He handed his ticket to the young Italian man who smiled. 'Thank you sir. I will collect your car. Please take a seat.'

The Ferrari arrived at the entrance of the hotel and he gave the young Italian concierge a twenty-pound note and thanked him. He drove out of Chelsea harbour and up onto the Kings Road. He was back in the car park of his building within ten minutes. He let himself into his flat and rushed into his bedroom. He took the wig out of his pocket and threw it onto the bed. He undressed and let the padding fall to the floor. He looked down at it and laughed. *That will keep the police guessing! I can't wait for Trudy to wake up!!* He wrapped a towel around himself and quickly took his camera and film into the dark room, before jumping in the shower.

He was back in the Ferrari and heading towards the office by nine o'clock. He was in charge in Roger's absence but wasn't too concerned about being over two hours late for work. The traffic was much heavier at nine o'clock and it took him forever to get down the Kings Road and onto Parliament Square. He smiled at the advert on the taxi next to him, '**www.motley.co.uk Professional Web Design. Affordable Prices**.' It reminded him that he needed to go online and order some more aftershave. He drove the same way every morning and for the first time, whilst stuck in traffic, he looked up at Big Ben and observed the intricate stonework and architecture of the old clock tower. *No wonder London was full of so many fucking tourists!* He had to admit Parliament Square was very impressive and he laughed at how he and so many other Londoners took it all so for granted. He went through all the landmarks he passed on his journey to and from work everyday; Houses of Parliament; Big Ben; Downing Street; Trafalgar Square; St. Paul's Cathedral; London Bridge. There were probably many more but he couldn't remember them all. *I should get in my taxi and start doing fucking guided tours!* He thought as he approached the office.

He dialled in a number on his mobile phone and waited whilst it rang. He was relieved when the ansafone clicked in. One of the girls had left a message and after the tone he left his. 'Trudy, what happened to you last night? You said you were going to the loo and that was the last time I saw you. I tried calling your mobile all night but it was switched off.' He grinned as he looked down at her phone on his passenger seat. 'Please call me as soon as you can. I'm worried. If it was something I said, at least let's talk about it. Call me please.' He parked the car in Roger's space below the building and made his way up onto the dealing floor.

'Oh, nice of you to join us Griffin! Where the fuck have you been?' Jamie was the first to begin winding him up.

'He probably overslept with his boyfriend!' Danny added.

He sat down at his desk. 'Okay, okay. Sorry guys. Trouble with my bloody washing machine. The house is flooded. Anyway, what have I missed?'

The boys on the desk had been quite busy but the early morning rush always subsided at around ten o'clock and he sat going through the trades on his screen. David came over with a cup of coffee for him. 'Here you go, Brian. Don't worry about the guys.'

'As if I would. It was nothing more than I expected. I knew with Roger away, I would be out on a bit of a limb. But, fuck 'em! They mean nothing to me. I'll just stab them in the back, if they're not careful.'

David knew he wasn't joking. That was why he had taken Brian the coffee. David had been brought up with the belief that being nice to the boss or stand-in boss, didn't do any harm. The boys might brand him a 'brown nose' but he preferred being on the right side of the management. 'Have you heard from Roger at all? Do you know what's happened?' David was genuinely interested. He liked Roger and was concerned about his boss.

'I haven't spoken to him, which is a good sign. He said he would only call if he needed me for anything.'

'Brian, one out!'

'Thanks.' He picked up the outside line. It was Roger. 'Hi Roger. We were just talking about you. Is everything okay?'

'No not really. Look, I'm not going to be in for a couple of weeks. There's quite a lot I need to do. I will call Michael and tell him. Is everything okay there?' I didn't really care about Kaplan Stewart right now, but I still wanted the guys on the desk to know that I was keeping an eye on things.

'Yeah, it's fine Rog. I'm looking after everything. It's in safe hands mate. Now please put the phone down and go and look after your sister. Is she okay?' *I'm always interested in my girls!*

'Yes thanks mate. She's going to be fine. I'm seeing Frank today to see if I can help him catch the bastard! I think Penny was able to provide a couple of new bits of info so Henson's quite excited.' I told Brian. I was glad that he was there to talk to and to look after things whilst I was working with Frank.

Fuck! That doesn't sound good. I don't want to be caught yet. I need to keep in touch with this. 'That's great news Rog. Say hi to Frank. Do you two fancy a drink one evening? You could probably do with having a night out and taking your mind off things, both of you.' He tried to sound sincere.

'Sounds good to me. I'm seeing Henson later; I'll suggest it to him. Thanks for looking after the show. I'll call you in a couple of days.'

He put down the phone and sat staring at the bank of screens in front of him. He was furious with himself. He didn't know what Penny had remembered or what she had told Frank and Roger, but whatever it was, Frank was obviously excited. *Fuck! What has that fucking bitch told them? If she fucking shits on me, it won't just be her neat little pussy she has to worry about.*

'You all right Brian?' David shook his shoulder.

He had forgotten that David was still stood next to him. 'What? Oh yeah. I'm fine, just a bit upset for Roger that's all. He's not going to be in for a couple of weeks.'

'Is everything okay? What's happened?' David looked very shocked.

'Yeah, Roger's fine. He doesn't want to talk about it and he's asked me not to say anything to anyone. Don't worry about it Dave. I need a piss.' He got up and walked towards the toilet.

At the end of his eventful day he drove home to Chelsea, excited at the prospect of developing his photos of Trudy.

FORTY

I rushed into the hallway where I had left my mobile phone. 'Roger, hi it's Brian.'

'Morning Griff. Everything all right?' I checked my watch; it was half past eleven. I was a bit worried, I hadn't been expecting a call from the office.

'Don't worry; there's no problem. It's just that Andrew Duncan has just called me and said you arranged to go out with him and his guys tonight. When I told him you were away he wanted to know if this evening was still happening. What do I tell him?'

'Oh shit! I'd completely forgotten. I can't let them down. Tell them I'll be at their offices at six. Thanks Griff.' A night out with clients was the last thing I needed tonight.

'No problem Roger. We had a good day yesterday. We did just over forty-five grand. Are you okay? How's Penny?' He needed to know.

'We're all doing okay thanks. Glad business is good. I'll call you later.' I put the phone down and sighed. It could have been worse. I liked Andrew. Mark and Gavin were good guys too. It would probably be a good night. I booked a table at The Rib Room in the Savoy Hotel. It was still one of London's finest restaurants and expensive to boot! I called Andrew just to touch base and told him that I was fine and that I would fill him in later.

I left my parent's house in the middle of the afternoon. I told my parents I would stay in London and probably see Henson the next day and be back late the next afternoon. Traffic was light and I arrived in South Kensington at four o'clock. I called the receptionist at Kaplan and asked her to book a taxi to pick me up at my flat at five-fifteen to take me to Morgan Stanley. I checked through my post; as usual it was mostly bills. There was one card from Emma. It was really sweet saying she was thinking of me and if I needed anything to give her a call. I felt terrible. I hadn't called her since I'd got the news about Penny. I wondered how she knew and began dialling her number at Holmes Place.

'Holmes Place Health and Beauty, can I help you?' A female voice answered.

'Yes. Can I speak to Emma Arnold please.'

'One moment please. I'll see if she's free.'

I waited for the receptionist to come back to me and wondered what I was going to say to Emma. 'Hi, Emma speaking.'

'Em. It's me. I'm sorry I hav...' I was interrupted.

'Roger! I've been so worried about you. Are you okay? How's Penny? Isabelle told me the news, it's just so terrible.' Emma's reaction was lovely and it made me smile.

'Honey, I'm fine and Penny's coping really well. I just feel so guilty for not calling you.'

'I did wonder when you were going to ring me, but I do understand. So where are you?' She sounded slightly cross.

'Thanks for not giving me a hard time. I've been staying down with my parents. I'm at the flat at the moment. I'd forgotten I was going out with clients tonight, Brian rang to remind me so I've just come up for the evening. I'm planning to stay in town tonight. Did you just say Frank had been out with Isabelle?'

'Yeah, I couldn't believe it either. They had a really good time and Frank was a complete gentleman apparently.' Emma laughed.

'Bollocks! No way, Frank a gentleman?! I don't believe that for a minute. I'm seeing him tomorrow so I'll get the full story then. I'm really sorry I didn't call you, I feel really guilty now.'

'Don't worry I understand, I'm just glad Penny is all right. When you say you are staying in town does that mean I can come over and stay with you?'

I couldn't believe I had been so insensitive. 'Yeah definitely! I would really love to see you Em. You've got a key so let yourself in and I'll see you when I get back.'

'Yippee! I'll be waiting in bed for you! Don't get too pissed Roger and try not to be too late, I'd love to sit and talk to you for a bit.'

'Damn! And here was me hoping I could just come home and ravish you!!' I joked. 'I'll try to get away as soon as I can.'

'See you later, I can't wait! Thank you so much for finally calling. I love you.' Emma whispered.

'I love you too, honey. See you tonight.' I put the phone down and felt a lot better. I had missed Emma more than I'd realised and couldn't wait to see her. I went to the fridge and got out a cold bottle of Krug and put it in a special bottle cooler I'd bought in New York. It would keep the champagne cold for about ten hours, long enough I thought as I took it into my bedroom and placed it on my bedside table with two champagne flutes. I left a note telling her to open the champagne and to save me some.

The taxi arrived spot on five-fifteen and half an hour later I arrived outside the impressive offices of Morgan Stanley. I gave my name to the girl at reception and asked her to call Andrew Duncan for me. I was told he would be down shortly and the receptionist suggested I take a seat.

Andrew and the guys came bounding out of the lift and over to where I sat. 'Hey Hamilton! How you doing Buddy? Where have you been hiding? We read about your sister in the papers, so sorry mate. Is she okay?'

I got up and greeted my top customers. 'Hi guys! Yeah, she's fine thanks.'

We headed out and into the cab still waiting outside. We were going for drinks first at a private members bar I had joined many years ago. I tipped the cabby and led my guests into Ricardo's. My father had been a member since his Formula One days along with the many other celebrities that frequented the exclusive club.

Julie, the stunning receptionist greeted us and took our coats. 'Fuck me Roger, she gets it!' Mark whispered to me.

'Oh yes, I bet she does. Not from me though, unfortunately!' I laughed.

'Thank you Mr Hamilton.' Julie said as she handed me the cloakroom token.

'She is one horny woman!' Mark struggled to take his eyes off her as we walked into the bar. He nearly smashed his head into the doorframe as we entered, much to our amusement!

'Mark, are you okay? You look all starry-eyed.' Andrew laughed.

'What can I get you all to drink? Beer Andrew?' I asked. He only drank beer and wine. I had never seen him drink any sort of spirit.

We sat at one of the tables near the bar and discussed what had happened to Penny and all the events of the past few days.

'I bet your mate Frank is under pressure to find the guy?' Andrew was very supportive and wanted to know if he could help in anyway or if I needed him to speak to Michael Irwin about allowing me all this time off.

'Thanks Andrew, but I think Michael is okay about it at the moment. The desk is in good hands with Brian in charge. They seem fairly busy so I don't think I'm missed too much!' I laughed.

'We fucking miss you, Roger. Our line doesn't get picked up half as quick when you're not there. I did a decent swap with your boys today, four hundred million six-oh-fours into three hundred million nine-three-oh-twos! I made a real killing on it. The market moved my way; six-oh-fours are easier and nine-threes have gone bananas. There's a big shortage out there and I feel a lot of pain coming down my phone line! I spoke to Higgsy and I know he's short.' Andrew winced at me.

'He must be doing his bollocks. Last I heard he was short of a couple of hundred, a point lower down. He's been trying to buy 'em back all week!' Mark added.

'God! He must have been gutted when that swap went through.' I said, shaking my head. All the traders talked shop during the early part of any evening out. They couldn't help it. I put it down to them unwinding from the stress of the day. They were all under extreme pressure and most of them couldn't just switch off at the close of business. For us brokers it was much easier. We never had outstanding positions that might make or lose the firm a fortune overnight. We could simply walk out the door and tomorrow was just another day with a clean sheet of paper. Andrew and the guys were paid a lot more money than most of the brokers but in return they were expected to make their banks a huge amount of money. There was no way I could perform with that amount of pressure on me all day, everyday.

The waiter came over with yet another round of drinks and we knocked them back as quickly as the last.

'Where are we dining tonight Roger?' Gavin asked.

'The Rib Room.' I said matter of factly.

'A very fine choice Mr Hamilton!' Andrew extended his hand to congratulate me.

I looked at my watch and realised time had raced on. 'Can I have the bill please, Harry?'

'Right away Sir.' The waiter rushed over to the bar.

'Table's booked for eight, we'd better get going.' I said to Andrew. I signed the bill and left a tip on the silver tray.

'Your car is waiting Mr Hamilton.' Julie said through the door of the bar.

We walked out and the driver held the door open for us.

'No way! Fucking brilliant!!' Mark laughed and slapped me on the back as he got into the silver stretch Bentley.

The smell of leather hit you as you got in. There was a bottle of Krug in an ice bucket on the table. The interior was vast and very sumptuous. There were two rows of cream coloured seats facing each other with a wonderful mahogany table in the middle. There were six cut-crystal champagne flutes in a wonderful, glass case.

'Roger, this is top notch mate.' Gavin winked at me, as the driver set off.

'Get the cards out then!' I joked, pretending to shuffle an imaginary deck and deal them out. I poured the champagne out and toasted the guys.

'To your sister and I hope and pray you find the guy that did it.' Andrew said, very sincerely. I was very touched and felt slightly light-headed.

'I think I'm getting pissed already!' I declared to my fellow passengers.

'That makes two of us then.' Andrew replied.

'Careful Andrew. It's dangerous to mix the grape with the grain!' Mark said, putting on a very exaggerated posh voice.

'Tonight, I don't care, mon ami!' Andrew replied in a pathetic French accent.

FORTY ONE

She was conscious but was struggling to recall anything. Her eyes were sore and she still had the taste in her mouth. It was like a bitter medicine similar to Paracetamol when it's been on your tongue for too long. She kept moving her tongue around inside her mouth, trying to produce enough saliva to swallow it away. Her back was agony and she realised she was lying on something hard digging into the small of her back. She sat up and discovered she was naked. Her head was throbbing and she had the worst hangover she'd ever had.

She looked around and began to panic. She was in a stunning bedroom with a beautiful marbled ensuite bathroom but what caused her concern was that she was lying half inside a wardrobe. There was a telephone next to the huge king size bed and she clambered out of the wardrobe and staggered over to the bed. She sat there for a couple of minutes, her head spinning. She tried to remember where she was; whose bedroom was she in? Why had she been hanging out the wardrobe? What had happened since her drink with Daniel? Was it his bedroom and if so, where was he? She could remember being in the bar with Daniel but nothing else. Her head hurt, she knew that much and as she thought this she became aware of another sensation. She had had sex, and it must have been rough sex because she was sore. This really upset her because she still couldn't remember a thing.

She shimmied over to the phone and stopped. Next to the phone was a pad with 'The Conrad Hotel' printed on it. She was in a hotel in Chelsea! She began to cry from the frustration of not knowing how she'd got there. She picked up the phone and called her house in Clapham. A voice she didn't recognise answered.

'Who's that?' Trudy asked.

This is reception madam, can I help?'

Trudy put the phone down without answering. She shook her head and then realised. She hadn't dialled a nine first, for an outside line! This time she was successful and on the fifth ring Tina answered the phone.

'Tina, thank God you're in. It's me, Trudy. I am really confused. Did I call you last night?' Trudy sounded groggy and her words came out clumsily.

'Trudy, you sound like shit girl. No, you didn't. Where have you been? The only message was from Daniel, saying how you stood him up last night. Now tell me what you been up to?'

'What! Oh shit. My head hurts. I didn't stand Daniel up last night at all. He met me at the house and then we went to Bar Excellence. I've just woken up and I can't remember a thing. I'm in a hotel in Chelsea! What did he say on the message?'

'He sounded truly concerned. I can't remember exactly, but I saved the message for you. I think he said you went to the loo and that was the last he saw of you. He left his mobile number for you to call.' Tina sounded excited, 'so, you better tell me what you've been playing at? Who were you with? A hotel in Chelsea? He must have money!'

'Tina I told you. I can't remember. I'm in this beautiful bedroom with the most fantastic bathroom and yet I don't know who I was with or how I got here. It's a bit of a scary thought really. I'm going to......'

The door of the bedroom was flung open and two policemen and two ambulance attendants came rushing in. They seemed surprised to see Trudy sitting on the bed. One of the officers turned to the chambermaid who had just come in. 'Is this the *dead* lady?' he asked with deep sarcasm.

'Um yes. I think it is her. I didn't say she was dead. It was that doctor who said she was dead.' The maid was very emotional.

Trudy had dived under the covers to hide her nudity. 'What the fuck is going on? Get out!'

'I am terribly sorry madam. We were told that there was a dead woman in your room. It's obviously not you. Do you mind if we take a look around?'

Trudy was shaking as the ambulance lady came over to see her. She sat down next to Trudy. 'Are you feeling okay?' she asked as she picked up Trudy's wrist and began taking her pulse.

'I think so. Not dead anyway!' Trudy laughed nervously.

The paramedic smiled and said that Trudy's pulse was a little on the slow side. 'Are you sure you feel all right? You look very pale.'

'Yeah, I think I just overdid it a little last night. I'm fine.'

'No one in there.' The young policeman told the other officer as he came back out the bathroom.

'We are sorry to have disturbed you.' The officer said to Trudy, almost bowing at the same time. 'Come on Perkins.'

The policemen and paramedics left closing the door behind them. Trudy sat stunned, staring at the door for ages then went into the bathroom. She sat on the toilet and winced slightly at the pain. She got up and put on the crisp white bathrobe from the back of the door and looked back into the bedroom, still very confused. She had forgotten the phone call and the handset was lying off the hook on the floor. She looked down and noticed it and quickly put it to her ear. 'You still there Tina?' The line was dead. She replaced the handset and it rang almost immediately.

'Good morning Miss. I am sorry to disturb you. Rupert Dawson speaking; I am the General Manager of The Conrad. I am so sorry about the disturbance that just happened. I assure you that I am looking into the matter with the police and I will find out who played this terrible prank. Would you like me to send you a continental breakfast up to your room, compliments of the hotel?'

'That's very kind, but I don't eat breakfast. Please don't worry, I will be checking out soon. Before you go, can you tell me who booked this room?'

'Of course miss. It was a Mr Lucky. He has already settled the bill. I sincerely apologise for this little problem and please do call me if you need anything.'

Trudy replaced the phone and slowly sat up in bed. Mr Lucky. What kind of a name is that, she thought and shook as a shiver ran down her spine. I don't know a Mr Lucky. She got up and went back into the bathroom. She decided to run a bath and poured lots of bubble bath under the running taps. The smell of fresh lavender began to relax her as she brushed her teeth, using the contents of the little hotel travel bag. She could still taste the chemical flavour and so brushed her teeth again. Her hair was all matted and her eyes were very blood shot. She looked tired and there were wrinkles on her forehead and around her eyelids.

She was impressed by how quickly the bath filled and she stepped delicately in. The water was hot but not too hot. Just right she thought as she began to sit down. The lather was thick and silky but as the water touched her bottom, she winced in pain. She was very sore. It must have been one great night. If only I could remember it, she thought as she lay back in the bath. She closed her eyes and tried to remember Mr Lucky.

She was back at the house in Clapham by midday and Tina was there to greet her as she opened the front door.

FORTY TWO

'Morning Roger. Good to have you back. How's your sister?' David asked as he took his jacket off, and placed on the back of his chair.

'Not too bad thanks, David.'

It was twenty past seven and the dealing floor was slowly filing with brokers and the noise rose with their arrival. I had missed the rough and tumble of dealing and the buzz and energy of the twentieth floor. I would still prefer to be working with Frank, helping him catch the rapist, but I had a mortgage and bills to be paid. I knew that Michael would only allow me so much time off and I didn't want to leave the guys for too long. More importantly, Electronic Trading started today and I had to be there to sort out any hiccoughs. It was the holiday season and if there were empty seats then lines wouldn't be picked up fast enough and the clients would get pissed off and take their business to one of the other broking firms. With the end of the quarter looming ahead, I had to maximise profits for bonus time, not just for me but also for the guys.

'Did Griff tell you about his party?' David asked, leaning on one of his screens, sipping his coffee. 'He should be bringing the invites in today, he's had them printed especially.'

'What's he celebrating? He hasn't mentioned it to me.' I asked sharply, a bit pissed off I hadn't been invited.

'Well, I dunno really. He's been a bit weird about it. Something to do with his numbers coming up and he said he has won at last, whatever that meant. Danny thinks he's won the Lottery!' David laughed, as he tossed his coffee cup into the bin behind him.

'Sounds a bit mysterious.' I saw Brian enter the dealing room. 'I'll quiz him myself. Hey Griffo, where's my invite?' I shouted at him as he approached the desk.

'Morning Roger, nice to see you. Your invite's in my case.' He informed me tapping his briefcase. 'I wanted to surprise you,' he glared at David, 'but obviously some loud mouth has told you.'

David shrugged apologetically and sat down, to hide behind his screens.

'Come on, let's go into my office Brian. You can give me my invite, explain the celebration and we can go through the last few weeks at the same time. You have the Con, David.'

'Aye, aye Captain. I concur.' David stood and saluted.

As I entered my office I noticed the photo of me and Penny and it brought back all the awful memories of when my parents had called to tell me about her rape. I composed myself and sat down.

'So what's this party in aid of?'

Brian handed me an invitation. It was plain white card, gold edged with black embossed type face:

> **Brian Griffin invites**
> **Roger and Emma**
> **to celebrate**
> **Being the Best of the Best**
> **'AT LAST WE HAVE A WINNER!'**
> **at an afternoon barbeque on**
> **11th July from 1 o'clock**
> **'til late at**
> **Flat 6**
> **217 Kings Road**
> **London**
> **R.S.V.P**

'Well I'm still none the wiser! It's not to celebrate England winning the World Cup, that's for sure!' I joked.

'Let's just say, I'm pretty chuffed with myself. I've been trying to achieve something for a long time and at last I've done it!' Brian smirked.

'I don't bloody believe it. You have haven't you? You of all people!' I slapped the desk and pretended to be angry. Brian's face changed and he seemed oddly nervous. 'You don't need the bloody money. You've won the Lottery, haven't you? How much have you won? You've won the fucking National Lottery you lucky bastard!' I was convinced, and really excited. I didn't know anyone that had actually won and here I was talking to a winner.

Brian laughed. 'Yes, in a way you could say that. I haven't actually won the lottery but I've been trying to achieve something for a long while now and I've finally done it. I had to rape a few people along the way but it has been good fun, Rog. I'm so excited.' Brian didn't notice me grimace when he mentioned raping people, but I let it go. 'I don't want to tell you any more just yet. I will announce it all officially at the party.'

'You can't leave me hanging like this Brian.' I grumbled. 'Give me a clue.'

'Sorry Roger. All will be revealed in good time. Will you and Emma be able to come? Are you both free that weekend?'

'I think we can make it, but I'll have to check with the 'boss' first.' I told him.

'I've got an invite for your parents and Penny too. Do you think she'll come? How is she now?' Brian produced two more invites from his briefcase.

'She seems to be okay thanks. I'll give her the invite but I won't promise. I think it will do her good and she knows most of the guys on the desk, so maybe. I do know mum and dad won't be able to; they will be in Germany for the Grand Prix. They're guests of Ferrari and they are having dinner with the Schumacher's the week before.'

'Awesome! What a life. It's another world. Perhaps they can all pop over on Michael's jet after qualifying for a cocktail or two.' He shook his head in disbelief.

I laughed with him and thanked him for the invites. We then spent twenty minutes or so discussing business. It had been pretty quiet with no real problems. Jamie was still getting in late and had paid no attention to Brian's warnings. He'd been out for lots of long lunches and had come back very pissed on three separate occasions. Brian also told me E-Trading had been delayed due to some technical problems. Our engineers were struggling to fix a bug in the coding.

'Okay, well I'll see how it goes this week. I'll give him another written warning on Friday and if nothing changes, he's out at the end of the month. Obnoxious little prick.' I was angry and disappointed with Jamie, but not altogether surprised. The trouble with being from a privileged background like Jamie was you sometimes took it all for granted. I was relieved that E-Trading was delayed. I would rather have a hassle free day to get back into things.

'How's the hunt for the rapist going?' Brian asked. 'Is Frank any closer to catching him?'

'I'm not sure, but we're meeting up for a beer tonight so I'll find out then. Why don't you join us?' I suggested.

'Yeah, great. I've got no plans.' He smiled as he left the office and made his way back to the desk.

FORTY THREE

The upstairs bar of Corney and Barrow was busy for a Monday night. There were a group of LIFFE guys in the corner drinking champagne and being very loud. They all still wore their various brightly coloured trading jackets unique to the London International Financial Futures Exchange; red and white stripes, blue & green and a couple of reds. All locals wear a red jacket. Locals are individuals who are self-employed and punt the futures market for their own financial gain. They fight harder than most when in the dealing pit and try to out bluff the big boys from the main financial institutions, mainly due to the fact it's their money on the line. Roger knew a couple of locals who had lost their life savings trading financial futures. It was a very volatile market and there was no margin for error in the frenetic dealing pits. The traders all scream at each other trying to get their trade filled first. They did this by being the loudest and waving frantically, trying to get the attention of all the other dealers, who themselves, were also screaming! It was just one big, bun fight and not a market Roger would ever want to be in. Most of the successful dealers were loud-mouthed yobs from London's east end. You didn't need manners or any customer care skills on the LIFFE floor.

'Obviously had a good day.' Brian flicked his head over towards the group.

'Wish we could say the same.' I threw my eyes up at the ceiling. It had been another classic Gilt Monday. No bloody business and all the brokers trying to book the lunch slots before anyone else! I had spent some of the afternoon talking to Michael Irwin and explaining the lack of business. He was far more interested in business than poor Penny.

I had arranged with Frank to meet in the City. We were going to have a few drinks and then an early curry in Brick Lane. I said I would meet Frank in South Kensington but he said he was more than happy to get out of the area. The cases were getting to Henson and I think he needed to take time away from it.

'What would you like, Roger?' Brian asked with his Platinum Amex out and ready in his hand.

'Corona with a slice of lime please Griff.'

Brian had a Bud Ice and we stood at the bar trying to ignore the boisterous gaggle in coloured jackets behind us.

'They are so bloody common.' I commented, sounding like a real snob.

Brian grinned at me and we clinked beers. 'What time's Frank meeting us?'

'He said about six but it depends on what time he can escape. He's a bit pissed off with work I think. He's been burning the candle at both ends so don't mention the rapes until he brings it up. He may not want to talk about it.'

'No probs. I know the form, we'll just talk about football and women!' He laughed. 'So I guess that's it for Jamie then?'

'He obviously didn't realise that I was going to be back this week. Eight thirty is a bloody piss take. Monday morning; he's had two days to relax and rest. He probably spent the whole weekend clubbing and doing drugs. Yeah, he's history. I'll give him his final written warning and see what happens. Bloody red-tape. If I had my way, I'd sack him now. I'll have quiet word with Peter Jarvis too, just to warn him that if Jamie doesn't get his act together, he'll be fired at the end of the month.'

'Don't you think Jarvis will say something to Jamie?' Brian asked.

'That's exactly what I think will happen. Then if I do fire Berry, at least Jarvis can't accuse me of not trying to do anything or complain that I should have told him.' I smiled. It was all so bloody political. If I had a crap broker on my desk, I should be able to do what I want; if I want to sack him that should be my prerogative. But every trader felt he owned his broker and if you sack a broker, you always run the risk of upsetting the traders. Normally, I wouldn't mind, but we needed Peter Jarvis' business, so for once I would have to tread carefully.

'Is this where the big dicks hang out?' Henson slapped me on the back and smiled at me, as I turned round.

'Hi Frank. You'll have to stand over there, that's where the little wieners hang out mate!' I laughed, shaking his hand. 'You remember Brian?'

'Hi Brian, how's it going?'

'Hi Frank, good to see you again.' Brian said, shaking hands.

'Vodka, lime and tonic?' I asked Henson.

'I've got a tab running Rog. I'll get this.' Brian jumped in.

'Wonderful. Just what I need. It's great to get away from bloody South Kensington.' Henson stretched his huge frame and yawned. 'How's the world of high finance boys?'

'It could be better to be honest. First day back and there's mutiny in the ranks. Probably have to sack one of the guys at the end of the month.' I commented.

'Not you Brian, I hope?' Frank smirked at Brian who was within ear shot at the bar.

'I don't plan on departing just yet Frank.' Griffin smiled back.

'So how are you Roger? I've missed you, you old tosser!' Henson made light of his comment.

'Well that makes you an old tosser too then, you old tosser!' I retorted. 'I've missed you too mate. Talk about a stressful time!'

'I can't believe what you and poor Penny have been through. How is she?' Frank asked, with real concern in his voice.

'She's not too bad, considering. She's just beginning to come out of her shell now. She seems to be more comfortable with discussing her ordeal now.

I think she wants this bastard as much as we do. How did the interviews go with the cab drivers?'

'Still got twenty or so to see. Not one decent suspect. With seven rapes we know about, every single one of the drivers has an alibi on at least one of the dates. That's why I'm really hopeful that we'll catch the bastard out, he's got to have been busy with a relevant excuse on every date we ask. All the witnesses the drivers have given us to back up their stories, have been spoken to and they all match. The other problem we have is he could be working in collaboration with someone else.'

'How can you tell the stories are all true? Wouldn't it be very easy for someone to lie?' I asked, taking a swig of my drink.

'Yeah, of course it would, that's what makes it so difficult.'

'What's difficult?' Brian asked, as he returned with a fresh round of drinks.

'Cheers, Brian.' Frank raised his glass, before taking a huge gulp. 'Roger and I were just discussing this bloody taxi driver rapist, but you don't want to be bored with it all.' Henson pulled out a cigarette and offered one to both Brian and myself.

'No thanks. Don't worry; you won't bore me with the details. Carry on. How's it going?' Brian asked. *Me bored, you stupid Fuck! I know more than you could imagine!*

'Frank has been interviewing a load of cab drivers to see if they all have alibis on the relevant dates. He was just telling me how it was all going.' I recapped for Griffo.

'You have to rely on your instincts sometimes and whilst it's difficult to know for sure, it is normally easy to notice if someone is lying to you. We get sent on all sorts of training courses. You can always read it in the person's eyes when they lie. But it is still an uphill struggle sometimes. I was telling Hamilton, we've only got twenty or so cab drivers to interview and then I'm at another bloody dead-end.' Frank took a big draw on his cigarette.

'Is there a chance this guy, isn't a taxi driver?' I asked Frank.

'Don't you start!' Frank moaned. 'Yes, there is and it's seeming more and more likely.'

'Then you haven't got many other leads, I take it?' Brian asked.

'No not really.'

'Bollocks Henson. Yes you have! What about all the info I gave you that Penny remembered?' I reminded my friend.

'Brian, what would I do without my mate Roger?' Frank joked. 'He's right. Penny did come up trumps and we have got plenty of new avenues to explore. I don't really want to go through them all now, but it should really help.'

'Oh come on Frank, you can tell us.' Brian put his arm round him. *Come on tell me. I need to know what you know for fucks sake!*

'Enough talking shop.' Frank wasn't going to be moved. 'Have you spoken to Emma recently Roger?'

'Yes. Why? What's it got to do with you, you nosey wanker!' I punched him gently on his huge arm.

'It's just that Isabelle mentioned that Emma was concerned that she hadn't heard from you.' Henson, rubbed his arm, feigning a pained expression.

'Oh yes, Isabelle. How is your love life blossoming? You sly old fox. He had a blind date at my place and the next thing I know, he's in a deep and meaningful relationship!' I told Brian.

'Fuck you Roger. We saw each other for a curry. Hardly deep! He's just jealous, Brian because she's a complete babe.'

'That's true, I couldn't believe it when she turned up for the dinner party. I think I just stood there with my mouth wide open. But I must admit, I'm very happy with Emma. I finally called her last week and we had a wonderful night of passion after I'd been out with Morgans. She was at home waiting for me!'

'Oh yeah. Tell me more.' Frank demanded.

'Sorry mate. On a need to know basis and you don't need to know! Let's just say we had a good time and I relieved myself of the pressure that had built up recently!' I finished my beer. 'Another round I think.'

Brian once again jumped up and ordered the drinks. I took the opportunity to quickly ask Frank some more about the clues Penny had provided.

'Well, too be honest, I haven't got round to checking out the aftershave lead. I'm going to pop into Harvey Nichols or Harrods tomorrow; they have the biggest perfume halls in London. I thought I could either get a collection of all the aftershaves or maybe we could get Penny to pop in with me to see if she can identify the smell.'

'I'll tell you what; I'll call Penny in the morning and see if she's ready to face the world again. I know she's been suggesting to mum she's ready to go back to work.' I told Frank.

'Ok that's great news. If you're absolutely sure she's ready then I'll try and see someone at one of the stores to make an appointment. It would be great if we can pin down the make of aftershave the sick fuck wears. Speaking of sick fucks, what are you wearing today, that's quite unusual?' He asked me, almost choking on his drink whilst laughing.

'Fuck you Frank.' I flicked my fingers at him. 'Armani; it doesn't get much more common! What about you? You always have that sweet smell of success about you!' I joked.

'I've got a few favourites. I'm quite into Davidoff at the moment; Blue water and Isabelle approves. It's all so bloody expensive though for us poor coppers!'

'What about you Brian?' I asked as he came back with more drinks.

'What?' He looked puzzled.

'What aftershave have you got on? We're discussing the poofy subject of Eau de Cologne!' I laughed and put my arm round Henson and kissed him.

'Piss off, you great queer!' Frank laughed.

'I buy mine from France. It's called Chamois. There's a perfume factory near Nice I found on the Internet. Wonderful selection.' He told us.

I leant over to get a whiff. 'Wow, I like that. It's quite heavy still considering it's nearly seven. What time d'you put it on this morning?'

'Oh about six thirty. It's not cheap but at least it lasts.' Brian swigged his beer.

'You flash bugger!' Henson commented. 'I'm definitely in the wrong bloody business!'

I laughed with him and said, 'You should see his bloody car mate!'

'What is it?' Frank asked.

'Oh, just a black taxi!' Brian joked and we all burst into laughter.

FORTY FOUR

I got in at seven and logged into Bloomberg. I had been very careful last night and didn't feel anywhere near as bad as usual after a night out with Henson. We'd had a curry in Brick Lane and I was at home by eleven thirty; early by our normal standards. I went straight into the World Cup pages to check out my positions. I was far more relaxed about it all now. I was still up over two thousands pounds and there was no way that I would lose it all by the Finals.

A light lit up on my phone board and I clicked in to answer it. 'Morning, Roger Hamilton.'

'Roger, come on up. I need your help on something.'

The phone went dead. It was Michael Irwin. I got up and made my way out to the lifts. He needs my help, I wondered. I know what that's all about!! The British Grand Prix, I'll bet.

I entered Michael's inner sanctum and knocked on his door.

'Come in.' Michael shouted. When he saw me he smiled and said, 'Ah Roger, good of you to come up so swiftly. I just want to say how deeply sorry I am about your sister. It must be truly awful for your whole family right now. If there is anything I can do, please just say the word. Dean asked me to pass on his best wishes too.'

'Thanks Michael. That means a lot. I'm sorry I was away for so long. The guys seem to have held the desk together well.' I appreciated his kind words.

'Roger, I don't give a fuck about the profits on your desk buddy. We're talking about family here. You just relax and take as much time off as you need. You are an integral part of this firm and I don't want you worrying. OK?' Michael smiled at me.

'Thanks. I get the message.' I smiled back.

'Ok, Staff and the Grand Prix.' Michael got straight back to business. 'Let's do the Grand Prix first. I know you have contacts in the right places and I need four Paddock Club tickets for this weekend. You can arrange that for me, can't you?'

Just because of who my dad was, I hated the way people assumed he wouldn't mind helping them. I liked Michael, but I was uncomfortable with him putting on me like this. 'Yes, Michael. That shouldn't be a problem. I'll call you later and let you know how much.'

'You just pay for them and put them through on your expenses Roger. Now you need to cull some guys from your desk. Have you decided who? I want three of them out by end of trading today. You tell my secretary the names and I'll make sure Paul has their redundancy letters ready by 3pm.'

'I have to decide on the third person but that should be OK.'

'Good man Roger. Keep up the great work and your bonus next quarter should be even bigger.' Michael picked up the phone and began dialling, his usual signal that our meeting was over.

I stood in the lift and went through all the guys on my desk. I hated days like today. Being the boss has some nice perks, but making people redundant was not one of them. Jamie was going, David was going, but the third fallguy was going to be a tougher decision. Mike was in the firing line, but he was married with three kids and a big mortgage and if I had to do that, I really wouldn't feel good. Jonathan was the more likely bet, but he did more business that Mike. I'd need to discuss this with Brian and Eddie. As the lift arrived at my floor, I hoped they were both in. I walked back into the dealing room and was relieved to see both Eddie and Griff sat at the desk. No one else was in and I asked them both to come into my office.

'Morning guys. I've just had a meeting with Michael and today is the day. He wants the desk down to nine men by 5pm today. I need your opinions. As we discussed the other day, we all know the favourites, but I need to finalise this now so I can let Michael know and then Paul can draw up the papers.'

Paul was Kaplan's lawyer and he ran a small legal department of three people.

'When you gonna do the deed?' Eddie asked.

'Papers should be ready by 3pm Michael said, so sometime after that.' It was never nice having to call people in and tell them to their faces that they were no longer needed. I was dreading it, but in a way I was looking forward to finally getting rid of Jamie.

'So who's on the list then, Roger?' Eddie asked. 'Am I right to assume the three of us are safe?' He grinned and nudged Brian.

'Eddie, I'm glad you find this amusing. You haven't had the best year really so do me a favour, just keep the clever comments to yourself for now.' Eddie was a pain in the arse sometimes and all I wanted to do was get the final three decided before the rest of the team arrived. 'The others will be in shortly and I just want us to decide on the right three.'

'Sorry Rog.' Eddie said genuinely. 'Well Berry has got to go, David wouldn't be missed and then it's either Mike or Jonathan, in my opinion.'

Brian nodded in agreement. 'They are the four suspects, I think it's got to be Berry, David and Mike.'

'Suspects!' I laughed. 'It's not a criminal investigation Griff. I'm not sure about Mike. It's close between him and Jonathan but I would prefer Jonathan to go.'

'Why? Because he hasn't got a family?' Eddie asked quite aggressively. 'Mike may be married with kids, but he's crap. He fucked up that six three's oh four trade yesterday and nearly cost us twenty grand and he's always too scared to go on and ask for business. At least Jonathan makes an effort.'

'Yeah, but Mike is a face. He's well known and liked in the market and he is great at the old entertaining.' Brian was with me on this one.

'He's a broker, not a bloody comedian. He may be well liked but he's crap. Berry, David and Mike are my votes.' Eddie was adamant.

'Brian what do you think?' I had already made my mind up.

'Mike does get some decent clips from the Credit Suisse boys and I think we would suffer more from the market reaction to us letting Mike go than Jonathan. Jonathan does try hard, but his results are clear. He's not making the grade and I think he would be very quickly forgotten.'

'Whatever.' Eddie had given up.

'Eddie, we're all in this together. I know you and Mike don't always see eye to eye and yes I agree with you, he's slow at times and his keyboard skills aren't great but..'

'You aren't kidding!' Eddie interrupted. 'He could never be a secretary. It would take him a week to type one bloody letter!'

We all laughed at Eddie's comment. 'But, he is well liked as Brian said. So it's Jamie, David and Jonathan. Thanks guys. We'll do it at about 3.30pm. I'll give you both a nod when the paper work's done.'

'Roger, were you serious about my year being crap?' Eddie was hurt. 'I thought I'd been doing really well.'

'You're a muppet, Eddie. I just wanted to shut you up. You're not in my inner circle for nothing you doughnut! Now get out and go and get some bloody prices on the screen.' I loved winding Eddie up.

Our legal team finished the paperwork by two and it was brought down to my office where I checked through it all. We were going to be shelling out just over seventy grand in redundancy money but it would save us over two hundred grand in salaries. A commotion on the desk disturbed my studying and I rushed back into the dealing room.

'I was fucking first. Danny saw me signal I was the next buyer you prick.' Gary screamed across at Jamie.

'No you wasn't. I shouted 'second buyer' and Mike filled me. Fucking hand signals no one can see don't mean you get the trade.'

'Fuck off Berry. I was first and you know it. And you should have filled me, not that little cock sucker, you old tosser. Why don't you all just fucking wake up a bit.' Gary was red in the face and not going to back down. He still had his client on the phone too, which didn't impress me. 'I'm trying to sort it out for you know, Si. You should have got fifty. I'll sort it out.' Gary turned back to the desk, 'Si reckons he's bought fifty so just fucking tell Peter that you fucked up and he ain't got any.'

'Jamie was the next buyer not you Gary, That's why I sold him fifty and not you.' Mike defended his actions.

'Oi, calm down Gary.' I was back at my desk and it was imperative that I took control.

'I'm fucking calm thank you. Tell that little prick he's wrong.' Gary replied.

I spoke to Griff to find out what happened and he explained Jamie was the second buyer and Gary had tried to sneak Simon into the trade.

'Jamie tell Peter he's got fifty and Gary tell Simon that you didn't get him in, but you'll work a forty eight bid for him.'

'No way. I bought the second fifty Roger. Now you're the fucking boss. You fucking SORT IT OUT!' Gary shouted at me, as he smashed his handset into his phone board, sending pieces of fragments flying in all directions and stormed off the desk. 'You fucking tell Si,' he added as he disappeared into the smoking room.

I called Si and explained what had happened. He was not at all happy but he did understand and he was pleased Gary was only trying to help him out by getting him into the trade. I explained he had just tried it on and Simon found it very amusing that Gary had tried to sneak him into the trade.

I looked over at Jamie who was looking very pleased with himself and he was on the phone, presumably talking to Peter and explaining how great he was to have got him in as the second buyer. I walked into the smoking room to have a quiet word with Gary.

'Gary, don't ever speak to me like that again. I don't need to be told how to do my job and I don't need to tell you trying to sneak your client into trades is not your job. Just because you shout loudest and scream obscenities at the other guy, doesn't give you the right to get in on a trade.'

'He's a little prick and always will be. I signalled as he shouted and I reckon I was first.' Gary took a drag on his cigarette.

'Griff told me what happened and you were not first, Jamie was. Now that's it and I don't want to hear you whinging about it when you get back to the desk. I spoke to Si and he's fine. He's happy you tried to get him in and understands. He's bidding forty nine and says he should get them.' I turned to walk out.

'How come Berry is still here anyway. Why haven't you sacked him yet. He's a fucking waste of space and always has been.'

'Gary, I understand your frustrations but you have to have faith in what I'm doing. Believe me, it will all be sorted. Now just calm down and don't ever speak to me like that in front of the rest of the guys. You'll need to call an engineer down to sort out your phone board too. You're lucky I'm not going to take the cost of a new one out of your salary.' As I walked out, he said he was sorry.

At three thirty I asked Eddie and Griffo to meet me in my office. I then walked back out to the desk and asked Jonathan to follow me.

FORTY FIVE

The phone rang twice. Penny was gazing out of the window, taking in the wonderful view down to the lake.

'Penny darling.' Her mother shouted. 'It's Lucy on the phone for you again.'

Penny knew she would have to talk to her flat mate at some point. Lucy had called four times in the last week and Penny had refused to take any of her calls so far, each time asking her mother to make an excuse.

'Penny, you can't keep avoiding her darling.' Her mother appeared in the doorway.

Penny had been delaying the inevitable for long enough and had been toying with the idea of returning to London and going back to work. Maybe Lucy would convince her it really was a good idea.

'Penny, are you going to speak to Lucy?'

'Yes I think I will, Mummy.' Penny got up from the armchair and kissed her mother on the cheek. 'I think it's time I got my life back in order.'

Penny's mother smiled and hugged her daughter tightly. 'I'm so very proud of you darling. Please only go back if you feel ready, there is no pressure. You know that your father and I will have you here as long as you wish.'

'Of course I do Mummy. You and Dad have been lovely and so generous as usual, Thank you for being here.'

Penny picked up the phone in the hall. 'Hi Lucy.'

'Oh Penny! Hi! How are you?' She could hear the joy and relief in Lucy's voice.

'I'm okay thanks. I'm sorry I haven't returned any of your calls. I just wasn't ready. I ..'

'Hey, don't worry. I just wanted you to know that I am here for you if you need me. The flat feels really empty without you.'

'Not for long Lucy. I'm coming back.'

'No way?' Lucy sounded really excited. 'Oh that's great news. When?'

'Probably next week I think. I've given it a lot of thought and I'll probably be going back to work too. How is everything at Marbles?'

'Work's just the same and everyone's been asking after you.' Lucy's toned changed. 'It must have been so terrible, I'm so sorry I left without you.'

'Lucy, it wasn't your fault. It was just one of those things, and anyway something good may come out of it yet.'

'What do you mean Penny?'

'Well, I've been helping the police with their enquiries and I can remember the aftershave he wore. I'm going with the police to sample loads of different aftershaves sometime next week. I will definitely know it if I smell it. I spent ages deciding if I wanted to go to the police or not, but Roger helped me make my mind up. His friend, Frank Henson is leading the investigation and I couldn't just sit and mope around, feeling sorry for myself. I had to try and help.' Penny felt really good telling her flat mate and getting it off her chest. It felt like a big weight being lifted from her slim shoulders.

'I'm so proud of you. I don't know if could be so brave in your situation. Anyway when are you coming back up to town? I'll make sure I'm here when you arrive.'

'I'm not sure. I've only just decided I'm coming back. I think I've been hiding down here for long enough. Mum and Dad have said I can stay here for as long as I need, but I woke up this morning and for the first time really missed London and you and the flat. So let me have a chat with my parents and I'll give you a call later this week.'

'Oh Penny, I'm so thrilled. I can't wait to see you. You let me know when you're going to be back, and I'll cook us a wonderful supper.'

'Thanks Lucy. I'll speak to you soon. Bye.'

'Bye Penny. Take care.'

Penny put the phone down and turned round to find her mother stood, smiling in the doorway. 'I think I'd better put the kettle on.' She said, putting her arm around Penny and leading her into the kitchen

FORTY SIX

Tina closed the front door and followed Trudy into the kitchen. She took the lid off the kettle and filled it with cold water and switched it on.

'So what the hell happened to you last night? The Conrad Hotel! My, my.' Tina smirked at her house mate.

'I don't know, honey. I have no idea. One minute I'm drinking with Daniel and next I'm lying on the floor of a hotel room, naked. This isn't funny Tina.' Trudy had sat down at the kitchen table.

'I know, I'm sorry. I kept Daniel's message if you wanna hear it.'

Trudy jumped up and over to the ansafone and hit the play button.

A mechanical voice came over the speaker. 'You have one old message. Message one'.

Daniel's voice came over the speaker:

'Trudy, what happened to you last night? You said you were going to the loo and that was the last time I saw you. I tried calling your mobile all night but it was switched off. Please call me as soon as you can. I'm worried. If it was something I said, at least let's talk about it. Call me please.'

'Well, that doesn't make things any clearer.' Trudy said with her hands on her hips. 'Maybe I should call Daniel to see what he knows. Oh God. This is awful.'

'Hey, it's Okay. Let me make you a cuppa. Tea or coffee?' Tina asked, reaching into a cupboard.

'Coffee would be great thanks.'

'So what do you remember?' Tina asked as she poured he piping hot water into each of the mugs.

'It's all quite foggy really. It started off really good. We got a cab to the bar and Daniel and I were just getting to know each other. He's a really successful businessman. He was very charming and it made a refreshing change to share a drink with a gentleman and not some drunken letch at Paradise.'

Tina grinned, knowing exactly what her friend meant. She sipped her coffee and listened as her friend ran her through the events of last night. She smiled at Trudy's recount of the moment the hotel manager burst in on her, sitting naked on the bed! 'So the last thing you can recall is coming back from the loo and that's it?

'Yeah, then I woke up on the floor of the hotel room. It's well strange. I know I had sex last night but can't remember anything. I spent the whole journey home trying to remember more, but I can't, I just can't."

'How much did you drink last night Trudy? Do you think you just had too much and blacked out?'

'No. I've never blacked out, you know me. I can drink like a fish. No, it's more than that. I felt bloody awful when I woke up on the floor and I had this strange chemical taste in my mouth. It was like I had chewed twenty Paracetamol before going to bed. No, it definitely wasn't booze.'

'That sounds like drugs. Did you do anything last night? Cocaine or Speed?' Tina asked.

'No. Not that I can remember anyway. And if I did, I've never had a taste like that before.'

'So if you didn't spend the night with Daniel, who did you spend the night with?' Tina was concerned about Trudy.

'I have no clue. The manager told me that the room was booked in the name of Mr Lucky. Can you believe that, Mr Lucky.'

'You gotta be kidding me. Mr Lucky? Someone's winding you up Trudy.'

'I hope it's just a wind up. Especially when you think that they thought I was dead. The room maid called the police. Apparently, some guy told her I *was* dead. He'd said he was a doctor. I've got to call Daniel.'

Trudy picked up the telephone and ferreted round in her handbag for the piece of paper with his number on. She found it and dialled his number. It went straight onto ansafone, so she left a message asking him to call her back as soon as he could.

'It was just the ansafone.' She told Tina, as she sat back down. 'I can't stand this. Whoever this guy was, I could have some awful disease like syphilis or even Aids. I don't know if he wore protection. I don't know anything. I could have been raped for all I know.' Tears began to slide slowly down Trudy's cheeks.

'Hey girl. It's gonna be cool. You hear me. Daniel will call you back and explain everything.' Tina had gone round to comfort her housemate. 'I think this house has had enough trauma to last a life time.'

As if by magic, the phone began ringing. Both girls jumped and Tina reacted first.

'Hello?'

'Hi, is Trudy there? It's Daniel.'

'It's Daniel.' Tina mouthed silently, raising her eyebrows. 'Hang on a second.'

With her hand placed firmly over the mouthpiece she asked Trudy if she was ready to talk to him. Trudy nodded and took the phone. 'Daniel, hi. What happened last night?'

'Hi Trudy. I was kinda hoping that you might be able to tell me. I thought we were getting along great. What did I do wrong? Was it something I said?'

'What? What are you talking about?' Trudy was confused.

'You go off to the toilet and that's the last I see of you. You never came back. Don't play games with me Trudy. I hoped we could have had something. Where did you go? Was it something I said?'

'Daniel. Stop. I don't remember anything from last night. I can recall drinking with you, I know I went to the toilet, I remember coming back and the next thing I am waking up on the floor of a hotel room. Please tell me you were there with me. Tell me you had to leave early for a meeting or something.'

'Trudy, I have been worried about you. I tried calling your mobile all night and it was switched off. What do you mean a hotel room?'

'I mean I woke up this morning in The Conrad Hotel in Chelsea. Did you book a room there for us?'

'No. I wouldn't have been so forward. It was our first drink. Trudy, I'm just glad that you're all right. So why did you abandon me?'

'Daniel, you're not listening to me!' Trudy was upset. She had hoped Daniel would be able to fill in the gaps. 'I didn't walk out on you, at least I didn't plan to. I really like you and I had been looking forward to our date for days. I wouldn't have walked out on you.'

'Okay, so you say you didn't walk out on me, then what happened. You went to the loo and I never saw you again. How do you think I feel?'

'Oh Daniel, I know how it must sound, but I just can't remember anything. I am so scared. Anything could have happened to me and I have no idea.'

'Okay, okay. Look I gotta go. When you know what happened give me a call.'

'Daniel, can I see you again?' Trudy didn't want him to put the phone down. 'Wouldn't it be nice to finish that drink?'

'Yeah, sure. Call me next week. I gotta run.'

FORTY SEVEN

The stupid little bitch. She suspects nothing, but that won't last long. He thought as he clicked his mobile off. It would only be a number of days before her memory returned. It would be patchy at first, but he would make sure whatever she did remember, he would be there to manipulate it into the untruth of his choice. *I'll call her Saturday night to book dinner. That way I can find out what the slag remembers.*

Leaving the dealing desk, he headed out to the lifts. Having made the company plenty of money already that morning, he'd decided to take the rest of the day off and had hoped to sneak out unnoticed.

'Brian, where are you off to?' I shouted after him, having seen him put his jacket on. He still had swaps working and hadn't left any instructions.

'Don't you remember? I told you on Monday, I've got to go to Hertfordshire to sort out some family business. I've taken a half day.' *You're a fucking nuisance Hamilton. Get off my back.*

'What about your nine three's oh two, seven's oh two swap and the long swaps you're working?' I'd followed him into the lobby.

'Shit, sorry Roger. Got so much on my mind. Get Gary to keep an eye on them for me would you? The terms and sizes are written down on my pad. I've got to go.'

He jumped into the lift and left me standing there. He was certainly in a hurry and I thought how peculiar he could be sometimes, as I returned to the desk. Must be some bad family news or something.

Smirking at himself in the mirror as the lift carried him down to the ground floor, he wiped his hand through his thick blond hair. *Family business my arse. More like none of your fucking business Roger!*

His yellow Ferrari got him home in record time and he was back in Chelsea by eleven o'clock and once inside his flat, he unlocked the annex. The next place was ready, number twelve. *Crosby you'd better watch out. I'm a coming to get you boy!*

Rushing round his apartment like a man possessed, he changed out of his City attire into more comfortable clothing. He adorned a green polo shirt, jeans, no pants, socks and slip on Gucci loafers. He checked his little bag of goodies and placed them on his coffee table ready for later. Getting out two wraps, one Speed and the other Cocaine, he opened them both on the table. He pulled the top off the Bud Ice and placed it in readiness next to the wraps. He licked his finger and dipped it into the Speed and popped it into his mouth and licked the white substance off. He grimaced at the taste and swigged down three quick gulps of beer to get rid of the taste.

The Cocaine was so much smoother but at five times the price, it should be, he thought as he organised two neat lines of the powder and snorted one up each nostril. To finish off the cocktail he downed two pills and smiled.

Nine three's oh two, seven's oh fucking two's! Who gives a shit? Roger you're mistaking me for somebody that gives a fuck! I've got better things to do buddy, like get myself an afternoon babe!

Picking up his jacket and car keys he headed out for the afternoon. He drove the Golf steadily down the Kings Road towards his lock up. *This afternoon is going to be fun.* The last couple of outings had been organised with military precision, but today he was just going to trawl the streets until he found babe number twelve.

The traffic heading into town wasn't too bad and he was soon in Knightsbridge. Approaching Hyde Park, he joined the end of the queue of taxis outside one of London's finest hotels, The Lanesborough. As he had all afternoon, he was very content to listen to the radio whilst the effects of the cocktail of drugs slowly took hold. He was looking for a rich lady today and he was also planning to leave a new clue for the nice Mr Henson, as he was obviously in need of some assistance.

By one o'clock his taxi was the first in line. So far he had watched an elderly couple and two gentlemen climb into the taxis in front of him and his taxi was next in line. *I can feel lady luck shining on me today and I'd be happy to ride her anytime!* He laughed and began jigging his legs in anticipation.

The huge doors of the hotel swung outwards and a young, but wealthy looking couple emerged. The man was in his early thirties and was wearing a finely tailored grey suit with a crisp white shirt and a sharp, contrasting red tie. He looked incredibly confident as he strode towards the taxi. His companion looked about six years younger and her suede trousers fitted her perfectly, as did her pink shirt, which was open at the neck, to accommodate her stylish Hermes scarf. The Dolce & Gabanna sunglasses were slid back on top of her head, to keep her hair from blowing in the wind and she swung an elegant Luis Vuitton handbag by her side.

'Could you take us to Heathrow Airport please.' The man requested, in a broad Texan accent.

Sure JR. You all just pop yourself inside my safe little cab, with your purdy little wife and sit back and relax buddy. God Bless America! 'Of course, Guv. Hop in.' He grinned at his passenger, as he released the door lock for the Hotel concierge to let them in.

The concierge loaded up the boot with their matching Louis Vuitton luggage and said, 'I hope you have a very pleasant trip, Mr Rodrigues. See you soon, no doubt.' He added, tipping his top hat.

'Why thank you John.' Mr Rodrigues said, placing a twenty pound note into John's palm.

'Which Terminal?' He asked, laughing inside to himself. The rear view mirror gave a perfect reflection of Mrs Rodrigues for him to check her out through. She turned her long black hair back and over both ears and pulled out a small make-up mirror and began to look over her soft features.

'Three.' Mr Rodrigues replied, as he closed the door.

I could do them both with the ether and then see how easily Mrs Rodrigues' suede pants come off!

As the taxi headed west down the Cromwell Road he considered the possibilities and how amusing it would be to attempt doing Mrs Rodrigues. Watching her in the mirror, she looked safe and happy, chatting with her husband. *If only you knew who your driver was! You wouldn't be so fucking happy then, would your Mr and Mrs Roddy!*

He knew of a couple of secluded roads he could duck down on the way to Hammersmith. The combination of drugs had got his imagination working overtime. His knuckles were white from gripping the steering wheel so hard, and as his pulse raced, his breathing increased and his eyes felt like they were on stalks. Smiling as he thought of his next move, he knew today was going to be very productive. He imagined how the police would be stunned he had attacked the wife with her husband in the cab! *Then they would be really pissed off. They would know I will stop at nothing. Poor old Detective Henson, I know how hard it is to catch someone like me, don't worry though. I'm gonna leave you a little clue to help you out.*

Going over the Hammersmith flyover, he realised he'd missed his turning. He could still duck down over Chiswick Bridge, but that could be complicated. He learnt on a sales course a few years back that piss poor planning equals piss poor results. He wasn't prepared so decided against his plans for Mr & Mrs Rodrigues. *They'll be plenty more opportunities at Heathrow,* he smiled, winking at Ms Rodrigues as she caught his eye. *You don't know how lucky you are!*

Arriving at the huge London airport, he dutifully dropped his passengers off and even helped them with their bags.

'Hey! Are they Gucci's?' Mrs Rodrigues asked him, looking down at his shoes.

'Yeah.' He grunted.

'Wow! Cabbies in London must do real well, Marty. He's wearing Gucci's, honey.'

Ignoring her, he put their suitcases onto a trolley and turned to Marty Rodrigues, 'That's twenty nine pounds please.'

'Here's fifty and keep the change.' Mr Rodrigues put his arm around his wife and they headed off with their trolley of luggage.

'Are they Gucci's?' Stupid rich bitch. Of course they are! You don't think I'm really a cab driver do you? I just do this for fun!! You don't know how lucky you are. I could have ruined your life!

He drove off and joined the end of the taxi rank at arrivals. The queue moved very quickly as the late afternoon flights came in thick and fast. *Thank you, thank you, thank you!* He smiled as the young lady approached his cab.

FORTY EIGHT

Trudy lay in her bed, unable to sleep. She had been awake since four o'clock and couldn't stop thinking about Wednesday night. She had been staring up at the ceiling for hours and as she glanced out through her curtains, she noticed the sun was already up. Her room overlooked the road and already there were cars moving about and people out walking their dogs and going about their business. She glanced at her Gucci watch; it was eight fifteen. She let the curtain fall back against the window and tuned onto her side, one hand under her two pillows. She stared at the promo poster of Elvis Presley that adorned her wall, but she wasn't really focusing on The King.

She had woken up remembering the night out with Daniel. For the first time she remembered going to the toilet and actually returning to the table and sitting with Daniel. She had led there ever since thinking she must be imagining it. Daniel had told her she hadn't returned from the loo. So why could she recall sitting at the table with him again? The longer she thought about it, she remembered more. They had left together and she could recall sitting in a taxi with him. But she didn't know whether to believe it. He had left an ansafone message saying he was concerned about her, so she couldn't have been in a taxi with Daniel.

Trudy tried to go back to sleep and free her mind of all the thoughts spinning round and round inside her head. But each time she closed her eyes, the mystery of Wednesday night immediately popped back and she began to go through the whole episode again, desperate to fill in the missing blanks. Each time she concentrated on the events from that night she fitted a new piece to the confused jigsaw in her mind. The problem was Trudy didn't believe her memory. She didn't know whether she was dreaming or simply imagining it all, desperate to find the truth and forcing her mind to make it all up.

Whipping off the duvet, Trudy climbed out of bed and headed downstairs, putting her dressing gown on as she left her room. The house was deadly quiet and the other girls were all still sleeping. Tina and Wendy had worked last night so they wouldn't surface until after lunch. Trudy needed a strong coffee and filled the kettle and sat at the kitchen table waiting for it to boil. She ruffled her long blonde hair and flicked it back over her forehead. Why was life so complicated, she asked herself. All she wanted was a steady relationship and just as she'd found herself a nice guy, it had all gone weird and crazy. Daniel was such a gentleman; he was stylish, good looking, fit and rich. What more could a girl want from a man! Daniel was also great company and Trudy had really enjoyed their short time together that night. They had got on well and the conversation had flowed with no awkward moments. And yet, she had walked out and left him in the bar and somehow ended up in The Conrad Hotel with a stranger!

It didn't ring true and she decided she needed to speak to Daniel to find out if he really was telling the truth. Perhaps he had taken her to the hotel and in the morning he'd had to rush off for work the next morning. But if so, why had he lied to her? It was still too early to call, she thought as she poured the hot water into the mug of milk and coffee granules. She stirred her drink and sat again. They had got in the taxi and she could remember getting out and feeling incredibly light headed. But where were they? She was trying hard to see the next few scenes in her mind. It was like trying to recall a film she had seen but later struggled to remember certain scenes.

Her mug of coffee began trembling in her hands as she recalled the next scene. She fought to catch her breath and had to quickly put the mug down before it spilt. She was in the reception of the hotel and was with Daniel! It was Daniel! She closed her eyes and again waded through her memory and confirmed her fears. She could remember getting out of the cab with Daniel and going into the Conrad Hotel. She had spent the night with him and yet he had lied and even gone to the trouble of leaving a message on the ansafone at the house. Why?

She needed to know and she rushed to phone and began dialling Daniel's number.

FORTY NINE

Sloshing the liquid back and forth, slowly the image appeared on the photographic paper. Grinning, he took a long swig of his beer from the bottle in his hand. He felt through the darkness and gently placed the bottle onto the worktop. The girl's face appeared in black and white, showing off her beautiful features cleanly and crisply. He stared into her dark eyes and then plucked her from the chemical depths and hung her up to dry on the line above him, carefully placing a cloths peg on the corner, making sure not to encroach on the image.

Rebecca Jones had climbed into the back of his taxi at Heathrow Airport and had asked to be taken to Broadgate in the City. He'd gladly obliged and had enjoyed the view in his mirror. She was dressed to kill in a sharp suit with a short grey, pleated skirt and a simple white shirt. She had a lot of paperwork with her and wore a sexy pair of tortoise-shell glasses to assist her pretty little green eyes and her black hair was trimmed into a neat bob. She was very fit and he'd enjoyed watching her slender legs strutting towards his cab when she'd first approached.

Travelling to the City had given him plenty of time to think of a suitable location to perform his latest magic. Thursday late afternoon in the City was always busy but he knew plenty of little side streets that would lend themselves perfectly. In the end he'd plumped for somewhere a bit more daring. The Kaplan Stewart Offices were on Canon Street and where better than just round the corner. He'd parked in Chapel Street just down from Canon Street tube station at six twenty, making up an excuse and then dived into the back and on her. She had struggled slightly, but it had made no difference. Once unconscious, he'd had his way with her on the floor of his taxi in broad daylight! He noticed whilst searching her handbag she worked for Bloomberg as a product trainer. Bloomberg provided specialist financial information systems and Bloomberg terminals could be found in almost every dealing room across the square mile.

After he'd taken her photo, he'd placed a packet of Cocaine in her handbag, right at the bottom amongst some old tissues and having checked for passer-bys, he then dumped her on the pavement along with the handbag. He'd then driven one block to a phone box where he'd double parked and jumped out to make a phone call. He'd dialled 999 and asked for the police. Explaining to the lady that answered, that he'd found a young lady in Chapel Street, he quickly replaced the handset when she asked for his details. Driving off, he'd headed west towards his flat, overjoyed at the thought of Frank Henson and his boys getting the news. *They would find the Cocaine and Rebecca would proclaim her innocence. Would they be clever enough to work out the Cocaine was mine? Probably not, being fucking thick.* He needed them to find Rebecca and he hadn't wanted to wait for her to pluck up the courage.

The clock is ticking ladies, we're deep into extra time and I've still got work to do. Come out, come out, wherever you are! Just three to go and then we'll blow the final fucking whistle!! He'd arrived at the lock up, switched cars and celebrated with a beer, once he'd got in.

He couldn't wait to see the next photo, of her lying in the doorway of the scooter shop. He began singing, *Me and Miss Jones!* His Frank Sinatra accent was a little corny but it made him smile. He placed another Agfa sheet in the tray and gently caressed the chemical back and forth over the paper. The glow of the dim, red light added to the tense atmosphere and his anticipation grew as he begged the image to appear. *This bit's almost as much fun as the adventure itself!* He sang at the top of his voice, stopping occasionally to check on the next photo.

He plucked the picture from the tray and gently shook it a couple of times. He held it up to the red light and admired his work. He had captured the light perfectly and laughed at the curious angle Rebecca was slumped at on the pavement, next to his taxi. *Poor little Rebecca. I'll have to invite you over to Kaplan for some training on my Bloomberg. It would be nice to catch up. Just to check you're okay and you have fully recovered from your ordeal.*

He poured the chemical from the tray into the sink and swilled the tray with cold water. He tidied up his utensils and switched off the red light and left his darkroom. Having got another beer from the fridge, he switched on his hi-fi and sat in his armchair. He flicked it on to Radio One and listened to the Pete Tong dance music show. Trudy came into his head and reminded him there were still some awkward moments to deal with. It wouldn't be long before she knew it was him with her in the hotel room. He would have to convince her she was imagining it. Maybe he could go round and see her to talk it through. He would explain he had left the bar and taken a taxi home where he got a take away pizza. He could call them to confirm it if she wished. He would begin dialling his phone and she would stop him, because she would want to believe him. He would make her believe him, to give him more time to plan his next few attacks.

The next few weeks were going to fun and it was now time to speed up the operation. *Let the final phase begin.* Laughing, he rose from his chair and began dancing to the music.

FIFTY

Frank had organised everything with the manager of the two department stores for next week and they would arrange to have a full collection of the aftershaves and eau de colognes ready for sampling. Frank explained it was a very delicate matter and he didn't want any unnecessary attention or publicity.

The cleaners he noticed, as he flicked his cigarette, had emptied the ashtray and he smiled as he thought of Roger and how surprised he'd be to see an empty ashtray on his desk. Time for a coffee, he thought and got up from his chair. The phone rang as he went for the door. No peace for the wicked.

'Henson. Yes, sure. Put them through.' It was an officer from the City police that wanted to speak to him about the cases he was working on. Detective Chief Inspector Lodge came on the phone and explained a woman had been found last night. She had been raped. The police had received a phone call from an anonymous caller who told them of the whereabouts of the woman. The call had been made from a phone box in Mansion House, about a five minute walk from the street where she had been found. DCI Lodge explained she had been unconscious when the officers arrived at the scene. She hadn't been robbed, there was no money missing from her purse. She had been taken to Guys Hospital where she had been examined. They had found semen they were able to collect. It was at forensics and the results would be known later that afternoon. Frank said that he would be right over and arranged to meet DCI Lodge at the hospital.

Frank slammed the phone down and smashed his fist down on his table, making the ashtray jump. The fucking bastard had struck again. The fact the woman had been found unconscious was enough for Frank. Why had he called it in though? He obviously wanted her to be discovered. Why? Frank walked down to the coffee machine with hundreds of thoughts whizzing in and out of his head. He watched the cup fill with the brown liquid and sugar and took it back to his office. He added the name Rebecca Jones to his file and sat staring at his wall. I feel like this bastard's playing with me. He knows I've got fuck all and it's like he's trying to help me now.

He tried calling Roger but he was away from his desk. Frank didn't leave a message. It was strange the attack had happened outside his patch. All the other rapes had taken place within three miles of his station and yet for some reason, he'd raped this victim in the City. Bloody City police and their elitist attitude, he thought. Frank had worked with the City police before and hadn't enjoyed the experience. The DCI had been so far up himself it was a wonder that he hadn't walked with a limp. They felt they were special because they were quite a small unit that covered just a two-mile radius, protecting some of the richest people and institutions in the capital. And Frank hadn't been allowed to forget it last time. The DCI had kept dropping snide remarks about how wonderful his force was compared to the normal, run of the mill forces elsewhere in London.

The DCI had changed and Frank hoped that this would make for a slightly nicer experience this time. He picked up his jacket and headed downstairs. He informed the desk sergeant that he was going to Guys Hospital, as he went to the car park. The traffic wasn't too bad and he made good time getting across to London Bridge. He parked underneath the huge hospital and made his way to Ward 6. He flashed his badge at the nurse on reception and explained he was meeting DCI Lodge. The nurse smiled and asked Frank to follow her. She knocked a door marked private and opened it.

'DS Henson I presume.' A man in a smart grey suit, white shirt and blue tie stood with his hand outstretched.

'Yes.' Frank took the hand in his and shook it. 'You must be DCI Lodge?'

'Call me Oliver. Thanks for coming over.' DCI Lodge gestured for Frank to sit down. 'We are very happy to let you deal with this. I'm not the sort of DCI that insists on keeping control of every case on my patch. It's quite obvious to me your man attacked this young lady. So I am very happy for my team to liase with you fully on this. It's your case DS Henson, and all I ask is that you keep me posted.'

'Thanks Oliver. Please, call me Frank.' Henson was amazed at DCI Lodge's reaction. Not at all like the old DCI, but Frank was very pleased. 'I can assure you that my team and me will keep you fully informed.'

'Frank, it is vital that we don't cause too much of a scene here. We have a large number of very wealthy and successful women in the City and I don't want them panicking unnecessarily. I have put a complete press ban on this incident and I don't want little pieces leaking to any of the bloody tabloids.'

'I quite understand Oliver. So what exactly happened?' Frank knew the protocol and just wanted to get to the chase.

FIFTY ONE

'Hi Trudy, how are you?' *Shit, the little bitch has remembered! I need time to think.* He thought as he answered his mobile. 'Can you hang on a sec? Let me turn my bath off.' He lied.

Placing his mobile on the table, he walked into the lounge and stood looking down on the Kings Road below. He opened his box and pulled out some Speed which he quickly dipped his finger into and then onto his tongue. The can of Coke next to the box was swiftly drunk and the vile bitterness of the powder quickly dispersed. He repeated the process then went back to the phone. The drugs effect would take a while but the simple fact he'd taken his 'medicine' made him feel better equipped to deal with Trudy's call.

'Sorry about that Trudy. How are you? I'm glad you called. I was beginning to think you didn't want to know me any more.'

'Daniel, I need to ask you a question and I want you to answer it honestly. Will you promise me you'll do this.' Trudy's voice trembled down the line.

'Of course I will. Are you okay? You sound weird.'

'Weird is not the word Daniel. I don't know what to think right now. I have been struggling to remember why I woke up on the floor of the Conrad Hotel on Wednesday and why I left a man I'd just met that I really liked. It made no sense until yesterday. I woke up yesterday morning and slowly my memory began to return. I've been trying to get hold of you since then.' Trudy paused for a moment. 'Daniel, you took me to the hotel didn't you?'

He waited to make her sweat a little. 'Trudy, I don't know what this silly game is that you're playing, but I'm not laughing. No, I didn't take you to a hotel and I still want to know why you never came back from the loo that night. You left me sitting there like a lemon. I was really concerned and I eventually asked the manager of the bar to go and check the toilets. She didn't find you and at that point I rushed out onto the street to look for you.' His voice sounded genuinely worried and stressed.

'Come on Daniel. Don't mess around. I know that you took me to that hotel. We left the bar and got a taxi and we went to the Conrad hotel. We were stood in reception together waiting for the lift. It was you! What are you trying to do to me?' Trudy voice had raised an octave and her breathing was heavier.

'Trudy, listen to me. I went home feeling upset you had dumped me. I got myself a bottle of wine and ordered a pizza from Dominos. I've got the receipt at home; I'll show it to you. I didn't go to any hotel with you Trudy I wish I had, but I didn't. What about the room? What name was it booked in?' He knew he was safe on that count.

'It wasn't your name, but so what. You could have given a false name' she argued.

'Oh Trudy, why would I? Come on, this is ridiculous! Maybe this guy you think is me, the guy that took you to this hotel, maybe he's someone else. Someone you don't want me to know about. Trudy, I really thought we could have had something. I don't know what you want me to say.' *Stupid, fucking bitch.* This was harder than he had expected.

'I want you to admit that you left the bar with me on Wednesday night and you took me to the Conrad Hotel,' she demanded.

'I've told you. After the manager checked the toilets, I went looking for you and then I went home. I then called and left an ansafone message for you and ordered an American Hot pizza from Dominos. I can't admit to something that never happened, Trudy. I'm sorry, but I can't lie.' *Well, not much anyway! By the way, you were a great fuck. Far more responsive than my usual girls!* Smiling into the handset, he waited for Trudy to respond.

Trudy wasn't so sure now. Daniel sounded so sincere and maybe it hadn't been him. Maybe she just wanted it to have been him, and for him to say it was all just a misunderstanding and that she didn't have to worry. But, instead, he was telling her he went home and had a pizza and had been really worried about her all night. So who did she go to the hotel with?

'Daniel, I am so confused. You have to believe me when I say I was sure you and I went to the hotel together. But I know how crazy that must sound to you. Did I have a lot to drink?'

Good girl! She was beginning to doubt her memory. 'You did have a few Jack Daniels and Cokes and you did stumble when you got up to go to the loo, but you weren't drunk, if that's what you mean?'

'Look, Daniel, I need to find out what happened that night. I don't know what to think. I've got so many images rushing around my head. I'd better go.'

'Trudy, can we meet? I don't want you to think badly of me. Let's meet and you can ask me face to face. Trudy, this sounds really serious. I didn't take you to a hotel, so someone did if your memory is right. Now if you thought it was me, and I promise you it wasn't, and you truly don't know who it was, that's scary. ' *Come to Daddy, you know it makes sense.*

'Tell me about it Daniel! I've been really worried ever since I heard your ansafone message. I still can't understand why I left you at the bar.'

'Trudy, let's meet. I really want to help you. I don't want you to worry. Everything is going to be fine, I promise.' *You are going to be famous, bitch. One of Daniel Freeman's little girls. Then you'll know the truth!*

'Let me sleep on it. I'll call you tomorrow.'

FIFTY TWO

I met Penny at her flat in Fulham at ten thirty. I had taken the day off so I could accompany my sister on the search for the aftershave worn by her attacker. Frank had organised a meeting with the managers of Harvey Nichols and Harrods to sample their complete range of men's aftershave and eau de cologne. Penny was convinced she would know it if she smelt it again and so Frank was very hopeful of a result today.

I set the alarm on my BMW and rang the bell to Penny's flat. The intercom crackled with Penny's voice and the door buzzed just long enough for me to let myself in. Penny greeted me with a huge hug and ushered me into her flat. The flat was simple and stark and had a damp, stuffy smell to it. It reminded me of the numerous flats I'd rented in the early days of my career. Landlords in London took the piss and got away with daylight robbery. I knew Penny was paying £175 a week for her room. That's just over £750 a month! That is way too expensive for what she got and not only that, it seemed that her flat mate was a messy cow.

'Don't look in there, Roger. That's Lucy's room.' Penny grimaced and stuck her tongue out in disgust. 'I was hoping she might have got a bit tidier in my absence. Fat chance! She's got worse.'

'It's a bomb site. How can she live like that?' I put my arm round my sister. 'So you gonna make me a coffee or what?'

'Have we got time? Didn't you say Frank's expecting us at eleven?'

'It's only ten minutes round the corner. I need caffeine, please.' I sidled up to Penny and begged her.

'Okay. I could do with a cup of tea too. So how's work?' Penny asked as she got two mugs out.

'It's been kind of tough recently. Michael Irwin has told me to reduce the size of my desk. I had to make three of the guys redundant on Monday. Not an easy task.'

'That's terrible. Does that mean you are in danger too? Is your desk losing money?'

'No. I'm fine and we're making shit loads of money. It's because the company's bringing in a new electronic trading system and it's eventually going to replace most of us. So they want to reduce numbers now, mainly to help pay for the investment in the new technology. So it's all fun and games at the moment!'

'The price you pay for living the life of a City hotshot!' Penny joked, as she handed me my coffee.

'Umm, that's good. So how are you doing? What's it like to be back?'

'I thought it would feel really strange, but I feel great and I'm so glad to be back at work too. The guys and girls there have been great.' Penny sipped her tea thoughtfully. 'Lucy has been really sweet. She cooked me a fabulous supper when I got back here and she has been looking after all my clients. Yeah, it is good to be just getting on with my life, but I'm not looking forward to today.' Her expression changed, as she looked down at the floor.

'Hey, it will be fine. That pretty little nose of yours will track the scent down and then we are one step closer to finding this bastard.' I rubbed her shoulder.

We sat in the messy lounge and talked about mum and dad and how happy they were. Penny said she'd enjoyed her time with them and they had both been really sweet and caring. She and dad had spent many hours playing 'Cluedo', the detective/murder board game. It was dad's favourite and he never seemed to tire of it. They'd played with mum and Susan, our housekeeper, as often as possible as it was useless playing with just two. It was great to see Penny back to her old self.

We left to meet Frank and arrived at reception a little after eleven. A constable led us to Henson's office.

'Now be prepared. You think your flat's messy. Wait 'til you see Frank's office!' I winked.

'Guv, the Hamiltons to see you.'

'Thanks, Randall. And don't call me Guv. We're not on the bloody Bill!' Frank opened the door with a beaming grin. His stubble was thicker than usual, the long hours beginning to show. 'Hi, come in.'

We shook hands and he kissed Penny on both cheeks. He held her slightly tighter than usual, as this was the first time he'd seen her since the rape. 'How you doing Penny? You look really great. Thank you so much for agreeing to do this today.'

'That's okay Frank, anything to help. I'm good thanks.' Penny replied, as Frank released her.

His office was the usual chaos, with paper everywhere and two ashtrays full of fag butts. The stale smell of old cigarettes hung in the air and somewhere in amongst the mess, Frank's phone was ringing.

'Excuse me. Henson.' Frank took the call.

'Can you deal with it Dave. Go through the notes and we'll sit down later this afternoon and decide the best course of action.' He put the phone down. 'More bloody red tape. Anyway, can I get you guys a drink?'

'No thanks.' I replied. 'I just had a coffee at Penny's.'

'I'm fine too thanks Frank.' Penny stated.

'We're going to Harvey Nicks first then Harrods. Shall we go now? I told the manager we would be there sometime after eleven.'

'Are you going like that Frank, you scruffy fucker?' I joked. He was his usual, casual self with a grubby white T-shirt, jeans and a brown sports jacket. His cowboy boots gave him more of a fashion director look than a policeman.

'Yeah, what's wrong with this?' He asked, brushing down his sports jacket. 'Penny, what do you think? Will I do?'

'I should say so Frank. You always look great.' Penny smiled.

'You can't ask her. She's biased. She'd say you look good in an old duffel coat.' I protested.

'Well I would look good in an old duffel coat. Thanks Penny. Shall we go?' Frank linked arms with my sister and they skipped out of Frank's office.

I followed them downstairs and into the car park at the back of the station. There was a new seven series BMW waiting for us with a driver.

'Fuck me Frank. Are you paying for this?' I joked, as we approached the car.

'No but you and all your other taxpaying mates are! I explained to the Chief that Penny was coming in today so he kindly said we could use the Diplomatic car. We do get some perks, Roger.'

I was impressed and it would certainly save us trying to find a parking space in Knightsbridge, I told Frank. Frank chatted casually as the driver picked his way through the heavy streets of South West London. Sloane Street was packed as usual and we crawled our way towards Harvey Nichols. The driver pulled up outside and jumped out to open Penny's door.

Frank led us through the doors of the exclusive department store and into the perfume hall. He approached a lady behind one of the counters and asked for Mr Birch and explained we had an appointment. The lady picked up the phone and after a short conversation, she asked us to follow her. She led us round to the lifts and asked us to go to the 4th floor where we would be greeted.

Mr Birch was a tall, slim, good-looking gentleman in his early forties and dressed impeccably. He welcomed them to Harvey Nichols and into a long, narrow boardroom. The table was covered with an amazing number of aftershave bottles of all shapes and sizes. They sat at the other end and a waiter appeared and asked them if they would like a drink.

Henson looked at his watch and asked for a cold beer. 'It's nearly lunchtime and I don't go in for this not drinking on duty lark. It helps keep my mind clear, know what I mean Roger?' He laughed.

'You keep me out of this. Gin and tonic please.'

Penny had a sparkling water and Mr Birch a glass of dry white wine.

Frank took control of the meeting and explained the bare minimum to Mr Birch. He had spoken to him last week and arranged to have their complete selection ready for today.

'Mr Henson, Harvey Nichols prides itself in stocking the widest range of perfumes and aftershaves in the country. If it's not here, it's not available to buy anywhere in the UK. You will see there are plenty of sampling papers for your use. The best way to test any scent is on these absorbent paper sticks. My assistant, Vivian, will spray each scent onto a paper stick and each stick will be recorded with the brand name of the scent.'

' Well, it sounds like you've got it all prepared. Penny if you're ready, shall we begin?'

'Yes, sure.' Penny walked to where Vivian was sitting and sat next to her. They smiled at each other and Vivian picked up the first bottle and sprayed one of the paper sticks.

Frank and I stood in the corner, watching from a far. I was trying to count the number of bottles; there must have been over a hundred, all different shapes and containing a wide spectrum of colours. Soon the room began to get heavy with the different fragrances and I began to feel a little sick. I took a big swig of my gin and tonic and felt slightly better. Frank and I whispered about the cases.

'So, how's it all been going mate?' I asked him. 'Your six o'clock shadow's becoming more of a midnight mass of hair.'

'Yeah, I know. If I'm still awake when I get home later, I'm going to trim it. We're still struggling to keep up with this bastard, Rog. He struck again on Friday.' Frank put his hand up to stop me interrupting. 'He's playing with me Roger. He raped a woman in the City, near your bloody office in fact and then called the police! He wanted us to know.'

'Are you sure he called it in?'

'Yeah. It was a man and he just gave the street name and said a woman had been raped. Before the switchboard operator could ask any questions he hung up. It's him all right and he wants us to know. Why? I've been thinking it all through. There is always a chance that this lady might not have called the police. He didn't want to take that chance. The City police found over a gram of Cocaine in her handbag and the lady swore blind that she has never used drugs of any sort. So they think he planted it there. But why? It's as if he wants to be caught.'

'Are you serious? Why would he want to be caught?' I couldn't believe he would go through all the pain and humiliation of having his identity revealed. 'And why the Cocaine? What's he trying to tell you?'

'He's a loser Roger. He's desperate for recognition. He is a weak person who wants the fame and celebrity status these rapes will bring him. The Cocaine is just him having a laugh, trying to get his victim in trouble. Most rapists and child abusers have one thing in common; they are obsessed with power, because they haven't got any. At the rate this guy's going, he's going to be one of the most prolific rapists ever. Do you remember a guy called Dan Crosby?'

'No, not really. Should I?'

'Not especially. But he was convicted of raping twelve women in 1980. He went down for twenty years. It was all over the papers and on the telly. I found the file and went through it the other day. One fucked up person. He actually raped sixteen women, the other four came forward after he'd been caught.'

'I do remember it vaguely. Twenty women, shit that's a lot. How many has our tosser raped so far?'

'Seven that we know about, but that won't be all. There are always a number of women who won't come forward, either because of fear or embarrassment, or they don't want to have to go to court.'

'Sounds like we need all the evidence we can get. Penny. How you getting on.' I stood up and went over to check on Penny.

'No joy so far, but still got about twenty more to try.'

'Keep sniffing Pen. No pressure but we need a result today.' I stroked her hair as she began sniffing yet another sample.

FIFTY THREE

I followed Frank up the stairs and back into his office. It had been a stressful afternoon and having dropped Penny back at her flat, we had returned to the station to go through all the evidence. It wasn't looking good and today we had hoped for a break, a break that never came. Penny had sniffed her way through some two hundred fragrances at both Harrods and Harvey Nichols and Frank had finally uncrossed his fingers as the lid on the last bottle was put back on. He and his team had really needed a result from my sister's sampling today. Penny was still adamant that she knew the smell and would recognise it if she smelled it again.

Frank plonked himself down and held his head in his hands. 'I get a bit excited, think I see a slight glimmer of hope, think we're turning a corner and it just ends up being another bloody dead-end.'

'Hey come on mate. Every negative has a positive. We now know whatever this aftershave is, it's got to be pretty specialised. It must be from an exclusive perfume manufacturer. This means that this cab driver has expensive tastes. Now, to me that doesn't sound like your run of the mill cabbie and he can afford Cocaine.' I was trying to remain focused. It was tough because I too was disappointed. Like Frank, I had expected Penny to find the aftershave her attacker had worn. So I did understand how Henson was feeling but I needed to keep his mind on the job.

'Yeah, you're right Roger. But you know, it's so hard waking up every day knowing you're no nearer the truth and meanwhile the sick fuck is still out there and he could be about to strike at any time. I'm just desperate to catch this psycho and today I let my emotions take over and felt certain by now we would know the brand of aftershave.' Frank shook his head.

'Yeah, but you know what Frank? I'm relieved in a way. What would you have done if the aftershave this guy wears had been Cacherel or Polo. How on earth would we have tracked him down? There must be thousands and thousands of men in London who wear them. At least we now know this aftershave is more exclusive so therefore when we do trace it we should stand more chance of finding him. If it's exclusive, there can't be so many customers in London, you know?'

'Yes, you're right mate. You should be a copper! I need a coffee, come on let's go to my wonderful little vending machine.' He smiled and slapped me on the back as he passed me.

'Good idea.' I didn't want vending machine coffee, but I did need caffeine so it would have to do. I followed Henson along the corridor. 'Frank, we will get this guy. I can feel it. Let's go through everything together and see where we are.'

Frank agreed and having got our cheap plastic coffees, we headed back to begin our brainstorming session.

'Frank, I was thinking about what I said just now. This elusive fragrance is a bit exclusive for a London cab driver. Do you still think you're looking for a taxi driver?' I didn't think so.

'Do you know what, I'm still waiting for my team to bring me the results of all those interviews and alibis. I remember young Dave saying a similar thing after the third rape. I told him not to be so stupid. But at that time we still had over eighteen thousand drivers to weed our way through. But, you're right. It seems far more likely that the rapist is not a cab driver.' Frank tapped his pencil against a pile of papers in his in-tray.

'So, if I wanted to buy a black taxi, where or how would I do it?'

'Great question Rog. I have no idea, but Dobson is looking into that at the moment.' Frank reached into the expanse of paperwork and pulled out a green folder. He opened it and scanned one of the sheets of paper. 'There's only one company that manufactures the taxi, London Taxis International and they are in Kent. I think you have to produce documents to show you are a licensed driver with the London Carriage Office. Also, all London taxis now have to have licensed number plates too. They have to be renewed annually so our guy must know all this. Any taxi not licensed is very easy to spot and would be pulled and checked.' Frank explained. 'And from the number of attacks our man has committed, we have to assume that he's done plenty of driving around London over the last few months.'

It was impressive listening to Frank reason everything through and even though his desk was a mess, he knew where every file and folder was. Rather than having a filing cabinet, it seemed that Frank used his desk as his filing system. There was no way I could work in a state of disarray like my mate, but it obviously worked for him. The cigarette smoke was beginning to irritate me so I asked Frank to open a window.

'The other lead we should have is he takes photos of all his victims. Well, it would appear he does. Three of the girls can remember seeing a flash and one heard a camera clicking and Penny says that she can remember a feeling of being photographed. So what can we assume from that?' Frank sat studying me.

'He's an amateur photographer. He collects pictures of all his victims. He's a sick fuck! Do you think he keeps them in an album?' I joked.

'That's exactly what I think Roger.' Frank was far more serious than I'd expected. 'He's documenting everything. He's keeping mementoes of his escapades. But there's more. What else Rog?'

'I don't know Frank. Come on, you're better at this stuff than me. What else?'

'The photos, what else could we know?' He paused to give me time to think. My mind was blank. Frank continued. 'To get the pictures after he's taken them, he needs to develop them.'

'Right!' I jumped back in. 'Of course. So where does he get them developed? What kind of film does he use? What make of camera is it?' I was in the flow.

'Atta boy Hamilton. We'll make a detective out of you yet! Exactly. He has to develop them somehow, so someone must have seen the photos. But our guys have tried every developer they know from Boots to Jessops online and nothing. So we figure he must have a dark room and develops them himself. So that leaves us with the brand of film and the paper he uses to develop the photos.'

'Shit. So where do you start? What a nightmare mate. No wonder you need the aftershave lead.' I realised the only break we were going to get was if he messed up next time. And that meant having to wait for more rapes and innocent victims. 'There must be something else we can do.'

'Roger. We'll get there; somehow we will get this pervert. We know now that he dabbles in drugs. Where would he be getting his coke from?'

'Shit! In this city he could be getting it from anywhere. There must be thousands of pushers in London.'

'Yep. You're right and I have no way of tracing that coke. It makes me fucking sick thinking he could be out there right now, about to strike again.' Frank shook his head.

I got up and went to the window. I watched a young girl walking towards the Kings Road and the traffic buzzing along and I couldn't help thinking what an awful job Frank's was. The world never stopped. The clock of life just kept ticking and people everywhere were going about their normal business and amongst them were some truly weird and sick freaks that didn't deserve the freedom they had. Poor Frank and his team, meanwhile, were banging their heads against brick wall after brick wall. I reached into my jacket for my fags and felt a card.

'Oh Frank. I almost forgot. Brian gave me this to give to you.' I handed Frank the invite to Griffo's party. 'He's having a party next week and wanted you to be there. Maybe you could bring Isabelle?'

'Excellent. I could do with a bit of a wild night. I haven't been to a party in a long while.'

FIFTY FOUR

The phone rang three times before my father answered.

'Hi Dad, it's me. I need to ask you a favour.'

'Oh dear! I know that tone Roger. What do you need this time?' Dad joked. I was always going to him for advice on various things and I always relied on my dad to supply me with tickets for the Autosport Award Dinner every year. He always tried to wind me up and pretend everything I needed was a huge problem to him.

'Well, I hate to ask, but I'd like to race for the Jordan team next year. Can you sort it out for me, Dad. I'm free for a test session at Silverstone next week.'

'Yeah no problem son. I'm sure Eddie Jordan won't mind removing Trulli or Frentzen to make room for a driver of your calibre.' My father chuckled. How are you Roger?'

'Great thanks Dad. Are you and Mum keeping yourselves out of mischief?'

'We seem to be. Now what's this favour you need?

'Michael Irwin has asked me if I can get him four tickets with hospitality for the British Grand Prix. I wouldn't mind if it was for a friend. I very nearly didn't call you at all. Why should I have to pander to people like him?' It really pissed me off.

'Hey, now come on Roger. You know how it is in business. You scratch his back and he scratches yours. He's your boss Roger. You do things like this to keep him sweet.'

'I know what you mean Dad, but you help him because that's what he expects and count your lucky stars that he's still employing you!'

'Roger, I understand how it is. How do you think it was working with Bernie in the old days, just as he was rising up through the ranks and becoming more powerful with each race? It was no different. I will gladly get Michael Irwin the tickets he needs, but he'll have to pay for them.'

'That's no problem Dad. I'll give you the cash next time I see you. Thanks for doing this. I know what you mean about Michael, he pays me well so I shouldn't begrudge it so much. Are you going to be there?'

'I am actually. Eddie has invited me and I'm sure if you and Emma wanted to come along, he wouldn't mind. You could meet me at Battersea and we can all fly in together. What do you think?'

'Dad, that sounds great, but I may have to take clients. Can I let you know?' My dad was generous to a fault.

'Yep, of course. Just make sure you do before next week. If you need tickets for anyone else, let me know.'

'Thanks Dad.'

'How's Penny? Didn't you and Frank see her earlier this week for this aftershave thing?'

I smiled at my dad's vagueness. 'Yes. She seems really good. She agreed to help Frank with the investigation. She was trying to find the fragrance her attacker was wearing the night he assaulted her. We went to two big stores in London and Pen must have sniffed her way through nearly two hundred different aftershaves and eau de colognes. Frank and I were hoping she would come up trumps, but she didn't.'

'What a shame. But if Penny says she can still remember it, I'm sure she's right. It must be bloody awful for poor old Frank. How is he? Is he doing OK?'

My father had always been very fond of Henson and even though he didn't see much of him these days, dad always asked how he was. 'He's as well as can be expected. I think he's finding it all very stressful and just desperate for a break, you know? He just needs a bit of luck, but the trouble with police work is you can't rely on bloody luck.'

'Well, send him my regards anyway and tell him to come and see us sometime. How's work? Have this bloody Labour Government messed things up for you guys?'

I laughed. 'Not half. They are paying off debt like it's going out of fashion. At this rate we won't have any bonds left to broke! I think I'll join the police force. At least there are always plenty of bloody criminals to catch. But, business is actually quite good. It will slow down, but it's fine at the moment. I'd better run. Thanks for sorting out the tickets. I'll call you and let you know if Emma and I can make it.'

As I clicked the line off, I felt a slap on the back. 'Roger, my old mucker. How the fuck are you?'

I turned round to see Spanner stood over me. He worked on the Forwards desk behind mine and was a big burly guy who drank too much, ate too much and talked too much! He was known as Spanner because he used to be a car mechanic before he came into broking.

'Spanner! How are you?' I swung the chair next to me round, and invited him to plonk his big backside down.

'Alright mate. Biz is shit but what do I care? They're still paying me!' He chortled loudly. 'How you doing on the World Cup then?'

I hadn't checked my positions for ages. Getting involved in Frank's investigation had taken my eyes off the ball. 'To be honest mate, I've been so bloody busy I haven't checked for a while.'

'Busy? You guys? You gotta be fuckin' kiddin'! We do more in most mornings than you do all week!' He punched me playfully, and I could feel the bruise immediately forming! He was right. His desk was one of the busiest on our floor. We struggled to hear our customers some mornings when Spanner and his henchmen were screaming at each other.

'Spanner, you'd better make hay while the sun's shining. You're fucked once the Euro kicks in. Give it a couple of years and you'll be back under a car fitting exhausts again.' I winked at him, just so that he knew I was kidding and I could avoid another punch. 'How are your bets doing?'

'Superb mate. You know me. They don't call me golden Spanner for nothin'. Everything I touch turns to gold. I sold yellow cards and I'm long of the Frogs, so I should be all right. Going long of England wasn't a great move. Fucking twats couldn't play netball, let alone football.'

'So Roger, who do you think's going to make the finals? I reckon it's gonna be a Holland and France.'

'Bollocks. There is no way the Dutch will beat the Brazilians. Nope, it's gonna be Brazil and France and Brazil will win three, nil and make me even richer.' There was nothing like a bit of banter to help on a boring Tuesday.

'Well, we'll see won't we. So how much you up then?'

'It looks like just over two grand so far.' I smiled at Spanner.

'Not bad.' Spanner began walking away.

'Hang on mate.' I called him back. 'What about you?'

'Not that much, you lucky tosser.' Spanner gave me a wanker sign as he scuttled off.

I work with such nice people, I thought, sarcastically, as I sipped my coffee.

FIFTY FIVE

The rain outside matched Penny's mood. The doodles on her pad had started as a few distracted patterns but had slowly grown into a wild patchwork of blue lines and shapes. She had been working a Veuve Clicquot guest list for the World Cup final in France, but couldn't concentrate. Her mind was on yesterday's aftershave hunt. Penny had been convinced she would find the fragrance amongst the vast array put in front of her. She knew how desperate Frank was for a new lead and wanted to help. But it also went much deeper than that; it wasn't just about the investigation or simply catching the bastard. To Penny it was about her fellow victims and preventing the next one from suffering like she and the others had, and if she'd identified the fragrance yesterday, it might just have helped. It was only a small clue, but bigger crimes had been solved from smaller clues.

Penny was so angry the bastard who attacked her was still at large. Living his life and enjoying himself and probably planning his next assault, while Penny was just about managing to begin again. His memories were sick and twisted whereas hers were painful and impossible to erase. She was going to have live with it for the rest of her life. Parcelled up in the 'I've been raped' box along with all the other innocent victims. She knew some girls would bury it and pretend it didn't happen but that wasn't Penny. She was a fighter and she was prepared to do anything to get this bastard caught and behind bars, even if it meant standing up in court to give evidence. If that's what she had to do, Penny was prepared. She couldn't just let him get away with it.

'Penny, how's the guest list coming along?' Lucy interrupted Penny's thoughts. 'The guest list. How's it coming along?' Lucy could see tears on Penny's cheeks. 'You okay Penny?'

'Yeah sure. I'm fine.' Penny looked away and wiped her cheeks. 'It's coming along okay. I've had trouble getting hold of Elton John's people and as we thought, Joan Collins is not in the slightest bit interested in football.'

'Surprise, surprise. Why don't Rupert and his people think about these things logically?' Lucy shook her head. 'I'm going to lunch, come with me. When we get back, we can attack the list together.'

Penny was glad of the offer and they headed out the door and into the heart of Soho. The company's offices were in Golden Square, the hub of the media, advertising and PR circus. There were loads of trendy bars and restaurants and pubs all within a square mile and some of London's finest restaurants were only streets away. The girls decided on a coffee first and went into Starbucks. Penny ordered a latté and Lucy a cappuccino with two sugars. They sat at the long bar by the window, where they could watch the world go by. Lucy knew Penny was upset but decided against prying too much. The night that Penny returned to the flat, they'd had a good talk and she'd opened her heart over a bottle of red wine and pasta. Even though Penny had gone into details and discussed how she felt and how determined she was to get her life back on track, Lucy still couldn't imagine fully how she would feel if she'd had gone through Penny's ordeal.

'It's so good to have you back Penny. I've really missed you at work and at the flat.' Lucy tried to cheer her friend up.

'Thanks. That's a lovely thing to say. I couldn't stay cooped up here for much longer and anyway, being back at work takes my mind off everything.'

'So are you going to France or do I have to? I suppose I have to.' Lucy decided to change the subject back to work.

'Why don't we both go?' Penny thought it would be good to go to the World Cup finals. She wasn't that interested in football, but both her brother and dad hadn't stopped going on about it and she had got swept up in the media hype. She never liked to admit it, but she had become a bit of a Ronaldo fan! She told Lucy and they both laughed. Lucy said it was worth watching them just for their sexy legs and pert bums. They agreed they would both go and as Penny pointed out; from the size of the guest list, they would both be needed just to socialise and ensure the clients were enjoying themselves.

Veuve Clicquot didn't do things by halves and they had asked for a full corporate event to be organised. The lucky invitees were to be flown by helicopter from Battersea in London to a private site just outside Silverstone, where they would be picked up and taken to the British Grand Prix. There they would enjoy all the benefits of Paddock Club VIP tickets before flying to Birmingham, where there would be a fleet of private jets waiting to take them to Paris. There they would enjoy a four-course meal before watching the World Cup final from the best seats in the stadium. It was being called the ultimate day of sport.

'Roger is going to be so envious when I tell him. You know he works in the City and he has clients that expect this kind of package all the time. They are so arrogant, Lucy, it's unbelievable. They call up and say "Get me tickets for Wimbledon will you?" and then put the phone down.'

'No way. That is so rude. How does Roger put up with it?' Lucy was amazed.

'Luckily, Roger has some really nice clients and they don't try it on too much. He wouldn't let them anyway. Even his boss asked Roger to get him some tickets for the Grand Prix. Roger was so angry, but daddy is so generous he told Roger it would be fine. I am so glad we work with refined clients like Veuve Clicquot. I couldn't work in the City.' Penny commented, finishing the dregs of her latté. 'To be honest, I can't believe I've agreed to it, but I'm going to a party with Roger tomorrow night. I'm not sure I'm ready for a crowded room full of guys from the City.'

'Oh I don't know, that sounds like my kind of party Penny! Whose party is it?'

'It's Roger's number two, Brian Griffin. He's a really nice guy and he's organised a barbeque and the invites are nice, but I didn't want to go. But you know Roger, once he got going I couldn't refuse him and I think he's right, it should do me good.'

'Penny, you'll have a great time. Just go and enjoy yourself. Where is it?'

'On the Kings Road somewhere, so I'm staying with Roger.'

'That's nice, I know you'll come in on Monday and tell me you had the best time. How did you get on with the police the other day?'

'Oh it was so disappointing Lucy. I was really hoping that I could help but it was a bit of a waste of time really.' Penny told Lucy all about the day she'd spent sniffing aftershaves.

'That's not a waste of time Penny. At least now they know it's a slightly more exclusive brand. And more to the point, at least you are trying to help. I am so proud of you.'

'Shall we go and grab a sandwich?' Penny suggested, as Lucy polished off her drink.

The girls left Starbucks and headed for their local sandwich shop, unaware they were being watched.

FIFTY SIX

The slot in the turnstile swallowed the ticket and he pushed the metal arm forward and walked out of Leicester Square tube station. *Fucking people, fucking foreigners everywhere. Why did people use the tube? It was filthy, it stank and it was full of fucking commuters.* But parking in the West End was a nightmare and he knew the tube would be the easier option for today's fun. Barging between groups of tourists, he made his way along Charing Cross Road and up to Shaftesbury Avenue.

Today, he was going to be a peeping tom. He was visiting some of his previous girlfriends and Penny Hamilton was first on his list. Plus, he wanted to check her out again, before his party tomorrow night. He opened his wallet and pulled out her driving licence to look at her photo again. The picture wasn't too clear but he would know her when he saw her. He knew from previous conversations with Roger she worked for Marble Mayhew, a PR agency in Golden Square.

Turning right into Greek Street would take him into the heart of Soho. This place wasn't his favourite. A lot of the bars in the area were gay bars and he grimaced as he passed two guys holding hands. *You fucking poofs. You'll be next. Before I go down I'll take a couple of you with me.* He hurried up Greek Street and into Soho Square where he turned left and before long he was in Golden Square. The address was firmly imprinted on his mind and he stood outside looking at the brass plaque. Turning round he spotted a seat in a café opposite. *Perfect. A cappuccino and a newspaper will hide me nicely as I wait for you Penny.* He asked the waiter if they had a toilet he could use and was directed downstairs. Once in the cubicle, he unravelled a packet of Speed and took two generous portions and winced at the taste. Two pills followed them and he took a couple of swigs from the cold tap on his way out.

He sat sipping the hot coffee, with the newspaper on his lap. Jigging his leg impatiently, he checked his watch. It was eleven forty and he was hoping Penny would be taking an early lunch. He picked up the newspaper and noticed an article about him on page three. 'Serial Rapist strikes again.' London police are on red alert now as another girl is raped in the capital. She was found in Chapel Street last Thursday. Police are appealing for witnesses who may have left work between six and six thirty that evening. There are plenty of pubs in the locality and police are hopeful that someone will have seen something.

He smiled as he read the article. *I chose Chapel Street because it's a dead end and it's the quietest street in the area. Witnesses, they'll be lucky.* He closed the paper and glanced up from the table.

It was another twenty minutes before Penny Hamilton appeared from the front door of her office, with another girl. He quickly put his coffee cup back on the table and sat upright, not taking his eyes off the two girls. He smiled as he watched Penny flick her hand through her hair, and then apply lip balm. *I remember those lips! She looks as good as ever!* He looked round desperately for a waiter so he could settle his bill. *There is never a fucking waiter when you want one.* He finally caught the attention of one and asked for the bill. He looked back across at the girls as they began crossing the road. His breath grew rapid as the girls came nearer and as they passed the café, he held his breath. *Penny, you look great. I can still see those amazing breasts of yours sitting pert and proud below that beautiful face. You ready to party tomorrow night baby?* Penny and her friend disappeared into Starbucks three doors down and he quickly plonked some coins onto the bill that the waiter had finally brought. He hurried out of his seat and followed the girls into Starbucks.

They were deciding on what to have and he stood quietly in line behind them. As he breathed in, he could detect Penny's perfume lightly wafting his way. He felt a flicker in his crotch and smiled. *See you tomorrow night honey!* He took in one final waft and turned on his heels and left. *It's nice to know she's doing okay.*

He headed back to the tube but changed his mind as he reached Shaftesbury Avenue. He hailed the black cab that was approaching and jumped in. He told the driver that he wanted to go to Fulham Broadway.

Sitting in the back of the taxi gave him time to mull things over. *Frank Henson would be sifting through the details of Rebecca Jones' attack by now.* Smiling, as he looked out of the window, he imagined Frank trying to work out why he had called the police to report his attack. *The stupid fuck! I suppose you want me to wipe your arse too!* He went through all the girls he'd raped so far. He knew exactly how many more would take him over the crucial target of twenty. He'd missed Amanda Worthington and today he was going to pay her a little visit too.

He asked the taxi driver to stop outside Fulham Broadway tube station. He threw the driver a tenner and walked across into Harwood Road. About fifty yards along on the left was Foxtons, where he hoped to find Miss Worthington. He walked straight past once, just to have a look in, to check to see if she was in. *Bingo! Hi Amanda honey. You're looking good considering everything you've been through.*

'Good afternoon. Can I help you?' Amanda asked the gentleman that had entered.

'Yes. I'm looking for something a little bit special and I heard that Foxtons would have something up my street.' *Good to see you again Amanda.*

FIFTY SEVEN

'Do you know where the loo is Roger?' Penny asked.

'Yeah, there's one just down the hall or I think he's got an ensuite in his bedroom. Just follow the hall down past the dining room.' I told her. I took her glass as she handed it to me.

Penny squeezed her slim frame through the smoky crowd. The hallway was filled with guests and the toilet was locked, so she headed for Brian's ensuite. She passed the dining room that was laid out with food and drink. There was a long table against the far wall with an array of delicacies, from sandwiches to chicken satay; and king prawns to fresh lobster. Brian hadn't skimped on the catering and there were five or six waiters stood, ready to serve, dressed very smartly in black and white.

Penny tried the door next to the dining room and was surprised to find it locked. The door next to it was slightly ajar and from a quick glance she realised it was Brian's bedroom. She entered and noticed how unusually tidy the room was. Unusual because it was a man's bedroom, she thought as she went into the bathroom.

The bathroom was clean and bright, almost clinical with white tiles on the walls and black and white tiles on the floor. Penny was amazed to find the loo seat down and smiled as she sat down, even the loo roll was velvety soft, she thought as she gently felt the paper. She almost expected to find a couple of labrador puppies frolicking around her ankles. As she relieved herself she noticed the huge bath with side taps and the amazing power shower in the far corner of the large bathroom. It was just like Roger's she thought as she pulled her knickers back up. As she washed her hands, she examined the small shelf above the basin and her gaze was drawn to a bottle of aftershave. It was an unusual shape and the glass was a bright green with a silver lid. Penny washed her hands with the wonderful Molton Brown sandalwood soap. She dried her hands and picked up the green bottle. 'Chamois' by Fragonard, read the label. Penny unscrewed the lid, lifted the bottle up to her nose and immediately dropped it. The glass smashed on impact spraying liquid over the bathroom floor.

Penny began trembling uncontrollably and staggered back against the door. She couldn't take her eyes off the light brown liquid slowly spreading over the black and white tiles. She was frozen to the spot and her mind was devoid of all thoughts. Her breathing was out of control and she spun round to reach for the key, fumbling furiously with it, trying to unlock the door. She was panicking badly now and was hyperventilating. Try as she did, the key refused to turn and Penny began to sob. The smell of the aftershave was still deep within her nostrils. The same smell from that night at Paddington. It was the aftershave the rapist had been wearing when she'd been attacked. Deep, musky, almost burnt almonds with the tiniest hint of tobacco. Still the key wouldn't turn and Penny sank to her knees and just shook.

She couldn't believe the coincidence that Brian wore the same unusual cologne that the guy who attacked her had worn. She hadn't really held out much hope for Frank and his team tracing the aftershave, particularly when they had sifted through every conceivable brand Harvey Nichols and Harrods sold. Yet, here she was trapped in a bathroom in Chelsea, probably within a quarter of a mile of where she'd been raped, on the same road where the police had found her, and she had just discovered the very brand they had been looking for. It was all she could smell. The stylish bottle was now in pieces and the air was thick with the smell and she shuddered as she breathed in an invisible cloud of the acrid scent. It brought back so much hurt and pain. What were the chances of finding someone in West London, where all the rapes had happened, who used Chamois? Slim to virtually impossible and yet Brian used it! Could it have been Brian? Don't be so stupid, she told herself. There must be lots of guys in London who bought the same brand. Brian works with Roger, they've been friends for years. But she couldn't shrug off the slight nagging doubt. It could simply be a coincidence or it could be one huge nightmare.

Penny got up and went over to the sink. She looked terrible, her eyes were really bloodshot and her mascara had run down both cheeks. She needed to calm down if she was to make it back to Roger without causing a scene. She just wanted to get out now. She washed her face in the sink and removed and reapplied her mascara and some lipstick and began to fell slightly better. She looked down at the mess on the floor but couldn't bring herself to clean it up. She took a deep breath and turned the key again. The door unlocked and Penny breathed a big sigh of relief. She quickly checked her face and hair in the mirror before opening the door and jumped back in terror!

'Hi Penny. I didn't mean to startle you. Sorry I didn't realise anyone was in here.' Brian was stood in his bedroom half naked, his hunky chest and biceps standing proud. 'Is everything OK? You looked a bit stressed.'

Penny struggled to keep her breathing under control. 'Uuh. Yeah, I'm fine, just a bit embarrassed. I'm really sorry, but I accidentally dropped your aftershave bottle and it's smashed on the floor.' She was holding it together well.

'Penny, don't worry. It's not a big deal.' Brian pulled on an Armani shirt, jet-black and perfectly pressed. 'I have plenty more where that came from. Sorry about my state of undress, I just spilt beer over myself.'

'I didn't clean it up 'cause there's bits of glass everywhere. Have you got a cloth?' Penny noticed his eyes and was beginning to panic again.

'Don't worry about it. I'll get one of the waiters to come in and clean it up.' Brian approached her. *I could have you again right here, you little bitch. You have no idea who I really am do you?* He gently rubbed her shoulder and said 'Get back to the party and enjoy yourself.'

Penny didn't need to be asked twice. She made her way back to the crowded room where she'd left her brother and quickly found him.

'Roger. I want to go and I want to go right now, please.'

'Penny, what's the matter?' I was concerned.

'Everything!' Penny was trembling. 'Can we just go?'

'But the party hasn't got going yet Pen. What's the big hurry? We don't even know what Brian's celebrating yet!' I couldn't understand it. I knew that she would enjoy herself if only she would just relax. I had spent all week trying to convince her to come and now we were here, she wanted to leave. But she did seem very troubled. 'Penny, if you want to go, we'll go, but aren't you hungry? What about all the lovely food next door? And what about Frank and Isabella?'

'They'll be fine. Come on please.' Penny was desperate to get out and couldn't bear to be in Brian's flat for a moment longer. 'And sod Brian and his bloody food.'

I wanted to explain to Henson, but he'd gone to the kitchen with Isabella and it would take me forever through the rugby scrum of people. 'It's only nine thirty, shall we grab some food somewhere?'

'Whatever. Let's just go.' Penny grabbed my arm.

'I should thank Brian.' I suggested, but Penny was already by the front door.

We headed to the lift and waited. Penny played nervously with her necklace, saying nothing. We got onto the Kings Road and headed up towards Sloane Square.

'What do you fancy for dinner? We could eat at Benihana if you like.'

'I just want a coffee.'

'Ok, how about MacDonalds?' I took Penny's hand as we made our way up the steps and into the burger bar.

We ordered a couple of coffees and sat in a booth over looking the Kings Road.

'Roger, how well do you know Brian?' Penny asked me, stirring sugar into her polystyrene cup.

'I've worked with him for five years. Why?'

'He wears Chamois by Fragonard.' Penny's eyes began to well up.

'Penny what's wrong? What do you mean he wears whatever it was you said?' Penny looked as if she was about to burst into tears.

'He wears that aftershave. That bloody aftershave.' She took a sip of her coffee. 'It's the one we've been looking for.'

'I don't follow. What's Brian's aftershave got to do with …' I stopped mid-sentence. I suddenly understood what Penny meant and felt a huge rush of adrenalin. 'You mean Brian wears the same aftershave as..'

'Yes!' Penny burst into tears and fumbled in her handbag for a tissue. I reached across for her hand and rubbed it caringly. I hated to see my sister go through such anguish. She blew her nose and wiped the tears from her cheeks. She looked at me through bloodshot eyes.

'I noticed the bottle on a shelf above his basin and when I smelt it, I panicked and dropped it. It smashed on his bathroom floor. I knew I'd recognise it if I smelt it again, but I didn't expect to feel like that. It was horrible Roger. It was like being back in the taxi.' She stopped and hugged her cup with both hands and stared deep into her coffee.

'What's it called?' I asked.

'Chamois. By Fragonard.' Penny shook her head and looked out of the window.

My eyes followed hers outside. The road was still busy and the light of the dusk evening meant most cars had their headlights on. A '**www.ntwebhost.co.uk Professional Web Hosting. Your Choice.**' advert whizzed by on the side of a red double decker bus. It made me think I could look for the aftershave company on the Internet.

'Chamois.' I repeated. I vaguely remembered Griffo discussing it with Frank and me a few days ago. I think it was French, but then I was no eau de cologne expert. I stuck to mainstream brands like Hugo Boss and Ralph Lauren. 'I'll call Frank and let him know.' I stated, as I pulled out my mobile.

'No, not yet Roger. Call him tomorrow. I need to think this all through and discuss it with you. It's all so muddled.'

I put the phone down and looked at Penny. 'We will catch this bastard, you do believe that don't you Penny?' She nodded slowly. 'What did you mean when you asked me how well do I know Brian?'

'I don't know.' She blew her nose again and scratched her pretty head. 'When I came out of the bathroom, Brian was stood in his bedroom and I just felt really weird. You know? It's difficult to explain. He didn't have a shirt on and his body was amazing, very muscular and I suddenly flashed back to that terrible night and even though the bastard seemed overweight, I remember his arms being really muscular and his eyes.' Penny shook her head again, as if she was trying to shake off those memories.

'Pen, I'm sorry but I cannot believe for one minute that Brian Griffin is the rapist. That's absolutely ridiculous!' I protested. I felt for Penny and what she had been through, but there was no way that Griffo was a rapist.

'I know Roger, but he's got the same horrible eyes and he's muscular and he wears the same fucking aftershave! I can't help how I feel.'

I had met Brian in the early nineties when he joined Kaplan from Butlers. He was flash, drove a 355 Ferrari Spider, fancied himself, but he also seemed slightly odd. He didn't have a girlfriend, very rarely went out and tried to avoid client entertainment as much as possible and always returned home to some stately home in the country at the weekends. The number plate on his car was "DAN 20" which I'd quizzed him about. He'd told me it had been his mother's and when she'd died, he'd kept it until he could drive. He'd had it on every car he'd owned. He never talked about his family and most of the guys on the desk thought he was gay. But he was a brilliant broker and that's why Gareth Miller had employed him. I was amazed he wore the same aftershave and it was one hell of a coincidence, but there was no chance Brian would have raped Penny, let alone the other twelve or however many there had been so far. 'No way, Penny.'

'It was him, I know it Roger. I just know it.' Penny was shaking again.

'Penny, I work with the guy, I've got drunk with him. He's my number two. My right hand man. Brian is not this bastard that Frank's looking for.' I argued.

'I know how crazy it sounds Roger. Please believe me. I just have this awful foreboding.' She squeezed my hand hard.

'If you hadn't smelt the aftershave you wouldn't be thinking like this. Let's just take it slowly. I will speak to Frank and we will find out who or what Fragonard is and where they are located. I'm sure Henson and his team will be able to acquire a list of retailers who stock the stuff and then they will be able to trace the customers who have bought Chamois. The main thing that you are forgetting is that Brian is not a taxi driver.'

'Oh Roger. I know, I know. You are right. I'm not thinking straight. I have been cooped up at Mum and Dad's for too long and the first night I have out for ages turns out to be the night from hell. I'd just begun to get over it and now I'm as scared as ever.'

'Penny, I know it's hard, but you must try and look on the bright side. We now know the brand of aftershave and you've got nothing to be scared of. I will not let anything else ever happen to you, I promise, and I promise that we will get this guy.'

'Thanks Roger. Can we go home now please?' Penny stood up and gave me a big hug.

She was staying with me and Emma and we were spending Sunday at our parent's house. We walked back to my car and I drove us the short distance to South Kensington. I'd decided not to drink so I could drive. That way we didn't have to rely on taxis, as I knew that Penny wasn't ready to face that ordeal yet. Emma was still at the Holmes Place party when we got back. It was just gone ten thirty and I asked Penny if she wanted a drink.

'No thanks. I'm going to bed. I've had enough for night! Thanks for being so understanding.' She kissed me and headed off to the spare room.

'There's a clean towel on your bed. Sleep tight.'

FIFTY EIGHT

I didn't sleep well and I rose early and sat watching Transworld Sport on Channel Four. I was worried about Penny. Taking her to Brian's party had turned out not to be such a great idea. She seemed okay after we'd left MacDonalds but before going to bed, Penny had made me promise I would speak to Brian. She was still convinced that Brian was the rapist and she was horrified I was going to the British Grand Prix with him today.

I was taking Andrew Duncan from Morgan's and Brian was taking Tony Stewart from Lehman's. It should be a great day and we had both been looking forward to it. Brian was meeting me at my flat and we were jumping in a cab and picking the customers up on the way to Battersea Heliport. Dad had organised everything for me and Michael Irwin had also been very pleased with the package Dad had managed to get sorted for him. Should keep him happy for a while.

Brian had tried to persuade me to include tickets to the World Cup final in Paris but I couldn't really justify the expenses. Penny and her flatmate Lucy were doing the ultimate day of sport, which comprised of the Grand Prix and then going straight to the cup final in Paris. Penny had told me that it was costing Veuve Clicquot two thousand pounds a head and there was no way that Michael Irwin would wear that.

I knocked gently on Penny's door and asked her if she wanted a coffee. She had to be back at her flat fairly early so that she and Lucy could get over to their offices where they were meeting all their clients.

Brian arrived about ten minutes after Penny left and as I buzzed him in, I felt my stomach knot up at the thought of confronting him. I was still convinced that Penny was wrong and it was just a coincidence Brian wore the same aftershave as the guy Frank was hunting. I had worked with him for years and there was no way he was a rapist. I took two deep breaths as I opened the front door.

'Hi Roger. This is going to be a blast. I could hardly sleep last night with excitement.' Brian shook my hand and I directed him in. 'What happened to you and Penny last night? You left so early, you missed all the fun.'

'Penny didn't feel well. So what were you celebrating? We left before your big announcement.' I couldn't bring myself to confront him as soon as he'd arrived.

'Oh nothing. It was a wind-up. If everyone thought it was more than a simple party, I knew more people would turn up.'

'You crafty bugger. So you haven't won the Lottery then?'

'No mate, well not yet anyway.' *All in good time Mr Hamilton!*

I checked my watch. 'The cab should be here by now. I booked it for ten. Let's go.'

'I saw one sat outside, I wondered if it was ours. Hope it's not that bastard Frank's looking for, driving it.'

'Let's hope not.' There's no way Brian is our man, I thought, not with comments like that. He thinks just like me. 'Do you wonder every time you get in a taxi Brian? Cause I know I do. Silly really, but I can't help it.'

Of course I don't, you stupid fuck. I know it's me!! He laughed. 'Yeah, I can't help it either. It always makes me think of poor old Frank and his investigation. How's it going?' Brian asked, as we headed down to the taxi.

'Still pretty slow but,' I took in a deep breath and watched Brian's face very closely without blinking. I may as well get it over with sooner rather than later. 'Penny thinks she knows who did it. She is convinced her attacker is ……you.' I let my statement hang in the air. We were stood on the pavement next to the taxi. His face didn't change, nothing, not even a flinch, and then a look of complete shock. Was it him?

'Me! You've got to be kidding! Where the hell did she get that idea? Are you winding me up mate?' *Jesus, fucking H Christ! Fucking Bitch! What does she know? Is he bluffing? Frank must have uncovered something, but what? Be calm, Daniel, calm down. You can deal with this. I need something to get me through this. This is not happening.*

'No I'm not winding you up.' I didn't want to side with him yet. I didn't believe Penny either, but I had to suss him out. 'She is convinced you are the rapist. Tell me Brian. It's you, isn't it?' I took a couple of steps back from him for effect.

I could run now. He wouldn't catch me. I could disappear and neither he nor Henson would find me. If I stay and he does know it's me, then I'm in all sorts of shit. But does he know anything or is he just joking? No. I can't run. I haven't finished the job yet. No way. I have to deal with this. I can't let this be the end. He's gotta be winding me up and if not I'll convince him. Buy myself a little time. He rummaged quickly in his jacket pocket where he had some Cocaine and took a pinch between his fingers in readiness. 'Bollox you bastard!' He laughed, approached me and went to playfully punch me. 'You are winding me up. Frank's put you up to this, hasn't he, the tosser? You wait 'til I see him next.'

I smiled. He was acting just as I would if someone had accused me of the same thing. 'No, Frank didn't put me up to this Brian, Penny did.' I paused as we got into the cab. 'It was your party last night. I know this sounds ridiculous, but she does think that you are the guy that attacked her.'

'Come on Roger. If you believe her then you're…'

I interrupted. 'Of course I don't. Do you think I'd have got into the back of this cab with you if I did! But Penny and I left very early because she had been spooked. She told me that you wear the same aftershave as the one her attacker was wearing on that night.'

'Is that it?' Brian laughed and looked away. *That should hit the spot,* he thought as he swiftly whipped his hand from his pocket and into his mouth in one slick move. 'So because I wear the same brand as some sicko, I'm now the rapist. Come on Roger, this is insane!'

'Look Brian, we've worked together for a long time, you're my number two, and we're drinking buddies. If anyone knows you, it's me and I know you're not a sicko, as you put it. I know how crazy it sounds, but Penny was really shaken up last night. She's my sister and I have to believe her when she tells me something.'

'Roger, she used the toilet in my bathroom and she accidentally dropped and smashed a bottle of my aftershave on the floor. She was acting strangely, but when I asked her if she was okay, she said she was fine. And surely there must be millions of guys that wear my brand of aftershave? So does this mean that they're all the rapist too?'

'Well, that's just it, Griffo. There aren't loads of other guys that wear it.' As the taxi headed for Battersea I explained to Brian all about Penny's sniffathon at Harrods and Harvey Nichols last week and how Chamois wasn't among the wide selection. 'It seems to be rarer than rocking horse shit mate. As you told Frank and me last time we went out, it's an exclusive brand. But it's not just that, Penny said that she just had this weird feeling, she described it as a woman's intuition. She is convinced it's you, but I told her she was being silly. I'm sorry mate. I had to ask you, just to see your reaction.'

'You do believe me Rog, don't you. I don't want to be another one of these guys that has to defend himself in court just because a woman cries rape.' *You're too soft Roger Hamilton. You trust your old mucker Brian. You know I'm telling the truth. It wasn't me, honest!* 'Sorry, I didn't mean that Penny's crying rape. I know how terrible it is, what she's been through.'

'I always doubted you were the rapist mate, don't worry. I tried explaining that to Penny over a cup of coffee at MacDonalds. Just because you wear that aftershave doesn't make you the prime suspect. I tried telling her she wasn't thinking straight and that she had to put it into perspective. If you're asking me for my honest opinion, then no, I don't think you are the rapist. But you've got to admit it's a spooky coincidence!'

'Too weird! I'll have to change brands. I've been wearing it since I discovered it on holiday in the South of France. Would it help if I spoke to her, face to face? I would be very happy to meet up with you and her and talk it all through with her. The last thing I want is for Penny to think I'm that bastard.'

'I don't know, maybe. I'll talk to her and explain I have spoken to you and there is no way you are the rapist.' I shook my head. 'I'm sorry, Griffo. I can't even believe we are having this conversation. It's all so fucking crazy. You drive a Ferrari not a bloody black cab.'

'Thanks Rog. Thank you for believing me. So what now?' *He's got to tell Frank and no doubt he'll want to interview me. Shit! What if he wants to take a urine or blood sample? I cannot let that happen. No way! This is way to* fucking close for comfort. *I still have work to do and can't let this get out of hand, not yet.*

'Well, I know for definite Frank will be pleased to have a break and he and his team will have to get a list of people who buy the aftershave. You will have to be eliminated from the enquiry. I'll tell Frank what happened. I can't wait to see his face when I tell him you wear Chamois!! He'll probably want to talk to you, just to wind you up! Anyway, look, there's Andrew. Let's forget it for now.' I asked the driver to pull over.

Forget it. How the hell was I supposed to just forget it? Penny fucking Hamilton had a lot to answer for. Just as I'm nearing the end, she comes along and messes the whole fucking plan. Well, she was going to have to pay.

FIFTY NINE

The drugs were beginning to take effect and as he sat in front of his computer, he recalled yesterday's events. Roger had really worried him with the accusation and even though he should have enjoyed himself at the Grand Prix, he hadn't been able to stop thinking about his next plans. He knew that the net was closing in and he must speed up his outings. Slamming his hand down next to the keyboard, he remembered Wendy Winger. He was determined to have her. If she got into the back of his taxi he would do her then, but she would recognise him and then he would be in trouble. He would have to time it so she was the last. *That would be nice. Very fitting the babe of all lap dancers, Wendy Winger, is the last victim of the most prolific serial rapist of all times. Daniel Freeman. My name will go down in history.*

He typed a website address into the computer and waited whilst he was connected. The page opened on the Paradise Lap Dancing Club website. He clicked on the 'girls' menu button and waited whilst the page loaded. He swigged on his Bud Ice as the page appeared. It listed all the girls along with a small image next to their names. Guiding the mouse over Wendy Winger's picture, he clicked and waited. He reached for his cigarettes and lit one, taking in a deep breathe before placing it in the ashtray. A page appeared on the screen with ten images of Wendy. It was a striptease beginning at the top of the page, ending in a topless picture of her with a pair of skimpy knickers.

He jumped up from his seat and went to his magic box. He did a couple of lines of Cocaine and then popped two pills. Finishing his lager he reached for his jacket; picked up his keys and headed out the door. Once in his taxi he placed the cotton wool, ether and gloves on the floor next to him, ready for when they would be needed.

Looking at the Paradise website had really got him going and so he'd decided to head for Stringfellows nightclub in Leicester Square. Peter Stringfellow, the club owner, had imported lap dancing from the USA and his trendy nightclub became a lap-dancing club on Mondays to Thursdays. They had a topless only rule, which meant that the standard of girls was much higher than most other clubs.

He pulled up on the taxi rank outside the club and parked. He didn't want to just sit outside and wait. *I'm gonna go and hand pick myself a sexy maiden for the night.* He entered the club, paid the twenty-pound entrance fee and wandered to the stairs at the back of the club. The floor below housed the main stage with a vast seating area based around it. The whole place was full of men in suits who were drinking to excess and the majority of them had a women dancing for them. *Where the fuck do these women hang out when they're not working? I never get to meet them. And now I've got to pay them just to see their tits. It's a bizarre fucking world.*

He stood at the bar drinking a bottle of Bud Ice for a few minutes taking in his surroundings and checking out all the ladies. There was a brunette with legs up to her armpits he couldn't take his eyes off. She had danced for the same man in a suit for the last six songs and he was getting agitated now. The drugs had taken effect and he was feeling hot and horny and bloody impatient. He approached the brunette as she had her back to her client and he whispered in her ear. She smiled and winked at him and said she would come and find him at the bar. She told him her name was Angie.

He checked out some of the other dancers as he walked back to his spot at the bar and was very impressed. He watched a blonde with fake tits wobbling them in some guys face in perfect time to the music. *It was a very sad place really. It was full of wankers with far too much money, wasting it on tarts when they could be using their money to benefit charities or some of the millions of starving people around the world. Money, the root of all evil,* he thought. *No that's wrong, I'm the root of all evil and if Angie plays her cards right, she'll get my root tonight!*

Her smiled as Angie approached and held out his hand to welcome her.

SIXTY

I flew back to Battersea with Brian and the clients. It was very cloudy and our Captain Mark had done really well to guide the helicopter in between the low hanging cloud. We arrived safely at just after five o'clock.

'So much more civilised than fighting in that traffic! Thanks Roger, what a great day.' Andrew had enjoyed the flight more than the race I think!

'My pleasure, Andrew. I'll speak to you in the morning.' I said goodbye to Brian and Tony Stewart and we all went our separate ways. There were four cars waiting to take us all home and I went straight to my flat and Emma was there to greet me.

"Hi darling. How was the race?" Emma gave me a huge hug and a kiss on the lips.

"It was great, Schumacher should have won but Coulthard went like a dream and won, much to the delight of that smug old Ron Dennis. At least a Brit won at Silverstone so it was good." Emma knew how big a Schumacher fan I was.

"Never mind, your Dad reckons that he'll win the title, so the fact that Coulthard has won one race won't make any difference. Would you like a drink?"

"Yeah, a glass of white wine would be great. What time are Frank and Isabelle coming over?" I checked the time; it was five forty.

"Isabelle said about six thirty. We didn't know what time you would be back. How was the flight? The weather's pretty bad."

"Not too bad actually, but you know what Mark's like, he's such an experienced captain. And I love a bit of risk, you know that." I smacked her bum as I headed into the bedroom.

Frank was coming round to watch the World Cup Final with me, and Emma had insisted that he bring Isabelle. Neither of the girls was really into football, but the glamour and the passion of the World Cup never failed to grab most people. Emma was more interested in the players' bums than anything else, so I knew what she and Isabelle were going to be watching during tonight's game.

I didn't bother with a shower, but I changed into slightly more comfortable jeans and a shirt and collected my wine from Emma. I embraced her and our lips met and our mouths parted to allow a passionate kiss.

'Em, I'm sorry that I haven't been myself over the last week or so. Penny's …'

Emma kissed me again and then said, 'Shh, you don't have to explain. I understand what you are going through. I just hope that Frank can catch this freak before too many other women have to suffer.'

'I promise I'll make it up to you before the end of summer. Maybe we can go away for a couple of weeks? Mauritius would be nice, wouldn't it?'

'That would be fab!'

'I'm hoping that Frank will have had some joy with the taxi and aftershave leads.'

'Did you speak to Brian about Penny's feelings?'

'Yeah. I confronted him before we left this morning. I wanted to get it out of the way early. It's not him. I know him too well. He was just so shocked. He drives a bloody Ferrari not a black taxi, and anyway most of the guys on the desk think he's gay.'

'But, you got to give some credence to a woman's intuition.'

'Yeah, I know. It really spooked Penny. But Brian did say he would speak to Penny face to face if it would help. I've worked with the guy for years, Em. I think Penny was just so shocked to smell the aftershave we'd been looking for that she panicked and drew the wrong conclusion. Just because he wears the same brand of aftershave as the attacker doesn't make him a rapist.'

'I know. But it *is* a coincidence. So have you spoken to Frank today about it?'

'No. I did try him just before the race began, but I couldn't get him. They'll be here soon.'

'I thought I'd just bung a couple of pizzas in the oven with a salad. That will be alright won't it?'

'Perfect!'

Frank and Isabelle arrived with beers, wine and a bunch of flowers for Emma. The girls stood in the kitchen chatting and Frank and I sat in front of the telly watching the match pre-amble. I told him all about the events of the party and what Penny had told me.

'But you know Brian, don't you?' Frank looked unconvinced.

'Exactly. I told Penny it was just a coincidence. Just because he wears Camois or whatever it's called doesn't mean he's the rapist, and he drives a Ferrari not a black cab.' I explained to Frank.

'A Ferrari? You're kidding me?'

'Didn't you know? Yeah he bought it with one of his bonuses last year. It's a bit ostentatious for my liking but each to their own. Anyway, I confronted Brian this morning, before we left for the Grand Prix. He pretty much reacted the way I would if someone had accused me of being the rapist. He thought I was winding him up at first, well he actually thought you had put me up to it! He then realised I was serious and told me not to be so stupid and he said he would meet with Penny if I thought it would help. It's not him Frank.'

'Well, I don't doubt it for a minute, but I should speak to him anyway. If he agrees to let us take a DNA sample, then we can very quickly eliminate him from the investigation. So how's Penny, is she okay? Must have been pretty hard for her, having all those memories brought back.'

'I think she's okay. She really feels for you and knows how much you need a break.'

'Good old Penny. She's always had a soft spot for me.'

'Yeah okay mate, no need to let it go to your head. She wants to help your investigation not your ego.' I wound him up.

'Well, it does seem strange the rapist struck in the City. Why would he change locations, when all the others had been in and around a one-mile radius? It makes no sense. Anyway, let's forget it for now. My head's been hurting all weekend and it will be nice to watch the Brazilians stuff the French. How have your bets been doing?'

'Bloody good thanks. I'm up just over two grand and so tonight's game is pretty irrelevant. I'm long of both teams, so who ever wins, it won't matter.'

'Why is it money always goes to money? You're a lucky fucker Hamilton. So do you want a little side bet on tonight's result? I'll have a straight tenner with that Brazil win.'

'If you want to give me your money, that's fine by me mate. A tenner it is. Come on you Frogs!'

SIXTY ONE

I sat in my chair and waited for the screen to refresh. The World Cup final had been perfect for me. France had beaten Brazil 3-0 in a very strange game. The Brazilians didn't seem to want to play and the newspapers were full of stories about match fixing and how Ronaldo had been feigning injury. The French had played well, but Brazil did not look or play how they should have done. I totted up my bets and I had made a total of two thousand, nine hundred pounds! Not bad for just over a month's work, and all tax-free which was even better. And to top it all, I'd taken a tenner off Henson!! He was not happy! My big win had been on yellow cards. I had sold the total at 290 and the make-up was 250. I had sold fifty pounds a card. Two thousand pounds profit. It was mad and could so easily have gone the other way.

'Hamilton, you counting out your winnings?' Spanner shouted over as he walked in.

'Of course mate. Didn't do too badly. I told you it would be France v Brazil in the final. Stick with me Spanner and I'll look after you.' I joked, rubbing my hands together for effect.

He grimaced and walked over to his desk. It was seven fifteen and I was still the only person in from my desk. I had hated sacking Jamie, David and Jonathan. Jonathan and David had taken it in their strides, but Jamie had gone mental, saying we were making a big mistake and he would go to one of our competitors and take Peter Jarvis' business with him. It wasn't nice to sit and listen to, and I felt a massive rush of relief when it was finally over. I then called a desk meeting for five thirty and explained to the rest of the team what had happened. Later on I took Mike out for a private drink to explain how close he had come and he needed to buck his ideas up. He looked deeply shocked and expressed his gratitude. I told him he'd always had my vote, but that Eddie was gunning for him. I told Mike, not to worry and that as far as I was concerned, he was a market face we needed and couldn't do without.

'Morning Roger.' Mike strutted across to his seat.

'Bloody hell Mike, that's six days on the trot now. I'm impressed.'

'I told you I was going to buck up my ideas Roger. I don't want to let you down. Eddie can go shit in his hat, but I'm not gonna let you regret your decision to keep me. D'you want a coffee?'

'No thanks Mike. I'll get Sally to nip downstairs when she gets in.'

I was pleased that Mike was making an effort. It really helped my conscience and his getting in early had been noticed by everyone on the desk. Eddie was still surly and complained it wouldn't last. 'Give it a couple of weeks and he'll be back to old ways.' Well for now he was doing a good job and I was chuffed. I'd got a lot of flack from some of the others desks. Spanner had slagged me off for being so mean and he wound me up saying that business must be bad for redundancies to happen. I ignored all the comments and jibes. What most of the brokers on the floor failed to realise was the E-Trading system was going to replace them all within time. Spanner and his guys were going to have a rough ride next year when the Euro came in. Once all the European currencies disappeared they would have very little cross currency dealing left and then they too would be hit with salary reductions and redundancies.

The start of the morning was fairly slow, but our screens were full of prices thanks to Andrew and Tony who'd given us loads of orders to show thanks for the trip to the Grand Prix. Tony was a huge David Coulthard fan and Andrew and I had been cheering for Michael Schumacher. The only thing I missed was Murray Walker's commentary on television. It was never the same being at the race.

Andrew's squawk crackled in action. 'Roger bid three for sevens oh two, bid six for nine threes oh two, offer big Greeks at forty, make thirty five forty two in tens oh one, bid double oh for tens oh three and offer six and a half oh threes at 27 plus.' The squawk went dead.

I clicked into Andrew's line and thanked him and quickly input all his prices. You had to concentrate the whole time and be ready to react when your client shouted prices down the open squawk. It wasn't difficult and after a few years it became second nature. You could be having a laugh and joke with a colleague or talking on the phone to a mate and you could still listen to the squawks and input prices, almost without thinking. It was the part of the job I really enjoyed, the action and thrill of seeing the desk suddenly burst into life. As soon as the prices appeared on the screen all the other brokers would shout the prices to their customers, hoping they could get a counter price and eventually do a trade. We got a percentage of every trade, which went into a bonus pool, but it wasn't for the desperation of needing the extra money the guys wanted to deal. It was really to stave off the boredom that existed most of the day. I did enjoy the kudos that came with saying you worked in the City, but the reality was very, very different. I always said to Frank one day I would like to sneak in a secret camera for a fly on the wall documentary, just so that people could see what it was really like.

As I sat thinking, a classic thing happened that would have been perfect for my documentary. There was an unwritten rule in the dealing room you didn't wear old worn out shirts to work. We were all paid well enough to afford new ones. Rodney, on Spanner's desk had come in wearing an old pink shirt and one of the elbows had worn through. Our attention was drawn over to their desk by his cries of 'NO!'

Spanner and three others had hold of Rodney and Darren had hold of his shirt and was poking his fingers into the hole in the elbow whilst tugging violently at it. Eventually it ripped and Rodney's left sleeve came off. It didn't stop there. Most of the dealing floor had come over to watch the ensuing fun. Rodney then literally had the shirt ripped off his back, much to the delight of the girls watching. Rodney took it in his stride; he had to because he knew the rules. He pulled out some money from his pocket and gave them to the junior on the desk and told him to go and buy a new shirt for him. Now topless, he sat back down in his chair and carried on as if nothing had happened. He got a very loud, raucous round of applause from the dealing floor and then it was back to business.

I tried to explain to Emma some of things that went on at work, but I think it must have sounded very childish and unbelievable from her reactions. There was an article written in The Times newspaper that referred to City dealers. It said because we were stuck in rooms that had very little light and had to be at our desks for long hours at a time, we were like caged animals and a psychiatrist in London had actually treated a few brokers for 'Caged Animal Syndrome'. Apparently it sent us a little loopy and we did crazy things because we were bored and it was a mild form of madness. Like a lion stuck in its cage, walking up and down endlessly, looking out between the bars, this psychiatrist said it was the same for us. Every now and then we had to let off steam. Emma had shown me the article and the guys and I had had a bloody good laugh about it. But, watching Rodney sitting topless in his seat, maybe we *were* all slightly mad!

SIXTY TWO

Trudy was sitting with Debbie in the lounge watching television. She wasn't really paying attention because she couldn't stop thinking about Daniel. He had definitely taken her back to the Conrad Hotel. Her memory had completely returned last night and she now knew for certain what the events of last Wednesday had been. She had returned from the toilet and carried on drinking with him. They had then left and taken a taxi to the hotel. She remembered feeling very strange, almost as if she had had an out of body experience. She could remember Daniel taking her up in the lift. She could remember he had to support her in the lift, to stop her falling. Once in the room, Trudy fell onto the bed, relieved to be able to rest.

An advert break came on and Debbie said she was going out. As she left the room, Trudy recalled Daniel taking her clothes off and then beginning to perform sex with her. Trudy jumped up and ran out after Debbie.

'Debbie, wait!'

'Trudy, what's up?' Debbie had her handbag over her shoulder.

'Debbie, can I talk to you?' Trudy asked, awkwardly.

'I'm going shopping, you can come with me if you want.' Debbie offered. 'I'd quite like the company to be honest.'

"Yeah, why not, I'd like that. Hang on, just let me get my handbag." Trudy smiled at Debbie, as she turned away.

As they walked to the tube station, they talked. 'So what did you want to talk to me about?'

'I know I have no right to ask this, but do you remember anything about your attack?'

Debbie's face changed and she looked angry. 'I don't want to discuss it Trudy.'

'I know you don't Debbie. I'm not trying to be nosey at all. It's just that I think I might have been..' She hesitated. 'I think I might have been raped too.'

Debbie stopped walking and turned to her friend, her face full of concern. 'What do you mean, think? You would know, believe me.'

'I know. I've been going nuts over the last few days. Do you remember my date with Daniel? Well, I woke up on the floor of the Conrad Hotel.'

'Tina did tell me. I'm sorry that I've been keeping myself to myself lately but you know?'

'I understand completely Debbie. That's why I wanted to confide in you. I knew you'd know what I was talking about. I told Tina what happened but now I feel completely different. It's so weird, like my memory has just returned.'

They carried on walking and Trudy filled Debbie in on everything she had remembered. Trudy told her it was only in the last day or so that her memory had come back completely. She knew she had been taken to the hotel and

Daniel had his way with her and yet she hadn't remembered until today and thinking back now, she didn't feel that the memories were hers. It was as if she was remembering someone else's experience.

'I wouldn't have had sex with him on the first date, you know me Debbie. There's no way. But I know he had sex with me. I'm sorry to bring those awful memories back for you, but I wondered if you could remember anything about your attacker.'

'Not sure really. I'm so sorry about Daniel. Wendy had told me that you were really keen on him. So do you think you were drugged or something?'

'It's the only conclusion that I can come up with. I woke up with a weird sort of chemical taste in my mouth. I've heard of girls being drugged and then raped but I never really believed it to be honest. There was a programme on TV about it a while ago and all the girls seemed to be fine and in full control, but in reality, they were just passengers being taken for a ride that they had no way of stopping. It was awful, and I think I must have been drugged.'

Debbie smiled kindly at her friend and rubbed her arm for comfort. 'So why did you ask about my attacker? You don't think that Daniel is the serial rapist do you?'

'No! He drives a Ferrari not a black cab. I don't know really. It's all just so weird. Why would Daniel want to drug me? He could have had me nicely, if he'd just waited. He didn't have to drug me, I was a sure thing, you know!' Trudy laughed and Debbie joined in, as they reached the platform of the tube station. 'It just doesn't make any sense. And I remember when I first met Daniel that night that his car had broken down. He was standing in the kitchen when Wendy came in and she went berserk at the sight of him. Apparently he'd been in Paradise the week before and had been really nasty to Wendy, asking if he could have sex with her and how much she charged. He blamed it on the amount he'd drunk but Wendy didn't seem that convinced. She did not like him, you know?'

'Don't tell Wendy this, but after you agreed to go on a date with Daniel she came and spoke to me. She said she didn't trust him and that she wanted to stop you from seeing him. I told her to chill and just let you have some fun. I'm so sorry Trudy. I wish I'd listened to Wendy now.'

'So do you know what I'm gonna do? I'm calling the police when we get back. He has violated me and I feel so used and dirty. He's gonna pay for this. Why didn't you go to the police Debbie?'

'I don't know. Too scared I suppose. I don't want to have to stand up in court and face all those people and especially the bastard that raped me. Think about it long and hard before you do call the police.'

'Why? I've made my mind up. I've confronted him and he just tries to make up stories about how I deserted him and disappeared from the bar. He tried to make me believe that someone else must have drugged my drink and taken me to the hotel. At the time, I kind of believed him. It all seemed so feasible and now that my memory has somehow returned, I know he's lying and it was him who took me to the hotel and I want to know why. If I call the police, maybe he might just begin telling me the truth.' Trudy had made her mind up.

The girls had had a great morning shopping and Trudy had bought herself a couple of summer dresses and a new pair of shoes from Bulgari as therapy. She had a very healthy bank balance and loved nothing more than a day at the shops. She thanked Debbie for inviting her and Debbie thanked Trudy for being such great company.

'I can't remember the last time I enjoyed myself like that Trudy. Thank you so much. We'll have to do it again soon.'

'Definitely honey. How are you fixed tomorrow?' Trudy joked, as she skipped upstairs.

Once in her bedroom she picked up the telephone and called directory enquiries. She got the telephone number for Clapham police Station and redialled. She spoke to a policeman about her ordeal and he told her she should come straight down to the station. He explained there would be a female officer present to make things easier for her and he reassured her they treat all cases like hers very seriously.

SIXTY THREE

Frank Henson was driving to work thinking today was going to be a good day. He didn't know why, but he'd woken up in a very good mood. The results from the Rebecca Jones case had confirmed the attacker was their man. The DNA taken from the semen sample matched. Rebecca had been very cooperative when Frank had questioned her in hospital. She couldn't remember much, but she did recall the sound of a camera clicking very quickly, like it was taking lots of pictures, and also a camera flash. Whilst he'd had the rag clamped on her face, he had told her to be quiet and he wouldn't hurt her. His voice had been very deep and he had been wearing an Arsenal cap.

The team had also been working through the different aftershave companies and the remaining taxi driver interviews. Frank now knew the rapist was not a London taxi driver. All the checks were complete and all the registered black, new shape taxis had been verified. Frank was now stumped. The rapist was not one of the eighteen odd thousand taxi drivers. No, he was one of the thirty odd million men in England!

Walking along the corridor of the police station, he noticed one of his team come rushing towards him. 'Frank, we've just had a call from Clapham CID. A girl that thinks she's been raped, but this one's a bit different.'

'I'm just getting a coffee and I'll be right in.'

Frank wasn't quite as excited as the young detective. Another poor woman had been violated and still he was no nearer to tracking the assailant down. He got his coffee and went into his office. On his desk was a new file with a woman's name on, Trudy Lloyd. The report had come from Clapham and as Frank read through it, he realised why the detective had said it was different. The girl had been drugged, probably by the "date rape" drug, Rohypnol. Clapham had only passed it on to him, just in case there were any similarities with his cases. The victim, Miss Lloyd, had told the police that her attacker's name was Daniel Webster. She knew he lived in London, but not where exactly. He had picked her up on the night concerned.

Frank read through the rest of the file. His attention was drawn to one of the details lower down the page. Miss Lloyd said that her Mr Webster drove a yellow sports car; she thought it was a Ferrari. Frank drew on his cigarette and looked thoughtfully out the window. Ferrari, he thought. He had been chasing rapists for nearly fifteen years and they normally didn't have wealth. Why would someone who owns a Ferrari be a rapist? Rapists were normally power seekers and surely a man that drives a Ferrari would have all the power he needed? Frank also noticed that Mr Webster had a very deep voice. But there was something else nagging at the back of his mind.

'What have you found?'

'Not sure, but maybe Clapham were right to pass this on to us. A couple of the victims said our guy had a deep voice didn't they?' Frank was sure of this.

'Yeah, they said it was gruff and deep. Why?' Dobson asked.

'This guy had a very deep voice, but he drove a Ferrari, not a black cab.' Frank had his eyes closed and was trying to think. His mind was trying to tell him something but he had so much crap going through his head. He reached for the phone and began dialling Roger's number.

'Kaplan Stewart.'

'Yeah hi, is Roger there please.' Frank heard the broker shout out Roger's name. 'No sorry mate, he's not at his desk.'

'Do you know where he is? I need to talk to him.' Frank demanded.

'Who are you, a bloody copper?' The broker joked. 'He's not here, that's all. I ain't his mother. Might be at lunch.'

'Well, I am a bloody copper actually. Can you tell him DS Henson called?'

The broker's toned changed completely. 'Yeah sure, sorry about the joke. I'll tell him.'

Frank put the phone down and lit another cigarette. 'Dobson, run a check on a Daniel Webster, he lives somewhere in West London. See what you can find, any previous, the usual stuff. Also check with Arsenal Football Club; see if they can let you have a list of season ticket holders. Miss Jones said he was wearing an Arsenal baseball cap and so did Penny.'

SIXTY FOUR

It had been a good night and very entertaining. I had taken Andrew and the boys from Morgan's to Gordon Ramsey's restaurant in Chelsea. We'd had a phenomenal meal with some outstanding wines. Jean-Claude Bruton, the maitre d' was his usual charming self and as efficient as ever.

We'd had a bottle of Dows Port 1954 decanted and once polished off, Gavin had convinced us all to go gambling. He had recently joined the Ritz Casino in Piccadilly and was keen to invite his boss, Andrew. I just went along for the ride and to pick up the drinks tab, of course!

'So what are you gonna play, blackjack?' I asked Gavin, as I paid the cab driver.

'Always blackjack. Roulette is a mug's game and I haven't got to grips with craps yet. Come on Roger, stick with me and I'll make you rich!' Gavin promised, putting his drunken arm around me as we entered the club.

Gavin signed us all in and we wandered into the exclusive casino. The first thing I noticed was the two huge crystal chandeliers hanging high above the gaming tables and the noise of people losing money. The odds were stacked safely in favour of the house and I was going to keep my losses down to the cash I had in my wallet, two hundred and fifty pounds.

I got a round of drinks in and watched Gavin play blackjack. I sat with him for about twenty minutes until he had dropped just over a hundred pounds. Most people earn less than ten pounds an hour and Gavin had just lost ten times that in under half an hour. I shook my head as I walked over to the roulette tables. I stopped and watched a few spins of the wheel. I knew the odds of winning roulette were the worst in a casino, but I had a sort of system that worked sometimes.

I bet on zero, the 1st, 2nd and 3rd dozen and the columns, but not on the area of the last number. So for example, if 1 were the last number I would not bet on the 1st dozen or the left column. I would bet £20 on the 2nd and 3rd dozen, the middle and right column and £5 on zero. If zero came up, I'd win £175. If say, 36 came up I'd win £35 and if 1 came up again, I'd lose £85. So I knew my best and worst win/lose scenarios and I felt it worked a lot of the time.

So I watched the wheel spin and the white ball jumped and bumped and finally landed on 21. A guy next to me had £50 on 21 and had just made a cool £1,175 on one spin of the wheel.

I placed my bets and waited for the croupier to finish paying out the winning bets. I pulled out a Silk Cut and lit it with a match from a Ritz Casino box. Trying to control my nerves, I took a long hard drag. Even though I wasn't betting big, I still got butterflies when I gambled. I ordered a gin and tonic from one of the circling waitresses and held my breath as the croupier set the ball in motion.

'No more bets please,' she declared as the wheel began to slow.

'17 black,' she stated as the ball came to rest.

Yes! I thought. I had won £35. It was always a relief to win the first bet of the evening and my luck continued on the next couple of spins. I was up just over a hundred and took a long swig of my drink. It was one o'clock and I was quite pissed and very tired so I decided to have one last bet before heading home. I placed £100 on red; an even money bet and finished my drink as I watched the ball land on 35 black. I had lost my hundred quid and went to find Andrew. I found him on the blackjack table with Gavin. I told them I was tired and going home.

'Bollox Roger. Stay, this is fun mate. Have another drink.'

'No thanks, Andrew. I'm knackered and need my bed.' I told them I was leaving whilst I was still up.

'How much did you make?' Gavin asked me.

I waved a five pound note at him as I headed for the exit. I staggered up the stairs and thanked the doorman as he opened the door for me. I considered walking home, but it was too far and plus, it had started to rain. The traffic heading west was still busy, but I spotted a free taxi waiting at the lights. I rushed over to it, opened the door, got in and asked the driver to take me to Cadogan Gardens.

I was amazed at how many people were still out at this hour. I watched them rushing to get out of the rain, waiting in doorways and ducking under shop awnings. I sat and thought of Frank and the lap dancer. I had sneaked off during dinner and called Frank from my mobile. A lap dancer had called him and explained that a guy called Daniel Webster had raped her. At least that's what she'd thought had happened. She'd explained the whole story to Frank and he'd suggested she come down to the station to give a statement. She had seen Frank earlier that afternoon. Frank explained to me she thought she'd been drugged. Henson had told me that it was probably Rohypnol, known as the "date rape" drug.

But the most frightening break Frank had got from her was the guy, Daniel Webster drove a yellow Ferrari and that he had a really deep voice. Frank was convinced it was our man. I said I'd pop in to see Frank later on the following afternoon, or in fact today, I thought as I glanced at my watch. My mind went into over drive. The yellow Ferrari came rushing back into it and Brain Griffin's face came into my head.

I sat bolt upright in the cab and rubbed my chin. Brian drives a yellow Ferrari, Brian's voice is deep and he wears the aftershave Penny remembered. And Penny said it was Brian. Brian Griffin had to be the rapist!

I reached inside my jacket pocket to get my mobile. I had to tell Frank. I unlocked the keys and dialled Frank's mobile. "*The mobile you've called may be switched off. It may respond if you try again.*" The posh voice of the mobile network told me.

I called his flat and got the ansafone. Bloody ansafone. I left a message asking him to call me as soon as he got my message, no matter what time it was. I wanted to tell him in person, so I just said it was mega urgent and I thought I had the break he needed.

'Can you step on it please driver?' I shouted. I wanted to get home in case Frank tried me there.

SIXTY FIVE

He'd had fun with Angie Gregson after he'd persuaded her to meet him outside after the club closed. *Biggest mistake of her life. The stupid bitch.* He told her he would take her home and then had his way with her. Tonight he was on the prowl for number fourteen.

It had started raining a little after one and so the world and his wife wanted a cab. He'd left the light on but ignored most of the people that had frantically tried waving him down. He had stopped at some lights and hadn't put the handbrake on, riding the footbrake instead. The handbrake always automatically locked the doors on the cab. Without the handbrake on, the doors remained open.

Catching him by complete surprise, someone opened the back door of the cab and dived into the back. He immediately recognised the voice as the passenger said 'Cadogan Gardens please.'

Fuck! It's Roger Hamilton. Fucking hell! As if I'm not struggling enough already. Now I've got my fucking boss in the back. Shit. What do I do? Stay calm. It will be cool. No it won't you shcmuck. He'll recognise me and then I'm fucked? I've got to think.

He steered the cab down Piccadilly and through the underpass and into Knightsbridge. The doors of the cab remained locked whist the taxi was moving and so Roger wouldn't be going anywhere. His mind was racing and he was struggling to keep calm. He had sunk down in his seat and was leaning far to the right, hoping that Roger wouldn't be able to see him in the mirror. He had his Arsenal baseball cap on and the grey wig, but he was sure Roger would still recognise him. He couldn't take the risk. If he were to drop Roger off when he paid he would definitely recognise him. So he decided he could not let Roger leave the taxi.

As he thought this, his heart jumped again to begin an even faster beat. The drugs were rushing through his blood stream at break neck speed now and he had to think quickly. The destination wasn't far but nor was his own flat. It was half past one in the morning so there shouldn't be too many people out and about in the residential streets of South Kensington.

'Can you step on it please driver?' Roger commanded from the back of the cab.

It's the middle of the night, what's the fucking hurry Hamilton? Are you a tired little man? Never mind, I'll soon have you asleep! He accelerated slightly just to keep his passenger happy.

Five minutes later the taxi was outside Roger's flat. He quickly jumped out of the taxi and opened the door for his passenger. Roger was a bit pissed and stumbled up out of his seat. As Roger stepped out of the taxi, a rag was slammed into his face.

He held the rag hard against Roger's face at the same time forcing him back inside the taxi. Roger tried hard to resist but his strength was far inferior. Roger slumped into a heap on the floor. *You wanted to sleep, so sleep. That should keep you outta trouble for a while.*

He decided tonight a break with protocol was in order so he drove the taxi straight into the car park instead of swapping back to the Golf. With Roger it would have been too tricky trying to move him twice. He knew it would be fairly quiet and he was buzzing as he dragged Roger's limp body up to the flat.

Shutting the front door behind him, he let Roger's body drop to the floor. He sat down in his armchair and looked at his boss' body lying on the floor. He laughed at the fact he'd pulled it off. He couldn't believe that Roger was here in his flat, unconscious in his lounge. *Oh I'm sorry Rog, where are my manners? Can I get you a drink? I'm having a beer shall I get you one?* He kicked him gently as he passed him.

As he swigged his Bud Ice he decided what he was going to do with his prisoner. He unlocked the annex and dragged Roger in. He laid him up against the far wall and left a glass of water on the table. He checked his pockets and took the mobile phone he found and Roger's wallet. He also took his watch. *Sweet dreams Mr Hamilton. Don't worry about work. I'll make sure the desk keeps ticking over. It's in safe hands!* Making sure the door to the dark room was locked, he laughed and left, locking the annex door behind him.

SIXTY SIX

Brian got in at seven thirty to find Mike already in. 'Morning Brian.'

'Morning Mike, still getting in early? Good for you. Where's Roger?'

'No idea. He wasn't here when I arrived at seven fifteen. He was out with Morgan's last night, so perhaps he had a late one.' Mike suggested.

'Maybe. I'll call Andrew and check.'

He picked up his handset and hit the Morgan short line. 'Andrew are you there?'

'Yeah Hi.'

'Hi Andrew. It's Brian. What did you do with Roger last night? He's not in yet. We thought perhaps you guys had got him tanked up.'

'No, not at all. We all had a few too many, but Roger left before us. We were in the Ritz Casino and Roger left us in there, must have been about one-ish.'

'Maybe he's just overslept. I'll give it half an hour and try him at home. Thanks Andrew.'

'No worries. Whilst you're there Brian, bid thirty nine for nine threes oh two for me.'

He typed the price into his keyboard and the thirty-nine bid appeared on the screen in front of him. He squawked the bid down all the short lines then told Mike Roger had left the guys from Morgan's at a casino last night and he'd been the first to go home.

By eight o'clock Roger still wasn't in so just for show Brian called Roger's flat. There was no reply so he left a message on the ansafone. 'Hi Rog. It's Griffo, just wondering where you are. It's eight am and I hope you haven't overslept. Roger wake up! When you get this message, give me a call and let me know you're okay.'

The morning flew by and at lunchtime Brian went to the toilet. He took a newspaper with him so the guys knew he'd be five or ten minutes. He settled in trap three and quietly snorted some coke. He smiled. Everything was cool and going to plan. The guys didn't suspect anything. Their boss was missing in action, but anything could have happened to him. He couldn't wait for the newspapers to get a sniff. He could just imagine the headline. "More worry for the Hamilton family." What would Frank make of it all? He would love to see his face when he finds out Roger is missing.

Back at the desk David called his name, 'Brian three out for you. It's Penny.'

He feigned concern and grimaced at David. 'Got it thanks.' He clicked into line three, 'Hi Penny. It's Brian.' *You remember me don't you?*

She was very short with him. 'Where's Roger?'

'No idea. He didn't show up this morning. He was out on a late one last night, but it's not like him to oversleep. I called his flat and left a message.'

'Okay, thanks.' Penny hung up.

Brian smiled at the handset and clicked the line out. *Poor little Penny. Nobody knows where your brother has gone.* About an hour later Frank Henson called to speak to Roger. Brian spoke to him and told the same story. Henson said Roger had called him very late last night, in fact, early that morning and had left a message on Frank's ansafone. He'd sounded pissed and had said something about needing to talk to Frank urgently and having the break he needed. Brian promised to get Roger to call him, if he called in.

The break he needed. What did Hamilton know? This was getting way out of hand. So close and yet so far. He grinned at the thought of Roger being awake now and panicking at the collage on the wall of the annex. *I'll be home soon Roger. I think we need to have a little chat.*

SIXTY SEVEN

I woke with a horrible chemical taste in my mouth and sinuses. The taxi driver had drugged me last night as I'd arrived home. I rubbed my eyes and took in my surroundings. But where was I now? This wasn't my flat.

As I looked around the room the enormity of the situation hit me. The serial rapist had kidnapped me! I was in a room with one table and a chair. Adorned on one of the white walls were pictures and details of different girls. The photographs were very graphic and I turned my head away to grimace. The sick fuck had turned this room into some kind of shrine for all the girls he'd raped. Each girl had her pictures and details on the wall. I suddenly realised that Penny would be up there. I found a photo of her pretty face and couldn't avoid noticing the other photos in her collection. I broke down and began crying uncontrollably.

I had to think. Crying wasn't going to get me anywhere. Wiping my eyes with the backs of my hands, I got up and went to the door. I tried to open it but it was obviously locked. I went to check the time but noticed my watch was missing. I rubbed my wrist where it should have been and tried to think. I had been in the back of the taxi and we'd pulled up outside my place. I had gone to get out and the driver had opened the door for me. As I'd stepped out, he'd slammed something into my face, a rag of some sort. I smelt the ether immediately and had tried to fight, but the taxi driver was incredibly strong. That was all I could remember. And try as I might, I couldn't remember how I'd got into this room.

I sat on the chair and looked at the stuff on the table. There were loads of contact sheets of photos of women. I threw them back down in disgust. Next to them there was a pile of driving licences. They all matched the victims on the wall. He had obviously taken them from his victims when they were unconscious. I flicked through them and noticed there were a couple missing. I thought not everybody carried his or her driving licence with them. But what I immediately worked out was the attacker had raped more than seven, in fact eight with the lap dancer, Frank now knew about.

I remembered my feelings about Brian from last night. Could I be in Brian's flat? I thought back to his party and tried to remember the layout of his rooms. I got onto the floor and lay spreadeagled as I tried to look under the door. The carpet was too thick and I couldn't see anything. I tried the door again as I got up and kicked it in frustration. I saw a glass on the table and sniffed its contents. I was bloody thirsty and took a small sip. It appeared to be water and my sip confirmed this. I was just about polish off the drink when I thought, what if I am stuck in here for days? I should just sip the water in case I am locked in here for some time. I took a big swig and another smaller swig and put the glass back down. I swished the water around inside my mouth, hoping it would take away the taste. It did slightly.

I turned back to the door and began banging loudly on it with both my palms. I also shouted, 'Help! Please somebody help me. Help me please!' I stopped to listen. Nothing. There were no noises or sounds of any sort. I was completely alone.

SIXTY EIGHT

Emma tried calling Roger again. His mobile was still switched off. He never turned his mobile off, not after the incident when Penny had been raped and his parents couldn't get hold of him. Emma was beginning to worry. She had called his office and been told that he hadn't turned up for work. She decided to call Frank. She dialled Directory Enquires to get the number for Chelsea police Station.

'Police, can I help you?' a voice asked.

'Yeah, I'm trying to get hold of detective Frank Henson.'

'You mean detective sergeant Henson. I'll try and put you through. One moment please.'

'DS Henson.' Frank answered.

'Frank, thank God. I am so worried. Have you seen Roger at all? It's Emma.'

Frank sat up in his chair and flicked his hand through his long hair. 'Emma, hi. No I haven't. I tried calling him at work earlier and they said he'd overslept or something. So I left a message on his mobile.'

'His mobile is always on Frank. He never turns it off, not after his parents couldn't get hold of him when...' her voice trailed off. 'Anyway, he's not answering the phone at the flat either. I'm really worried. Where could he be Frank?'

'Emma. It's going to be fine. He's probably gone away on business and forgotten to tell anyone. Look, I'll go over to his flat now with one of my guys and see if we can find him. Have you got keys?'

'Yes I have. Shall I meet you there? I've finished for the day now. I can be there in half an hour.' Emma suggested.

'Great. See you at Roger's at six o'clock. And try not to worry Emma, it will be fine, he'll turn up I promise.'

'Thanks Frank.' Emma liked Frank and was thankful that he'd been there. She got her bag and left the club.

Frank put the phone down and lit a cigarette. He was puzzled. Roger calls him at one o'clock in the morning saying that he has urgent news, something about the break he needs and then goes missing. If Roger hadn't planned to be in a meeting then Frank would be concerned. His friend had never missed a day's work through drink and he was sure that Roger wasn't about to start breaking habits like that. He was going to call Roger's parents, but thought better of it. He didn't want to create unnecessary alarm. He would go over to Roger's and meet Emma and see if they could discover anything at the flat.

Frank arrived at 26 Cadogan Gardens slightly early and sat outside in his Sierra. He had DC Dave Dobson with him who was a good detective. He'd come across from Uniform about six months ago and had shown a good aptitude for the job since then.

'Frank, how much would it cost to live here then? Over a hundred grand or more?' DC Dobson asked.

'Oh much more than that Dobson. I think Roger paid about two fifty for his flat.'

'Bloody hell! How many bedrooms has it got, four or five?'

Frank laughed. 'No just the two. I'm always taking the piss out of him for paying over the top for his shoe box.'

Dobson laughed too. 'I didn't realise the houses round here were that much. Oh well, I suppose I can dream. Maybe once I've reached the dizzy heights of Chief Inspector.'

'Even then it would be tough Dave. So did you enjoy the interview with Miss Lloyd?' Frank had invited Dobson to attend the interview of Trudy Lloyd. Frank smiled as he recalled the look on Dobson's face when she walked in.

'She was a real looker, but I found it all very disturbing to be honest with you. It really winds me up there are sick men like him around out there. I just want to catch him as much as you do Frank.'

'Good man Dave. We'll get the bastard. It's all beginning to slot into place now. Did you speak to Ferrari head office at Egham?'

'I did. They do have a database and they are going to send me their current list of owners. The lady I spoke to also recommended the Department of Transport. But trying to get through to the right person there is taking much longer. The usual Government red tape.' Dobson shook his head.

'Good work Dave. What about Daniel Webster? What did you find? Has he got any previous?'

'I looked up his details on the system and there were only four Daniel Webster's and none of them live in London. None of them had any previous. They all live up north, the closest to London lives in Manchester. So I don't think she's given us the right name.' The young detective explained. 'I spoke to the membership department of Arsenal Football Club and they faxed over a full list of all the season ticket holders. There's no Daniel Webster listed.'

'Call Miss Lloyd tomorrow and make sure she's got the bloody name right. Okay, here we go, I think this could be Emma now.' Frank had spotted her red hair flowing in the breeze.

SIXTY NINE

'Oh Daniel. Have you had workmen working in your flat today?' Mrs Laidlaw had appeared from nowhere, as he'd got out the lift.

'Er, yes I have. Why?' *What the fuck is the old bag talking about now?*

'Oh I thought so. I heard lots of banging and shouting coming from inside your flat.'

'Well, nothing to worry about then is there, Mrs Laidlaw?'

'No, but I didn't see them leave. Oh well, must have missed them whilst I was making tea. Would you like a cup Daniel? Earl Grey, It's freshly brewed dear?'

'That's kind but I'm going out soon. But thanks anyway. Mrs Laidlaw, do you spend all day spying through your door?'

'Well really Daniel. Of course I don't. I was just concerned, I thought you might have had burglars are something.'

'No just workmen. They should be back again tomorrow so don't be surprised if you hear more noise.' With that, Daniel closed his front door behind him, leaving his nosey neighbour outside.

'Honey I'm home!' He shouted towards the annex door. 'Roger did you miss me?'

I had been drifting in and out of light sleep when I heard the voice. I sat up and listened. There was a knock on the door. 'Hello, let me out, please help me I've been locked in. Please open the door.' I pleaded with my rescuer.

'No chance Roger. I'm so sorry boss. But you're going to have stay put for sometime. You know too much.'

Shit! My heart sank as I recognised Brian's voice through the door. I was right. Brian Griffin was the rapist. The sick fuck. He worked on my desk, I'd worked with him for over seven years and he had violated my sister. How could he? Not just my sister, but all the other women too. How could he have been doing it for so long and I hadn't noticed? Surely I there must have been some clue? I had been searching for this fucker with Frank and the whole time he was sat on my dealing desk. He was my number two for fuck sake! He was my friend. Some fucking friend. I stood with my head in my hands, as all these thoughts rushing through my head.

'Brian you fucking bastard! How could you? You are going to pay for this. Open the fucking door now, you prick!' I banged both fists, hard against the door.

'Roger, that's not a nice welcome. Calm down, before you upset me.'

'Upset you? I'll fucking upset you given half the chance. Open the fucking door now Brian and I'll show you what upset really means.' I was still reeling. I could not believe that the guy Frank and I had been looking for had been right under my nose the whole time.

'Don't play the tough guy, Hamilton, it doesn't suit you. The door's locked, bang as hard as you like, it isn't going to open.'

'Fuck you Griffin! Why, just tell me why? You sick bastard!'

'We've got plenty of time for talking Roger, but first I've still got work to do. I hope you like my wall. A little tribute to all my little bitches. There are some spaces I still need to fill Rog. Oh and don't worry about work. The guys are fine. We had quite a good day today actually, so you haven't been missed too much.'

'Open the door Brian. Let's talk about this man to man. Come on.' I wanted to get my hands on him and give him a piece of my mind. He needed to be taught a lesson and I was stuck behind this bloody door. I was so fucking frustrated and just wanted to rip Brian's fucking head off. The more I thought about it the more it wound me up. He had raped Penny and then carried on as if nothing had happened. He sat in my office with me whilst I told him that Penny had been raped. How could he?

'Yeah right. I'll open the door and you'll try to escape. No chance Roger. If you promise to be a good boy, I might let you have some food and another drink. But not right now. I have to go out. I just wanted to check you were okay. I don't want the star of the show dying on me, well not just yet.'

'You're fucked anyway Griffin. Whether you open the door or not, Frank will know where to find me. I left him a message on his ansafone last night. He'll be here before you know.' I was bluffing and hoped that Brian would panic into doing a deal with me.

'Yeah sure Roger. That's not what he said when I spoke to him this morning. He'd got your message but he didn't say anything else. He assumed that you had gone on a business trip or something. And even when he does become suspicious that dumb fuck will take forever to work it all out. Why d'you think I've done the wall tribute? I want to make it as easy for thick old Frank as possible.' Brain began laughing hysterically.

'You might be in control right now, but you'd better make the most of it. I'll make sure that you wipe the grin off your face. You won't get away with this Brian, you fucking wanker.'

'I don't want to get away with it stupid! But I'll come out when I'm ready and not before. So don't even think about playing the fucking hero here Roger. You are in way too deep and I don't want you thinking you're Riggs from Lethal Weapon. This isn't the movies Roger. This is real life and things don't work out the way you want in reality. Hollywood may let the good guys win, but not this time. I'm the only winner here, you hear me Hamilton? Anyway, I'd love to stop and talk, but I gotto go. People to see, things to do, money to spend, girls to rape. See you later Roger. Don't wait up.'

SEVENTY

I slammed my hands against the door in frustration and listened to Brian laughing as he shut his front door. Once again I was completely alone and absolutely helpless. I knew who the rapist was and there was nothing I could do about it. He could be about to rape his next victim and I was unable to do anything. He'd taken my mobile, my lifeline. I felt helpless and began to search the room again for any kind of way out. I felt inside my jacket pocket and smiled as I found my Mont Blanc biro at the bottom of one of the pockets. It must have slipped down, I thought as I sat there clicking it.

There were no windows at all, very weird I thought as I walked over to the other door. It too was still locked. I gave up and sat back down in the chair. With my pen I began making notes on the back of one of the contact sheets. Frank didn't suspect anything. But he knew that the rapist drove a Ferrari. Surely sooner or later he would tie the two together. He knew Penny thought it was Brian, so at some point he should draw the correct conclusion. But what Brian had said did concern me. Frank wasn't the cleverest cookie in the jar and I couldn't afford to wait for too long. Brian had sounded very volatile, a little wacky. Not like the Brian I knew from the dealing room.

I knew it had to be evening. There had been some light coming through the gap under the door and that was slowly fading, plus Brian had come home, so I assumed he must have finished work. I looked down at my wrist, a slight tan mark where my watch should have been. So I'd been in here for about a day. Emma would be concerned by now and hopefully she would call Frank. The guys at work would also be wondering where… I realised Brian would manipulate that situation and keep the guys calm. They wouldn't think I'd been kidnapped. They would probably assume I had decided to take some time off and no doubt Griffin would convince them of some cock and bull story.

Reaching for the glass I took a swig and finished what was left of it. I hoped that Brian would give me some food and water. I was starving. I had four walls to stare at and I was beginning to feel what it would be like in prison. But I stopped myself. I had no sympathy for anyone who ended up in prison. I was a true believer in a proper judicial system that dealt fairly and justly with each crime. The problem in today's society was the system had softened over the years. We now believed everyone deserved a second chance. Second chance maybe, but what of perverts like Brian Griffin? He had no right to any sort of second chance. Constant re-offenders did not deserve any kind of chance. As far as I was concerned, he had forfeited any right to live or breath on this planet. We were far too soft. We pandered to the minorities who say we can't play God and just kill people for wrongdoing. I wasn't talking about petty crimes. In my book, someone like Brian hasn't simply been wrongdoing. He's been raping innocent women who had done nothing to provoke his attacks, except getting into the back of his taxi. He had no rights in my view. He had made his bed and I was going to help him lie on it.

I didn't necessarily believe an eye for an eye was right either. But when somebody commits serial rape, murder, paedophilia, burglary or car theft, I believe they should be punished properly. Putting someone away for 7 or 8 years and then letting them out after 4 or 5 years for good behaviour in my opinion is wrong. So many of them come out and re-offend. They learn new tricks in prison, from other re-offenders. If the same person keeps coming back in front of the judges time and again, surely the system isn't working.

A lot of the guys I knew in the City were in favour of a vigilante system of some sort. A system where a crack squad of men and women went out under the cover of darkness and dealt with the scum once and for all. They wouldn't be missed and it would make the world a safer place to be. But you speak to the pacifists among us and they immediately argue, "Oh but what if they get the wrong man, what if he's guilty?" Well I'm talking about a crack squad of vigilantes that only responds to orders from the Prime Minister. There would be a system in place where the Prime Minister would be informed of the need to eradicate a person or persons and he would put the call in. I had discussed this with many of my good friends, not so good friends, clients, parents and they all agreed it would be a good thing. We are too soft on the criminals of today and we need to send them a new message.

I had scribbled notes all over the back of the contact sheet, but there was nothing I could do from my prison room. I was the innocent victim and yet I was the one locked up. I was thirsty and needed a cigarette. Come on Frank, work your magic and get me out of here.

SEVENTY ONE

Frank, Dobson and Emma looked all over Roger's flat and found nothing. No clue of where he could be. There were three messages on his ansafone, one from Brian, one from Penny and one from Emma. They all expressed their concern and asked him to call them as soon as he got their message.

Emma dashed in through the door expecting to find him lying in bed. Frank on the other hand was more realistic. He'd seen people disappear before. They just vanished without any reason. But he knew Roger wasn't like that. He'd known him since school and he knew how committed Roger was to the case. Roger wanted this guy almost more than Frank. There was no way he would just disappear at a time like this.

Emma explored through Roger's desk and the only thing she found to surprise her was a receipt from the lap dancing club he and Frank had visited a few weeks ago. Frank had laughed at her reaction.

'Oh God. Do you think he's run off with one of these blonde bimbos Frank?' She asked, waving the receipt at him. 'Don't laugh at me, this could be serious!'

'I know Emma, but I know how much you mean to Roger and I know he wouldn't do the dirty on you. He's prime time in love with you, so put away silly thoughts like that right now. That receipt is from a very drunken night he spent with me. We ended up in this club and that's it.' Frank explained calmly. 'Now, without wanting to cause you too much concern, I wish it was that simple. I think there's more to this than meets the eye.'

'What do you mean?' Emma looked uneasy.

'Well, you say you've spoken to his parents and they don't know where he is. I've spoken to Brian and he and the guys at work haven't heard from him, I haven't got a clue where he is. But Emma, I don't want you to worry. We will find him.'

'I know you will Frank. I'm just so pleased that you are here. Would you like a coffee, I can pop the kettle on quickly?' Emma smiled.

'Yeah that would be great. Dave, just call in and tell them we'll be another half an hour.'

Driving back to the station, Frank decided to pay a visit to the Conrad Hotel.

'Where we going Frank?' Dobson asked, realising Frank had taken an unplanned turn.

'I've had an idea and thought we should follow up on it. We're going to The Conrad Hotel. Trudy Lloyd said something about the room being booked by a Mr Lucky. That's got to be a piss take. I just want to go through the guest register.'

Dave Dobson was twenty-three and loved working with Frank. He had learnt so much from him over the past few months and to have a case like this one to work on, was the best training a young detective like him could get.

'What are you hoping to find?'

'Not sure. I don't want to miss anything. If this Daniel Webster or whatever his name is, took her to the hotel, maybe there was another room booked in his name. I also think someone at the hotel must have seen them arrive and I just hope we might be able to obtain some kind of a description.'

Dobson pulled up outside the hotel and the doorman opened his door. He and Frank walked into the reception and they both whistled quietly at the grand entrance and long marble hall. Frank explained they were there to see the manager and the receptionist made a quick call. Within minutes the manager appeared.

'Gentlemen, Rupert Dawson, I'm the general manager.' He extended his hand to Frank.

'Evening, I'm DS Henson and this is DC Dobson. Thank you for agreeing to see us.'

Following the hotel manager, Frank shook his head at Dobson as they walked past the impressive piano bar. Mr Dawson led them into his office and they sat down round his desk.

'So how can I help you gentleman?'

'I have a few questions I'd like to go over with you concerning the evening of Wednesday the 1st of July. A Miss Trudy Lloyd was discovered by one of your room maids in Room 343 and mistakenly assumed dead.' Frank was referring to a notepad on his lap. 'You may remember this incident? Miss Lloyd told me that you called her to apologise for inconveniencing her. She said you were very nice.'

'Well we do try to please all our guests and the incident you refer to was a little embarrassing and I was simply trying to ensure our guest wasn't too upset. Has she reported the hotel to the police?' Rupert Dawson seemed very concerned.

'No, worse I'm afraid. She was raped that night in the hotel room and has reported it to us. I am very keen to learn more about the man who booked the reservation that evening.'

'How terrible. I will do anything I can to assist you.' The manager said, rubbing his chin. He turned to a PC monitor on his desk and began tapping on the keyboard. 'Let me check for you. The room was booked in the name of Mr Lucky.'

'Yeah, we have that on file but what I want to know is how the bill was settled. Do you have an address and credit card details?'

'No. It seems that Mr Lucky settled with cash and he didn't fill in his address on the form. You have to understand, Mr Henson, I run a five star hotel and many of our guests have, well let me say, discreet needs. Not all my guests use their real names due to the prying nature of the media and a lot of them use cash. The Lord giveth and the taxman taketh away!' Mr Dawson joked, laughing for emphasis.

'I don't consider rape to be a discreet need Mr Dawson.' Frank was pleased to see Mr Dawson's smile disappear. 'Now do you or any of your staff remember this Mr Lucky? It would really help us if someone can give us a description of him. Also, can you let me have a list of all the hotel guests on that evening?'

'Yes of course. I will find out who was on reception that evening, shouldn't take too long. Can I get you gentlemen some coffee?'

Frank and Dave sat there going through the list of guests Mr Dawson had printed out for them, sipping on the freshly ground coffee. Frank smiled at the thought of his mate, Roger. Roger would love this coffee and I would prefer my instant coffee from the vending machine. He wondered where Roger could be and sat there pensively looking into his coffee cup.

'Frank, there was no Daniel Webster staying that night and Mr Lucky's Christian name is Larry. Definitely sounds like a piss take.'

'I think that's right. Were there any other similar names?'

'There were no Webster's at all.' Dobson informed his boss, still going down the list. 'There was a Daniel Freeman staying. He's the only other Daniel.'

'Okay, let's call it a night. Bring the list with you and check up on Daniel Freeman, just in case.'

SEVENTY TWO

I heard Brian come back in. I had fallen asleep and had lost track of time. I rubbed my eyes and as I yawned I realised that I was very thirsty. I got up from the chair and knocked hard on the door.

'Brian, I'm thirsty. Any chance of having that drink you promised me?' I shouted through the wood.

'Hi Roger. I had to take the taxi back to my lock up, just to be on the safe side. Don't want your mate the copper finding my black cab. No chance of that though. That tosser Henson couldn't find a fucking convict in a prison. I'll bring you a drink in a minute.'

I glanced round the room for something I could use as a weapon. I could use the chair to hit him with. That was my best plan and so I stood poised over the chair ready to strike. About five minutes later, Brian returned.

'Roger, I've got you a drink and something to eat. Now I know how thirsty and hungry you are so I presume you're going to be a good boy and not do anything silly. But I know if I was you, I would be ready to pounce, so I'm warning you don't be stupid. Now I'm coming in.' He unlocked the door using the key and as he quickly pushed the door open, he jumped back.

I lifted the chair above my head and as the door opened I released the chair violently. The chair flew at the door but Brian didn't appear. Shit!

'Too predictable Hamilton.' He laughed, as he entered the room.

Brian entered the room with a plate in one hand and a gun in the other. The gun was pointed straight at me. 'Now, move away to the other side please Roger.' Brian waved the pistol, directing me to the far wall. I had no choice but to comply.

Brian placed the plate of sandwiches on the table and backed out of the room. I thought about running for the door, but Brian reappeared with two glasses of water. Placing them on the table he said, 'Smoked salmon on brown bread. I hope you approve. I don't want to be remembered as being tough on my prisoner.'

The gun was still pointed at me so I remained where I was. 'Brian, just tell me why? None of those girls deserved what you did? You're a good-looking guy; you could have any girl you want? Penny still has nightmares about her attack. Why Brian? I don't understand?'

'Roger, you wouldn't understand. Every one of those pretty little bitches deserved it. They play with men like we are just pawns in a chess set. They are too beautiful for their own good and they needed to be taught a lesson. Just eat your food and don't worry about it. All will be explained when I'm ready to let the tale be told.'

'Make the most of this Brian. Once Frank realises where I am, you are gonna pay, big time.'

Brain laughed at me and shook his head. 'Frank won't be a problem Rog. I'm calling him tomorrow morning to tell him that you've called from New York. You had to go over for an emergency meeting regarding E-Trading and you will be gone for a few days. That will buy me a nice bit of time to add a couple more to my collage!' Brian laughed and backed out the room, locking the door behind him.

I was completely unable to help and there was nothing I could do to warn Frank. I picked the chair up from the floor and sat at the table. The sandwiches did look good and although Brian's comments had taken my appetite away, I knew I had to eat to keep my energy up.

SEVENTY THREE

Frank called Dobson on his extension and asked him to come into his office. Frank had one of the many folders open on his desk and was looking at the list of guests from the Conrad Hotel. It was four o'clock and he had been going through all the main points from each of the cases to try to find some common threads. He knew that with Penny and Trudy's statements he was a lot closer to the truth but he was missing something, something vital.

'Frank, you wanted me?' Dobson stood in the doorway.

Frank's phone rang and as he answered it, he told Dobson to sit down. 'DS Henson.'

'Hi Frank, it's Brian. I've got some good news. Roger's just called me from New York. He's been there since Tuesday. Michael Irwin and Dean Gilkey, the big bosses, called him over for some important meeting. Roger says he's going to be away until sometime next week. I told him everyone was really worried and he said he just hadn't had time to call you. He said he would later in the week. He also said he'd tried to get hold of Emma a couple of times. I promised him I would call you and Emma to let you both know.'

'That's great news. If you speak to him again, tell him he's a tosser from me.' Frank leant back in his chair, sliding his hand through his long hair in relief. 'Thanks for calling Brian. Do you know where he's staying in New York?'

'He didn't say, but I can find out and...' There was a shout in the background. 'Frank. I gotta go.' The line went dead.

Frank put the phone down and said, 'Bloody City dealers! You can never have an uninterrupted conversation with them. That was Brian. Roger's in New York. He got called over on some urgent business. I'd better call Emma.'

'That's good news. At least we know he's safe.' Dobson added.

Frank called Emma and was told that she was taking an aerobics class. He left a message asking her to call him when she could.

'What a relief!' Frank really was delighted to hear that his old friend was safe and sound in New York. It still didn't make it right Roger hadn't called him, but he could now concentrate on the job in hand. 'Right Dave. Did you get hold of Trudy Lloyd?'

'Yep. She said she was sure his name was Daniel Webster. I also looked up Daniel Freeman. He is registered as the owner of a flat on the Kings Road and of Rushden House, Chalfont St Giles in Hertfordshire. I looked up his name on our history files and found a newspaper article dating back to 1979. His mother, a Denise Freeman had died in a house fire and Daniel had survived.'

'Um, not one I remember. What was the address of the flat?'

'Flat 6, 217 Kings Road. Shall we go and check it out?' Dobson was keen and stood in readiness.

'Flat 6, 217 Kings Road.' Frank repeated thoughtfully. 'Why do I know that?' He slammed his hand down. 'Oh Shit! It's Brian Griffin's flat. Roger and I went to a party there last weekend. Dave what did you find from Ferrari?'

'I'll be back.' Dave dashed to his desk and then back into Frank's office. 'I don't believe it Frank. Look here, there's a Daniel Freeman listed, registration "DAN 20".'

'So Daniel Freeman must be our man. Maybe Brian just rents the flat. I need to speak to Brian to find out who this Daniel Freeman is. It would be good to speak to Roger too to find out what he wanted to tell me.'

Frank dialled Roger's work number and the phone was picked up almost instantly. 'This is Frank Henson. Can I speak to Brian Griffin please?'

'Hi Frank. Has Roger called you yet?' Brian sounded upbeat and happy to hear from the detective.

'No. Look I'd like to meet up with you, today if possible. There are a couple of things I need to ask you. Are you free for a drink later?'

Fuck! What does thick old Henson know? Has he put two and two together and finally got four? I can't meet him tonight, no fucking way! 'Sorry Frank, I'm out with customers tonight, how about tomorrow night? Anything I can help you with now?'

'Tomorrow night's fine.' Frank wanted to meet him face to face. 'Shall I meet you in the bar over the road from you? Say six o'clock?'

'Six is great. See you tomorrow.'

'He didn't sound too concerned.' Frank told Dobson, as he replaced the receiver. 'He's busy tonight. I'm going to call Roger in New York.'

Frank called International directory inquiries and got the number for Kaplan Stewart's New York office.

A clear and confident American female answered the phone. 'Good morning, Kaplan Stewart International. How may I direct your call?'

'Yeah hi. I am calling from London. I am trying to get hold Roger Hamilton. Is it possible for you to put me through?'

'Roger Hamilton works in our London office. I can't put you through directly, but if you need the number…'

Frank interrupted her. 'No it's okay. Roger is over there on business with Dean Gilkey and Michael Irwin.'

'I'll put you through to Mr Gilkey's office. Who can I say is calling?'

'It's Frank Henson.'

Frank looked at Dave and threw his eyes up to the ceiling. After a few seconds a different lady spoke. 'Good morning Sir. I understand you wanted to speak to Mr Roger Hamilton?'

'That's correct. He's over there seeing Dean Gilkey and Michael Irwin.'

'Mr Gilkey is on holiday at the moment and I have no record of Roger Hamilton coming over, are you sure you have the right dates?'

'Yeah. He should be there? Are you certain that Roger Hamilton's not there.'

'Yes I am Sir. He couldn't even be visiting Mr Irwin either. Mr Irwin is in London and not due over here until the beginning of August.'

Frank explained to Dave that Roger wasn't in New York. 'Why would Brian lie to me?'

'Because he's trying to hide something? Maybe there is more to Brian renting the flat, maybe Brian is……'

'Daniel Freeman! Quick Dave, get online and check for a Brian Griffin living at Flat 6, 217 Kings Road or anywhere else in London.'

Dave jumped onto Frank's PC and began tapping away. 'Frank, look.' Dave spun the screen round for Frank to see.

"Brian Griffin deceased 1966. Still born." It was the only listing of Brian Griffin in London. There were fifteen others, but none fitted the rapist's age.

'It's got to be him Frank.' Dobson was excited and animated.

'Hang on. Let's just go over everything to make absolutely sure. I don't want to rush in like a bull in a china shop if we're wrong. I can't believe it would be Brian. He's worked with Roger for years.'

'But didn't Penny Hamilton say that she had a weird felling about him? You said she'd told Roger it was Brian.'

'Yeah, she did, but I never believed it. Roger even spoke to him and he reacted in the way you would expect. Roger was convinced it wasn't him, but Daniel Freeman stayed in the Conrad Hotel the same night Trudy Lloyd was date-raped, he drives a Ferrari. Hang on, Ferrari.' Frank tapped the desk as he thought. 'Roger told me that Brian drives a Ferrari. We were about to watch the World Cup final at his place and he'd been telling me how Brian had reacted at the accusation. Brian Griffin drives a bloody Ferrari too! Brian lives in Daniel Freeman's flat and he wears the same aftershave as the attacker and Penny says it's him.'

'But what about the black cab?' Dave asked.

'Don't know. We need to find out if a Daniel Freeman has bought one recently. Also Dave, check out all the camera shops in the Hertfordshire area. Maybe he deals up there.'

'If Brian owns a Ferrari, then he must be on the owners list. I'll check that too.'

'Good idea Dave. He must be on it because Roger told me he bought it with one of his bonuses. We've got twenty-four hours to make certain that Brian Griffin aka Daniel Freeman is our man. We'll meet back here at 8am and then I think we should pay Brian a visit.'

SEVENTY FOUR

Brian Griffin put the phone down and headed straight for the safety of trap three. He shut the toilet door and sat on the loo seat. He unwrapped the packet and snorted two fingers of coke. He shook his head. *This is turning into a fucking nightmare. I'm not ready and yet the net is closing in. I need more time. Maybe I'm paranoid and Henson knows jack shit. Why would he know anything? Unless another one of the bitches had come forward with more clues. Fuck! What now? I need to sort out Roger. If the police come snooping, I don't want them to find Hamilton in my flat.*

At four thirty, when the markets were shut and business was nearly done for the day, Brian made his excuses and headed home. Setting off early meant he missed the usual rush hour traffic. The journey took less than twenty minutes.

Slamming the front door shut, he went straight to his box of tricks and licking his fingers he took two big dabs of Speed. He closed his eyes at the taste and quickly took a beer from the fridge. The long gulps immediately took away the horrible taste and he smiled at the thought of the Speed mixing with all the Cocaine he'd taken on the way home. *Right, it's time to sort out my mate Hamilton.*

Unlocking the door to the annex, he walked in gun in hand. 'Right Hamilton. No more time for any of your fucking games. I want to know what you've said to Frank Henson.'

I was stunned at Brian's anger. I had never seen this side of him and it scared me. 'I haven't spoken to Frank for a couple of days. Told him about what exactly?'

'He called me today. He wants to meet me tomorrow for a few questions. I don't like this heat one bit Hamilton. I'm not ready for your mate to fuck things up for me now. I want you to call him and tell him you're in New York. You've been head hunted and you had to slip over there quietly.'

'No way Brian. You must be fucking joking. I'm not going to help you and your sordid little game. Forget it. You call Frank and tell him yet another lie, but don't get me involved.'

'You're already involved. You know everything Roger.' Frank began dialling a number on the handset. 'Now ask for Frank Henson and fucking tell him.'

'Sod off Brian. Never.' I stood where I was, making no attempt to take the handset from him.

There was a bloody loud bang as Brian fired the gun. I dived onto the floor and covered my head. I couldn't feel anything, so I didn't think I'd been hit. *He's a fucking lunatic. How could I have worked with him for so many years and not seen the signs?* My heart was racing and I could feel my hands and arms shaking.

'Now take the fucking phone Hamilton and tell Frank before I fire the next one into your head. Take the fucking phone.'

Brian was leaning over me and shouting. I looked up to see his face. It was burning red with anger and he looked like he meant every word. The gun was less than an inch from my head. I took the handset and heard a woman's voice saying hello.

'Hi can I speak to DS Henson please. It's Roger calling from New York.'

'Don't try anything clever, Roger.' Brian warned me, the gun still next to my head.

'Hi mate, it's me. I'm in New York.'

'Roger where the bloody hell have you been. I've had Brian on the phone lying to me. He told me that you were in New York but I've been on to your office in New York and they say they haven't seen you. Where the fucking hell are you, mate. Is everything all right?' I could hear the worry in Frank's voice. I had to somehow give him a clue.

'No. I'm here in secret. It wasn't my plan. I got called over at the last minute. I've been headhunted and they wanted me to come over to see them. I should be back soon.'

'Why haven't you called? You said you knew something and needed to tell me. What was it Rog?'

'Yes.' I prayed that Frank would understand.

'What's wrong Roger? What do you mean yes? Are you OK?'

'I've got to go now mate.' Brian was waving the gun at me and he quickly clicked the phone off.

SEVENTY FIVE

Mike and Janet Hamilton were having breakfast and Mike was reading the paper when the phone rang. Susan walked into the conservatory and explained that Penny was on the phone.

'Thank you Susan. I'll go.' Janet got up to take the call.

'Mum hi. Have you heard from Roger at all?' Penny sounded more serious than usual.

'No why darling? Should we have?'

'I can't get hold of him. I spoke to his work and Brian told me he's gone to New York on business. I always speak to him at least once a day. I can't believe he's gone to America without telling me.'

'Well maybe he's just really busy. He always calls us at the weekends. I wouldn't worry Penny.' Her mother reassured Penny.

'I wouldn't normally but I just spoke to Emma. She and Frank went to his flat and there was no sign of him and Emma's really worried too. He would have told either you and dad, or me and Emma if he were travelling abroad. I am worried Mum.'

'Now listen. I'm sure it will be all aright. I'll speak to your father and see if he has any suggestions. But if Brian says Roger's in New York on business, then he must be. They can't survive without your brother at work and if they are not concerned, I don't think we should be.'

Janet walked back into the conservatory and told her husband what Penny had said. Mike said he would call Kaplan Stewart and speak to Michael Irwin. 'He should speak to me. I got him those tickets for the British Grand Prix. I'll call him now.'

Mike Hamilton called Michael Irwin and was told by Michael's secretary he was unavailable all day. Mike left a message asking Michael to call him on his home number as soon as he could. He explained it was a private matter.

Mike spent the rest of the morning sitting in his sunny conservatory, reading the paper. When the phone rang at noon he assumed it would be Michael Irwin so was surprised to hear Penny's voice.

'Daddy, I've just spoken to Frank and he said Roger has called from New York explaining that he is over there seeing a company that want him to work for them.'

'Do you mean he's been head hunted?'

'Yes, that's what Roger told Frank. It all makes sense now. No wonder Brian seemed a bit vague. Roger wouldn't want his work colleagues to know another firm had approached him. Just thought you and Mummy should know. Sorry to have alarmed you both earlier.'

'Don't worry love. I'm pleased that he's okay. Head hunted hey? Sounds very glamorous! Are we seeing you this weekend Penny?'

'No, Lucy and I are staying in London. It does seem strange Roger hasn't called any of us to share the news.'

'Probably just playing his cards close to his chest. I wouldn't worry Penny.'

SEVENTY SIX

'It's got to be him Frank. It all stacks up to the same conclusion.' Dave Dobson had got in early and was sat sipping coffee with his boss.

Lighting his fourth cigarette of the day at eight fifteen, Frank nodded in agreement. The stubble on his face was a bit too long, he thought as he rubbed his cheek. His long hair was more of a mess than usual but the white T-shirt he wore was clean on and looked a lot fresher than him or Dobson.

'Okay, so Brian Griffin, Daniel Webster and Daniel Freeman are all the same guy. They all live in Flat 6, 217 Kings Road, they all drive a yellow, 355 Ferrari Spider, they all wear Chamois by Fragonard, they all rape women and we know that they all drive a black cab. We need to find the taxi. He must keep it somewhere.'

'I checked all the camera shops in the Hertfordshire area yesterday afternoon and I finally spoke to the owner of Barry's Camera Shop in Harpenden. Barry Riley recalled a very rude man who drove a yellow sportscar. He was unnecessarily rude Mr Riley told me and he had noted down the number plate. "DAN 20". He said the man's name was Griffin. He had received an email from him ordering some special photographic paper.'

'Bingo!' Frank shouted and slapped Dobson on the back, nearly making him choke on his coffee. 'Right, fuck the taxi details, we have enough to arrest him on and we can see what the fucker tells us. Let's go Dave.' Frank had picked up his jacket and was on the way out the door before Dave had time to put his coffee down.

On the way across London, Frank organised two other cars to meet them outside number four Cannon Street. Frank and Dave raced across town with the blue lights flashing and siren blaring. As the car approached the City, Frank turned off the siren and lights, as he didn't want to warn Brian Griffin of their presence. He parked outside the impressive office block and got out to brief the officers in the other cars that had already arrived.

Frank and Dave closely followed by the other officers dashed through the revolving doors and into reception. Frank flashed his warrant card and asked the security guard where he could find Brian Griffin.

'I'll show you. He works on the twentieth floor on the Gilt desk. There are over two hundred brokers on that floor so I'll show you where his desk is.'

Frank instructed two officers to go with him and Dave, three to wait at the entrance and the other two to wait by the lifts on the ground floor. The security guard explained that there were fire exits on every floor.

'Okay thanks, but I don't think he'll make a break and if he does, he won't get far.' Frank smiled.

The lift travelled quite quickly Frank noticed as the security guard asked him what Brian had done. Frank explained that he was just wanted for questioning. The lift opened on the twentieth floor and Frank could already hear a constant drone of noise coming from round the corner.

'You won't be able to hear yourselves think in there!' the guard joked. 'Okay follow me.'

Around the corner they were greeted by a set of glass doors and through them could be seen the dealing floor. There were desks, screens and people everywhere. Dave let out a low gasp. The guard swiped a card past a panel to the left of the doors and there was a click as the lock released.

'Follow me. The Gilt desk is just up here to the right.'

The noise from the dealing room erupted as the doors opened and Dave and Frank struggled to take it all in. There were banks of screens spread almost symmetrically on every desk. The desks were all separated and Frank assumed these were all the different markets Roger had told him about. Across the middle of the dealing room, hanging from the ceiling were five clocks, all telling different times and under each clock was a capital city. The time was nine fifteen in London; four fifteen pm in Hong Kong and three fifteen am in New York. Some desks were busier than others and one of the biggest desks was frenetic as they passed. There were six guys all screaming at each other and it all sounded like a foreign language to Dave.

As they approached the Gilt desk Frank spotted Brian Griffin on the phone, standing and dealing with one of the other guys on Roger's desk.

Right you bastard; let's see what you've got to say for yourself, Frank thought. 'Come on Dave, I see him, let's go!'

SEVENTY SEVEN

Friday's could be busy, but in the middle of summer the Gilt desk was normally very quiet, as a lot of the bigger players would take long weekends. "Sell in May and go away" was an age-old adage in the City, but Brian hadn't stopped dealing since the market had opened. He was in the middle of a swap for Morgan's and as he stood dealing with Mike, he noticed Frank Henson. *Fuck! Fuck! Fuck! Fuck!*

'Brian, I'll sell on, keep going.' Brian heard Andrew shout down the handset, but he wasn't reacting. He was stuck to the spot, frozen at the sight of the detectives and the security guard heading briskly over to his desk.

'Griff, am I done?' Mike shouted at him. 'Griff, I'll buy another fifty.'

'Did he say fifty? Brian I'll sell another hundred, just keep going. Come on.'

'I'll sell.' Up jumped another broker, with a second seller of the swap on the phone.

'Brian, are you gonna sell me my fifty or do I deal with David?' Mike screamed at him.

'Mike I'll sell you fifty, if I can. Get me in when you can. Griffo, are you gonna trade or not?'

'Brian, are you still there? Come on I can hear the other brokers. You've got a buyer, sell him the nine three's oh two. I'll even sell them straight if I have to. Brain are you listening?' Andrew was getting agitated now.

Brian was shaking now and he suddenly snapped out of the trance and dropped the phone. He quickly took his jacket off his chair, picked up his mobile and ran towards the back of the room.

'Brian, where are you going for fuck sake? Am I done?' Mike shouted after him.

He looked over his shoulder and saw Frank break into a run. 'Stop him. Brian stop!' Frank shouted. He put his radio to his mouth and informed the other officers that the suspect was making a break for it and to standby.

Brian made it to the Fire Exit and ran his pass over the panel. As he was senior management the card worked and the door opened. He slammed the door shut behind him and he sprinted down the stairs, three at a time.

'Get this bloody door open now!' barked Frank. The security guard fumbled for his pass and finally got the door open. Frank and the guard ran through the door. Dave said he'd go the other way and ran back through the dealing room and out to the lift.

Fucking Henson. Fuck, fuck, fuck! Got to stay cool. This is okay. I can handle this tosser. The games have well and truly begun, but are you up to the challenge Frankie? 'You'll never catch me alive copper!' He screamed back up the stair well. He smiled on reaching the third floor. On the ground floor, the stairs led straight into the car park only used by a handful of senior brokers. *Nearly there! You can do this, be cool. This is all Hamilton's fucking fault. I'm gonna make that son of a bitch pay.*

Frank was fitter than the guard and was two floors ahead of him, but still some seven or eight floors behind his suspect. As he sprinted on down the stairs, he was pleased to know he and Dave had come to the right conclusion that Brian Griffin was their man. As soon as Brian fled, he knew for certain, but now he was worried the bastard would get away. He didn't know where the exit came out and he doubted if Dave would get down the lift in time. The other officers were covering the entrance but Frank doubted whether Brian would come out that way. As he ran he radioed the station and asked for a car to be sent to 217 Kings Road and to be on the look out for a yellow Ferrari 355 Spider, registration DAN 20. If he headed for the flat Frank wanted to make sure he'd be caught there.

Brian was out the door and into the car park. *What a fucking loser! Where's your back up team Henson!* He laughed as he blipped the alarm and jumped into his car. He slammed the gear stick into first and wheel spun towards the barrier. Usually he would pause to key in the six-digit code, but today he blasted straight through the wooden barrier, laughing as it splintered across his windscreen. He deftly held the back end as he skidded out and left onto Cannon Street and up towards Mansion House. He saw two police cars in his mirrors, still parked outside. *See you later, Henson. You snooze you fucking lose!*

Frank arrived on the ground floor his lungs aching and struggling for air. He saw the broken barrier and radioed Dave. He and the other officers had just got to the front of the building in time to see Brian drive off. Frank ran out onto the road and was met by Dave. He jumped into the police car and Dave sped off in chase. The other traffic quickly moved out of their path and Frank was confident they would catch the Ferrari. Still assuming that Brian would go to his flat he told Dave to head for the embankment. It would be quicker as there were large stretches of two lanes, which meant they should be able to go faster. He was in constant contact with control and other cars were now on alert and looking for the sports car.

Dave sped onto the beginning of the embankment under Blackfriars and saw the Ferrari in the distance. 'There he is!' He planted his foot to the floor and the Vauxhall Omega responded.

Brian saw the patrol car's lights in his mirror. 'Get out the way you fucking morons!' He shouted at the other cars. His headlights were on full beam and he had one hand pressed hard on the horn. The police car was gaining on him in all this traffic. He had to think fast. He knew the route back to his flat well and he knew most of the short cuts. He knew soon there would more police cars involved. Henson was dumb, but not that dumb. He would have called for support and so he would have to be clever with his route home.

As the yellow Ferrari raced up to Embankment Station he flicked it right, straight through the red light and onto Northumberland Avenue. A police car coming down the other way tried to cut him off, but Brian was too quick. He flicked it round the police car closely avoiding the parked cars and left the police car crashing into the car behind him. Brian drove on up to Trafalgar Square and somehow managed to squeeze through and onto The Mall. This was risky as there were always plenty of police at Buckingham Palace.

There were tourists everywhere down the Mall and Frank had called a hold to the other police cars. He didn't want an accident here, not in front of Buckingham Palace. Dave had caught up with him and was close enough to read the number plate on the Ferrari. Frank called patrol and asked if they could get a helicopter up to keep track from the air. He was told to standby.

'Don't get too close Dobson, just sit on his tail and we'll follow him home. This cunt is going down for twenty years and I want the pleasure of slapping the cuffs on and seeing him in the dock. I don't want any heroics, you know? This could so easily go wrong and we get buried in a month of paperwork with a dead suspect killed whilst we were in pursuit.'

SEVENTY EIGHT

The only way he was going to have any chance of getting back to his flat was if he ditched the car. *But where? If I can get past Buckingham Palace and down to Knightsbridge, I can take one of the cut throughs round the back of Sloane Street.* He put his foot down and safely made it past the Palace and up to Admiralty Arch. He drove on to Brompton Road. He changed his mind and went straight past Harrods and checked his mirrors. The police had dropped back slightly and this was the chance he needed.

At Felton Flowers he suddenly spun the wheel left and turned on to the beginning of the Fulham Road and then immediately right then right again into an NCP car park. He stopped at the barrier and jumped out, throwing the keys to an attendant. 'Happy Birthday! Keep it, I don't think I'll need it anymore.' He said running out onto the street, leaving a very bewildered NCP employee looking at the Ferrari.

Smiling as two police cars whizzed past, still on the Brompton Road, he hailed a passing taxi and jumped in. 'Kings Road please, down by Henry J Beans. Get me there in five minutes and you can keep the change.' He leant forward and passed a fifty pound note through the gap in the partition.

'Right. Thanks very much.' The cab driver sped off down the Fulham Road and into Sydney Street and turned right on to the Kings Road and pulled up outside the American Diner.

'Thanks.' Brian shouted, as he leapt out the cab. He ran back up the road towards Sloane Square to his flat. As he approached he saw two police cars parked outside. There were plenty of shoppers and tourists he could mingle with and he knew they were on the look out for his Ferrari and would not be expecting him to turn up on foot. He still had the upper hand and that pleased him.

He decided to walk past once just to check out the situation and then thought better of it when he heard the distant sirens coming down from Sloane Square. *I'll race you Henson. Bet I get there first. You won't be expecting to find your mate Hamilton there now will you. Well, he'll be dead, by the time you and your cronies manage to get in. They think it's all over..*

SEVENTY NINE

'I can't believe the fucking scumbag's got away. How did you lose him Dave?' Frank was livid. They'd spent months chasing this guy and now, just as they were so close, he'd got away. 'It's a fucking yellow Ferrari, Dobson! You can't miss it. They're not your everyday Ford fucking Mondeo.'

'Sorry Frank. He was up ahead and the next minute he was gone. He must have turned off somewhere.' Dobson was angry with himself. This could have been a great moment to shine in his boss' eyes and he'd blown it.

'Oh really! No shit Sherlock! Just get to his flat as quick as you can. Control, come in.' Frank's radio crackled.

'Go ahead 29'

'Is that chopper in the sky yet?'

'It's just taken off from Battersea, should be with you in five Sir.'

'Roger, out' He shook his head. Five minutes would be too long.

Frank radioed the other cars and told them to get to 217 Kings Road as soon as possible. They would try to apprehend Daniel Freeman there. Hanging on to the handle above the door, as Dave swung left on to the Kings Road, Frank played with his moustache with the other hand. He couldn't believe Brian, Daniel Freeman, had got away. He was convinced he would go to his flat. If he didn't they would be struggling and it would turn into a long waiting game. They had played that game before with a paedophile in Hammersmith a few years ago. He and another policeman had staked out the guy's flat and had sat there taking it in turns to watch the flat for nearly two days before the guy finally showed. He didn't fancy going though all that again. Why hadn't Roger called? He wanted his mate to be included in all this. They had found the rapist and Roger didn't even know.

Dave spotted the other cars parked outside the suspect's flat and with the lights and siren still blaring he did a U-turn and pulled up next to them. There were two policemen outside the flat and they were frantically trying to get in to the building.

EIGHTY

He took a deep breath and followed a crowd of Japanese tourists up towards his flat. He got alongside them and took his door keys out in readiness. His heart was in overdrive and he was struggling to keep it together. As he got to his door he quickly crept into the doorway and without looking round unlocked the door and quickly slammed it behind him. He heard a couple of shouts from outside and ignored them running upstairs to his flat. He didn't want to risk the lift and once outside his flat he unlocked the door and knew he was safe at least for a short time. He heard all the flat buzzers going, including his own as the police downstairs sought entry. He knew Mrs Laidlaw would oblige so decided time was against him and moved fast.

He was really angry Frank had got so close so soon. He thought it would have taken longer and realised it had been a big mistake to do Trudy. *Fucking bitch!* As he thought about her he was reminded of Wendy Winger and how he wanted to have her. He kicked his coffee table over and punched the kitchen door as he passed. *Fucking hell! Why did Henson have to get in the fucking way now? Roger was going to pay. It's his fault. He shouldn't have been involved but his sister had to be another one of those pretty bitches.* He grabbed a beer and sat in his chair. What had happened? It had all been going to plan and then his cock had taken over and he'd had to play boyfriend/girlfriend with Trudy. He took two big gulps and wiped his mouth with the back of his hand.

Finding his gun in the drawer of the bureau, Daniel walked over to the annex. 'Roger, I've got you more food, now stand back and be a good boy.'

Daniel took in a deep breath, quickly snorted some more coke and began to unlock the door. He had decided Roger had to pay and if he was going to be caught now, he may as well kill him and give Frank something to be very sorry about. He may not have reached Crosby's target, but he would still be remembered. *Henson, you won't ever be able to forget me!*

I stood against the far wall. I had my Mont Blanc biro in my hand and decided if I got the chance I was going to try to overpower him. I couldn't stay in here any longer. I had to alert Frank somehow and sitting in this fucking room every day was driving me insane. I watched the door open then froze as Brian appeared with the gun.

'Hi Roger. Have you got any last requests.' Brian smiled.

'Hey now look Brian. It doesn't have to be like this. We can…..'

'Roger don't call me Brian. The name's Daniel, Daniel Freeman. Now you're wrong, it does have to be like this because Frank is downstairs and I am trapped in this fucking flat. I knew I should have got rid of him a while ago.'

I was really scared now. I may have been mega successful, my dad was famous, I had never wanted for anything in life but here I was facing a lunatic with a gun pointed at me and he'd just asked me if I had any last requests. I was about to die and had to think. I had to buy some time. 'Daniel, just tell me why? What did Penny do to deserve that?'

'Penny is the same as them all; she's a pretty little bitch. My mum was a pretty bitch and she got her dues. They will all pay. Dan Crosby is a fucking loser and I deserve his title. Frank has got in the way, but not for long. If I have to shoot my way out I will and Wendy is still going to get it. And Trudy needs another visit, they're all bitches Roger, you know? Fucking pretty little bitches the lot of them.'

Daniel was babbling and I knew I was in serious danger. This lunatic was definitely capable of killing. Dan Crosby was the guy Frank had told me about. 'Who's Dan Crosby?'

'He's a fucking low life loser, that's who he is.' Daniel snapped back at me. 'A serial rapist and I want his record. Now Roger I want you to turn around and face the fucking wall.'

EIGHTY ONE

Frank jumped out the car and ran over to the flat. 'What's going on?'

'We think he's inside Sir. We saw someone sneak in about five minutes ago and we can't open the door. It opens outwards so we can't kick it open.'

'Why weren't you watching the flat?'

'We were but we were looking out for a yellow Ferrari and he surprised us Sir.'

'For fuck sake! Okay, look we need to get this fucking door open.'

'I've rung ever buzzer, but still had no luck.'

'Well, buzz them all again. Just get this fucking door open!'

'Hello.' A lady's voice came out of the intercom.

'Hello madam. This is Detective Sergeant Henson. We need to get into this building. Please can you release the lock for me.'

'Can you show your ID to the camera please.'

Frank held his warrant card up to the camera and the old lady opened the door. Frank and his team went rushing through and up the stairs. 'Check for a back exit and two of you cover the lift.' His adrenaline was pumping now and he took the steps three at a time.

They found Flat 6 and Frank pounded on the door. 'Brian, open the door.'

'His name's Daniel, Officer.' Mrs Laidlaw was stood in her doorway opposite. 'Is he in trouble?'

'You could say that madam.' A female officer replied and ushered Mrs Laidlaw back inside her flat.

'Daniel open this door now.' Frank signalled for the battering ram to be used and two burly officers stepped up to the door. With three attempts the door cracked and gave way, just as Frank heard two gunshots from within.

Frank stepped through the splintered door and into the flat. 'Fuck me!' He let out in anguish as he took in the scene.

EIGHTY TWO

I stood there not knowing what to do. If I turned around I would be shot, but if I didn't I would probably be shot anyway. I decided to try to stall him. 'Daniel what good will killing me do?'

'It will upset that fucker Henson that's what. Now turn round, I don't want to see your face Roger. Turn round and stop fucking looking at me!'

I suddenly heard Frank shouting and knocking on the door. Daniel looked towards it and I took my chance. I pounced on him and tried knocking the gun away but his grip was strong. I stabbed my pen into his neck sinking it a couple of inches into his flesh and he let out a blood-curdling cry and the gun went off. One shot and then another. I felt the vibration up my arm as I was still holding his wrist. The bullets thudded into the thick wall behind me and I bit into Daniel's arm finally making him drop the gun. Blood was spurting out of his neck now and I was hit again and again by blood splatters as Daniel spun round in agony. I kicked the gun away into the corner and then charged Daniel shoving him out into his lounge and up against the big French windows. The windows gave way with our weight and the glass cracked. I grimaced and flexed as we fell through the thick glass and on to the patio on his balcony. Daniel's neck was bleeding badly now and he seemed dazed. I stood up and brushed the glass splinters off my shirt, noticing I too was bleeding in a couple of places.

'Roger, help me, please do something mate. My neck hurts, please help.' He was gasping for breath and holding his neck, my pen still in place. I could actually see the thick, red fluid running slowly over his hand and along his wrist. I began to gag and struggled to stop myself throwing up.

I walked over to him and knelt down beside him. I reached over and he smiled, thinking I was going to try to stem the bleeding or something. Instead, I wiggled my pen further into his neck and whispered into his bloody ear. 'You deserve to die Brian. You are one sick motherfucker.' I said, wiggling the pen more aggressively.

'Roger, please help me. Come on mate. Please?' His voice gurgled from all the blood, as he pleaded with me.

I could not believe he had raped my sister and all those other women. The pictures from his wall came back to haunt me and I shuddered. I knew Frank and his team would have the door open in no time. But, if Brian lived, he'd go to court and probably be put away for ten or fifteen years. Penny's life would never be the same, or any of those other poor victims of his. Anyone committing crimes like his did not deserve the right to live and so I decided there and then this included Brian.

'Fuck you Brian! You think I'm going to help you when you've violated my sister. Fuck you!' I punched him in the face as hard as I could, breaking his nose. Blood began to ooze slowly from his left nostril. 'Rot in hell

Griffin!' I ripped my pen out of his neck and the blood spurted freely onto the tiled floor. I then whispered to him, 'Dan Crosby is still the greatest. You're just a fucking loser!' For good measure, I kicked him as hard as could between the legs and watched him curl up in agony. I stumbled back, breathing heavily and watched the life slowly ebb out of him.

'Roger! What the fucking hell are you doing here.' Frank appeared in the lounge. He saw Brian's body and said, 'What's happened here?'

I couldn't speak. Brian had got his just desserts and deep down I was happy but the stress of the last couple of days had finally hit me and I was tired, very tired. My ears were still ringing from the gunshots and I couldn't stop shaking.

'Are you okay. I heard the gunshots. Are you hit?'

'No. I'm okay mate.'

'I thought you were in New York?'

'It's a long story Frank. But I told you we would get this bastard and we have.'

I didn't glance back as Frank helped me out of the flat and downstairs.

Printed in the United Kingdom
by Lightning Source UK Ltd.
2099